Prai

bestse

“Palmer proves that love and passion [illegible]d even in the most dangerous situations.”

—*Publishers Weekly* on *Untamed*

“You just can’t do better than a Diana Palmer story to make your heart lighter and smile brighter.”

—*Fresh Fiction* on *Wyoming Rugged*

“Diana Palmer is a mesmerizing storyteller who captures the essence of what a romance should be.”

—*Affaire de Coeur*

“The popular Palmer has penned another winning novel, a perfect blend of romance and suspense.”

—*Booklist* on *Lawman*

“Diana Palmer’s characters leap off the page. She captures their emotions and scars beautifully and makes them come alive for readers.”

—*RT Book Reviews* on *Lawless*

Dear Reader,

I can't believe that it has been thirty years since my first Long, Tall Texan book, *Calhoun*, debuted! The series was suggested by my former editor Tara Gavin, who asked if I might like to set stories in a fictional town of my own design. Would I! And the rest is history.

As the years went by, I found more and more sexy ranchers and cowboys to add to the collection. My readers (especially Amy!) found time to gift me with a notebook listing every single one of them, wives and kids and connections to other families in my own Texas town of Jacobsville. Eventually the town got a little too big for me, so I added another smaller town called Comanche Wells and began to fill it up, too.

You can't imagine how much pleasure this series has given me. I continue to add to the population of Jacobs County, Texas, and I have no plans to stop. Ever.

I hope all of you enjoy reading the Long, Tall Texans as much as I enjoy writing them. Thank you all for your kindness and loyalty and friendship. I am your biggest fan!

Love,

Diana Palmer

NEW YORK TIMES BESTSELLING AUTHOR

DIANA PALMER

LONG, TALL TEXANS:

Rey

Stuart

Previously published as
A Man of Means and *Winter Roses*

HARLEQUIN® SPECIAL RELEASE

ISBN-13: 978-1-335-00709-4

Long, Tall Texans: Rey/Stuart

Rey
First published as A Man of Means in 2002.
This edition published in 2019.

Stuart
First published as Winter Roses in 2007.
This edition published in 2019.

Recycling programs for this product may not exist in your area.

This edition published by arrangement with Harlequin Books S.A.

For questions and comments about the quality of this book, please contact us at CustomerService@Harlequin.com.

HARLEQUIN®
www.Harlequin.com

Printed in U.S.A.

CONTENTS

A prolific author of more than one hundred books, **Diana Palmer** got her start as a newspaper reporter. A *New York Times* bestselling author and voted one of the top ten romance writers in America, she has a gift for telling the most sensual tales with charm and humor. Diana lives with her family in Cornelia, Georgia. Visit her website at www.dianapalmer.com.

Books by Diana Palmer

Long, Tall Texans

Fearless
Heartless
Dangerous
Merciless
Courageous
Protector
Invincible
Untamed
Defender
Undaunted

The Wyoming Men

Wyoming Tough
Wyoming Fierce
Wyoming Bold
Wyoming Strong
Wyoming Rugged
Wyoming Brave

Morcai Battalion

The Morcai Battalion
The Morcai Battalion: The Recruit
The Morcai Battalion: Invictus
The Morcai Battalion: The Rescue

Visit the Author Profile page
at Harlequin.com for more titles.

REY

CHAPTER ONE

MEREDITH JOHNS GLANCED around her worriedly at the out-of-control Halloween partygoers in their colorful costumes. Meredith was wearing an outfit left over from college days. She made a good salary at her job, but there was no money for little luxuries like Halloween costumes. She had to budget just to be able to pay the utility bill in the house she shared with her father.

The past few months had been traumatic, and the wear was telling on her. She needed to get out of the house, Jill, one of her colleagues, had said firmly—especially after her most agonizing experience at home. Meredith was reluctant. Her father was only just back at their house after three days. But Jill was insistent. So she'd put on the only costume she had, a bad choice in many ways, and walked the three blocks to her friend's downtown apartment. She grimaced at her surroundings. What an idiot she'd been to come to this wild party.

But it really had been a tumultuous week for Meredith and she'd wanted to get her mind off her troubles. Her father's violent behavior at the house they shared was unnerving. They were both still grieving, but her father had taken the tragedy much harder. He felt responsible. That was why a scholarly, conservative college professor had suddenly retired from his job and turned into an alcoholic. Meredith had tried everything she could think of to get him into treatment, but he refused to go on his own accord and the treatment facilities which would have taken him wouldn't unless he went voluntarily. Only a violent episode that had landed him in jail had temporarily spared her of this saddening experience. But he was out three days later and he had a new bottle of whiskey. She still had to go home after the party. He'd warned her not to be late. Not that she ever was.

Her grey eyes were sad as she sipped her soft drink. She had no head for alcohol, and she was as out of place here as a cup of tea. Not only that, her costume was drawing unwanted attention from the men. So was her long blond hair. It had been a bad costume choice, but it was the only thing she had to wear on the spur of the moment. Going to a Halloween party in her street clothes would have made her stand out, too.

She moved away from a slightly tipsy colleague who wanted to show her around Jill's bedroom and unobtrusively put her glass on a table. She found Jill, pleaded a headache, thanked her for a "good" time and headed out the front door as fast as she could. Once on the sidewalk, she drew in a long, sweet breath of fresh air.

What a bunch of wild people! She coughed delicately, remembering the unmistakable smell of that smoke that had been thick enough to obstruct clear vision inside. She'd thought it would be fun to go to a party. She might even meet a man who would be willing to take her out and cope with her father. And cows might fly, she told herself. She hadn't been out on a date in months. She'd invited one prospective date to her home for supper. But after a good look at her father, who was mean when he drank, the prospective suitor took off. Her heart wasn't in it, anyway. Recently she'd given up trying to attract anyone. She had her hands full already. Her grief was still fresh, too.

An odd noise attracted her attention as she started back toward her own house. She felt self-conscious in her getup, and remembering the lewd remarks she'd drawn from a man who was normally very polite and gentlemanly, she was sorry she hadn't had a coat to wear. Her clothes were mostly old, because by the time she made the mortgage payment and took care of the bills, there wasn't much left over. Her father couldn't work and wouldn't get help, and she loved him too much to desert him. It was becoming a costly proposition.

She wrapped her arms around herself and hoped she was covering up enough skin to discourage stalkers. But her skirt was very short and tight, and she was wearing fishnet hose, very high heels, a low-cut blouse and a flaming pink feather boa. Her blond hair was loose around her shoulders and she was wearing enough makeup to do justice to a ballet recital. She winced, hoping she hadn't been noticed. She'd gone to the party as a burlesque dancer. Sadly she looked more like a professional hooker in her garb.

She rounded a corner and saw two shadowy figures bending over what looked like a man on the ground.

"Hey! What do you think you're doing there?" she yelled, making as much noise as possible. Then she started running toward them and waving her arms, yelling threats as she went.

As she expected, the surprise of her aggressive presence shocked them into retreat. They jumped up and ran away, without even looking back. The best defense, she thought with faint amusement, was always a good offense. It was a calculated bluff, but she'd seen it work for women smaller in stature than she was.

She ran to the downed man and examined him the best she could in the dim glow of the streetlights.

Concussion, she thought, feeling his head and encountering a metallic smelling wetness. Blood. He'd been hit on the head by his assailants, and probably robbed as well. She felt around under the jacket he was wearing and her hand touched something small and square on his belt. She pulled it out.

"Aha," she said with a triumphant grin. A man dressed as well as he was could be expected to have a cell phone. She dialed 911 and gave the operator her location and the condition of her patient, staying on the line while the dispatcher got an ambulance en route.

While she waited for it, she sat down on the pavement beside the man and held his hand.

He groaned and tried to move.

"Don't do that," she said firmly. "You'll be okay. You mustn't move until the EMTs get here. I haven't got anything to treat you with."

"Head…hurts."

"I imagine it does. You've got a heck of a bump. Just lie still. Feel sick, sleepy…?"

"Sick," he managed weakly.

"Lie still." She lifted her head to listen for the ambulance, and sure enough, a siren sounded nearby. The hospital was less than two blocks from her home, maybe four from here. Lucky for this guy, whoever he was. Head injuries could be fatal.

"My…brothers," the man was whispering brokenly. "Hart… Ranch. Jacobsville, Texas."

"I'll make sure they're contacted," she promised.

He gripped her hand, hard, as he fought not to lose consciousness. "Don't…leave me," he ground out.

"I won't. I promise."

"Angel," he whispered. He took a long, shaky breath, and went back into the oblivion he'd left so briefly. That wasn't a good sign.

The ambulance rounded the corner, and the headlights spilled out onto Meredith and her patient. She got to her feet as two EMTs, one male and one female, piled out the doors and rushed to the downed man.

"Head wound," she told them. "Pulse is slow, but steady. He's coherent, some nausea, his skin is cold and clammy. Blunt force trauma, probably mild concussion…"

"Don't I know you?" the female EMT asked. Her face brightened. "Got you! You're Johns!"

"That's me," Meredith said with a grin. "I must be famous!"

"Sorry, not you—your dad." She winced at the look on Meredith's face.

Meredith sighed. "Yes, he spends a lot of time on ambulances these days."

"What happened here?" the woman asked quickly, changing the subject. "Did you see anything?"

"I yelled and scared off two guys who were bending over him," she volunteered. "I don't know if they were the ones who hit him or not. What do you think?" she added as the woman gave him a professional once-over.

"Concussion, definitely," she agreed. "Nothing broken, but he's got a lump the size of the national debt here on his head. We'll transport him. Coming along?"

"I guess I should," Meredith said, waiting until they

loaded him onto the gurney. He was still unconscious. "But I'm not exactly dressed for visiting a hospital."

The EMT gave her a speaking glance. "Should I ask why you're dressed like that? And does your boss know you're moonlighting?" she added wickedly.

"Jill Baxley had a Halloween party. She thought I should come."

The other woman's eyebrows levered up. "Jill's parties are notorious for getting out of control. I've never even seen you take a drink."

"My father drinks enough for both of us," came the reply. "I don't drink or use drugs, and I need my head examined for going to that party. I escaped early, which is how I found this guy."

"Lucky for him," the woman murmured as they loaded him into the back of the ambulance. "Judging by his condition, he could have died if he hadn't been found in time."

Meredith climbed up into the back and sat down on the bench while the driver got in under the wheel and the female EMT called the hospital emergency room for orders. It was going to be a long night, Meredith thought worriedly, and her father was going to be very upset when she got home. He and her mother had been really close, but her mother had been fond of going to parties and staying out until the early morning; sometimes with other men. Recent events had made him dwell on that behavior. Her father seemed to have transferred that old contempt to her. It made her uneasy to think of arriving home in the wee hours. Anything could happen. On the other hand, how could she leave this man? She was the only person who knew who to contact for him. She'd promised to stay with him. She couldn't let him down.

HE WAS EXAMINED by the resident on duty in the emergency room, who diagnosed concussion. He'd been unconscious most of the way to the hospital, but he'd come out of it just once to look up at Meredith and smile, tightening his big hand around the fingers that were holding it.

His family had to be notified, and Meredith was coaxed into making the call to Jacobsville for the harassed and overworked emergency room staff.

She was given a phone and a telephone directory which also listed Jacobs County, of which Jacobsville was the county seat. She looked through it until she found a listing for Hart Ranch Properties, Inc. That had to be it.

She dialed the number and waited. A deep, drawling voice answered, "Hart Ranch."

"Uh, I'm calling for a Mr. Leo Hart," she said, having found his driver's license in the wallet his assailants hadn't had time to steal. "He's at Houston General…"

"What happened?" the voice asked impatiently. "Is he all right?"

"He was mugged. He has a concussion," she added. "He can't give the staff any medical information…"

"Who are you?"

"I'm Meredith Johns. I work…"

"Who found him?"

"I did, actually. I called the ambulance on his cell phone. He said to call his brothers and he told me where they were…"

"It's two o'clock in the morning!" the voice pointed out angrily.

"Yes, I am aware of that," she began. "It only happened a little while ago. I was walking down the street when I saw him on the sidewalk. He needs his family—"

"I'm his brother, Rey. I'll be there in thirty minutes."

"Sir, it's a long way to Houston from where you are. If you drive that fast…!" she said at once.

"We have an airplane. I'll get the pilot out of bed right now. Thanks." He added that last word as if it hurt him, and hung up.

Meredith went back to the waiting room. Ten minutes later, she was admitted to the room where the victim had been examined.

"He's conscious," the attending physician told her. "I'm going to admit him overnight, just to be sure. Any luck with his family?"

"His brother is on the way, in his own plane, apparently," she said. "I didn't get a thing out of him. Sorry."

"People get upset and they don't think," the resident said with a weary smile. "How about staying with him? We're understaffed because of that respiratory virus that's going around, and he shouldn't be alone."

"I'll stay," she said with a grin. "It's not as if I have a hectic social life."

The resident pursed his lips and smirked at her outfit.

"Halloween party," she said, grimacing. "And next time I get invited, I'll have a broken leg, I swear it!"

FORTY-FIVE MINUTES LATER, there was a problem. It was six feet tall, had black hair and dark eyes and it erupted into the hospital cubicle like an F-5 tornado, dressed in jeans and boots and a fringed rawhide jacket thrown carelessly over what looked like a beige silk shirt. The wide-brimmed hat slanted over those threatening eyes was a Stetson, one of the most expensive made, with its distinctive feathered logo pin on the hatband. He looked impressively rich, and excessively angry.

The man was livid when he saw his big brother, still drifting in and out of consciousness, on the examining table. He gave Meredith a scrutiny that could have peeled paint off old furniture, his eyes narrowing contemptuously on her costume.

"Well, that explains why you were on the street at two in the morning," he snarled angrily. "What happened? Did you feel guilty and call for help after you tried to roll him?" he added sarcastically.

"Look here," she began, rising.

"Save it." He turned to the big man on the table and laid a lean, strong hand on his brother's broad chest. "Leo. Leo, it's Rey! Can you hear me?" he asked in a tone that combined affection with concern.

The big man's eyes blinked and opened. He stared blankly up at the leaner man. "Rey?"

"What happened to you?" Rey Hart demanded gently.

Leo grinned wearily. "I was thinking about new forage grasses and wasn't paying attention to my surroundings," he murmured drowsily. "Something hit me in the head and I went down like a brick. Didn't see a thing." He winced and felt clumsily in his pockets. "Damn! My wallet's gone. So's my cell phone."

Meredith started to tell him that she had the phone and wallet in her purse for safekeeping, but before she could speak, Rey Hart gave her a furious, speaking glance and walked out of the cubicle like a man hunting a fight.

His brother drifted off again. Meredith stood beside him, wondering what to do. Five minutes later, Rey Hart walked back in accompanied by a tall man in a police uniform. He looked familiar, but Meredith couldn't quite place him. She knew she'd seen him before.

"That's her," Rey told the policeman, indicating Meredith. "I'll sign anything necessary as soon as I see that my brother's going to be okay. But get her out of here."

"Don't worry. I'll handle it," the policeman said quietly. He handcuffed Meredith with easy efficiency and pulled her out of the cubicle before she could protest.

"I'm being arrested?" she exclaimed, stunned. "But, why? I haven't done anything!"

"Yes, I know, I've heard it all before," the officer told her in a bored tone when she tried to explain what had happened. "Nobody's ever guilty. Honest to God, dressed like that, out on the streets alone after midnight, you were bound to be up to no good. What did you do with his cell phone and his wallet?"

"They're in my pocketbook," she began.

He confiscated it from her shoulder and propelled her out of the building. "You're going to be in a lot of trouble. You picked the wrong man to rob."

"See here, I didn't mug him! It was two men. I didn't see their faces, but they were bending over him as I came down the sidewalk."

"Soliciting is a felony," he pointed out.

"I wasn't soliciting anything! I'd just come from a Halloween party dressed as a burlesque dancer!" she raged, furious that she was being punished for having done someone a good turn. She read his name tag. "Officer Sanders, you have to believe me!"

He didn't say a word. He drew her with him, firmly but gently, and put her into the back seat of the police car.

"Wait," she told him before he could close the door.

"You get my wallet out of my purse and look in it. Right now," she insisted.

He gave her an impatient look, but he did what she asked. He looked through the plastic inserts in her wallet and glanced at her with a changed expression. "I thought you looked familiar, Johns," he murmured, using her last name, as most people she knew at work did.

"I didn't mug Mr. Hart," she continued. "And I can prove where I was when he was being mugged." She gave him her friend Jill's address.

He gave in. He drove to Jill's apartment, went to the door, spoke to an obviously intoxicated and amused Jill and came back to the squad car. He let Meredith out of the back of the squad car and took off the handcuffs. It was cool in the night air, and Meredith felt self-conscious and uncomfortable in her garb, even though the police officer knew the truth now.

"I'm really sorry," he told her with a grimace as he met her grey eyes. "I didn't recognize you. All I knew was what Mr. Hart told me, and he was too upset to think straight. You have to admit, you don't look very professional tonight."

"I do realize that. Mr. Hart cares about his brother, and he doesn't know what happened," she pointed out. "He walked in and saw his brother on the table and me dressed like this," she indicated her clothing, "and his brother said his wallet and cell phone were missing. He doesn't know me from a stump. You can't blame him for thinking the worst. But those two men who hit him would have gotten his wallet if I hadn't come along, and they're still on the loose."

"Can you show me where you found him?" he asked.

"Of course. It was just down the sidewalk, that way."

She led and he followed her, with his big wide-angle flashlight sweeping the sidewalk and the grass as they walked. She pointed to an area of flattened grass. He left her on the sidewalk and gave the area a thorough scrutiny, looking for clues. He found a candy wrapper and a cigarette butt.

"I don't guess you know if Mr. Hart smokes or likes candy?" he asked.

She shook her head. "Sorry. All he told me was his brothers' names and where they lived. I don't know anything more about him."

He stood up. "I'll ask his brother later. Wait here while I call for one of the technicians to bag this evidence," he told her.

"Okay," she said agreeably, drawing the feather boa closer. It was getting cold standing around briefly clad, waiting for crime scene investigators. "Somebody's going to love being turned out of bed to come look at a cigarette butt and a candy wrapper," she stated with helpless amusement.

"You'd be surprised at what excites those guys," he chuckled. "Catching crooks isn't exactly a chore to them. It's high drama."

"I hope they catch these two," she said firmly. "Nobody should have to be afraid to walk down the streets at night. Even after dark, dressed like this, alone," she added pointedly, indicating her clothes.

"Good point," he was fair enough to admit.

He called in his location and requested crime scene technicians. Meredith was ready to go home, but she couldn't leave until she'd given the policeman a statement for his report. She sat in his car, with the overhead lights on, writing out what she knew of the attack on Leo Hart. It didn't take long, because she didn't know much.

She handed it back to him. "Can I go home now?" she asked. "I live with my father and he's going to be upset because I'm coming home so late. I can walk. It's only about three blocks from here."

He frowned. "Your father is Alan Johns, isn't he?" he asked. His expression changed. "Do you want me to go with you?"

She didn't usually flinch at facing her irate parent. She was gutsy, and she could handle herself. But tonight, she'd been through a lot. "Would you?" she asked, uneasy because her fear was visible.

"No problem. Get in."

He drove her to her house and went to the door with her. The house was dark and there was no movement inside. She let out a sigh of relief. "It's okay. If he was awake, the lights would be on. Thanks, anyway," she said with a smile.

"If you need us, call," he said. "I'm afraid I'll be in touch again about this. Rey Hart already reminded me that his brother is our state attorney general. He's not going to let this case go until it's solved."

"I don't blame him. Those guys are a menace and they're probably still running around looking for easy targets to rob. Take care."

"You, too. And I'm sorry about the handcuffs," he added, with the first smile she'd seen on his lean face since her ordeal began.

She smiled back. "My fault, for wearing a costume like this on the streets," she admitted. "I won't do it again. Thanks for the ride."

Back at the hospital, Rey Hart sat by his brother's bedside until dawn, in the private room he'd obtained for him. He was worried. Leo was the hardiest one of the lot, and the most cautious as a rule. He was the prankster, always playing jokes, cheering them up in bad times. Now, he lay still and quiet and Rey realized how much his sibling meant to him.

It infuriated him that that woman had thought nothing of robbing his brother while he was sick and weak and helpless. He wondered what she'd hit him with. She wasn't a big woman. Odd, that she'd been able to reach as high as Leo's head with some blunt object. He recalled with distaste the way she'd been dressed. He was no prude, but in his early twenties he'd had a fling with a woman he later found out was a private call girl. He'd been infatuated with her, and thought she loved him. When he learned her profession and that she'd recognized him at once and knew how wealthy he was, it had soured him on women. Like his married brothers had been, and Leo still was, he was wary of females. If he could find a man who could bake biscuits, he told himself, he'd never let even an old woman into the house ever again.

He recalled their latest acquisition with sorrow. He and Leo had found a retired pastry chef who'd moved in with them—the last of the Hart bachelors—to bake their beloved biscuits. She'd become ill and they'd rushed to the drugstore to get her prescriptions, along with candy and chocolates and a bundle of flowers. But her condition had worsened and she'd told them, sadly, that the job was just too much in her frail state of health. She had to quit. It was going to be hard to replace her. There weren't a lot of people who wanted to live on an isolated ranch and bake biscuits at all hours of the day and night. Even want ads with offers of a princely salary hadn't attracted anyone just yet. It was depressing; like having Leo lying there under white sheets, so still and quiet in that faded striped hospital gown.

Rey dozed for a few hours in the deep night, used to sleeping in all sorts of odd positions and places. Cattle ranchers could sleep in the saddle when they had to, he thought amusedly, especially when calving was underway or there was a storm or they were cutting out and branding calves and doing inventory of the various herds.

But he came awake quickly when Sanders, the police officer who'd arrested that woman last night, came into the room with a murmured apology.

"I'm just going off shift," Officer Sanders told Rey. "I thought I'd stop by and tell you that we've gone over the scene of the attack and we have some trace evidence. The detectives will start looking for other witnesses this morning. We'll get the people responsible for the attack on your brother."

Rey frowned. "Get 'them'?" he queried. "You've already got her. You arrested her!"

Officer Sanders averted his eyes. "Had to turn her loose," he said uneasily. "She had an alibi, which was confirmed. She gave me a statement and I took her home."

Rey stood up, unfolding his intimidating length, and glared at the officer. "You let her go," he said coldly. "Where's my brother's cell phone?" he added as an afterthought.

The policeman grimaced. "In her purse, along with his wallet," he said apologetically. "I forgot to ask her for them when I left. Tell you what, I'll swing by her house and get them on my way home..."

"I'll go with you," he said curtly. "I still think she's guilty. She's probably in cahoots with the guys who attacked Leo. And she could have paid someone to lie and give her an alibi."

"She's not that sort of woman," the policeman began.

Rey cut him off angrily. "I don't want to hear another word about her! Let's go," he said, grabbing his hat, with a last, worried glance at his sleeping brother. He wondered how the policeman could make such a statement about a woman he'd just met, but he didn't really care. He wanted her in jail.

HE DROVE HIS rental car, with the off-duty policeman beside him, to Meredith's home, following the directions Officer Sanders gave him. It was in a run-down neighborhood, and the house was in poor condition. It only intensified Rey's suspicions about her. She was obviously poor. What better way to get money than to rob somebody?

He went to the door, accompanied by the policeman, and knocked. Hard.

He had to do it three times, each with more force and impatience, before someone answered the door.

Meredith Johns was disheveled and white-faced. She was clutching a bulky washcloth to her face and wearing a robe over the clothes she'd had on the night before.

"What do you want now?" she asked huskily, her voice slurred and jerky.

"Been drinking, have you?" Rey Hart asked in a blistering tone.

She flinched.

Officer Sanders knew what was going on. He read the situation immediately. He stepped past Rey, grim and silent, grimacing when he saw Meredith's face. He went by her and into the living room and began looking around.

"Hard night, I gather? It must be a continual risk, in your profession," Rey said insinuatingly, with a speaking glance at her dress in the opening of the old, worn robe. "Do your marks make a habit of beating you up?" he added with cold contempt.

She didn't answer him. It was hard to talk and her face hurt.

Officer Sanders had gone into the bedroom. He came back two minutes later with a tall, disheveled but oddly dignified-looking man in handcuffs. The man, who'd been quiet before, was now cursing furiously, accusing Meredith of everything from prostitution to murder in a voice that rose until he was yelling. Rey Hart looked at him with obvious surprise. His eyes went to Meredith Johns, who was stiff as a poker and wincing every time the man yelled at her. The policeman picked up the telephone and called for a squad car.

"Please, don't," Meredith pleaded, still clutching the ice-filled cloth to her face. "He's only just got out..."

"He isn't staying. This time, he's going to be in jail for longer than three days," the officer said firmly. "You get to the hospital and let one of the residents look at you, Miss Johns. How bad is it? Come on, show me," he demanded, moving closer.

Rey stood by, silent and confused, watching as Meredith winced and moved the bulky cloth away from her face. His breath was audible when he saw the swelling and the growing purple and violet discoloration around her eye, cheek and jaw.

"God Almighty," Rey said harshly. "What did he hit you with?"

"His fist," the policeman replied coldly. "And it isn't the first time. You have to face facts, Miss Johns," he told her. "He isn't the man he used to be. When he drinks, he doesn't know what he's doing. He'll kill you one night when he's like this, and he won't even remember doing it!"

"I won't press charges," she said miserably. "How can I? He's my father! He's the only family I have left in the world…"

The policeman looked at her with compassion. "You don't have to press charges," he told her. "I'll provide them myself. You'd better phone your boss and tell him you won't be in for a few weeks. He'll have kittens if you walk into the office looking like that."

"I suppose he would." Tears ran down her pale cheeks, all the more eloquent for being silent. She looked at her raging, cursing father and sadness claimed her features. "He wasn't like this before, honest he wasn't," she told them. "He was a kind, loving, caring man."

"Not anymore," Officer Sanders replied grimly. "Get to the hospital and have your face seen about, Miss Johns. I'll take your father outside until the unit comes…"

"No," she groaned. "Please, spare us that! I can't bear to have the whole neighborhood watching, hearing him…like that, again!"

He hesitated. "Okay. I'll watch for them out the window. The unit can drop you by the hospital, since it's going there first…"

"I'll take her," Rey said at once, without wondering why he should do such an about-face. He didn't trust the woman, or even totally believe her story. But she did look so pitiful. He couldn't bear to leave her in that condition to get to the hospital. Besides, whatever her motives, she had gotten help for Leo. He could have died if he hadn't been cared for.

"But..." she began.

"If," he added coldly, "you change clothes first. I am *not* being seen in public with you in that rig!"

CHAPTER TWO

MEREDITH WISHED SHE felt up to a fight. Her long blond hair was down in her face, her grey eyes were sparking fire. But she was sick to her stomach and bruised. She would rather have gone to bed if these stubborn men would just have let her alone. But her face could have broken or shattered bones. She knew that. She grimaced, hoping her insurance would cover a second "accident" in as many months.

When the unit arrived, Meredith turned away from the sight of her raging father being carried off and closed the door. Probably it wasn't surprising to the neighbors anymore, it happened so often. But she hated having everyone know.

"I'll get dressed," she said in a subdued tone.

Rey watched her go and then shoved his hands into his pockets and looked around the room. It was shabby. The only bright things in it were books—hundreds of them, in bookcases and boxes and stacked on tables and chairs. Odd, he thought. They were apparently short of cash, judging by the worn old furniture and bare floor. There was only a very small television and a portable stereo. He glanced at the CD case and was surprised to find classical music dominating the discs. What a peculiar family. Why have so many books and so little else? He wondered where the woman's mother was. Had she left the father, and was that why he drank? It would have explained a lot. He knew about missing parents, especially missing mothers—his had left the family while the five Hart boys were young, without a backward glance.

Minutes later, Meredith came back, and except for the bruised face, he might not have recognized her. She was wearing a beige sweater set, with a tweed coat over it. Her blond hair was in a neat bun and her face devoid of makeup. She wore flat-heeled shoes and carried a purse that looked new.

"Here's your brother's cell phone and his wallet," she said, handing it to him. "I forgot to give them to Officer Sanders."

He glared at them and put them in his pocket. He wondered if she'd have given them back at all if he hadn't come here. He didn't trust her, regardless of what the policeman had said. "Let's go," he said stiffly. "The car's outside."

She hesitated, but only for a minute. She wasn't going to be able to avoid a checkup. She knew the problems that negligence could cause. Even a relatively minor problem could become major.

Unexpectedly Rey opened the car door for her. She slid in, surprised to find herself in a new luxury car. She fastened her seat belt. His brother, Simon Hart, was state attorney general. Rey owned a ranch. She remembered how his injured brother, Leo, had been dressed last night, and her eyes went to Rey's expensive hat and boots and silk shirt. Of course, they were a wealthy family. Considering her state of dress—or undress—the night before, she could understand his misgivings about her character.

She sat wearily beside him, the ice-filled cloth still

in her hand. She held it to the side of her face that was bruised and hoped that it would spare her some of the swelling. She didn't need a doctor to tell her that it was a bad blow. The pain was almost unbearable.

"I took a hit to the face a few years ago in a brawl," he volunteered in his deep, slow drawl. "It hurt like hell. I imagine your face does, too."

She swallowed, touched by the faint concern. Tears threatened, but she never cried now. It was a weakness she couldn't afford.

He glanced at her, puzzled. "Nothing to say?"

She managed to get her voice under control. "Thank you for taking me to the hospital," she said huskily.

"Do you usually dress like that when you go out at night?" he asked belatedly.

"I told you. There was…a Halloween party," she said. It hurt to talk. "It was the only costume I had."

"Do you like parties?" he asked sarcastically.

"My first one…in almost four years," she managed to say. "Please…hurts…to talk."

He glanced at her and then was quiet. He didn't like her. He didn't trust her. Why was he taking care of her? There was something unexpectedly vulnerable about her. But she had spirit.

He walked her into the emergency room. She filled out forms and was ushered back into a treatment cubicle while Rey sat in the waiting room between a squalling toddler and a man coughing his head off. He wasn't used to illness. He'd never seen much of it, and he didn't know how to cope with it. Accidents, sure, he was good hand in an emergency, and there were plenty on ranch. But he hated hospitals.

Meredith came back a good thirty minutes later with a prescription and a frown.

"What did he say?" he asked conversationally.

She shrugged. "He gave me something…for pain," she said, waving the prescription.

"They sent me to a plastic surgeon," he volunteered as they went through the automatic door.

She didn't speak.

"I had a shattered bone in my cheek that they couldn't repair," he persisted.

"I'm not…going…to any damned…plastic surgeon!"

His eyebrows arched. "Your face could be distorted."

"So what?" she muttered, wincing because it really did hurt to speak. "It's not…much of a face, anyway."

He scowled. She wasn't pretty, but her face had attractive features. Her nose was straight and elegant, she had high cheekbones. Her mouth was like a little bow, perfect. Her eyes, big and grey, fascinated him.

"You should go," he said.

She ignored him. "Can you…drive me by the pharmacy?"

"Sure."

She gave him directions and he waited while she had the prescription filled. He drove her back to her house and left her there reluctantly.

"I'll be at the hospital with Leo if you need anything," he said as if it pained him to say it.

"I don't need any help. Thanks," she added stiffly.

His eyebrows arched. "You remind me of me," he murmured, and a thin smile touched his lips—a kind one. "Proud as Lucifer."

"I get by. I really am…sorry about your brother. Will he be all right?" she asked at her door.

He nodded. "They want to keep him for two or thre days. He'll want to thank you."

"No need. I would have done it for anyone."

He sighed. She was going to look bad for a long tim with her face in that condition. She'd been beaten and h felt responsible, God knew why. He took a breath. "I' sorry I had you arrested," he said reluctantly.

She pursed her lips. "I'll bet…that hurt."

"What?"

"You don't apologize much, do you?" she asked, a if she knew.

He scowled down at her, puzzled.

She turned away. "No sweat. I'll live. So long."

She went in and closed the door. Rey, who'd don without companionship for a number of years, sudden felt alone. He didn't like the feeling, so he shoved it o of his mind and drove back to the hospital. He wouldn see her again, anyway.

LEO CAME BACK to himself with a vengeance late th afternoon. He had Rey lever the head of his bed up a he ate dinner with pure enjoyment.

"It's not bad," Leo murmured between mouthfu "But I wish I had a biscuit."

"Me, too," Rey said on a sigh. "I guess we could b a restaurant, as a last resort," he added dejectedly. "O that serves breakfast."

"Who was that woman who came in with me?" asked Rey.

"You remember her?" Rey was surprised.

"She looked like an angel," he mused, smilin "Blonde and big-eyed and all heart. She held my ha and sat down on the sidewalk in the cold and talked to me until the ambulance got there."

"You were unconscious."

"Not all the time. She even came in with me on the ambulance," he said. "She kept telling me I was going to be all right. I remember her voice." He smiled. "Her name was Meredith."

Rey's heart jumped. He felt uneasy. Leo usually didn't pay much attention to strange women. "Meredith Johns," he agreed.

"Is she married?" Leo asked at once.

Rey felt threatened; it irritated him. "I don't know," he said.

"Do you think you could find somebody who knows how to get in touch with her?" his brother persisted. "I want to thank her for saving me."

Rey got up from the chair where he'd been sitting and walked to the darkened window, peering out through the blinds while he played for time. "She lives near the place where you were attacked," he said finally, unable to lie.

"What does she do for a living?"

"I don't know," Rey said, feeling uncomfortable. He couldn't get her father's accusing remarks out of his mind. She'd said she was dressed up for a party, she'd even found someone to give her an alibi, but Rey didn't completely believe her. What if that whole defense was a lie? What if she was some sort of prostitute? He didn't want his brother getting mixed up with a woman like that. He didn't trust women, especially strange women. Then he remembered her poor, bruised face and he felt bad about his suspicions.

"I'll ask one of the nurses," Leo said abruptly.

"No need," Rey told him. He turned back around

with his hands in his pockets. "If you're determined, I'll go get her in the morning and bring her in to see you."

"Why not tonight?"

Rey let out an impatient breath. "Her father roughed her up because she got home late last night. I took her to the emergency room this morning before I came back here."

Leo's eyes narrowed and went cold. "Her father beat her? And you took her back home to him?" he said angrily.

"He wasn't there. They took him off to jail," he said. His face hardened even more. "She'll have a hell of a bruise. They said she couldn't go back to work for a few weeks." He moved one shoulder restlessly. "Considering the way they live, I don't know how she'll manage," he added reluctantly. "They don't seem to have much. Apparently the old man doesn't work and she's the only one bringing home any money." He didn't volunteer his opinion of how she made it.

Leo leaned back against the pillows. His big frame was without its usual vibrance. His dark eyes were dull, and his lean face was drawn. His blond-streaked brown hair was unkempt, and looked odd in the back where they'd had to shave it to put stitches in. It was a reminder of how tricky head wounds were. Leo was very lucky not to have brain damage. Rey thought about the assailants and his eyes blazed.

"I'm going to phone Simon tonight," he told Leo. "I'm sure the local police will do all they can to catch the guys who waylaid you, but they'll work even harder if they get a call from the state attorney general."

"There you go again, pulling strings," Leo mused.

"It's for a good cause."

"Did you find my wallet and my cell phone?" Leo asked.

"The woman had them. They're in my pocket."

"Good. I didn't think she had anything to do with mugging me. Don't forget your promise to bring Meredith here in the morning," he said.

Now it was "Meredith." Rey didn't like the whole idea of having Leo around the woman, but he didn't have a legitimate reason for keeping her from Leo's side. It would sound even more suspicious if Rey started throwing out sarcastic remarks about her. Leo did love to pull his chain.

"Okay," he said reluctantly.

"Good man," Leo replied with a wan grin. "Nothing like family to look after you."

"Next time, watch your back instead of daydreaming about forage grasses," Rey said firmly. Then he leaned forward in the chair. "So, tell me what sort of grasses the Cattleman's Association is advocating."

REY GOT A hotel room near the hospital, so that he could have a bath and get some rest. The night staff had the phone number, so they could call him immediately if he was needed.

He phoned Simon before he went to bed.

"Leo's been mugged?" Simon exclaimed. "And you didn't call me last night?"

That tone was still intimidating, even though Rey was thirty-one. Simon was the eldest of the five brothers, and the bossiest, next to Cag.

"I was too upset to phone anybody," Rey returned, "and too busy trying to handle…another problem that cropped up. He's all right. Honest. I didn't find out until the early hours of the morning, and it's been a long day. He was already out of danger before it occurred to me that I needed to let you know."

"All right," Simon said, sounding as if he was more relaxed. "Do they have a suspect?"

"No. I thought we did, but it turned out to be a dead end," he added, without going into details about Meredith Johns. "There were two of them, and they haven't been caught. It's a miracle he wasn't killed, and that they were stopped in time before they robbed him. You might give the local police chief a call. Just to let him know we're all interested in solving the case."

"You want me to use my influence for personal gain?" Simon drawled.

"Hell, yes, I do!" Rey shot back. "This is our brother, for God's sake! If a big, strong man like Leo can get mugged in a residential neighborhood, so can anybody else! It doesn't say a lot for the security in this area."

"No, it doesn't," Simon agreed. "I'll point that out to the police commissioner, first thing tomorrow. Then I'll run down to Jacobsville and get Cag and Corrigan and we'll be right up to see about Leo."

Rey chuckled. It was the first bit of humor he'd felt so far. The five brothers rarely went so far as to gang up on people, but considering the size and reputation of them, they got results when they did. This was an emergency, anyway. They could have lost a brother. The perpetrators had to be caught.

"They should be home by now," Rey replied. "I couldn't phone them because they were showing those Japanese businessmen around the ranch and the town."

"I'll see how much luck they had. Japan is very careful

about its import beef. The fact that we run organically raised cattle will certainly go in our favor," Simon said.

"Yes, it will. Get some sleep. And don't worry about Leo. He's fine. I'd never have left the hospital if I'd had one doubt about that."

"I'll stop worrying."

"Give my love to Tira and the boys," Rey added.

"I'll do that. See you tomorrow."

Rey hung up, thinking about Simon and his family. Tira was redheaded and gorgeous, and the boys favored both of them, although they had Simon's dark eyes and hair. Corrigan and Dorie had a boy and a girl. Cag and Tess had just a boy, but they were talking about how nice a daughter would be. Meanwhile, Rey and Leo enjoyed being uncles, but had no interest in joining the ranks of the married.

If it wasn't for those biscuits, Rey thought miserably. It was going to be expensive to have the local café make biscuits for them every day until they employed a new biscuit maker, but if they got desperate enough, and offered enough of an incentive, they could probably manage it.

Turning his attention elsewhere, Rey gave a thought to poor Leo with his stitches and his headache, and another to Meredith Johns's bruised face. Tomorrow, he'd have to deal with Leo's request to see her, and he wasn't looking forward to it. He wished he knew why.

REY WENT TO Meredith Johns's house the next morning after he'd had breakfast. It took her a minute or two to answer the door, and for an instant, he thought that perhaps she might not be in any condition to answer it. She'd been badly bruised.

But she opened the door and peered up at him bravely, even though she looked like a refugee from a bar brawl. Her left eye was swollen shut completely now.

"Leo wants to see you," he said easily, noticing how the top of her blond head only came to his shoulder. She wasn't tall. Even bruised, her face had a beautiful complexion. Her mouth was pretty. He shook himself mentally. "He wants to thank you for what you did. He remembers that you rode in on the ambulance with him. You didn't tell me that," he added with faint accusation.

"I wasn't thinking," she said. "I was worried about what would happen when I came home late."

"Have you heard any more about your father this morning?" he asked grimly.

"They're going to charge him with simple battery," she said heavily. "I can't afford a lawyer. He'll have a public defender and he'll probably have to stay in jail for a few weeks." She looked up at him. "It will be a godsend, you know, because he'll dry out completely."

He hated the compassion he felt. "Did your mother leave him?" he asked.

She averted her face. She couldn't bear to talk about it yet. "In a way," she said huskily. "Are you going to drive me?" she added, glancing at him over her shoulder. "The bus doesn't run for another thirty minutes."

"Sure," he agreed.

"Then I'll get my jacket and purse."

She went into another room and came back quickly, leading the way out the door. "Is he conscious now?"

"Very," he murmured dryly. "When I left him, he was telling a nurse what she could do with the wash basin, and how far."

She chuckled. "He didn't seem like that kind of man,"

she murmured. “I had him figured for a gentleman, not a renegade.”

“We’re all that kind of man,” he replied.

“All?”

He led her to the car and put her into the passenger seat. “There are five of us. The other three are coming up this morning to have a talk with the police.”

“I remember. You said that your brother was the attorney general.”

“He is,” he replied. “We tend to stick together.”

Her eyes went to his hands on the steering wheel. He had nice hands, very lean and strong with neat, clean fingernails. He was a tough-looking man, like a cowboy.

“How’s your face?” he asked unexpectedly.

She shrugged. “It still hurts. It will for a while, but I’ll be fine.”

“You should see that plastic surgeon.”

“Why?” she asked heavily. “My insurance won’t pay for cosmetic surgery, and there’s not much chance that they can do any major repair on tiny shattered bones.”

“You’re not a doctor. Stop giving yourself medical advice.”

She stared at him for a long moment and started to speak, then lost the opportunity when he pulled up in the hospital parking lot, cut off the engine and got out.

Rey waited for her and led her up to the floor where his brother’s room was located.

Leo wasn’t alone. Three other men were with him, one big and dark and missing an arm, the other lean and light-eyed and handsome, and a third big one with black eyes and a threatening face towering over both the others.

“That’s Cag,” Rey indicated the black-eyed man.

"Corrigan," he nodded toward the light-eyed man, "and that's Simon," he finished, smiling at the one-armed man. "This is Meredith Johns. She rescued Leo."

"Nice to see you and know who you are," Leo said, alert now and interested as his dark eyes swept over the neat woman just inside the door. "Miss Johns, I presume?"

She smiled self-consciously, because everybody was looking at her bruised face. "Yes," she said.

Simon Hart frowned when he got a good look at her. "What the hell happened to you?" he demanded.

"Her father," Rey said for her. "She got in late and he beat her up."

Leo looked suddenly as intimidating as the other three. "Where is he?" he asked.

"In jail," Meredith said heavily. "For several weeks, at least, and he'll have time to dry out."

"Good." Leo looked toward Simon. "Maybe you can find a way to get him into rehab before he gets out."

"I'll look into it," Simon said at once.

"And some counseling wouldn't come amiss," Rey put his two cents worth in.

"I'll see about that, too," Simon replied. "Nice to meet you, Miss Johns. We're all grateful for what you did for Leo."

"You're all very welcome," she replied. She clutched her purse, intimidated by the group of brothers.

"Come here," Leo said, holding out his hand. "They're big and they look tough, but they're really marshmallows. You don't have to feel threatened. I'll protect you."

"She doesn't need protecting from us!" Rey snapped.

The others gaped at him. It wasn't like Rey to act that way.

He cleared his throat. He didn't want them asking themselves embarrassing questions about his attitude. He shoved his hands into his pockets. "Sorry. I didn't sleep much last night," he explained.

Meredith went to stand beside Leo, who took one of her small, cold hands in his and looked up at her with interest.

"Have you seen a doctor?" he asked.

"Your brother took me to the emergency room yesterday," she said.

"Rey. His name's Reynard, but he's called Rey," Leo informed her.

She smiled. "You look much better today. Head hurt?"

"A bit, but my vision's clear and I'm not disoriented," he said, quoting the doctor. "I have a good prognosis."

"That's nice to hear. You were in pretty bad shape."

"I'd have been in a lot worse shape, but for you," Leo said. "I hear that you can't work out in public for a while, until your face heals," he added. "Can you cook?"

She blinked. "Of course," she said at once.

"Can you make bread?"

She frowned. "Bread?"

"More specifically, biscuits," he added, and had the oddest expression on his face.

She shifted her purse in the hand he wasn't holding. "Well, yes, those and rolls and loaf bread," she said, as if everybody could do it.

Leo shot a glance at Rey, who was just staring at him without daring to say a word. He knew what was coming, and he couldn't decide how he felt about it. He didn't want to think about it.

"How would you like a brief stay in Jacobsville,

Texas, in a big sprawling ranch house where your only job would be to make biscuits every morning?" Leo asked with his best smile.

Rey and the other brothers were staring at her, waiting. She wondered why. And Rey was frowning, as if he didn't like the idea at all. Probably he still secretly thought she was a hooker. He couldn't seem to credit her with any sense of decency.

She thought about his attitude for a few seconds, and decided that it wouldn't be a bad idea to take the job, and show him that you really couldn't judge a book by its cover. It wouldn't hurt that arrogant cowboy to be taken down a step or two, and she was just the girl who could do it.

She smiled. It hurt her face, but what was a little pain for a good cause? She turned back to Leo. "Mr. Hart, I think I'd like that job very much!"

CHAPTER THREE

"GOOD FOR YOU!" Leo exclaimed, animated and smiling. "You won't be sorry, Meredith. Honest."

She smiled back at him. He was nice, like a big brother. She liked him already. "I can do housekeeping, too," she told him. "I'll earn my keep."

"You'll go on salary, of course," he insisted. "It won't be a holiday."

"Nothing is a holiday with those two," Simon murmured dryly. "They aren't kidding about biscuits. They'll run you crazy baking them."

Rey and Leo gave their brother a disgusted look.

Meredith grinned. "I don't mind," she assured Simon. "I love to cook."

"It won't be that hard," Leo promised, with another speaking glance at Simon. "We just love biscuits. But we'll make you feel right at home. Anything you need, you can have—a new stove…" he added mischievously.

She thought about her father and her job, and her smile faltered. "I have to wrap up a few loose ends first," she began.

"No problem," Leo assured her. "I can't get out of here for another day at least, or so that doctor said," he added with impatience.

"You'll stay until he lets you out," Rey said firmly. "Concussions are tricky. You know that."

Leo grimaced. “I guess so. I hate hospitals.”

“I’m not too wild about them myself,” Rey had to agree.

“It would be a very sad world without them,” Meredith spoke up.

She seemed irritated, Rey thought, and wondered why. “I’ll run you back home when you’re ready,” Rey told her. “We’ll be in touch before we’re ready to leave.”

“All right.” She held Leo’s hand again and squeezed it gently, to the amusement of all the Harts except Rey. “You get better. I’ll see you soon.”

“Thanks again,” Leo told her with genuine gratitude.

“It was nothing.” She gave him another smile, tugged her hand free, and let Rey herd her out the door after a quick goodbye to the other brothers.

“I thought your brother was big until I saw all of you together. Goodness, you’re all huge!” she exclaimed when they were outside in the parking lot. She gave him a long scrutiny. “And there doesn’t seem to be an extra ounce of fat on any of you.”

“We don’t sit behind desks. We’re ranchers, not office workers, and we work hard, right alongside our cowboys,” he said. His dark eyes cut sideways. “Leo likes you.”

She smiled. “I’m glad, because I like him, too.”

That set him off and he tried not to let it show. He didn’t want her to like Leo. He wished he knew why. He glanced at her as he wove skillfully through traffic toward her house. “Do you have family besides your father?” he asked.

“A cousin or two near Fort Worth,” she said. She glanced out the window, absently rubbing the ring finger of her left hand, trying not to choke up over the question. "What is Jacobsville like?" she asked to divert him from any further questions.

"It's small," he said easily. "There are a lot of ranches in the area. We have good pasture and soil, and we get enough rain to manage healthy crops." He grinned. "A lot of us are heavily into organic cattle raising. And with the industry under threat right now, we'll probably keep our financial heads above water when some other ranchers are going under."

"I like organic food," she said. "It may have a few more blemishes and bug bites, but if it doesn't kill bugs, it won't kill me," she added with a grin.

He chuckled. "Good point. Do you like animals?"

"I love them. I'd like to have a cat, but it's not possible. Dad's allergic to them." She sighed wearily, leaning her head back against the headrest. Her bruises were still giving her a lot of pain. Her hand went to them and she winced.

"You should see that plastic surgeon," he reminded her.

She shook her head. "Can't afford it. Even if I could, I don't want to go through weeks of surgery."

He hesitated and then he shrugged. "Have it your way."

"I'll heal." She touched her cheek again self-consciously. "I'm not sure going to work for you is a good idea. I mean, people might think the five of you beat me up!"

He laughed wholeheartedly. "Nobody who knows us would ever think that. Especially," he added, "if you can bake. Simon was right. I'm afraid we're famous locally for our addiction to biscuits."

Actually they were famous a lot further out than Jacobsville, but he didn't want to make her think they were loopy.

She took the words at face value. "I like to cook."

He glanced at her again, taking in her very conservative way of dressing. "You don't look like the same woman I met just after Leo was assaulted."

"I almost never dress up," she confided. "And it really was a costume," she pointed out. "I wasn't lying. I don't make my living on the streets."

"How old are you?"

Her eyebrows arched. "Old enough."

"Are you over twenty-one?" he persisted.

"I'm twenty-three, almost twenty-four," she replied.

"And not married?"

"I've had responsibilities for the past few years," she said distantly, staring out the windshield. "My father has become the largest of them. I've been afraid to leave him alone."

"He's obviously dangerous when he drinks."

She hesitated, fingering her purse. "He seemed to lose himself in the bottle overnight. I thought I could handle him, control him, break the cycle. I couldn't even get help for him. My father doesn't think he has a drinking problem, so nobody would take him." She looked over at him. "I'm very grateful to your brother for his help. As I mentioned the night he was arrested, my father has only been like this for the past few months. It's not a long-standing problem. But I couldn't solve it alone."

"You're going to work for us," Rey said. "And it's not that much of a problem for Simon. He's good at his job."

"Is it a big ranch?" she asked unexpectedly.

"Enormous," he replied, "and one of five ranches we

own as a family. Things get hectic during roundup, as you'll find out if you're still there next Spring."

"I won't be," she said with some certainty. "When I heal, I have to get back to my job."

"What do you do?" he asked curiously. "Is it housecleaning or working as a cook in a restaurant?"

She almost bit her tongue at the demeaning comment. "You don't think I'm qualified to do anything else?"

He averted his eyes to the road. "I don't know you, Miss Johns," he commented carelessly. "But you seem pretty domestic to me."

She didn't feel well enough to retaliate. But one day, she promised herself, she was going to make him eat those condescending words.

"I've made beds and done light cleaning," she said, talking around her actual profession.

"Aren't you ambitious?" he persisted, with a faint frown. "Most women are, these days."

"That sounded bitter," she commented. "Did you get thrown over by an ambitious woman?"

"By a couple of them," he said curtly, and his expression became hard.

She hadn't thought of him that way. They'd been adversaries from the first contact. But it occurred to her as she gave him a quick, covert scrutiny, that he was a sensuous man. He wasn't handsome—except for Corrigan Hart, the rest of the brothers seemed cursed by a lack of conventional good looks.

But Rey had a lithe, graceful stride, and a strong face. He had good hands, clean and long-fingered. She liked the blackness of his straight hair, the high cheekbones, the long, thin, chiseled mouth. He was the sort of man who could have attracted women, except for his personality. The Harts didn't strike her as particularly gregarious or good mixers from her brief acquaintance with them. Leo was the one with the warmest personality. He made her feel at ease. The man beside her made her uncomfortable, insecure, nervous. She wasn't usually so strung-out by a man's proximity. Not that she'd had a lot to do with men in very recent years. Her father's overprotective, possessive nature had seen to that. He'd been so certain that she was going to end up like her mother.

She closed her eyes briefly, hating the memories.

"If you want to go and see your father before we leave for Jacobsville, I'll ask Simon to arrange it."

She stiffened. "I don't want to see him again until he's sober," she replied. "We both need time to get over what happened."

"Is your face the only place he hit you?" he asked unexpectedly.

"He got me in the back and the side, too, but those were only bruises. The doctor checked me over thoroughly." She sighed wearily. "I'm so tired," she murmured absently.

"I'm not surprised. You can get some rest. I'll phone you tomorrow, when we'll know more about Leo's condition and when he'll be released."

"Okay."

He stopped in front of her house and parked the car, walking to the door with her. He looked down at her while she fumbled the key into the lock. She was, in some ways, the most vulnerable woman he'd ever met. But there was steel in her makeup. He sensed that she wasn't like this usually, that she was fiery and independent and determined.

"This isn't the first time your father's laid into you, is it?" he asked suddenly.

She glanced at him, surprised. "No. But until this happened, it was more humiliating than painful." She frowned. "How did you know?"

He seemed concerned. "When I was in school, I had a couple of friends whose fathers got violent during binges. There's an…attitude, a posture, that people get when they've been beaten. I can't explain it, but I recognize it when I see it."

"Do you want to know what it is?" she asked with a world-weary smile. "It's a feeling of futility, of knowing that no matter what you do, you can't hold out physically against a man who's enraged and bent on hurting you. Because you know if you fight back, it will be even worse, maybe fatally worse. I don't like it," she added, her pale eyes beginning to glow, "and he's never getting the chance to do this again. He's my father. I love him, and I feel sorry for him. But I'm nobody's victim. Not even his."

He pushed his hands into his slacks' pockets and smiled at her. Her face was bright with color, and her eyes were alive, like peridots in sunlit water. He remembered her long blond hair around her shoulders and he wondered what she'd look like in pink silk. The thought shocked him and he scowled.

"Did I glue my nose on upside down?" she asked, raising her eyebrows.

He let out a short laugh. "No. I had a wild thought. Do you need an advance on your salary? I mean, is there anything you have to get for the trip that you can't afford?"

"I don't have a car," she began, and hated remembering why.

He glared. "I didn't say you were going to have to get to Jacobsville on your own. You'll go with Leo and me. Simon drove my car up from Jacobsville."

"Do I get to ride in the car, or have you got me earmarked for the trunk?" she returned.

He pursed his lips. Odd feelings were kindling inside him. "Keep that up and you'll be riding on the back bumper."

She wrinkled her nose. "Nice. Real nice. I can see you're going to be a great boss."

"If you don't burn the biscuits, I will be," he said.

"I'll stick close to your brother," she promised. "He'll protect me."

He didn't like that, but he wasn't going to let it show. "Leo's a tease," he said flatly. "Don't get your hopes up. He's not a marrying man. Neither am I," he added deliberately.

Her eyes widened. "Well, gee whiz, that's a major disappointment! And to think, I was only willing to take the job because of the marriage prospects!"

His face shuttered. "Sarcasm doesn't get you any points with me. I'm just making the position clear. We need a cook, not a prospective soul mate."

"Speak for yourself," she told him, turning back to her door. "I think Leo likes me already."

"I just told you…!"

She opened the door and looked back at him with pure irreverence. "Your brother can speak for himself. You don't own him, and you don't own me. I'll do what I please."

"Damn it…!"

"With charm like that, it's no surprise to me that you're still single," she said as she walked into the house.

"I can be charming when I've got a reason to be," he said icily. "But that's something you'll never know!"

"Lucky me!"

He started to speak, closed his lips tight, and walked back to his car.

She closed the door quickly and leaned back against it, almost shivering with anger. Of all the conceited, infuriating men she'd ever met, that one took the cake!

THE NEXT DAY, Rey phoned her midmorning to tell her that he and Leo would pick her up at one for the drive down to Jacobsville.

She had her suitcase packed and the house closed up when the big luxury car pulled into the driveway. It was a late-model car, and it looked odd, sitting in front of the shabby little house.

As she walked to the car, Meredith saw curtains fluttering and knew that the neighbors were getting an eyeful. They probably thought she was being carried off by the mob. That amused her and she smiled, glad that something diverted her mind from her father and her pain, and the misery of the past few months.

"We hadn't planned to ask you to help us move cattle," Rey drawled when he saw how she was dressed, in jeans and a striped shirt and boots.

"I haven't volunteered, either," she assured him. "But I didn't think you'd want me to do housework in a dress." She gave him a wry glance. "Those old black-and-white sitcoms weren't historically accurate, you know. I never saw a woman vacuum the carpet wearing a dress and high heels and pearls!"

"You can do housework in a suit for all I care, as long as you can bake me a pan of biscuits every morning," Rey said, taking the suitcase and putting it in the trunk.

"Good morning," Leo called from the open window of the front seat, grinning as Rey opened the back door and helped her inside.

"Good morning," she said brightly. "You look much better."

"I feel better, except for the headache." He gave her a long look. "You aren't in very good shape yourself. Face hurt?"

"Yes. I guess we're both like walking wounded, huh?" she asked with a grin as she leaned back into the warm leather seat.

"Maybe we should take a nurse with us," Rey muttered as he got in and started the car.

Meredith cleared her throat, but before she could speak, Leo turned to his brother. "I don't need nursing, thank you very much!" Leo said curtly.

"Neither do I!" Meredith agreed.

Rey glanced at them as he pulled out into the street. "I've seen accident victims who looked better than the two of you."

"Don't let him insult you, Meredith," Leo told her. "I'll tell you all about his weak spots so that you can deal with him."

She wouldn't have expected Rey to have any of those, but she was keeping her mouth shut and her options open for the time being. Her new boss looked formidable, and even Leo seemed curious about his lack of warmth.

"Are you all from Jacobsville originally?" Meredith changed the subject.

"No, we're from San Antonio," Leo said. "We inherited the Jacobsville property and it needed a lot of work, so we made it our headquarters. It's convenient to Houston and San Antonio, and frankly, it's isolated and gives us some privacy. We don't like cities as a rule."

"Neither do I," she said, recalling her grandmother's beautiful flower garden at the old place near Fort Worth. She smiled. "I wish Dad hadn't taken the job in Houston in the first place."

"What does he do?" Leo asked.

"He's retired," she said, not wanting to go into specifics. It hurt to talk about her family. Her father was a sore spot just now, anyway.

"Simon talked to the authorities," Rey interrupted. "They're going to make sure he gets counseling and he won't be released until he's kicked the alcohol habit." He glanced over the seat at her, his dark eyes intent. "They think it will be better if you don't have any contact with him for a few weeks, until he's through the worst of the withdrawal symptoms."

"I know about withdrawal," she replied, absently smoothing her hand over her jeans. "Bad habits are hard to break, even new ones."

"You two must read a lot," Rey replied. "I never saw so many books in one place as I did at your house. Even our library isn't that stuffed, and we all read."

"I love reading," she agreed. "We have a television, but neither of us had much time to watch it. Until recently," she added reluctantly, and winced at the thoughts that went through her mind. "I hope they get those men who mugged you, Mr. Hart," she told Leo fervently.

"Leo," he corrected. "It's really Leopold, but nobody calls me that," he added with a grin. "We're pretty informal with our employees."

"Do you have a lot?" she asked curiously.

"A good many in Jacobsville," he replied. "Although we don't have a full-time vet, we do have several accountants, livestock managers, computer programmers, salesmen…you name it, we've got one. It's big business these days to run cattle. We even have a man who does nothing but keep up with legislation that may impact us."

"Do you have dogs and cats?" she asked.

"Always," Rey replied. "We have border collies that help us herd cattle, and we keep cats in the barn to help handle the rats."

"We had a cat in the house," Leo added, "but it was Cag and Tess's, and they took it with them when they moved into their new house. At least she won't have to cope with Herman," he told his brother, and laughed.

Rey smiled involuntarily. "You might not have wanted to work for us if we still had Herman."

"Who's Herman?" she wanted to know.

"He was Cag's albino python," he told her. "He weighed a hundred and ten pounds and lived in a cage in Cag's bedroom. He gave Herman up when he married Tess. He said it would be crazy to keep an animal that big and dangerous around their son. They're still over the moon about that little boy."

"Yes, but there are people who don't even consider things like that," Meredith murmured absently. "I remember a little girl who had to have plastic surgery because she was bitten in the face by her father's pet boa constrictor."

"Herman didn't bite, but Tess almost had a heart attack when she first came to work for us and found him in the washing machine."

"I can sympathize with her," Meredith said. "I haven't come across many snakes. I'm not sure I want to."

"We have rattlers and water moccasins around the place," Rey told her. "You have to watch where you walk, but we've only had one person bitten in recent years. Snakes are always going to be a hazard in open country. You can't be careless."

"I'll remember."

"We've got a big garage apartment," Leo told her. "It's got picture windows and a whirlpool bath. Tess lived there until she and Cag married. I think you'll like it."

"I don't mind where I stay," she said easily. "I'm grateful to have a job at all. I really couldn't go to work in Houston looking like this. It would have been embarrassing for my boss."

"You won't have people staring at you on the ranch," Leo assured her. "And it won't take too long for those bruises to heal."

"I'll be fine, but you'll have to take it easy for a few days still, I'm sure they told you that," she returned at once. "No violent exertion. Concussion is tricky."

"I know that," Leo told her. "We had a man who was kicked in the head by a horse. He dropped dead three days later while he was walking into the corral. It was a hard lesson about head injuries. None of us ever forgot it."

She averted her eyes. She didn't like thinking about head injuries just now.

"I've got to stop for gas," Rey said as they reached the outskirts of the city and he pulled into a self-service gas station. "Anybody want something to drink?"

"Coffee for me," Leo said. "Meredith?"

"I'd like a small coffee, black, please."

"I'll go get it after I fill the tank," Rey said. He got out and started pumping gas.

Leo leaned his arm over the backseat and looked at Meredith openly, his dark eyes quiet and gently affectionate.

"You're still having a hard time with Rey, aren't you?" he asked her.

"He doesn't really like me," she confessed with a wry smile. "And I have to admit, he puts my back up, too. He seems to want to think the worst of me. He was convinced that I mugged you."

He chuckled. "You aren't tall enough to have knocked me out," he said. "But Rey doesn't like women much. He had a bad time of it with a young woman who turned out to be a call girl," he added, noticing absently how stunned Meredith seemed to be at that remark. "He had the ring bought, the honeymoon spot picked out, and then he found out the truth about her. It took him years to get over it. He was crushed."

"I guess so," she said heavily. "Good Lord, no wonder he thought the worst when he saw how I was dressed."

Leo frowned. "I just barely remember the rig you had on. What was it, some sort of costume?"

"I'd been to a wild Halloween party and had just escaped when I saw those men bending over you," she told him. "I ran at them waving my arms and yelling, and frightened them off."

"That was taking a hell of a chance!" he exploded.

She shrugged. "I've done it before," she said. "I learned it from my…from my brother's best friend," she amended, forcing the words out. It was much too soon to try to talk about her tragedy. "He taught karate in the military. He said that sometimes all it needed was a yell and the element of surprise to spook an attacker and make him run. It works."

"Not all the time," Leo said darkly, "and not for women. I'm all for equality, but most men are bigger and stronger than most women, and in hand-to-hand, you'd lose. You can't count on a man running, loud noise or not."

"Well, it worked for you," she amended, and smiled at him. "I'm glad, because I couldn't have wrestled those guys down."

He nodded. "See that you remember it," he told her. "Don't take chances. Get help."

"Some help those partygoers would have been," she scoffed. "Half of them were drunk, and the other half probably wouldn't have walked across the street to save a grandmother from a mugging!"

"Then why were you at a party with them?" he asked reasonably.

She picked at a fingernail. "A girl I know from work said I needed a night off and insisted that I come. I wore an old costume, the only one I had, and thought I'd enjoy myself. I don't do drugs or drink, and one of the men made a blatant pass at me." She wrapped her arms around her body in a defensive posture that betrayed her fear. "I was anxious to get away from the whole mess, luckily for you," she added with a grin.

"I don't like parties much, either," he said. "Getting drunk isn't my idea of a good time."

She glanced out the window. Rey had finished pumping gas and was inside the convenience store now. "Does he drink?" she asked.

"Very rarely. I've been known to, under provocation,

but Rey's levelheaded and sober. He can be mean, and he's got the blackest temper of all of us, but he's a good man to have on your side when the chips are down."

"He doesn't like me," she repeated.

"He'll come around, give him time," Leo told her. "Meanwhile, you've got a job and a place to stay while your face heals. We all have hard times," he added gently. "But we get through them, even when we don't expect to. Give yourself time."

She smiled. "Thanks," she said huskily. "You really are a nice man."

"Nice, clean, sober, modest and incredibly handsome," he added with a wicked grin. "And I haven't even gotten to my best points yet!"

"Compared to your brothers," she began, "you—"

The door opened before she could hang herself, and Rey shoved a cup of coffee at her before he handed the second one to Leo.

"It's hot," he told them as he slid in and took the soft drink out of his jacket pocket and put it in the cup holder.

"Cold caffeine," Leo said, shuddering. "Why can't you drink coffee like a normal man?"

"I drink coffee at breakfast," Rey told him haughtily.

"So do I, but you don't have to have rules on when to drink it!"

Rey started the engine with a speaking glance.

"See that look?" Leo indicated it to Meredith. "When he looks like that, you've already lost whatever argument you're in the middle of. We call it 'the look.' I once saw him break up a fistfight with it."

"I don't plan to argue," Meredith promised.

Rey gave her "the look," and it lingered before his attention turned back to the windshield.

Meredith sat back against the leather seat and wondered suddenly if she wasn't making the biggest mistake of her life.

CHAPTER FOUR

THE HART RANCH was almost as Meredith had pictured it, with neat wooden fences concealing electrified fencing, improved pasture land and cattle everywhere. There were also pastures with horses, and there was a barn big enough to store a commercial jet. But she loved the house itself, with its graceful arches reminiscent of Spanish architecture, and the incredible number of small trees and shrubs around it. In the spring, it must be glorious. There were two ponds, a decorative one in the front of the house and a larger one behind the house in which a handful of ducks shivered in the November sun.

"Do you have goldfish in the pond?" she asked excitedly as Rey stopped the car in front of the house on an inlaid stone driveway.

"Goldfish and Koi," he answered, smiling reluctantly at her excitement. "We have a heater in the pond to keep them comfortable during the winter. There are water lilies in there, too, and a lotus plant."

"Does the other pond have goldfish, too, where the ducks are?" she wondered.

Leo chuckled. "The other one is because of the ducks. We had to net this pond to keep them out of it so we'd *have* some goldfish. The ducks were eating them."

"Oh, I see." She sighed. "It must be beautiful here in the spring," she said dreamily, noting the gazebo and the rose garden and stone seats and shrubs around the goldfish pond.

"It's beautiful to us year-round," Leo told her with lazy affection. "We all love flowers. We've got some more roses in a big flower garden around the back of the house, near a stand of pecan trees. Tess is taking courses in horticulture and she works with hybrids."

"I love roses," Meredith said softly. "If I had time, I'd live in a flower garden."

"I suppose cleaning rooms is time-consuming," Rey murmured sarcastically as he got out of the car and went in the front door of the house.

Leo glanced at her curiously while Rey was out of earshot. "You clean rooms?"

"I don't," she told him with a sharp grin. "But I'm living down to your brother's image of my assets."

Leo pursed his lips. "Now, that's interesting. You sound like a woman with secrets."

"More than you'd guess," she told him heavily. "But none that I'm ashamed of," she added quickly, just in case he got the wrong idea.

"Rey doesn't like you, does he?" he murmured, almost to himself. "I wonder why? It's not like him to pick on sick people."

"I'm not sick," she assured him. "I'm just battered, but I'll heal."

"Sure you will," Leo promised, smiling. "You'll be safe here. The only real chore you'll have is baking. By the time you're completely back on your feet, your father will be sober and in counseling, and your home life will have changed drastically."

"I hope so," she said huskily.

He watched her eyes grow tragic and haunted. He

frowned. "Meredith," he said slowly. "If you need to talk, ever, I can listen without making judgments."

She met his clear dark eyes. "Thanks, Leo," she said with genuine gratitude. "But talking won't change a thing. It's a matter of learning to live with…things."

"Now I'm intrigued."

"Don't push," she said gently. "I'm not able to talk about my problems yet. They're too fresh. Too painful."

"And more than just your father, or I'm a dirt farmer," he drawled.

She shrugged. "Perhaps."

"Anyway, just take your time and let the world pass you by. You're going to love it here. I promise."

"Am I?" She watched Rey come back out of the house with an elderly lady in tow, wringing her hands on her apron.

"That's Mrs. Lewis," Leo told her. "We talked her into coming back to bake biscuits for us, even though she'd retired, but now we're losing her to arthritis. She's going to show you the ropes. But not right now," he added quickly.

"No time like the present," Meredith disagreed with a smile. "Busy hands make busy minds."

"I know how that works," Leo murmured drolly.

Rey opened the back door and helped Meredith out. "Mrs. Lewis, this is Meredith Johns, our new cook. Meredith, Annie Lewis. She's retiring. Again." He made it sound like a shooting offense.

"Oh, my, yes, I'm losing the use of my hands, I'm afraid," Mrs. Lewis said. "Glad to meet you, Miss Johns."

"Glad to meet you, too, Mrs. Lewis," Meredith replied.

"I'll take your bag to your room, while Mrs. Lewis shows you around the house," Rey added.

"She just got here," Leo protested.

"And there's no time like the present to show her the house," Rey replied.

"That's just what she said," Leo sighed.

Rey glanced at Meredith, who gave him a wicked grin and followed along behind Annie Lewis, who was making a valiant effort not to ask about the terrible bruises on Meredith's face.

"It's a big, sprawling house, and it takes a lot of cleaning," Mrs. Lewis said as she led Meredith down the long hall and opened doors to the very masculine bedrooms both with dark, heavy Mediterranean furniture and earth tones in the drapes and carpets. "The men aren't messy, thank God, but they track in all that mud and dust and animal fur! They had beige carpeting when I came here." She glanced at Meredith with a shake of her head. "Red mud just won't come *out* of beige carpet!"

"Or anything else," Meredith added on a soft laugh.

"They work hard, and they're away a lot. But the foreman lives in the bunkhouse with a couple of bachelor cowboys, and they'll look out for you."

"I don't know that I'll be here very long," Meredith replied quietly. "They offered me the job so that I can have time for these to heal." She touched her face, and looked straight at the older woman, who was struggling not to ask the question in her eyes.

"Nobody will hurt you here," Mrs. Lewis said firmly.

Meredith smiled gently. "My father got drunk and beat me up, Mrs. Lewis," she explained matter-of-factly. "He's a good and kind man, but we've had a terrible tragedy to work through. He hasn't been able to cope with it except by losing himself in a bottle, and now he's gone too far and he's in jail." She sighed. "I tried so hard to help him. But I couldn't."

Mrs. Lewis didn't say a word. She put her arms around Meredith and rocked her in them. The shock of it brought the tears that she'd held back for so long. She wept until her body shook with sobs.

Rey, looking for her, stopped dead in the doorway of his bedroom and met Mrs. Lewis's misty eyes over Meredith's bowed shoulders. It shocked him to see that feisty, strong woman collapsed in tears. It hurt him.

Mrs. Lewis made a gesture with her eyebrows and a severe look. Rey acknowledged it with a nod and a last glance at the younger woman as he walked back down the hall.

SUPPER WAS RIOTOUS. Meredith had made a huge pan of homemade biscuits and ferreted out all sorts of preserves to go with them. For an entrée, she made fajitas with lean beef and sliced vegetables, served with wild rice and a salad. Dessert was fresh fruit and fresh whipped cream, the only concession besides the biscuits that she made to fat calories. She'd also found some light margarine to set out.

"This is good," Rey commented as he glanced at her. "We usually have broiled or fried steak with lots of potatoes."

"Not bad once a week or so, but terrible for your cholesterol," she pointed out with a smile as she finished her salad. "Lean beef is okay for you, but not in massive doses."

"You sound like a dietician," Leo chuckled.

"Modern women have to keep up with health issues,"

she said evasively. "I'm responsible for your health while I'm working for you. I have to be food-conscious."

"That's fine," Rey told her flatly, "but don't put tofu and bean sprouts in front of me if you want to stay here."

Her eyebrows arched. "I hate tofu."

"Thank God," Leo sighed as he buttered another biscuit. "I got fed tofu salad the last time I went to Brewster's for supper," he added with absolute disgust. "I ate the olives and the cheese and left the rest."

"I can't say that I blame you," Meredith said, laughing because he looked so forlorn.

"Janie Brewster thinks tofu is good for him," Rey commented. "But she thinks he needs therapy more. He doesn't like fish. She says that has some sort of connection to his fear of deep water." He glanced at his brother with wicked affection. "She's a psychology major. She already has an associate degree from our local junior college."

"She's twenty," Leo said with a twist of his lower lip. "She knows everything."

"She just got her associate degree this spring," Rey added.

"Good. Maybe she'll get a job in New York," Leo said darkly.

"Why New York?" Meredith asked curiously.

"Well, it's about as far east as she can go and find her sort of work," Leo muttered. "And she'd be out of my hair!"

Rey gave him a covert glance and finished his fajitas.

Meredith finished her own meal and got up to refill coffee cups. She had a feeling that Leo was more interested in the nebulous Brewster girl than he wanted to admit.

"We need groceries," she told them when she'd served dessert and they were eating it. "Mrs. Lewis made me a list."

"You can use one of the ranch trucks to drive to town," Leo suggested carelessly.

Her fingers toyed with her fork. "I haven't driven in several months."

"You don't drive?" Rey exclaimed, shocked.

She couldn't meet his eyes. "I take buses." Cars made her feel guilty.

"Why?"

She remembered a day she should have driven. The memories were horrible…

"Meredith, it's all right," Leo said gently, sensing something traumatic about her behavior. "I'll drive you. Okay?"

"You won't," Rey replied. "You're in worse shape than she is. Which brings up another point. You don't need to be walking around town like that," he told her.

She wasn't offended; it was a relief. She even smiled. "No, I don't guess I do. Will you do the shopping?" she asked him, her wide, soft eyes steady on his.

He felt wild little thrills shooting through his body at the impact. It had been years since he'd been so shaken by eye contact alone. He didn't move. He just stared at her, his dark eyes unblinking, curious. His body rippled with vague hunger.

Leo, watching the eye contact, tried not to grin. He cleared his throat, and Rey seemed to remember that he had a forkful of fruit halfway to his mouth. He took it the rest of the way and chewed it carefully before he spoke.

"I'll get the groceries," Rey volunteered. He glared at both of them, noting the shaved place where Leo had stitches near the back of his head. "Obviously I'm the only one here who can walk around without drawing curious stares from bystanders!"

Leo buttered another biscuit. "That sounds like sour grapes to me. If you want attention, try walking around without your pants."

"I didn't say I wanted attention," Rey returned hotly.

"Good thing." He glanced at Meredith with a mischievous smile. "He looks like hell without his pants," he said conversationally. "Hairiest legs of the bunch."

"That's debatable," Rey shot back. "Yours aren't much better."

"What a good thing you two aren't Scottish," Meredith said demurely.

It took a minute for them to get it, then Leo burst out laughing, trying to picture his younger brother in a kilt. Rey lifted a corner of his thin mouth, but he wasn't in a smiling mood. It bothered him, that Meredith had been crying in Mrs. Lewis's arms, that she didn't drive, that she was so mysterious about her life. She was twenty-three, almost twenty-four. Most women by that age had been involved in a serious relationship, some more than one. Many had been married.

His heart skipped. Was that her secret? He remembered watching her rub her ring finger in the car. He glanced at it curiously. She didn't wear a ring, and there was no sign that she'd been wearing one there. She didn't act married. She hadn't talked about having a husband. She was single, apparently by choice. But had there been men in her past? He was still carrying scars from his one great love affair, from the deception he'd endured. Meredith had gone out walking to a party in a rig that made her look like a prostitute, and she'd been comfortable doing that. It wasn't something an innocent girl would have considered.

Knowing that, he looked at her in a different way, speculatively. She had a nice figure and she wasn't all flushing smiles like Janie Brewster when Leo was around. Meredith was oddly mature for her age, almost matronly. She seemed to be used to giving instructions, too. She was a puzzle that disturbed him. What if she was hiding something sordid in her past? He and Leo had taken her in on faith and pity, but now he wondered if they'd made a terrible mistake. If she were in league with the men who'd robbed Leo, they might have a dangerous situation developing. What if she'd planned the whole thing as a means to an end?

Basically Rey didn't trust her. He wasn't going to let down his guard, either, no matter if looking at her did raise his blood pressure. She wasn't going to know that she did. And he'd keep his eyes open, all the time, just in case.

THE DAYS TURNED to a week. Meredith's painful bruises faded slowly. She lost some of the brooding sadness that seemed to cling to her like the jeans she wore around the house when she was working. She found the slower, easier pace strange, and she missed the urgency of her daily routine. But as the days went by lazily, she realized that she hadn't really given herself time to think. She'd avoided it, ignored it, hoping that the past would vanish. Now she was face to face with it, forced to reflect on what had happened.

She sat beside the fishpond one sunny afternoon, between chores, and watched the goldfish under the surface of the dark water as they moved sluggishly. The water wasn't frozen, but it was cold. The pond heater only kept a small area heated, so the fish were limited in movement. She could imagine how it would be to sit here in the summer and watch them move around in their watery world, with flowers blooming all around.

She'd loved planting flowers. She missed her home, her bulbs and shrubs, the familiar things that she'd accumulated around her. Now it was all gone, sold without a second thought to make the memories bearable. It was too late, and she wished she'd been more sensible. There were things she should have kept. Mike's stupid baseball cap, the one he always wore on the rare occasions when he wasn't working, and when he went fishing. She missed her mother's collection of small silk Chinese boxes and her pretty evening gowns. She'd thrown all those things away. At the time, it had seemed reasonable to cut all the ties with the past. It didn't now.

The sound of a truck pulling up to the front door caught her attention. Rey and Leo had been out of town for two days, attending another cattle convention, this time in Denver.

They climbed out of the cab of the big six-wheeled pickup truck and retrieved their suitcases from the back, waving as the ranch truck pulled right out again and took off down the road.

Meredith got up and went to join them.

"Want some coffee and pie?" she asked with a smile.

"That would really hit the spot," Leo said, returning the smile. "I hate commercial flights."

"You're the smart guy who said our jet needed to be overhauled," Rey reminded him.

"It did," Leo replied.

Rey was looking at Meredith openly. "The bruises are fading," he remarked. "You have more color, too."

"I've been getting out in the sunlight," she replied easily. "I like to watch the fish, even though they don't move much."

"We might put a big aquarium inside," Rey remarked, unaware of his brother's quick, curious glance. "I like fish myself."

"They've done studies," Meredith volunteered as they stood aside to let her enter the house first. "They say watching fish swim is calming. It helps relieve stress."

"God knows, we could use some of that," Leo chuckled. "Especially when cattle prices fall and feed prices go through the roof."

"Cattle raising must be a complex process," she remarked.

"Very complex," Rey said. He frowned as he watched her walk. "Hip sore?" he asked.

She laughed self-consciously. "Well, yes, it is. How did you know?"

"You've got a light limp on the right side. Barely noticeable."

She rubbed her hip self-consciously. "I fell on that side, the night Dad hit me," she told him. "The floor's pretty hard."

"There's a whirlpool bath in your bedroom," Rey reminded her. "It'll help the soreness."

"I discovered that," she said, grinning. "What a luxury! We only have a shower at home, and it's temperamental."

Rey gave her a long look. "When we've had time to catch our breath, I'll see what I can find out about your father, if you'd like."

Her face brightened. “That would be nice.”

He smiled slowly, liking the way her pale eyes seemed to glow when she was pleased. She wasn’t bad-looking at all, and her figure was just about perfect. He wondered how she could have remained single for so long, with her homemaking skills, not to mention her sweet personality and that knockout body.

She was watching him with equal appreciation, and totally unaware of it. He had a lithe, powerful physique that made her think of rodeo. He walked with a unique sort of grace, and he didn’t stoop or slouch, ever. She liked his eyes best of all. They were almost a liquid-brown, and they had black rims around the pupils. He was rugged and sensuous, and she looked at his wide thin mouth and wondered for the first time how it would feel to kiss it.

Her thoughts horrified her. She dragged her eyes away and excused herself in an absolute fluster to go make coffee.

Leo lifted both eyebrows and stared at his brother after she was out of earshot. “Well, well,” he murmured. “You do seem to be making an impression on her.”

“Cut it out,” Rey said testily.

“And vice versa,” came the irritating reply.

Rey made a rough sound in his throat and stomped off down the hall to his room. He put down his suitcase, took off his suit and dress shirt and got into jeans and a checked long-sleeved work shirt. He glanced at himself in the mirror as he buttoned it, his eyes blank as he recalled the wild flush on Meredith’s cheeks. It shouldn’t please him. He didn’t trust her. She could be trying to play them all for suckers. But he smiled, just the same.

Meredith had coffee and cherry pie in saucers on the table by the time the brothers were changed and walking into the kitchen.

"Coffee's fresh," she said.

"Aren't you having any?" Rey asked.

"I have to get the clothes into the dryer," she excused herself with a quick smile. "Yell if you need anything."

She was gone in a flash.

Rey stared broodingly at his pie and frowned. She didn't want to have coffee with them. Why?

"You make her nervous," Leo said, answering the unspoken question. "She knows you don't trust her."

Rey frowned as he nibbled at his pie and sipped coffee. "I don't know her," he replied. He gave his brother a speaking glance. "We've always done background checks on employees," he added firmly. "I don't think we should make an exception of her, even though she's temporary."

"Translated, that means you want to know more about her than you do," Leo drawled, grinning.

"Maybe I do," Rey confessed. "But she's in a position to do a lot of damage if she isn't what she seems. You could have been killed, or suffered brain damage," he added quietly. "If she's in cahoots with the guys who mugged you…" He let the sentence trail off meaningfully.

Leo grimaced. "I don't like poking into peoples' private business," he replied. "But you're right. It's risky not to check her out."

"I'll get the agency on it first thing tomorrow," Rey said. He took another bite of the pie. "She's a hell of a good cook," he murmured.

"Makes good coffee, too," Leo commented.

They looked at each other and grimaced. It was going to upset Meredith if she found out what they were up to. But it was too much of a gamble not to find out what they could about her background and character. On the other hand, Leo promised himself, he was going to intercept that background check before Rey had a chance to see it. If Meredith had secrets she was hiding for a good reason, he wasn't going to give her away to Rey.

IT TOOK SEVERAL days for the private detective to get to the case and send a report to the Harts.

Rey was out of town at a one-day seminar on a new spreadsheet computer program the brothers were using for herd records when the report arrived. Leo carried the report into his office and closed the door while he read it.

When he finished, he let out a harsh breath. So that was Meredith's secret. No wonder her father drank. No wonder she was so reticent and quiet about her past. He smiled as he considered her true profession, and he was determined that Rey wasn't going to know about it until disclosure was inevitable. Rey was too prone to conclusion-jumping and rushing to judgment. It was about time he had a set down, and Meredith was just the woman to give it to him. Meanwhile, he'd let Rey work on hanging himself. Obviously Meredith was enjoying her anonymity, and considering the high-powered pressures of her daily job, it wasn't surprising that she found mundane housekeeping a nice change. It wouldn't hurt to let her enjoy the vacation from stress, without probing into her feelings. No doubt she still felt the grief, even after several months.

He touched the report with idle fingers, frowning as

he recognized one of the names on it. Mike had been a Houston policeman. He was also a friend of Colter Banks, a Texas Ranger and cousin of the Harts, who worked out of the Houston ranger office. It really was a small world. He wanted to tell Meredith that he remembered Mike, but he didn't want to blow her cover. He also didn't want her to know that they'd been checking up on her.

He put the file into the filing cabinet, deliberately putting it under the wrong letter of the alphabet. If Rey asked, he'd just tell him that the agency was working on it but had other, more urgent cases to assign agents to first.

MEREDITH WAS ALONE in the house when Rey came in, late that night, from his business trip. Leo had gone to dinner at the Brewsters' house again, presumably at the invitation of Janie's father, to talk about a new breeding bull the Brewsters were trying to sell him.

She'd just started the dishwasher and was ready to turn the lights off in the kitchen when she heard Rey come in.

He paused in the kitchen doorway, a black Stetson slanted over one dark eye, wearing a grey vested suit that clung lovingly to the hard, muscular lines of his tall body. Meredith felt ragged by comparison in her jeans and red T-shirt, and barefoot. Her hair was disheveled because she'd been scrubbing the floor with a brush, and she wasn't wearing makeup. She hadn't expected to see either of the brothers before she went to bed.

Rey's dark eyes went to her pretty feet and he smiled. "You don't like shoes, do you?"

She grimaced. "No, and it's not good to go without

them. No arch support." She studied his lean face. He had dark circles under his eyes. "Would you like some coffee and something to eat?"

"I would," he said heavily. "They gave me peanuts on the plane," he added with absolute disgust.

She chuckled. The sound was pleasant, and Rey was surprised at how it touched him to hear her laugh.

"I'll make you a nice thick low-fat ham sandwich with sauce."

"Thanks," he said, sliding a chair out so that he could straddle it. He tossed his hat into the chair beside him and ran a hand through his thick dark hair. "Make the coffee first, Meredith. I've got paperwork that has to be done tonight before the accountant comes to do the books in the morning."

"Can't it wait?" she asked gently. "You look worn to a frazzle. You need an early night."

His eyes searched hers intently. "I don't need mothering," he said, angered out of all proportion.

She flushed and turned away. She didn't apologize or say another word, but her hands shook as she filled the coffeepot and started it brewing.

Rey cursed himself silently for snapping at her. It was unkind, especially after she'd volunteered to feed him. She'd been working hard, too, he could see the spotless floor and the brush and bucket she'd been using on it. She must have done it on her hands and knees. It was a big kitchen, too. He wasn't the only one who was tired.

He got up from the chair and moved to stand just behind her. His lean hands caught her small waist and pulled her back against him. "I'm sorry," he said, his voice deep and husky with sudden emotion.

Her cold fingers came to rest on his and her whole

body went rigid as a flash of white-hot pleasure shot through it. She caught her breath. He heard it. His own body tautened and the hands around her waist suddenly grew possessive, rough, insistent, as they pulled her tight against him.

He could hear her breathing change. He could feel the faint tremor of her hands over his. Impulsively he bent his head and his mouth touched the side of her neck.

CHAPTER FIVE

MEREDITH KNEW HER knees were shaking. She hoped she wasn't going to fall on the floor at his feet with sheer excitement. It had been years since a man had made her feel such a rush of pleasure, and even then, it had been one-sided. She'd been crazy about a man who only saw her as a sort of unrelated sister. But even that wasn't as powerful as what she was feeling with Rey Hart.

His mouth became insistent as it moved slowly up her neck. He began to turn her, in the silence that was suddenly alive with passion. His hard lips traveled to the hollow of her throat, where a tiny pulse hammered, and then up to her chin. His teeth nibbled her chin, moving on to her lower lip. He tugged it away from the top one and tasted it with his tongue. All the while, his lean, strong hands were sliding up and down at her waist, smoothing her body completely against him.

His teeth nipped at her top lip with a sensual approach that made her breath shiver in her throat. He was experienced, far more so than she was. For all her professional capability, in this way she was a novice, and it showed.

He noticed her lack of sensual response with absent curiosity. She was attracted to him, that was obvious, but it was as if she didn't know what to do.

He guided her hands to his vest and flicked open

buttons while his lips teased around hers. She fumbled and he laughed softly, his nose rubbing against hers as he moved her hands and unfastened the buttons on his vest and shirt with deft efficiency. He coaxed her hands inside, against thick hair and hard, warm muscle, while his mouth began to bite at hers, tempting her lips to part. She was stiff, trying not to respond, but her body was hungry.

"Like this," he whispered gently, teaching her mouth the lazy, sensual rhythm he wanted from it. "Taste my mouth, the way I'm tasting yours. Don't fight what you're feeling."

She heard the words as if through a fog. She didn't understand what he was saying, but her body obeyed him. She was in a sensual limbo, her hands flat against his chest, her head lifted, her eyes slitted and looking up into his as he began to increase the teasing pressure of his mouth. She followed his lips. She relaxed into the curve of his powerful body with a little shiver.

He devoured her mouth roughly, again and then again, tempting her until her mouth followed his, returning the arousing pressure. She could see the glitter grow in his narrow eyes, feel the grip of his lean hands as he pushed her hips against the sudden hardness of him. She gasped with embarrassment and then lost all sense of it as his mouth opened and pushed down hard against her parted lips, drowning her in passion.

It was like flying, she thought dazedly. He hesitated for an instant and her eyes opened, drowsy and curious. Her mouth was swollen, soft, tremulous. She looked at him with fascination, utterly helpless in his embrace. He felt an unfamiliar protectiveness toward her. It had been years since he'd kissed an innocent. Meredith's lack of experience was obvious. He was enjoying it.

"Yes," he murmured gruffly, and he bent again. His arms enfolded her, tender arms that no longer forced her into intimacy. His mouth was tender, too, exploring hers with slow mastery, careful not to overwhelm her.

She sighed into his hard mouth, relaxing against him. Her hands moved restlessly on his broad, bare chest, and contracted in the thick mat of hair that covered him.

He lifted his head, staring down into her wide eyes with somber delight. His hands smoothed hers deeper into his thick hair and hard muscle. He traced the edges of her short nails with his thumbs. His breath was jerky. He didn't like having her see that he was vulnerable. There were too many things he still didn't know about her, and he didn't trust her. She seemed innocent, but he couldn't forget the dress she'd been wearing and the accusations her father had made about her. He didn't dare trust her on such short acquaintance. On the other hand, his body was singing with pleasure from the long, hot contact with hers. He couldn't force himself to let her go. Not just yet.

"Why did you do that?" she asked huskily.

One dark eyebrow lifted. He didn't smile. "Why did you let me?" he shot back.

She felt uncomfortable. Despite the effort it took, she moved away from him. He let her go with no show of reluctance. He watched her struggle for composure while he refastened buttons with easy confidence, concealing the effect she had on him. He didn't even look ruffled.

"The coffee must be done by now," he pointed out when she seemed unable to move.

She turned stiffly and went to fill cups and put them, along with cream and sugar, on the table.

While he fixed his coffee, she made him two thick ham sandwiches with hands that slowly lost their tremor. She was devastated by a kiss that didn't seem to have disturbed him at all. She remembered the sudden hardness of his body, but she knew all about anatomy. A man couldn't help that reaction to anything feminine, it was part of his makeup. It wasn't even personal.

Somehow, it made things worse to know that. She felt his eyes on her back, and she knew he was measuring her up. She had no idea why he'd kissed her, but she didn't trust his motives. He didn't like her. She couldn't afford to let her guard down. Rey Hart would be hell on a woman who loved him. She knew that instinctively.

By the time she had the sandwiches made, her hands were steady again and she was able to put them on the table with a cool smile.

"I have to tidy up the living room…" she began.

He caught her hand as she started past him. "Sit down, Meredith," he said quietly.

She sat. He sipped coffee and studied her for a long moment. "I talked to Simon while I was away," he said. "Your father has been released from jail and placed in an alcohol treatment center. It's early days yet, but the prognosis is good. It helps that he hasn't been drinking that heavily for a long time."

She looked relieved and anxiously waited to hear what else Rey had to say about her father.

He continued. "The therapist wouldn't reveal any intimate details to Simon, you understand, but he was able to say that your father had been unable to deal with a family tragedy. Now that he's sober, he's extremely upset about what he did to you." He looked grim. "He doesn't remember doing it, Meredith."

She averted her eyes to her coffee cup. For something to do, she lifted it and took a sip of blistering black coffee, almost burning her lip. "That's common in cases of alcohol or drug abuse," she murmured absently.

He studied her over the rim of his coffee cup. "You won't be allowed to communicate with him until he's through the treatment program, but he wanted you to know that he's desperately sorry for what he did."

She ground her teeth together. She knew that. Her father wasn't a bad man. Until he'd started abusing alcohol, he'd been one of the gentlest men alive. But, like all human beings, he had a breaking point which he reached when tragedy erupted into his life.

"He isn't a bad man," she said quietly. "Although I know it must have seemed like it."

"I've seen drunks before," Rey replied. "My brothers have gone on benders a time or two." He smiled faintly. "In fact, Leo holds the current record for damage at Shea's Bar, out on the Victoria road. He doesn't cut loose often, but when he does, people notice."

"He doesn't seem the sort of man who would do that," she remarked, surprised.

"We're all the sort of men who would do that, given the right provocation," he told her.

She smiled. "Do you get drunk and wreck bars?" she couldn't resist asking.

"I don't drink as a rule," he said simply. "A glass of wine rarely, nothing stronger. I don't like alcohol."

She smiled. "Neither do I."

He leaned back in his chair and studied her quietly. His hair was still faintly disheveled where her hands had caught in it when he was kissing her, and his lower lip was swollen from the pressure of her mouth. She knew she must look almost as bad. Her hand went unconsciously to her unruly hair.

"Take it down," he said abruptly.

"Wh…what?"

"Take your hair down," he said huskily. "I want to see it."

She'd just gotten her wild heart under control, and now it was galloping all over again from that sultry tone, from the dark, intent caress of his eyes on her face.

"Listen, I work for you," she began with a tremor in her voice.

He got up from the chair and moved toward her with a lazy, almost arrogant stride. He drew her up in front of him and started pulling out hairpins. Her hair, unbound, fell in soft waves down her back, almost concealing one eye.

"It's hard to manage when it's down," she said self-consciously.

"I love long hair." He tangled his lean hands in it and coaxed her face up to his. He searched her eyes at point-blank range. "I've kissed girls years younger than you who knew even more than I do. Why are you still a novice?"

She swallowed hard. He was making her knees weak again. She couldn't quite get a whole breath of air into her lungs. Her hands rested on his chest lightly and she felt her heart choking her with its rapid beat as she stared into his narrowed, dark eyes.

"What?" she asked, barely having heard much less understood the question.

His hands were exploring the cool length of her hair

with fascination. "You're not bad-looking, Meredith. Surely you've dated."

"Yes," she said, disconcerted. "But I'm old-fashioned."

Both eyebrows went up over a cynical smile. "That's a pitiful excuse in this day and age."

"Why?" she asked, her clear grey eyes staring up into his with no thought of subterfuge. "The whole reason for the women's movement is so that women can have the freedom to do as they please. I'm not promiscuous. Why should I need an excuse?"

He blinked. She made his question sound unreasonable. "I thought sexual liberation was the soul of the movement," he drawled.

"Being chaste is sexual liberation, in my book," she replied. "You'd be amazed how many women in my graduating class practiced abstinence."

"In high school, I gather," he said absently, tracing the length of her hair with his hands.

She almost corrected him, but then, she really mustn't destroy the illusions he had about her as a domestic. "Yes. In high school."

He moved closer to her, his lean body a sensual provocation that made her breath catch. He laughed softly. "Care to test the hypothesis?" he murmured softly.

"I work for you," she repeated, playing for time.

"So?"

"So it's not wise to mix business…"

"…with pleasure?" He caught her waist and drew her close. "It's been a while since I found a woman so desirable," he whispered, bending to her mouth. "Experience bores me. You," he bit off against her soft lips, "are a challenge."

"Thank you, but I don't want to be," she whispered, trying to pull away.

He lifted his head and searched her eyes. "No curiosity about the great unknown?" he taunted.

"No desire to treat it as a sophisticated game," she corrected abruptly.

He hesitated, but only for an instant. His lean hands contracted and then released her. He went back to his chair and sat down. "Touché," he said with a curious glance. "All right, Meredith, I'll sit here and eat my sandwiches and we'll pretend that we're still strangers physically."

"Good idea," she approved. She reached down for her half-empty coffee cup and put it in the sink.

He was halfway through a sandwich when she excused herself and went to fluff up the pillows in the living room and put magazines and books back in their places. Leo had left things strewn about before he'd gone to the Brewsters'. She was glad, because it gave her a valid reason not to sit next to Rey with her emotions in turmoil.

By the time she'd gone back to the kitchen, Rey had finished his sandwiches and coffee and was coming out the door.

"You're safe," he drawled. "I'm going to change and get to work in the study. Where's Leo?"

"Having supper at the Brewsters' house," she told him. "He said he'd be early."

"That means he'll be late," he mused. "Janie Brewster will have found twenty excuses to keep him talking to her father. She's one determined young lady, but Leo's equally determined. He doesn't want ties."

"Doesn't that sound familiar?" she murmured wickedly.

His eyes slid up and down her body in a silence that teemed with tension. "I never said I didn't want ties," he corrected. "I said I didn't want marriage. There's a difference."

"Don't look at me," she said carelessly. "I don't have time for relationships."

"Of course. All that cleaning must demand a lot of you," he said deliberately.

She flushed. He had no idea what her life was like on a daily basis, and she wanted very badly to tell him. But he was so almighty arrogant and condescending that he put her back up. She wasn't going to tell him a thing. He'd find out soon enough.

She put her hands on her hips and stared at him. "And what's wrong with being a housekeeper?" she demanded, going on the offensive. "Where would you and your brother be right now if there weren't women you could hire to bake and clean for you? I guess you'd have to get married then, or learn to cook, wouldn't you?"

He glared at her. "I could cook if I wanted to."

"You're the sort of man who makes a woman wish she didn't have a culinary skill to her name," she said icily. "You are so 'lord of the manor-ish,' Mr. Hart!"

"It isn't a manor," he pointed out. "They have those in England. We call this a ranch."

She glared at him.

He grinned. "You really do rise to the bait beautifully," he murmured, and something flashed in his dark eyes. "The sandwiches were good," he added.

She looked surprised. "Nothing but ham and a homemade sauce," she faltered.

"You do that a lot with food," he remarked gently. "I like the way you experiment with dishes. I even like the way you garnish the plates. You make things look appetizing."

She didn't realize that he'd even noticed. "I learned that from a dietician," she said without thinking. "If food is decorative, sometimes it makes up for bulk."

He smiled quizzically. "You can't decorate biscuits," he teased. "But you make really good ones."

"Thanks." She smiled back. "I'll tidy up the kitchen if you're through."

"I am. Don't stay up too late," he added and his eyes were suddenly bright with mischief. "You need plenty of rest so that you can make biscuits for breakfast!"

"Okay. I'll get an early night." She laughed and went on past him to the kitchen.

He stared after her for several long seconds with an expression that he was glad she didn't see. He liked the taste of her. That hadn't been wise, kissing her that way. He was going to have to make sure it didn't happen again. He didn't need complications.

NOTHING WAS THE same between Meredith and Rey after that day. They were aware of each other. It wasn't blatant, but she could feel tingling in her spine when Rey was in a room. It was instinctive. Her eyes followed him like puppies, and she flushed wildly when he caught her at it and gave her that amused, worldly glance.

Leo noticed, too, and it worried him that Rey was encouraging Meredith. He knew Rey too well to think he'd had a change of heart toward his bachelor status.

"You're leading her on," Leo accused his brother one evening when they were alone in the study with the door closed. "Why?"

Rey gave him a surprised glance. "You make it sound like a crime to flirt with her."

"In your case, it is," his brother said flatly. "You're a rounder. She isn't."

Rey shrugged. "She's not exactly off-limits," he told his brother. "Not at her age."

"And what do you have in mind? Seduction?" Leo persisted irritably. "She's already been damaged enough by what happened with her father. The bruises are barely healed, and the mental scars are still there. Don't play games with her."

"Aren't you self-righteous all of a sudden?" Rey shot back angrily. "You've been stringing Janie Brewster along for weeks, and we both know you don't have any intention in hell of getting serious about her. All you want is first chance at that damned seed bull they're thinking of selling! Does she know?" he added maliciously.

Leo's eyes began to glitter. "Janie is a child," he said furiously. "I pick at her, and not because of any damned bull. I'm certainly not hell-bent on seduction!"

"She's not a child," Rey countered. "You're leading her down a blind alley, when you know full well she's in love with you."

Leo looked shocked. "She's not in love with me! Maybe she's got a crush. That's all!"

"You don't see the way she looks at you, do you?" Rey replied solemnly.

Leo cleared his throat. "We're talking about Meredith," he said firmly.

Rey's eyes narrowed. "Meredith is an adult."

"And she works for us," Leo went on relentlessly.

"I'm not going to stand by and let you make an amusement of her."

"Jealous?" his brother taunted.

Leo was very still. "Is that the draw?" he asked softly. "Are we competing for a woman again?"

Rey's eyes flashed. "I would never have known about Carlie if you hadn't started propositioning her in front of me. Do you think I can forget that?"

"I keep hoping you will someday. She would have taken you for the ride of your life," Leo said quietly. "You're my brother. I couldn't stand by and do nothing."

Rey turned away with a muttered curse. Leo was right; he had saved him from even worse heartache, but the memory was still raw enough to hurt.

"Don't try to take it out on Meredith," Leo told him firmly. "She's had enough tragedy. Let her do her job."

Rey glanced at him over his shoulder. "I would, if she'd remember why she's here," he said venomously. "It's not my fault that every time I turn around, she's drooling over me! A saint could be tempted by a woman whose eyes worship him like that. I'm only human!"

"Don't raise your voice," Leo cautioned.

"Why? Do you think she's standing outside the door eavesdropping?" Rey drawled sarcastically. "What if she did hear me? It's the truth. She wants me. A blind man could see it."

"That's no reason to take advantage of her. She's not like your usual women."

"No, she's not. She has no ambition, no intellect. Besides that, she's so inexperienced, it's unreal. I never thought kissing a woman could be boring, until she came along," Rey added coldly, trying not to let Leo see how attracted he was to their housekeeper. "She's so naive, it's nauseating."

Outside the door, Meredith stood poised like a statue with a cup of coffee in a saucer shaking in her hands. She'd come to offer it to Rey, and overheard words that had never been meant for her ears. She fought tears as she turned around and went quickly and silently back down the hall to the kitchen.

Hearts couldn't really break, she told herself firmly, as she dabbed at the tears with a paper towel. She was just feeling the aftereffects of her devastating experience at home. It wasn't as if she was really drooling over Rey Hart.

She felt like sinking through the floor when she realized that she did spend an inordinate amount of time staring at him. He was handsome, sensuous, attractive. She liked looking at him. And maybe she was infatuated, a little. That didn't give him the right to say such horrible things about her.

If she hadn't been listening, she'd never have known about them in the first place. She'd have gone right ahead, mooning over him and having him know it and be amused by it. Her pride felt tattered. She'd never been one to wear her heart on her sleeve, but Rey had kissed her as if he enjoyed it, and she'd built dreams on those kisses. She realized now how truly naive it had been. The first man who paid her any attention in years, and she fell head over heels for him. Seen in that context, perhaps it wasn't surprising after all. She'd heard Leo accuse him of being a rounder, and she had to admit that his experience ran rings around hers. Apparently he was accustomed to playing sensual games with women. That was all those devastating kisses that had brought her to her knees had meant to him—just a game. And she'd taken it seriously!

Well, she told herself firmly, he needn't worry that she'd throw herself at his feet again. From now on, she was going to be the perfect employee, polite and courteous and eager to please—but she'd never stare at him longingly again. Thank God she'd overheard what he said to Leo. It had spared her a terrible humiliation. A little hurt now was far better than being wrung out emotionally down the road because she'd been ignorant of the facts. Wasn't she herself always telling people that the truth, however brutal, was always best in the long run? It was time to take her own advice.

WHEN REY AND Leo came in to breakfast the next morning, she put bacon and eggs and biscuits on the table with a cool, professional smile.

Rey was oddly subdued. He didn't give her the arrogant scrutiny that had become force of habit in recent days. In fact, he didn't look at her at all. Leo kept up a pleasant conversation about the day's chores. They were moving some sick cattle into a pasture near the house so the vet could examine them, and stock was being shifted into closer quarters as well, within easier reach of the hay barn.

"I thought you had those big round bales of hay?" Meredith asked curiously.

"We do," Leo agreed. "But we still bale it the old-fashioned way and stack it in the barn. You lose some of the round bales through weathering by sun and rain. The hay that's kept dry in the barn has less deterioration and better nutrition."

"But you feed more than hay?"

Leo chuckled. He buttered a second biscuit. "You are sharp. Yes, we have a man who mixes feeds for better nutrition. No animal proteins, either," he added. "We're reactionaries when it comes to ranching. No artificial hormones, no pesticides, nothing except natural methods of pest control and growth. We're marketing our beef under the Hart Ranch label, as well, certifying it organic. We've already got several chain supermarkets carrying our product, and we've just moved onto the internet to extend our distribution."

"That's amazing," Meredith said with genuine interest. "It's like having custom beef," she added, nodding.

"It is custom beef," Leo told her. "We're capitalizing on the move toward healthier beef. Quick profit methods are going to fail producers in the long run, especially with the current attitude toward hormones and antibiotics and animal-product proteins for feed. We think that once organic beef catches on, the market will justify the added expense."

"Word of mouth will take you far, too," Meredith said. "Hospitals teach nutrition these days, not only to patients but to the community. Tailored beef will find a market among consumers with heart problems, who'll pay the extra cost for healthier cuts of meat grown organically."

Rey was listening. He finished his biscuit and poured himself another cup of coffee from the carafe on the table. "J.D. Langley pioneered that organic approach locally," he remarked. "He and the Tremayne boys got into terrific fights with other producers at seminars for a while. Then we saw the disasters overseas and suddenly everybody else was jumping on the bandwagon."

"They'll be glad they did, I think," Meredith said.

"Which reminds me," Leo said, eyeing her. "Mrs. Lewis said her larder hadn't been opened since you came here. So…what are you making these biscuits with?"

She gave them a wary glance. "Light olive oil," she said slowly.

Rey gaped at his biscuit as if it had suddenly sprouted hair. "Olive oil?" he gasped.

"Listen," she said quickly, aware of horrified stares, "olive oil is so healthy that people who live on a Mediterranean diet have only a fraction of the vascular problems we have in abundance in this country. The fat content is still there, but it's a vegetable fat, and it's actually good for you. Until I told you, you didn't even know you'd given up great gobs of animal fat in those biscuits!"

The brothers looked at each other. "Well," Leo had to admit, "they taste just as good as the others did."

"That's true," Rey agreed reluctantly.

"And we're getting older," Leo continued. "We don't want clogged arteries giving us heart attacks and strokes."

"Or bypass surgery," Rey sighed.

"So I guess olive oil isn't so bad, after all," Leo concluded, with a grin at Meredith.

She grinned back. "Thank goodness. I had visions of being tarred and feathered," she confessed.

"I'm not giving up butter, though," Rey told her firmly, dipping his knife into the tub next to the biscuit basket. "Nothing tastes like real butter on a biscuit."

Meredith didn't look at him. She couldn't confess that what he was eating was not butter, but rather a light margarine that actually lowered cholesterol levels. She only smiled and poured herself another cup of coffee.

Leo and Rey had started moving bulls into the lower pasture, where new forage grasses were thriving even in autumn, when a mangy old longhorn bull suddenly jerked his head and hooked Leo in the shoulder.

Leo yelled and threw a kick at him, but the aggravating animal was already trotting nonchalantly into the new pasture without a backward glance.

"How bad is it?" Rey asked, leaving the cowboys to work the cattle alone while he looked at his brother's shoulder.

"Probably needs stitches," Leo said through his teeth. "Drive me to the house and let me change shirts, then you can take me to Lou Coltrain."

"Damned bull," Rey muttered as he put his brother into the ranch truck and took off home.

Meredith was sweeping off the back steps when they drove up. She gave Leo's bloodstained shirt a quick glance.

"Come on in here, let me have a look," she said gently.

Disconcerted, Leo let her remove the shirt from his shoulder and bathe the blood away with a clean cloth.

She probed around the edges of the cut and nodded. "You'll need stitches. Here. Hold this tight against the cut until you get to town."

"I need to change shirts," he began.

"You need to get to the doctor. Which one do you use?" she persisted, picking up the mobile phone she kept on the table.

"Dr. Lou Coltrain," he said.

"I'll phone and tell them you're on the way," she said firmly.

Rey gave her a curious glance, but he hustled Leo out the door and into the truck again.

When they got to the office, Dr. Lou Coltrain's nurse, Betty, came right out to meet them and guide them back into a cubicle.

Lou walked in, took a professional look at the cut, and grinned. "Stitches," she said. "How about a tetanus jab?"

Leo grimaced. "Well…"

She patted him on the shoulder that wasn't injured. "We'll have you fixed up and out of here in no time."

He sighed, glancing at his brother. "I hate shots."

Rey shrugged. "You'd hate tetanus more," he told Leo. "Besides," he added, "I hear she gives sugarless gum to the good patients."

Leo made a face at him.

WHEN LEO WAS stitched up and given his tetanus shot, Rey drove him back to the house, where Meredith made him a cup of coffee and cut him a slice of cherry pie, making sure he had a cushion for his back in the straight chair at the table.

Rey glared at the special treatment his brother was getting. "Maybe I should get gored," he commented drolly.

Meredith stared at him, and she didn't smile. "You'd get a vinegar dressing and a cup of cold coffee," she said.

He glared at her, too. He felt as if he'd been put in the corner without supper. It wasn't a feeling he liked. He gave them both a hard look and went back out the door, smoldering with bad temper.

CHAPTER SIX

"I SHOULDN'T HAVE said that," Meredith said wryly when Rey was gone. "I set him off again."

"It won't hurt him to have one woman who doesn't fall all over herself when he's around," Leo told her flatly. "Sometimes too much success can ruin a good man."

She toyed with her coffee cup. "Women like him, I guess," she said.

He gave her a quick glance that she didn't see before he started on his pie. "He's had girlfriends since he was in grammar school. But there was only one serious one. She turned out to be a real loser," he added quietly. "She soured him on women."

She sipped coffee. "You can't judge an entire sex by one woman," she pointed out.

"Well, we had our mother as an example, too," he continued. "She left Dad with five young boys and never looked back. We haven't been overawed with sterling examples of womanhood, although Simon and Corrigan and Cag have made good marriages in spite of that."

She smiled absently as she looked at him. "I had a brother of my own," she said without thinking.

"Yes, I know," Leo replied, surprising her into silence. "His name was Michael Johns. He worked for Houston PD."

Her gasp was audible. "How…do you know about him?"

"Remember Colter Banks?"

"Yes. Colter was Mike's best friend."

"Well, Colter's our second cousin," he told her. "I knew Mike, too. I'm sorry."

She clenched one fist in her lap and tried not to give way to tears. "Do the others…know?"

"No, they don't," he replied. "They weren't that close to Colter, and they never met Mike. I haven't told them, and I'm not planning to."

She searched his dark eyes. "What else do you know about me, Leo?" she asked, because of the way he was watching her.

He shrugged. "Everything."

She let out a long breath. "And you haven't shared it with Rey."

"You wouldn't want me to," he murmured dryly. "He's having too much fun being condescending. When the time comes, he's got a few shocks coming, hasn't he?"

She laughed softly. "I hadn't meant to be cloak-and-daggerish. It's just that it still hurts too much to talk about," she said honestly.

"Colter told me the circumstances. It wasn't your fault," he replied. "Or your father's. I gather that he drinks because he feels responsible?"

She nodded. "We both dined out on 'what-if' just after it happened," she confessed. "I know that it probably wouldn't have made any difference, but you can't help wondering."

"It doesn't do any good to torment yourself over things that are history," Leo said gently.

"I don't do it intentionally," she murmured.

"The first step was getting your father into treatment," he said. "Getting you out of your rut was the second. You don't have any memories to contend with here. I've noticed the difference in you just in the past week." He smiled. "You're changing already."

"I suppose so." She smiled back. "I've never even been on a ranch before. I could love it here. It's such a change of pace."

"When you're back to normal, we've got plenty of opportunity around here for your sort of job," he pointed out.

She chuckled. "Don't rush me. It's far too soon to think about leaving Houston." She didn't add that she didn't want to be that close to Rey, considering his opinion of her at the moment. "I've only been down here a week."

"Okay. I'll let it drop, for now." He leaned back in his chair and winced, favoring the arm he'd had stitched. "Damned bull," he muttered.

"Did they give you something for the pain?"

"No, and I didn't ask for anything. I have over-the-counter painkillers if it gets really bad. So far, it hasn't."

"You know, of course, that statistically farm and ranch work have the highest ratio of accidents," she said.

"Any job can be dangerous," he said easily.

She pursed her lips and lifted her coffee cup to them. "Your brother's a walking job hazard," she said thoughtfully.

"Oh? In what way, exactly?" he asked.

She wouldn't have touched that line with a pole. She laughed. "He's abrasive. I don't think he wants me here."

"I've noticed his attitude. I hope you haven't let it get to you?"

"I haven't. Anyway, he'll mellow one of these days," she said.

"He could use some mellowing. He's a disillusioned man."

She smoothed the lip of the cup. "Did he love her very much?"

He knew she was talking about Carlie. He sighed. "He thought he did. His pride suffered more than his heart." He hesitated. "I didn't help matters. I made a play for her deliberately, to show him what she was. That was a miscalculation. A bad one. He's never forgiven me for it. Now, if I pay any attention to a woman, he tries to compete with me…"

She noticed the way his voice trailed off, and she averted her eyes. "I get the picture," she said.

"It's not like that, not with you," he began.

She forced a smile. "He's not interested in me," she said bluntly. "And just in case you're worried that I might be falling all over him, there's no danger of that, either. I was outside the door when he was talking to you. I wasn't eavesdropping, but he was speaking rather loudly. I heard what he said. I'd have to be certifiable to lose my heart over a man like that."

He grimaced as he read the faint pain that lingered in her eyes. "I wouldn't have had you hear what he said for the world," he said deeply.

She managed a smile. "It's just as well. It will keep me from taking him seriously. Besides, I'm not really down here looking for a soul mate."

"Just as well, because Rey isn't any woman's idea of the perfect partner, not the way he is right now. I love him dearly, but I can afford to. It's another story for any woman who loses her heart to him." He studied her warily. "Just don't let him play you for a fool."

"I wouldn't dream of it," she said. "Even if I got the chance."

He nodded. He finished his pie and coffee and got to his feet. "I'd better change and get back to work. Thanks for running interference, by the way. You're a cool head in an emergency," he remarked with a smile.

"I've had lots of practice," she said modestly and grinned. "But try to stay away from horned things for a while."

"Especially my brother, the minor devil," he said, tongue-in-cheek, and grinned back when she got the reference and started laughing.

AFTER LEO WENT back to work, Meredith went out to gather eggs. It seemed very straightforward. You walked into the henhouse, reached in the nest, and pulled out a dozen or so big brown eggs, some still warm from the chicken's feathered body.

But that wasn't what happened. She paused just inside the henhouse to let her eyes adjust to the reduced light, and when she moved toward the row of straw-laced nests, she saw something wrapped around one nest that wasn't feathered. It had scales and a flickering long tongue. It peered at her through the darkness and tightened its coils around its prey, three big brown eggs.

Meredith, a city girl with very little experience of scaly things, did something predictable. She screamed, threw the basket in the general direction of the snake, and left skid marks getting out of the fenced lot.

Annie Lewis, who was doing the laundry, came to

the back door as fast as her arthritis would allow, to see what all the commotion was about.

"There's a…big black and white *snnnnnakkkkkke...* in there!" Meredith screamed, shaking all over from the close encounter.

"After the eggs, I reckon," Annie said with a sigh. She wiped her hands on her apron. "Let me get a stick and I'll deal with it."

"You can't go in there alone with the horrible thing and try to kill it! It must be five feet long!"

"It's a king snake, not a rattler," Annie said gently, recognizing the description. "And I'm not planning to kill it. I'm going to get it on a stick and put in the barn. It can eat its fill of rats and poisonous snakes and do some good out there."

"You aren't going to kill it?" Meredith exclaimed, horrified.

"It's a king snake, dear," came the gentle reply. "We don't like to kill them. They're very useful. They eat rattlesnakes, you know."

"I didn't know." Meredith shivered again. "I've never seen a snake except in a zoo, and it was a python."

"You'll see lots of them out here in the country. Just remember that if one rattles at you, it means business and it will strike. Rattlesnakes are venomous."

Meredith looked around as if she expected to be mobbed just at the mention of them.

"You can finish the washing," Annie said, trying not to grin. "I'll take care of the snake."

"Please be careful!"

"I will. After all, you get used to things like…"

Rey drove up and stopped the truck just short of the two women, exiting it with his usual graceful speed.

"What's going on?" he asked as he pulled a box of assorted bovine medicines out of the boot of the truck.

"There's a snake in the henhouse!" Meredith exclaimed.

He stopped with the supplies in his arms and stared at her curiously. "So?" he asked.

"I'm just going to move it for her, Rey," Mrs. Lewis said with a grin. "It sounds like a king snake. I thought I'd put him in the barn."

"I'll get him for you." He put the box on the hood of the truck. "Scared of snakes, are you?" he scoffed.

"I'd never seen one until a few minutes ago," she said huffily, and flushed. He was looking at her as if she were a child.

"There's a first time for everything," he said, and his eyes made a very explicit remark as they lingered on her breasts.

She gave him a glare hot enough to fry bacon, which he ignored. He walked right into the chicken lot and, then, into the henhouse.

Barely a minute later, he came back out with the snake coiled around one arm, its neck gently held in his other hand.

"Would you look at this, it's Bandit!" he exclaimed, showing it to a fascinated Mrs. Lewis. "See the scar on his back where he got caught in the corn sheller that time?"

"So it is!" she said. "Hello, old fella!" She actually petted the vile thing under the chin.

"How can you touch that thing?" Meredith groaned. "It's a snake!"

Mrs. Lewis glanced at Rey. "Reckon we should tell her that he used to live in the house?"

"Probably not," Rey suggested, aware of her white face. "I'll just stick him up in the loft. Come on, Bandit, I'll put you in a safe place."

Meredith was holding both chill-bump laden arms with her hands and shivering.

"There, there," Annie said gently. "He wouldn't bite you unless you provoked him. He's very gentle."

"If you say so."

"I do. Now you go back in there and get the eggs. Don't let Rey see how frightened you are. Trust me, he'll take advantage of it. You'll find rubber snakes in the refrigerator, the blender, the washer..."

"No!" Meredith exclaimed, horrified.

"Just grit your teeth and go back in the henhouse," Annie suggested. "Quick, before he comes back out."

Meredith took a quick breath and gave Annie a miserable glance, but she did as she was told.

Her skin crawled when she had to pick up the basket and gather the eggs, especially the ones the snake had been curled around. Now, every time she went to the henhouse, she'd be shivering with apprehension.

You've looked at gunshot wounds, accident victims, every sort of horror known to human eyes, she told herself firmly. *The snake wasn't even lacerated! So get it done and move on.*

She did, walking back out into the sunlight with a full basket of eggs and a forced look of composure on her soft face.

Rey was waiting for her, leaning against the bumper of the truck with his arms crossed and his hat pulled low over his eyes.

She didn't dare look at him for long. In that indolent pose, his lean, muscular body was shown to its very best advantage. It made her tingle to think how it had felt to be held against every inch of that formidable frame, to be kissed by that long, hard mouth.

"You get thrown, you get right back on the horse," he said with approval. "I'm proud of you, Meredith. It would be hard for even a ranch-born girl to go back into a henhouse where a snake had been lurking."

She took a slow breath. "We don't face things by running away from them, I guess," she agreed.

His eyes narrowed under the wide brim of the hat. "What are you running away from, Meredith? What is your father running away from?"

She clutched the basket to her chest. "That's nothing that you need to concern yourself with," she said with quiet dignity.

"You work for me," he replied.

"Not for long," she pointed out. "In another week or so, I'll be a memory."

"Will you?" He lurched away from the bumper and went to stand just in front of her, a tall and sensual threat. His fingers touched her soft mouth lightly. "Those bruises still look pretty fresh," he pointed out. "And you did ask for a month's leave, or so you said. Did you?"

She grimaced. "Well, yes, but I don't have to stay here all that time."

"I think you do," he returned. He bent and drew his mouth slowly over hers, a whisper of a contact that made her breath catch. He smiled with faint arrogance as he stood up again. "Anything could happen," he drawled. "You might like ranch life."

"I don't like snakes already."

"That was a fluke. They're generally hibernating by

November, but it's been unseasonably warm. Spring is generally when you have to watch where you put your hands. But you don't need to worry. I'll protect you from snakes. And other perils."

"Who'll protect me from you?" she asked huskily.

He raised an eyebrow. "Why would you need protection?" he asked. "You're well over the age of consent."

"I've lived a very sheltered life," she said flatly.

He pursed his lips as he studied her, examining the statement. "Maybe it's time you walked out of the cocoon."

"I'm not in the market for an affair."

"Neither am I." He smiled slowly. "But if you worked at it, you might change my mind."

"I don't think so," she said. Her eyes were cool as they met his. "I wouldn't want you to think I was 'drooling' over you," she added deliberately.

His face changed. He knew immediately that she'd overheard what he'd said to Leo. He was sorry, because it wasn't true. He'd been desperate to throw Leo off the track. He didn't want his brother to know how attracted he was to her.

"Eavesdroppers never hear anything good about themselves, don't they say?" he asked quietly.

"Never," she agreed. "Now, if you'll excuse me, I'll go wash the eggs."

"I said something else that you'll remember with sordid ease," he murmured as she started past him. He caught her by the shoulder and tugged her close, bending to drag his mouth roughly across hers. "But I didn't mean that, either," he whispered against her parted lips. "Your innocence makes my head spin. I lay awake at night thinking of all sorts of delicious ways to relieve you of it."

"You'd be lucky!" she exclaimed, shocked.

He laughed softly as he let her go. "So would you," he drawled. "I've been called 'sensual hell' in bed, and I can assure you it wasn't meant to be a derogatory remark."

"Rey Hart!" she burst out.

"But why take anyone else's word for it?" he teased. "I'll be glad to let you see for yourself, anytime you like."

"If you think… I have never…of all the…!"

"Yes, it does tend to make women flustered when I mention what a great lover I am," he said with a wicked grin.

She couldn't get one coherent sentence out. She stomped her foot hard, turned around, and stormed into the kitchen, almost knocking herself down with the door in the process. It didn't help that Rey stood out there laughing like a predator.

IF SHE EXPECTED Rey to be apologetic about what he'd said, she was doomed to disappointment. He watched her with narrow, assessing eyes as she went about her household duties. He didn't harass her, or monopolize her. He just watched. The scrutiny made her so nervous that she fumbled constantly. Her heart ran wild at the attention from those dark, steady eyes.

"Why don't you want to do something else besides keep house?" Rey asked her one evening when she was putting supper on the table. Leo, as usual, was late getting in. Rey had volunteered to set the table while she fixed Mexican corn bread and chili.

"Keeping house has less stress than most outside jobs," she said, not looking at him.

"It pays lousy wages," he continued, "and you could get into a lot of trouble in some households, with men who'd see you as fair game."

"Do you see me that way?" she asked, wide-eyed.

He glowered at her. "No, I don't. The point is, some other man might. It isn't a safe career. In a profession, there are more laws to protect you."

"Most professional people have degrees and such. Besides, I'm too old."

"You're never too old to go back to school," he replied.

She shrugged. "Besides, I like cooking and cleaning."

He eyed her curiously. "You're very good at handling injured people," he said suddenly. "And you're remarkably calm in an emergency."

"It's good practice for when I have kids," she said.

He drew in a short breath. "You like being mysterious, don't you?"

"While it lasts, it's fun," she agreed.

His eyes narrowed. "What dark secrets are you keeping, Meredith?" he asked quietly.

"None that should bother you, even if you found them out," she assured him. She smiled at him from the stove. "Meanwhile, you're getting fresh biscuits every day."

"Yes, we are," he had to agree. "And you're a good cook. But I don't like mysteries."

She pursed her lips and gave him a teasing glance over her shoulder. "Too bad."

He put the last place setting on the table and sat down at his place, just staring at her, without speaking. "You know," he said after a minute, frowning, "there's something familiar about your last name. I can't quite place it, but I know I've heard it somewhere."

That wasn't good, she thought. He might remember Leo talking about her brother. She didn't want to have to face the past, not just yet, when she was still broken and bruised and uncomfortable. When she was back on her feet and well again, there would be time to come to grips with it once and for all—as her poor father was already doing.

"Think so?" she asked with forced nonchalance.

He shrugged. "Well, it may come back to me one day."

Fortunately Leo came in and stopped his train of thought. Meredith put supper on the table and sat down to eat it with the brothers.

THE NEXT MORNING, Rey came out to the kitchen with a bright silver metal gun case. He set it down beside the counter, out of the way, before he started eating his breakfast.

"Going hunting?" Meredith asked impishly.

He gave her a wary glance. "Skeet shooting," he corrected. "The season's over, but I practice year-round."

"He won two medals at the World championships in San Antonio, this year," Leo told her with a grin. "He's an A class shooter."

"Which gauge?" she asked without thinking.

Rey's face became suspicious. "All of them. What do you know about shotguns?"

"I used to skeet-shoot," she volunteered. "My brother taught me how to handle a shotgun, and then he got me into competition shooting. I wasn't able to keep it up after I grad...after high school," she improvised quickly.

She didn't dare tell him she gave it up after she finished college. That would be giving away far too much.

He watched her sip coffee. "You can shoot, can you?" he asked, looking as if he were humoring her. He didn't seem to believe what she claimed.

"Yes, I can," she said deliberately.

He smiled. "Like to come down to the range with me?" he asked. "I've got a nice little .28 gauge I can bring along for you."

By offering her his lowest caliber shotgun, he was assuming that she couldn't handle anything heavier.

"What's in the case?" she asked.

"My twelve gauge," he said.

She gave him a speaking glance. "I'll just shoot that, if you don't mind sharing it. Uh, it doesn't have a kick or anything…?" she added, and had to bite her tongue to keep from grinning at her innocent pose.

He cleared his throat. He didn't dare look at Leo. "No," he said carelessly. "Of course it doesn't have a kick."

In truth, it would kick worse than any other of the four gauges, but Rey was planning to call her bluff. She was putting on an act for his benefit. He was going to make her sorry she tried it.

"Then I'll be just fine with that gun," she said. "More apple butter?" She offered him an open jar and spoon.

"Thanks," he replied smugly, accepting the jar. He put it down and buttered another biscuit before he spooned the apple butter into it. "Don't mind if I do. Leo, want to come along?" he asked his brother.

Leo was also trying not to grin. "I think I will, this time," he told his brother. This was one shooting contest he wasn't about to miss. He knew that Mike Johns was a champion shooter. If he'd been the one who taught his sister, Meredith would shock Rey speechless when she got that shotgun in her arms. He was going along. He didn't want to miss the fun.

"The more the merrier, I always say," Rey chuckled.

"Funny thing, that's just what I was thinking," Leo replied, tongue-in-cheek.

Meredith didn't say another word. She finished her breakfast, waited until they finished theirs, and put the dishes in the dishwasher. Then she dressed in jeans, boots, and a long-sleeved flannel shirt with a down-filled vest and a bib cap, and went off to let Rey show her how to shoot a shotgun.

THE TARGET RANGE was unusually busy for a lazy Friday afternoon in November. It was a cool day, with a nice nip in the air. Meredith felt good in the down vest. It was one she'd often worn when she went to the firing range with Mike in cold weather. Coats were cumbersome and often got in the way of a good, quick aim.

Rey and Leo stopped to pass the time of day with two elderly shooters, both of whom gave Meredith a warm welcome.

"This is Jack, and that's Billy Joe," Rey introduced the white-haired men, one of whom was tall and spare, the other overweight and short. The short one had walked briskly the short distance from the red pickup truck parked at the clubhouse, and he was out of breath already. "We all go to district, state and national shoots as a team from our club."

"But we get honorable mention, and Rey wins the medals," Billy Joe, the shorter man, chuckled, still trying to catch his breath. "We don't mind. We're just happy that somebody from our club breaks records!"

"Amen to that," Jack agreed, smiling.

"All right, let's get to shooting," Billy Joe said, turning back to his truck. "Stay where you are, Jack. I'll bring your gun, too!"

He turned back toward the truck, rushing and still breathless. Meredith frowned. His cheeks were unnaturally pink, and it wasn't that cold. His complexion was almost white. He was sweating. She knew the symptoms. She'd seen them all too often.

"You might go with him," Meredith said abruptly, interrupting Jack's banter with Rey.

"Excuse me?" Jack asked.

Just at that moment, Billy Joe stopped, stood very still for a minute, and then buckled and fell forward into a crumpled heap at the door of his truck.

Meredith took off at a dead run. "Somebody get me a cell phone!" she called as she ran.

Leo fumbled his out of the holder on his belt and passed it to her as she knelt beside Billy Joe.

"Get his feet elevated. Find something to cover him with," she shot at the other men. She was dialing while she spoke. She loosened the man's shirt, propping the phone against her ear—the worst way to hold it, but there was no other way at the moment—and felt down Billy Joe's chest for his diaphragm. "Get his wallet and read me his weight and age from his driver's license," she added with a sharp glance in Leo's direction.

Leo dug out the wallet and started calling out information, while Rey and Jack stood beside the fallen man and watched with silent concern.

"I want the resident on duty in the emergency room,

stat," she said. "This is Meredith Johns. I have a patient, sixty years of age, one hundred and eighty pounds, who collapsed without warning. Early signs indicate a possible myocardial infarction. Pulse is thready," she murmured, checking the second hand of her watch as she took his pulse with her fingertips, "forty beats a minute, breathing shallow and labored, grey complexion, profuse sweating. I need EMTs en route, I am initiating cardiopulmonary resuscitation now."

There was a long pause, and a male voice came over the line. With her voice calm and steady, Meredith gave the information again, and then handed the phone to Leo as she bent over the elderly man and did the spaced compressions over his breastbone, followed by mouth-to-mouth breathing.

Rey was watching, spellbound at her proficiency, at the easy and quite professional manner in which she'd taken charge of a life-or-death emergency. Within five minutes, the ambulance was screaming up the graveled road that led to the Jacobsville Gun Club, and Billy Joe was holding his own.

The EMTs listened to Meredith's terse summary of events as they called the same resident Meredith had been talking to.

"Doc says to give you a pat on the back." The female EMT grinned at Meredith as they loaded Billy Joe into the ambulance. "You sure knew what to do."

"Yes," Rey agreed, finding his tongue at last. "You've obviously had first-aid training."

He probably meant it as praise, but it hit Meredith in the gut. She glared at him. "What I've had," she emphasized, "is five years of college. I have a master's degree in nursing science, and I'm a card-carrying nurse practitioner!"

CHAPTER SEVEN

REY STARED AT his new cook as if she'd suddenly sprouted feathers on her head. His summation of her abilities was suddenly smoke. She was someone he didn't even know. She was a health-care professional, not a flighty cook, and certainly not the sort of woman to streetwalk as a sideline.

She nodded solemnly. "I figured it would come as a shock," she told him. She turned her attention back to the EMTs. "Thanks for being so prompt. Think he'll be okay?"

The female EMT smiled. "I think so. His heartbeat's stronger, his breathing is regular, and he's regaining consciousness. Good job!"

She grinned. "You, too."

They waved and took off, lights flashing, but without turning on the sirens.

"Why aren't the sirens going?" Rey wanted to know. "He's not out of danger yet, surely?"

"They don't like to run the sirens unless they have to," Meredith told him. "Some people actually run off the road and wreck their cars because the sirens rattle them. They use the lights, but they only turn on the sirens if they hit heavy traffic and have to force their way through it. Those EMTs," she added with a smile, "they're the real heroes and heroines. They do the hardest job of all."

"You saved Billy Joe's life," Jack said huskily, shaking her hand hard. "He's the best friend I got. Thank you."

She smiled gently and returned the handshake. "It goes with the job description. Don't try to keep up with the ambulance," she cautioned when he went toward Billy Joe's truck, which still had the key in the ignition. The two men had come together.

"I'll be careful," the older man promised.

"Whew!" Leo let out the breath he'd almost been holding, and put up his cell phone. "You're one cool lady under fire, Meredith."

She smiled sadly. "I've had to be," she replied. She glanced at Rey, who looked cold and angry as it occurred to him, belatedly, that she'd played him for a fool. "I can see what you're thinking, but I didn't actually lie to you. You never asked me exactly what I did for a living. Of course, you thought you already knew," she added with faint sarcasm.

He didn't reply. He gave her a long, contemptuous look and turned away. "I've lost my taste for practice," he said quietly. "I want to go on to the hospital and see about Billy Joe."

"Me, too," Leo added. "Meredith…?"

"I'll go along," she said. "I'd like to meet that resident I spoke with. He's very good."

Rey glanced toward her. "You'll get along. He keeps secrets, too," he said bitterly, and got behind the wheel.

Leo made a face at Meredith, opening the third door of the big double-cabbed truck so that she could sit in back. He put the gun cases in the boot, in a locked area, and climbed in beside Rey.

THE RESIDENT TURNED out to be a former mercenary named Micah Steele. He was married to a local girl, and he'd gone back to school to finish his course of study for his medical license.

"I couldn't very well carry a wife and child around the jungles with me," Micah told her with a grin. He was tall and big, and not at all bad-looking. She could picture him with a rifle in one arm. But now, in a white lab coat with a stethoscope thrown carelessly around his neck, he seemed equally at home.

"When's Callie due?" Leo asked.

"Any minute," he said, tongue-in-cheek. "Can't you see me shaking? I'm the soul of self-confidence around here, but one little pregnant woman makes me a basket case!"

"Callie's quite a girl," Rey agreed, smiling at the big man.

Micah gave him a look. "Yes, and isn't it lucky for me that you hardly ever went into her boss Kemp's office for legal advice, while she was still single?"

Rey pursed his lips. "Kemp eats scorpions for breakfast, I hear. I like my lawyers less caustic."

"Last I heard, the local bar association had you down as a contagious plague and was warning its members to avoid you at all costs," Micah replied wickedly.

"I never hit any local lawyers." Rey looked uncomfortable. "It was that Victoria lawyer, Matherson," he muttered. "And I didn't even hit him that hard. Hell, he's lucky I wasn't sober at the time! Otherwise, he'd have had twice the number of stitches!"

Meredith listened to the repartee with wide, fascinated eyes, but Rey wouldn't meet her eyes and Micah, too, cleared his throat and didn't pursue the subject.

"Matherson took a client who accused us of assault," Leo volunteered. "Cag had hit him, several times, after he got drunk and assaulted Tess, who's now Cag's wife. But the bounder swore that he was the injured party, that we falsely accused him and all took turns pounding him. He convinced a jury to award him damages. Not a lot of money," Leo added solemnly, "but the principle was what set Rey off. He was in a bad mood already and he had a few too many drinks at Shea's Bar, out on the Victoria road. To make a long story short," he added with a chuckle, "Matherson was having a quiet beer when Rey accused him of handling the ex-employee's case for spite because he lost an argument with us over Tess when he was handling her inheritance. Matherson took exception to Rey's remarks, and the two of them set about wrecking the pretty stained-glass window that used to overlook the parking lot."

"Used to?" Meredith fished, sensing something ominous.

"Yes, well, Matherson made a rather large hole in it when Rey helped him into the parking lot the hard way," Leo concluded.

Micah Steele looked as if it was killing him not to burst out laughing.

"He," Leo jerked his thumb toward Steele, "had to remove quite a number of glass particles from Matherson's rear end. *And* we got sued again, for that!"

"But the jury, after hearing Kemp's masterful summation of our grievances," Rey interrupted, "decided that Matherson was only entitled to the cost of the repair job on his butt. Shea had insurance that replaced the stained-glass window with one of comparable age and exclusivity." Rey smiled smugly. "And the judge said that if she'd been sitting on the first case, the rat Matherson was representing would have gotten a jail sentence."

Leo chuckled. "Only because Kemp put Tess on the stand and had her testify about what really happened the night Matherson's client took her on a date. The jury felt that Rey was justifiably incensed by the former verdict." He glanced at Meredith wryly.

"Yes, but I understand that Shea's two bouncers meet Rey at the door these days and won't let him in if he's not smiling," Micah contributed.

Rey shrugged. "I never get drunk anymore. I've learned to handle aggression in a nonphysical manner."

The other two men actually walked down the hall. Meredith noticed their shoulders vibrating.

Rey took a step toward Meredith, half irritated by the character assassination job his brother and Micah Steele had just done on him, and even more put out by Meredith's unmasking.

"You knew I had no idea about your education," Rey accused Meredith. "Why didn't you say something at the outset, when Leo first went to the hospital?" he demanded in a low, deep tone. "I may have jumped to conclusions, but you provided the springs, didn't you?"

She grimaced. "I guess so. But it was only a little jump from telling you about my job to talking about the reason Daddy started drinking. It's…still very fresh in my mind," she added huskily. "It's only been six months. The memories are—" she swallowed and looked away "—bad."

Unexpectedly he reached out and caught her fingers

in his, tugging her closer. The hall was deserted. In the background there were muted bell-tones and announcements and the sound of lunch trays being distributed. "Tell me," he said gently.

She bit her lower lip hard and lifted her tormented eyes to his curious ones. "Not…yet," she whispered tightly. "One day, but…not yet. I can't."

"Okay," he said after a minute. "But I'd like to know how you learned to shoot."

"My brother, Mike, taught me," she said reluctantly, staring at his broad chest. She wanted to lay her head on it and cry out her pain. There hadn't been anyone to hold her, not when it happened, not afterward. Her father withdrew into his own mind and started drinking to excess at once. Her job was all that had kept Meredith sane. She hadn't been able to let out her grief in any normal way.

Rey's mind was working overtime. He stared down at her, still holding her fingers entwined tightly with his own, and he frowned as bits and pieces of memory began fitting themselves together.

"Mike. Mike Johns." His eyes narrowed. "Our cousin Colter's best friend, and one of Leo's acquaintances. He was killed…!"

She tried to tug her fingers away. He wouldn't let her. He pulled her into his arms, holding her there even when she struggled. But a few seconds of resistance were all she had. She laid her flushed cheek against his broad chest and let the tears flow.

Rey's arms contracted roughly. He smoothed his hand over her nape, caressing, soothing. "There was a bank robbery in Houston," he recalled quietly. "Mike was a cop. He was at the bank with your mother. It was

Saturday. He was off duty, but he had his service revolver under his jacket." His arms tightened as her sobs grew painful to hear. "He drew and fired automatically, and one of the robbers sprayed fire from one of those damned little automatic rifles in his general direction. He and your mother died instantly..."

Meredith's fingers dug into his wide back. He rocked her, barely aware of curious glances from passersby.

"Both men were caught. You don't kill a cop and get away with it in Texas," he added softly. "They were arraigned and treated to a speedy trial just a month ago. You and your father testified. That was when your father really went off the deep end, wasn't it, when he had to see the autopsy photos..."

Micah and Leo came back down the hall, frowning when they saw the condition Meredith was in. Even as they watched, her eyes rolled back and she would have fallen to the floor except for Rey's strong arms lifting her.

Later, she wouldn't recall much except that she was hustled into a cubicle and revived. But when she started sobbing hysterically, they'd given her a shot of something that put her out like a light. She came to back at the ranch, in her own little garage apartment.

She opened her eyes, and there was Rey, sitting by the bed, still wearing the same jeans and shirt and boots he'd worn to the shooting range. Meredith was aware of the bedspread covering her up to her waist. Her boots were off, but she was also wearing the same clothes she'd started out in that morning.

"What time is it?" she asked in a husky, slightly disoriented tone.

"Five hours past the time you flaked out on me,"

he said, smiling gently. "Micah knocked you out. He thought some sleep might help." The smile faded into quiet concern. "You don't sleep much, do you, Meredith?" he asked surprisingly.

She sighed, brushed back her disheveled blond hair, and shook her head. "When I go to sleep, I have nightmares. I wake up in a cold sweat, and I see them, lying there on the floor, just the way they looked in those vivid crime scene photos." She closed her eyes and shivered. "People look so fragile like that, they look like big dolls, sprawled in pitiful disarray on the floor. Everybody stares at them..."

He brushed back her hair with a lean, gentle hand. "They got the guys who did it," he reminded her. "Including the trigger man. He'll serve life without any hope of parole. He'll pay for it."

Her pale eyes were tormented as they met his. "Yes, but it won't bring them back, will it?" she asked. "And do you know why they said they did it? For a bet. For a stupid bet, they killed two innocent people!"

"They also ruined their own lives," he reminded her, "and the lives of their own families."

She looked at him blankly, scowling.

"Don't you ever think about that?" he asked softly. "Criminals have families, too. Most of them have loving, decent parents who took care of them and disciplined them and blame themselves for what their children do. It must be pure hell, to have your child kill someone, and feel responsible for it."

"I haven't considered that," she admitted.

He continued. "When I was in high school, one of my best friends was arrested for murder. He killed the old man next door in the process of stealing his wallet.

He wanted to buy his girl a diamond necklace she liked, and he didn't have any money. He figured the man was old and didn't need money anyway, so he might as well take it. He was sorry about it, but he never figured on killing the man or getting caught."

"Was he a good friend?" she asked.

He looked at their linked fingers. He nodded. "We were pals since grammar school. He wasn't quite as bright as some of the other boys, but he had a gentle nature. Or so we thought." He met her eyes. "His mom and dad always had a houseful of other peoples' kids. They were everybody's mom and dad. It shattered them when Joey went to prison. Even the children of the old man felt sorry for them."

"Funny," she mused. "I never even thought of how it would feel to have a child or a parent or a sibling who broke the law in some terrible way." She met his eyes. "I guess I'd feel guilty, too."

"Most kids are raised right. But some of them have a wild streak that nobody can tame, others have poor impulse control. Many are handicapped. Nobody goes to jail because he wants to."

"I never thought of you as a sensitive man," she blurted out, and then flushed at the insult.

His eyebrows lifted. "Who, me? I stop to pick worms out of the highway so my tires won't bruise their little bodies, and you think I'm insensitive?"

It took a minute for the words to make sense, and then she burst out laughing.

"That's better," he said. He smiled and squeezed her fingers. "You're going to be okay. You've had a lot of traumatic experiences just lately. No wonder you caved in."

"Lucky for you," she shot back.

"Me? Why?"

"Because if we'd unpacked those shotguns, I'd have destroyed your ego," she said with a smug smile. "At Mike's gun club, they used to call me 'dead-eye.'"

"Oh, they did, did they?" he challenged. "Well, we'll see about that when you step up to my gun range."

She studied his lean face. He wasn't handsome, but he had strong, stubborn features. He was familiar to her now, almost necessary. She thought about going back to Houston with real panic.

He touched her cheek where the bruises were a mixture of purple and yellow, much less vivid now. "He really knocked you around," he said, and his face hardened visibly. "I don't care if a man is drunk, there's no excuse for hitting a woman."

"Shades of primitive man," she chided with a smile.

"Women are the cradles of life," he said simply. "What sort of man tries to break a cradle?"

"You have a unique way of putting things."

"We had Spanish ancestors," he told her. "They were old-world men, conquerors, adventurers. One of them made his way to Texas and was given a huge tract of land under a Spanish land grant, for services to the crown of Spain." He noticed a start of surprise on her face. "Do you know the legend of the Cid?"

"Yes!" she exclaimed. "He was a great Spanish hero. *Cid* is for the Arabic *Sidi* which means *Lord*."

"Well, our ancestor wasn't El Cid," he said on a chuckle. "But he fought his way through hostile neighbors to claim his land, and he held it as long as he lived. Our family still holds it, through our late uncle, who left us this ranch."

"This is the original grant?" she exclaimed.

He nodded. “It isn’t nearly as big as it was a couple of hundred years ago, but it’s no weekend farm, either. Didn’t you notice the antique silver service in the dining room?”

“Yes, I’ve been afraid to touch it. It looks very old.”

He smiled. “It came from Madrid. It’s over two hundred years old.”

“An heirloom!” she breathed.

“Yes. Like the ranch itself.” He tilted his head and studied her for a long time. “Now I understand. Your father wasn’t violent until the killer’s trial, was he?”

“No, he wasn’t.” She looked down at Rey’s big, warm hand wrapped around her own. It made her feel safe. “He told Mike to drive Mama to the bank,” she added reluctantly. “He had papers to grade. He couldn’t spare the time, he said, and he snapped at her when she protested that Mike was spending his day off, carting her all over Houston.” She glanced at him. “I was called in to work at a clinic my boss holds in the Hispanic community every Saturday. There’s a regular nurse, but she was at home with a sick child. I went to stand in for her.” Her eyes fell to his broad chest. “I could have asked someone to go in my place. I didn’t. So he and I both have our guilt.”

“Because you lived and they didn’t,” Rey said bluntly.

She gasped. “No, that’s not true!”

“It is true.” His black eyes held hers relentlessly. “The same thing happens to people who survive airplane crashes, automobile wrecks, sinking ships. It’s a normal, human reaction to surviving when other people don’t. It’s worse when the victims include close relatives or friends.”

“Where did you learn that?” she asked.

"From Janie Brewster," he said.

She frowned. "That name sounds familiar."

"We've mentioned her to you. She's the daughter of a neighboring cattleman," he related. "She got her associate degree in psychology from our community college, and now she's studying it in Houston," he added with a grin. "She's almost twenty. They let her take college courses while she was still in high school, so she's ahead."

"Oh."

"She's not hard on the eyes, either," he murmured, avoiding her eyes. "She and her father live alone. Leo and I have a standing dinner invitation, any time we care to show up."

She started to say "oh" again, and realized how juvenile she was behaving. She straightened her shoulders against the pillow that was propping her up, and tugged at the hand Rey still held. "Then if she can bake biscuits, you're saved when I leave, aren't you?" she asked coolly.

"Well, she can't exactly bake stuff," Rey had to admit.

"Why?"

"She has no sense of time. She sets the timer and it goes off, and she never hears it. So the chicken bounces, the heat-and-serve rolls usually come out black, and I won't even mention what happens to vegetables she tries to cook on *top* of the stove." He gave her a sad look. "She did try to make us a pan of biscuits once." He actually shuddered.

"Not a successful try?" she fished.

"We had to take the damned things home, or her father would never have let us near the Salers heifers he was offering for sale." He glanced at her. "Leo just bought us a big Salers bull, and we needed purebred heifers to breed to him. Purebred breeding stock brings a big price, especially if you show cattle and win ribbons." He shrugged. "So we took the biscuits home."

"Did you eat them?" she persisted.

He shook his head and he shuddered again.

"Then what did you do with them?" she asked, thinking he probably fed them to the cattle dogs or some livestock.

"Well, actually, we took them out to the skeet field and used them for clay pigeons," he confessed with a grin. "They were the best damned targets we ever had, but we didn't dare say where we got them!"

She put her face in her hands and burst out laughing. "Oh, the poor girl!" she chuckled.

"Don't worry, we'd never tell her," he promised. "But we did ask her for another pan of biscuits, without telling her why." He sighed. "That woman has a ready-made profession as a target maker, and we haven't got the guts to tell her so. Hell of a shame!"

She brushed at her eyes with the hem of her blouse. Poor Janie. And she'd been jealous.

"What does she look like?" she asked, curious.

"She comes up to my shoulder. She's got light brown hair, longer than yours, and her eyes are green. If she didn't know everything, and tell you so every time you saw her, she might get married one day."

"You don't want to marry her?" she teased. "Not even for an inexhaustible supply of skeet targets?"

"I don't want to marry anybody," he said bluntly, and he looked her straight in the eye when he said it. "I love my freedom."

She sighed and smiled. "So do I," she confessed. "I

don't think I could ever settle for diapers and dishes. Not with my background."

"You were a science major, weren't you?" he asked abruptly.

"Yes. Chemistry and biology, genetics—stuff like that. I made good grades, but it was hard work. Then I went right to work for my boss, straight out of college. I need to be two people, just to catch up. I run my legs off. The stress is pretty bad sometimes."

"No wonder keeping house and baking biscuits seemed like a holiday to you," he said to himself.

"It's been fun," she agreed. "I love to cook. I do it a lot, at home. I used to when Mama was alive," she recalled. "She hated housework and cooking. I came home from work and did it all."

"I've read about the sort of work you do," he commented, recalling articles he'd seen in the daily newspaper. "You're second only to a physician in authority. The only thing you can't do is write a prescription without his supervision."

"That's true." She smiled.

He studied her slender body, her exquisite figure nicely outlined by the garments she was wearing. "All those years, nothing but textbooks and exams and, then, a hectic career. No men?" he added, with a calculating stare.

"I dated," she replied. "I just couldn't afford to get serious about anybody. My father scraped and begged and borrowed to get the money to finance my nursing education," she told him. "Even Mike…contributed to it." She drew in a steadying breath and locked her fingers together on her lap. "It would have been so petty of me to throw all that up, just so I could go to parties and get drunk with the other students."

"Surely there wasn't much of that, at a community college?"

She laughed. "You'd be surprised. There was all too much, for my taste. But I didn't live on campus. I lived at home and commuted." She met his searching gaze. "That party I was at, when Leo was attacked—the woman who gave it was a college classmate who works for a doctor in our practice. I knew she sort of had a reputation. I guess I should have realized how wild things would get, but I was so depressed that I let her pressure me into going to the party. It was a mistake."

"A lucky mistake, for my brother," Rey said gently. "He might have been killed, if you hadn't come along when you did." He scowled. "You said, you ran at the attackers, waving your arms."

She nodded. "Mike taught me about shock tactics," she said sadly. "I was afraid it wouldn't work, but I had no weapon, no other way of stopping them. So I took the risk."

"I'm grateful that you did." He shook his head slowly. "But it was an act of lunacy, Meredith. You could have been lying on the grass next to Leo."

"But I wasn't." She hunched her shoulders as if she felt a chill. "I think there might be a force behind every single chain of events," she said thoughtfully. "I don't believe in chaos," she elaborated. "The body is such a messy, beautiful miracle. A single cell has chemical processes that are so complex, so meticulously crafted, that I can't believe life is an accident. If it isn't accidental, it has to be planned." She shrugged. "That's simple logic. That's why I don't think God is a myth."

They were silent for a moment. "You're the most intriguing woman I've ever met," he murmured, and his dark eyes fell to her soft, full mouth.

"Surely not?" she asked demurely. "I don't have any secrets left."

"That's what you think," he said in a soft, low tone.

She looked up and he moved toward her, one hand catching the wooden headboard as he levered his hard mouth down against her soft one.

Her hands instinctively went to his chest, but its muscular warmth was fascinating. She'd never done anything really intimate with her infrequent dates, having been completely turned off by men with fast reputations. She preferred gentlemen to rounders. She knew that Rey had been a rounder. She wanted to draw away. She really did.

But Rey Hart was completely out of her experience. He wasn't aggressive and insistent, as one of Meredith's rare dates had been. He didn't rush at her. He didn't insist. He wasn't insulting with the speed of his advances. He simply bent and kissed her, slowly and gently, with nothing more intimate than his hard, tender lips touching hers. He nibbled her upper lip and lifted his mouth slowly.

"You're doing a surfboard imitation," he murmured. "There's no need. I'm too good a cattleman to rush my fences."

She was trying to understand the slow, sensuous speech when his lips came down on hers again and caressed her upper lip. Her hands pressed flat against his muscular chest. She liked the way he felt. She could feel the quick, strong pulse of his heart under her palms. She could feel the growing rise and fall of his breathing.

His teeth nibbled her lips again, tenderly, and she found her hands moving under his arms and around him. She wanted to be held close, tight. She wanted him to envelop her against him. She wanted something more than this torturous teasing of his mouth on hers.

She made a husky, high-pitched little cry into his mouth and her nails bit into the solid muscles of his back.

"What do you want?" he whispered just above her lips.

"Kiss me," she moaned huskily.

"Kisses are dangerous, didn't you know?" he murmured, smiling against her responsive mouth. "They can be very addictive."

She was following his lips mindlessly. Her body was on fire. She'd never felt such headlong desire. Belatedly she realized that his hands were at her rib cage. Whether by accident or design, they were moving slowly up and down, up and down, so that his long fingers just lightly brushed the underswell of her breasts. It was extremely provocative. It was arousing.

She caught her breath as they moved ever closer to entrapment, and her eyes locked into his.

"Don't you like it this way?" he asked at her lips, brushing his mouth against them.

"Like…it?" she murmured mindlessly. Her body was reaching up toward those tormenting hands. She was shivering with every pulsating motion of her body, trembling with new and exciting surges of pleasure.

He laughed softly, sensuously. "Never mind." He lifted a hand to her hair and tugged out the hairpins, so that her beautiful long hair fell down around her shoulders. He tugged aside the top she was wearing, so that her shoulder was bare. Then he bent to it with his mouth, and she felt the warm, moist press of his lips right in the hollow of her shoulder.

Her nails dug into him. She lifted toward his mouth with a hoarse moan as she felt the slow tracing of his tongue against skin that had never known a man's touch. She was on fire. She was going to go up in flames right here. She didn't want to think, see, hear anything. She only wanted Rey to keep on touching her, to keep on holding her, to never, never stop…!

CHAPTER EIGHT

JUST WHEN THE world was spinning away in a warm, pleasurable oblivion, the sound of loud, urgent footsteps echoed down the hall and brought Rey upright.

He looked at her with narrow, blank eyes as the sound grew louder. He cursed under his breath and got to his feet, keeping his back to her as he moved to the window, gripped the curtains and stared out at the pasture beyond.

Meredith dragged the bedspread up under her arms, over her clothes, and tried to steady her breathing. When she remembered what she and Rey had been doing, she blushed.

The door, ajar, was pushed completely open, and Leo came in with a tray. On it were a china cup and saucer, with a silver coffeepot, a silver cream and sugar service and a napkin and spoon. On a china plate were some dainty little chicken salad sandwiches.

"I thought you might be hungry," Leo said with a gentle smile as he put the tray on her lap. It had legs, so it would stand alone over her lap. "Mrs. Lewis came over to fix supper, and I had her make you these."

"Thank you!" she exclaimed. "And thank Mrs. Lewis, too. I was just starting to feel empty!"

Rey made an odd sound and she reached for a tiny

sandwich very quickly, not daring to glance at him after the enthusiastic and unwise remark she'd just made.

Leo turned his eyes toward his brother. "Something wrong with you?" he asked curiously.

"Stomach cramp," Rey said without turning. "I had chili and salsa for lunch. Heartburn's killing me!"

"You should go and take an antacid tablet," Leo advised. "And drink some milk."

"I guess I'd better." Rey took a long breath and turned around, feeling more normal, finally. He glanced at Meredith. "I'm glad you're okay."

"I'll be fine. Thanks for the conversation," she said, and wouldn't meet his eyes. But she smiled shyly.

He just looked at her. Suddenly his dark eyes began to burn. He studied her intently, as if something had just happened that shocked him.

"Are you all right?" she asked impulsively.

He took a slow breath. He was still staring at her, to his brother's covert amusement. With her hair around her shoulders like that, sitting up in bed, smiling at him, he felt as if his whole life had just shifted five degrees. She was uncommonly pretty with her hair down. She had a warm, kind heart. She'd put her life on the line for a total stranger. Why hadn't that occurred to him in Houston, when they first told him that she'd saved his brother from attackers?

"Leo probably owes you his life," Rey said carefully. "But it bothers me that you risked your own to save him."

"Wouldn't you have done that same thing, even for a total stranger?" she mused.

He hesitated. "Yes," he said after deliberating for a few seconds. "I suppose I would have."

"See? You have all sorts of potential as a prospective husband," she added with a wicked smile, which got wider when he reacted. "You're sexy, you're rich, you drive a nice car, and besides all that, you like animals." She began nodding her head. "Definite potential."

His high cheekbones flushed and he glared at her. "I don't want to get married."

"Don't worry about it," she said soothingly. "It's perfectly natural for a bachelor to resist matrimony. But you'll come around." She wiggled both eyebrows. "If you get me a ring, I'll let you see my collection of used chewing-gum wrappers and bottle caps."

He was still glaring.

Leo chuckled. "I'd love to see your used chewing-gum wrappers, Meredith," he said enthusiastically. "In fact, I may start collecting right now!"

Rey stared a hole through his brother while, inside him, something froze.

"I'll even consider marrying you," Leo added wickedly.

She laughed, not taking him seriously. "Sorry. It's Rey or nobody. My heart's set on him." She frowned. "Pity I couldn't trade you something for him," she murmured to Leo.

Rey was getting angrier by the second, and uncomfortable at the idea that Leo was trying to cut him out.

"Make me an offer," Leo told her. "But he can't cook, and he has a temper worse than a sunburned rattler. Besides that, you can't domesticate him. He wears his spurs to the dinner table."

"So do you!" Rey accused.

"I sit more daintily than you do," Leo said imperturbably.

Rey rammed his hands into the pockets of his jeans and glared at Meredith again. "You can't give people away."

"I'm not trying to give you away," Leo said calmly. "I want to make a profit." He scowled suddenly and his eyes widened as he looked at his brother's boots.

Meredith was staring at them, too. She pursed her lips and exchanged a look with Leo.

Rey glared back at them belligerently. "What?" he demanded hotly.

Both Leo's eyebrows went up, along with both hands, palms out. "I didn't say a word!"

"Neither did I," Meredith assured him.

Rey looked from one to the other and finally looked down. There, on one of his feet, was a dainty little foot sock with a tassel on it, covering the steel toe of his brown cowboy boot. He'd unknowingly picked it up under Meredith's bed while he was kissing her.

Rey jerked it off, cursed royally, shot a furious glance at Meredith and his brother, who were trying valiantly not to look at him, and stomped out.

Helpless laughter erupted from the two people left in Meredith's room, and the sound of it infuriated Rey.

Leo was obviously ready to set up shop with their recently disclosed nurse, and Rey didn't like it. Leo was the plague of housekeepers everywhere, but he was also easier on the eyes than the other brothers, and he was charming. Rey had never learned how to use charm. He always looked uncomfortable when he smiled. Especially with women like Meredith, who was painfully shy and naive. He wasn't used to such women. But what made it so much worse was the dropping sensation in his stomach that he'd experienced when he'd stared at

Meredith. He hadn't had anything like that since Carlie, who made his pulse race almost as fast as Meredith did when he kissed her.

He could still taste Meredith on his mouth. She didn't know much, but she made up for her lack of knowledge with enthusiasm and curiosity. He thought about carrying the lessons much farther, about baring her to the waist. His heart began to slam into his throat as he tried to imagine what she looked like under her blouse. He already knew that the skin of her shoulder was warm and soft, like silk. He remembered her husky moan when he'd kissed her there, the way her fingers had bitten into his back like little sharp pegs.

He'd been away from women for a long time, but he still knew what to do with one, and his imagination was working overtime just now. Meredith had attracted him when she was just his cook. Now that he knew about the intelligent, capable woman underneath the flighty camouflage, he was fascinated with her. She was everything a man could wish for.

Not that she wanted him, oh, no. She'd made it plain. But that teasing speech about marriage had unnerved him. His freedom was like a religion. He didn't want to get married. Of course he didn't!

But it was natural to think of Meredith with children. He could picture her baking biscuits for him every morning and holding a child in her arms at night while they watched television. He could picture her playing catch with a little boy out in back, or picking wildflowers with a little girl at her skirts. She was kind and sweet. She'd make a wonderful mother.

There was her job, of course. He knew something about her profession, that it was supposed to be high pressure. She'd be called upon to make life and death decisions, to comfort the sick and grieving, to make herself involved in the daily lives of her patients so that she should counsel them on how to maintain good health. Besides all that, she had a college degree.

Rey was college educated, too, with a degree in management and a minor in marketing. He was the mind behind the business decisions, the coordinator of the labor pool, and the director of marketing for the brothers' cattle cooperative. He was good at what he did. He enjoyed conversations with other educated people, and he'd convinced himself that Meredith wouldn't know Degas from Dali, Domingo from Dwight Yoakam, Hemingway from Dr. Seuss. Now he knew better, and his respect for her increased.

She'd saved Billy Joe's life at the gun club. He recalled that she must have known what to do for Leo as well, when she'd found him after he was mugged. Leo really did owe her his life. She was competent, confident, and she wasn't hard on the eyes, either. She had wonderful qualities.

But he didn't want to marry her. He wasn't sure about Leo. His eyes narrowed as he recalled the way Leo conspired with her. Leo had known all about her already. Obviously they'd been talking together since her arrival at the ranch, because Leo hadn't been a bit surprised when she rushed over to manage Billy Joe's heart attack.

Why hadn't he noticed that? Leo had called for Meredith when he was in the hospital. He was obviously fond of her. Maybe he was interested in her romantically, too. He'd been interested in Tess, before Cag had walked off with her, but Tess hadn't realized it. Or if she had, she'd ignored it. Leo wasn't hard on the eyes, either, and when it came to charm, he had his share and Rey's as well.

As he walked down to the barn to talk to one of his men, Rey had a terrible premonition that Leo had been serious when he joked about being willing to marry Meredith. Would she be desperate enough, lonely enough, frightened enough, to marry Leo and give up her job and living with her father? Her father had beaten her badly. She might be looking for a way out of the torment, and there was Leo, successful and handsome and charming, just ready to take her in and protect her.

Rey felt himself choke on dread. He couldn't imagine living in a house with Meredith if she was married to his brother. He'd rather throw himself headfirst into a cement mixer!

But, then, Leo had been teasing. Leo was always teasing. Rey forced himself to breathe normally and at least give the appearance of someone who was relaxed. Sure, it was just a joke. He didn't have to worry about the competition. There wasn't any. He pulled his hat lower over his eyes and walked on down the aisle to the man who was doctoring a heifer.

SEVERAL DAYS LATER, Meredith received a huge bouquet of assorted roses from Billy Joe, now out of the hospital and back on the shooting range. She put them in water in the kitchen, along with the card, which the brothers blatantly read.

"He'd marry you," Rey drawled with pure acid in his tone as he dragged out a chair and sat down to lunch. "He's been widowed twenty years."

Meredith gave Leo a mischievous glance and fiddled with putting biscuits in a linen-lined basket. "He's not bad-looking for a man his age, and it wouldn't hurt him to have a nurse under his roof." She glanced at Rey's eloquent back. "But can he cook?"

Rey sipped coffee noisily.

"And does he slurp his coffee?" she added without missing a beat.

"That was done deliberately, to show you that I don't give a damn about manners!" Rey growled.

"All right, just don't expect me to take you to any nice restaurants while we're courting," she said easily, setting the basket of biscuits on the table.

"Lady, you aren't taking me as far as the mailbox," he said curtly.

He looked ferocious. That black temper was already kindling. Meredith studied his bent head curiously. You never knew about men. She'd seen some very mild-mannered ones come to the emergency room with wives who'd been beaten within an inch of their lives. It didn't hurt to see how far a man would go when he got mad. Especially after her experience with her father.

"You'll have to learn to scrape the mud off those enormous boots, too," she went on in a conversational tone. "And not slurp your soup. Your hair could use a good trim..."

"Damn it!"

He shot to his feet, eyes blazing in a rigid face, with a dusky flush creeping along his high cheekbones with all the warning color of a poisonous reptile.

Meredith stood her ground, watching him clench those big fists at his side.

"Rey," Leo cautioned abruptly, and started to get to his feet.

Meredith went right up to Rey, looking him in the eyes, quiet, still—waiting.

Rey was breathing through his nostrils. His jaw was clenched with fury. But intelligence won easily over bad temper. His chin raised slowly. "You're testing me," he said out of the blue. "You want to know if I'll hit you."

"It's something a woman needs to know about a man," she said very quietly. "And she needs to find it out where she can get help if she needs it." She didn't look at Leo, but Rey knew that was what she meant. She smiled gently. "No, you don't hit," she said in a soft, quizzical tone. "You do have a temper, but it's not a physical one."

He was still breathing through his nose. "If you were a man, it might be," he told her bluntly.

"But I'm not a man," she replied.

Her eyes were almost glowing with feeling. He got lost in those soft, warm, grey eyes. He hated the way he felt when he was near her. He'd been fighting it ever since he carried her up to her garage apartment after she'd fainted at the hospital. He liked the feel of her in his arms. He liked kissing her. He liked the way she picked at him and teased him. No woman had ever done that before. As his older brothers had been before they married, he was taciturn and uncommunicative most of the time. His very attitude put most women off.

It didn't put Meredith off. She wasn't afraid of his temper, either. She made him into a different person. It wasn't something he could easily explain. He felt comfortable with her, even while she was stirring him to passion. He could imagine just sitting in front of the television with her and holding hands, late at night.

The image intimidated him. He sat back down, ignoring Meredith, and started putting butter and strawberry preserves on four biscuits.

Leo gave him a measuring look. "Don't eat all the biscuits."

"I'm only getting my share. She," he jerked his thumb towards Meredith, "didn't make but eight this morning. That's one for her, four for me, and three for you."

"And why do you get four?" Leo asked belligerently.

"Because she proposed to me," he said with pure smug arrogance, and a look that made Leo's teeth snap together.

"I did not," Meredith said haughtily, sitting down across from him. "I said I was thinking of you as a marriage prospect, not that I actually wanted to go through with a ceremony." She cleared her throat. "I'll have to see how you work out."

Rey smiled faintly. "That sounds interesting."

He didn't necessarily mean what it sounded like he meant. She mustn't jump to any conclusions here. But her cheeks were getting very rosy.

He noticed that. It was a devilish game they were playing, and he could do it better. He stared pointedly at her soft mouth as he put a cube of fresh pear into his mouth, slowly and deliberately.

She felt very uncomfortable in odd places when he did that. She ate her beef and gravy and tried to ignore him.

"I like having fresh fruit," Rey said with a slow smile. He speared a grape with his fork and eased it slowly between his lips.

She moved restlessly in her chair. "It's healthy stuff."

"No wonder you were trying to get us to eat right,"

Leo said, trying to break the growing spell Rey was casting on her. "You teach nutrition, I suppose."

"In a way. I'm supposed to counsel patients on changing bad habits and making lifestyle changes when they're warranted," she explained. If only her hand didn't shake while she was holding the stupid fork. Rey saw it and knew why, and she hated that damned smug smile on his lean face!

He picked up a piece of perfectly cooked asparagus spear and slowly sucked it into his mouth, using his tongue meaningfully.

"I have to fix dessert," Meredith choked, jumping to her feet so quickly that she knocked her chair winding and had to right it.

"I saw that chair jump right out and trip you, Meredith," Rey commented dryly. "You ought to hit it with a stick."

"I ought to hit *you* with a stick instead!" she raged at him, flushed and flustered and out of patience.

"Me?" Both eyebrows arched. "What did I do?"

She pictured hitting him across the jaw with the biggest frying pan she had. It was very satisfying. Pity she couldn't do it for real.

She went to the cupboard and drew out the ingredients for an instant reduced fat pudding. She had some low-fat whipped cream in the freezer that she could top it with. Meanwhile, Rey would finish his meal and stop using fruits and vegetables to torment her with. She could have kicked him.

Behind her, Rey was talking comfortably to Leo about some new equipment they were ordering, and about routine chores that had to be completed before Thanksgiving this month and the Christmas holidays next month. Most of the ranch hands would have Thanksgiving, the day after, and that weekend free. Next month, they'd have Christmas Eve and Christmas Day free, along with four days before or after, depending on the schedule. Some of the men had families in far-flung locations and they had to travel a distance for the holidays. The Harts made a practice of giving the men time off to go home during the holiday season by staggering work schedules, so that there was an adequate crew here to work when days off were assigned.

Then they moved on, naturally, to a discussion about Thanksgiving dinner.

"You're going to stay until after Thanksgiving, aren't you?" Rey asked Meredith.

She had her back to them. "Yes, I'd like to," she said, because she'd already been planning special menus and light, noncaloric desserts for it. "Unless you're planning to go away for it," she added quickly.

"The family has a Christmas party, when we all get together. We sort of save Thanksgiving for just us, so the others can have the day with their wives and kids," Leo told her. "It's been sort of hit and miss since Mrs. Lewis has been plagued with arthritis. As you know, we got her to come back to work just briefly, but her hands won't hold out to make bread and do any scrubbing with them, despite medicine. She has her children up from Corpus Christi for the holidays and cooks for them. We sort of got leftovers."

She grimaced. "Well, I'll make sure you have a big Thanksgiving dinner this year," she said gently. "With all the trimmings. Including biscuits," she added when they both looked her way.

She finished whipping the pudding, and put it in

bowls in the refrigerator to chill before she sat back down. "That will make us a nice dessert tonight," she commented. "I don't suppose you want it any sooner?"

They shook their heads. "I've got a meeting with our marketing staff in half an hour," Rey said, checking his multifunction watch.

"And I've got to go over the new equipment list with our mechanic and see if we've got everything ready to order," Leo added.

"How about a nice Greek salad for supper?" Meredith asked. "I make it with feta cheese and black olives and eggs. I bought the ingredients yesterday at the store. Except for the eggs, of course. I'll get those out of the henhouse."

"Sounds nice," Leo said with a grin.

"Watch where you put your hands," Rey murmured without looking right at her. "I haven't seen my pet snake in the barn lately."

She gave him a cold look. "If I see him, I'll get him on a stick and put him right back in the barn," she said with pure bravado.

Rey glanced at her with dancing dark eyes. "I'd pay real money to see you do that," he chided.

So would I, she thought, but she didn't say it. She just smiled smugly.

The brothers finished their last swallows of coffee and went out the door still talking business.

Later, Meredith went out to the henhouse to gather the eggs, with her straw basket on her arm. Rey had unnerved her with his comment about the damned snake. Now she was sure it was in there, waiting for a gullible victim to frighten.

She took a deep breath and walked carefully into the

dim confines of the henhouse. She bit her lower lip and approached the nest slowly. She stopped dead. There was actually a snake in there. He was wrapped around the eggs. He was licking his snaky lips.

She shivered with fear, but she wasn't going to let the stupid thing make her a laughingstock twice.

She saw a long, thick stick on the straw-covered floor. She put her basket down, still watching the snake, and picked up the stick.

"It's okay, old fellow," she said to the snake. "It's okay. I'm just going to ease you out of the nest. Don't get mad, now. I won't hurt you. It's okay."

While she was talking, softly, she eased the stick under its coils and very carefully lifted it. It was very still, not moving its head except to hiss. So far, so good. She had it up on the stick. It was heavy.

As she pulled it out of the nest, she noticed that it was really quite long. It really didn't look much like that black and white one Rey had put in the barn. This one had a pretty brown pattern on its back and had a white underbelly. But, then, it wasn't striking at her or anything, so she wasn't worried.

She held it far out in front of her and stepped carefully out of the henhouse into the bright light. As she did, the snake hung from the stick, looking rather bored by the whole thing.

She carried it through the yard and out toward the barn. One of the men was standing by a truck, watching her progress. His jaw fell. She wondered what was wrong with him. Maybe he'd never seen a woman carry a snake around before.

"Nice day," she called to him.

He didn't answer. She shrugged and kept walking.

The barn was empty, except for the bales of hay that were stacked neatly on the bottom and the loft of the huge structure. Over against one wall there was a corn crib with stacks and stacks of dried corn, and a machine that shelled them.

"Here we go, old fellow," she told the snake. She eased him over the wooden box and slid him down into the piles of unshelled corn.

He drew back in a threatening pose and hissed at her again.

Odd, the shape of his head, she thought, frowning as she studied him. It looked like an arrowhead. That other snake's head had been rounded.

Well, it might be some other species of king snake, she supposed. Weren't there several?

She walked back out of the barn into the daylight, whistling softly to herself as she started back to the henhouse. She was so proud of herself. She'd gotten the snake on the stick all by herself, without screaming once, and she'd carried him all the way to the barn and put him in the corn crib. She wasn't afraid of the snake anymore. As Rey had said, they were beneficial. It wasn't right to kill something just because you were afraid of it, she told herself.

The man who'd been standing by the truck was nowhere in sight, but the truck was still running and the driver's door was standing wide-open. She wondered where the driver had gone. He must have been in a hurry for some reason.

Meredith went back to the henhouse, put the stick down, picked up her basket and went to gather eggs. There were no more snakes, but there were plenty of eggs. She could boil several to go in her nice Greek salad. The spinach she'd bought to make it with was crisp and cold and almost blemishless. The brothers would love a salad if it had enough eggs and cheese and dressing.

She got the last egg into the basket and walked back out again, pausing to reach down and pet one of the big red hens who came right up to her and cocked its head curiously toward her face.

"Aren't you a pretty girl?" she said, smiling. She liked the way the chicken felt. Its feathers were very smooth and silky, and the chicken made the sweetest little noises when she petted it. She'd never been around farm creatures. She found that she enjoyed the chickens and the cattle dogs and the endless cats that hung around outside begging for handouts.

Two other hens came up to her, curious about the tall creature in jeans and tank top. She petted them, too, laughing as they crowded close. But then one started to peck the eggs, and she stood up again.

She turned back toward the house, her mind on the snake and her bravery. She'd have to remember to tell Rey and Leo about it…

"Meredith!"

The loud, urgent deep voice sent her spinning around. Rey was running toward her, bare-headed, with the cowhand who'd been next to the running pickup truck at his heels.

"Hi, Rey," she said hesitantly. "What's wrong?"

He stopped just in front of her. He caught her a little roughly by the arms and took the basket away from her, setting it aside, while he looked at every inch of her bare arms and hands. He was breathing rapidly. He seemed unnaturally pale and tight-lipped.

"It didn't bite you?" he demanded.

"What?"

"The snake! It didn't bite you?" he snapped.

"No, of course not," she stammered. "I just got it on a stick, like you did, and put it in the corn crib."

"Get my Winchester," Rey told the other man in a harsh tone. "Load it and bring it back here. Hurry!"

"I don't understand," Meredith said with noticeable confusion. "What's wrong with you? Why do you need a gun?"

"Oh, baby," he whispered hoarsely. He pulled her against him and bent to kiss her in view of the whole outfit, his mouth hard and rough against hers. "Baby!"

She had no idea what was wrong, but she loved the faint tremor in his hard arms as they crushed her against his body. And she loved the way he was kissing her, as if he couldn't get enough of her mouth. He'd called her "baby..."

She held on and moaned under the crush of his lips.

He drew back. "I'm sorry. It was such a shock. I was scared out of my wits, I didn't even stop to grab my hat when Whit came into the office...!"

Her mouth was pleasantly swollen. She looked up at him dreamily and smiled.

"You don't have a clue, do you?" he asked huskily, searching her soft grey eyes.

"Mmm. About what?" she murmured, only half hearing him.

The other man came out with a rifle. He handed it to Rey. "Safety's on," the man advised.

"Thanks, Whit."

He moved back from Meredith. "I'll go kill it."

"Kill it?" Meredith exclaimed. "You can't! It will eat the rats, it's harmless…!"

"Sweetheart," he said very gently, "you were carrying a copperhead moccasin."

"Yes?" She stared at him blankly.

"It's one of the most poisonous snakes in Texas!"

She stood looking after him with her mouth open and her heartbeat choking her. She'd been carrying the damned thing on a stick, with it hissing at her. She felt the blood leave her head. Seconds later, she was lying on the hard ground. Fortunately she missed the basket of eggs on the way down.

CHAPTER NINE

"YOU'RE MAKING A habit of this lately," Rey murmured as he carried Meredith up the stairs to the garage apartment. "I never figured you for a fainter, Meredith," he added dryly.

He was still bare-headed, but he wasn't grim now. He was smiling.

"Of course I fainted! I picked up a poisonous snake!" she gasped, still in shock.

"Well, you've got guts, woman, I'll give you that," he said with a slow smile, shifting her a little closer. "Picked up a poisonous snake with a stick and carried it all the way to the barn, and it didn't bite you. Now I've heard everything."

"It did hiss a little," she recalled, shivering.

"It had eaten three eggs," he murmured. "Probably it was too busy digesting to care where it went at the time. Lucky for you."

She laid her cheek against his broad, strong shoulder and held on tight. She had a sudden thought. "It didn't bite you?" she asked worriedly.

"It didn't get the chance. Didn't you hear the shot? I got it as it was crawling down from the corn bin onto the floor." He chuckled. "If I hadn't gotten it, though, Bandit would have. King snakes are natural enemies of any poisonous snake. They eat them. I hate to kill even a copperhead, but we can't have poisonous snakes around the livestock, or the men. Or, especially," he added with a warm glance at her, "in the henhouse. At the very least, a bite from one can put a man in the hospital."

She shivered, and her arms tightened around Rey's neck. "I was so proud of myself," she murmured. "I had no idea I was taking my life in my hands. It didn't look exactly like the other snake, but the patterns were sort of similar. I know about snake bites because I've helped treat them, but I don't know one snake from another unless I see pictures of them!" she added defensively.

"You'll learn." He kissed her forehead with breathless tenderness. "My brave girl," he whispered. "You'll never know how scared I was when Whit came running to tell me what you were doing."

It made soft little ripples of pleasure run through her body when he said that. He was being protective about her. She closed her eyes and drank in the warm nearness of him, the easy strength of his arms as he carried her. She felt safe as she'd never felt in her whole life. It was nice to lean on somebody strong, just for a little while.

He felt the vulnerability. He told himself that he wouldn't take advantage of it, but who was he kidding? She was soft and cuddly like this, and it was almost an involuntary action when his mouth slowly moved over hers as he reached her door.

The pressure was light, comforting. She sighed under the warmth and delight of it, and her lips parted, just the least little bit.

His whole body contracted with desire at that faint response. He looked down into her half-closed, misty eyes with growing hunger.

The look was as new as the tenderness. She couldn't

tear her eyes away from that dark hunger in his. She forgot the snake, the scare, the people outside in the yard, everything. He bent back to her, and she met his mouth hungrily with her own, her arms clinging fiercely to his shoulders.

He groaned aloud. It was too soon, but he didn't care. He managed to open the door and close it behind them, making a beeline for the neatly made-up bed. He barely took time to put her down on the coverlet before his body slid against and over her own, his arms under her, taking his weight while his mouth made new, insistent demands on her innocence.

He lifted his head a torturous few seconds later, and his eyes blazed into her own. One lean hand slid deliberately under the hem of her tank top. At the same time, one long, powerful leg eased between both of hers and his hard mouth began to tease around the corners of hers.

"Danger will do it every time," he murmured deeply.

"Will…do what?" she asked, burning with new longings as his hand began to move up her rib cage toward the lacy little bra she was wearing under the top.

"This." His mouth opened on hers and became quickly insistent. While he kissed her, his fingers found the catch on her bra and flicked it open. She jumped when she felt his hand on flesh that had never known a man's touch before. He lifted his head and looked into her eyes. "I know. It's new territory," he said gently. His fingers stroked the delicate, warm flesh as lightly as a breeze. "Try to think of it as a rite of passage."

She felt strange new sensations. There was a tightening, a swelling, in her breasts as he touched them. She lifted involuntarily, and her eyes mirrored her surprise.

"Innocence is a rare, rare thing these days," he said at

her lips. "I respect it. And you'd better thank your lucky stars that I do," he added as his mouth bit hungrily at hers. "Because with an experienced woman, I'd lock the door and I wouldn't hesitate a minute."

She felt the words like the caress of his hands on her body. She moaned huskily under the demanding crush of his mouth. She felt his tongue tracing her lips, teasing under them, darting and touching and withdrawing. She felt his teeth, too, in a sensual caress that only intensified the new sensations he was teaching her to feel.

She felt her back arch again as he traced around the curves of her breast without ever touching the hard, taut nipple. She wanted him to touch it. Her body ached to have him touch it. She didn't understand why it should be such a violent, aching need…!

He laughed in a soft, sexy way against her lips. "Is this what you want?"

He caught the nipple between his thumb and forefinger and she lifted off the bed with a sharp cry. Heat spread over her, through her. Her short nails dug into his back fiercely and she gasped with pleasure.

"Baby," he groaned roughly, aroused by her unexpectedly ardent response. "Baby, you turn me on so hard…!"

The top was suddenly around her collarbone and his mouth—his mouth!—was right on her nipple, suckling her while his tongue tasted the hardness with a subtle caress that made her shiver. Her hands caught in the thick strands of his dark hair and held him to her body while he explored it with his mouth. She'd never imagined that she was capable of so much passion, and so unexpectedly swift. He could do anything to her, and she didn't have the willpower to stop him. Even a simple "no" was beyond her now. She wanted more. She wanted his eyes on her, his hands on her. She wanted his body closer.

As if he knew that, both lean hands smoothed up from her waist and onto her soft breasts. His fingers were rough from hard work, but their touch was pure heaven. She caressed his nape, moving rhythmically with each slow brush of his fingers, lost in pleasure.

He lifted his head to look at what he'd uncovered. She was beautiful, not too big or too small. She was just right. He loved the way her body moved when he touched it. He loved knowing how innocent she was. He'd never been with an innocent. Making love to one was a whole new experience, with levels of pleasure he'd never tasted. Her soft little moans excited him as much as those enthusiastic fingers caressing his back.

She felt his eyes and she opened hers, looking up at him. "Am I doing it right?" she whispered breathlessly.

His body tautened even more. "Yes," he whispered. "Just right."

He bent and drew his mouth gently over hers with a soft, cherishing pressure. He felt it open under his, felt her arms pulling at him. It wasn't a good idea to let this go any farther than it already had. While he was thinking it, he was moving slowly between her long legs until his body rested in the fork of hers. He eased down against her, letting her feel the slow burgeoning of his body against her belly.

She caught her breath.

He heard it, and lifted his head. His eyes were smoldering with desire, his body was rigid with it. He was getting little surges of insistent pleasure that ran the length of his spine. Her hips moved as if they were responding helplessly to the touch of him. She was making him ache like hell.

His hand moved to her hip and bit into the soft flesh, stilling the faint motion of her hips instantly while he rested on the elbow of his other arm. "Meredith," he said softly. "That will get you seduced. Right now."

She felt hot all over. Her mind seemed barely under her control. She searched his dark eyes with wonder. Her hands were against his shirt, right on the buttons. She felt him against the lower part of her body, and it felt right. It felt wonderful. She wanted to writhe under him and tempt him into intimacy.

His hand contracted and he gave her a wise, challenging stare as he read the look on her face. "Don't do it," he said huskily. "I'm years ahead of you in experience, but I can still lose my head. You don't want me to do that. Not really."

She pulled at a stabilizing breath. Her heart was still whacking around at the walls of her chest, as if she'd been running a race. "Are you sure I don't want you to do that? I mean, if you get pregnant, I'll marry you," she said breathlessly, and with deathbed humor. "Honest!"

He looked at her as if he couldn't believe his ears. The passion drained out of him, replaced by howling amusement. He started laughing. "Damn you, that wasn't fair!" he accused.

"Well, I like that! You're laughing, and here I've made you a solemn promise," she persisted, eyes twinkling.

"Hell!" He rolled away from her and sat up on the edge of the bed to run a lean hand through his disheveled hair. He glared down at her. "Now you've got fingerprints and lipstick and perfume all over me. The men will laugh themselves sick if I go to work smelling like a flower garden."

She tugged down her top and gave him an impish grin. "We could rush into my bathroom and shower it off, together," she offered wickedly.

He laughed again. He'd never laughed as much in his life as he did with her. Was this the way she'd been, before the tragedies of the past year that had marred her life? She'd said she didn't date much, but how in the world could men ignore a sweet, pretty little woman like that?

"I can't believe you spend your weekends watching television with your father," he murmured.

"I don't. I work."

He frowned. "On the weekends?"

She sat up, reaching under her blouse to refasten the bra he'd unsnapped. She wondered why she didn't feel embarrassed. "Seven days a week, for the past six months," she said honestly. "Before that, six days a week, and I had to rest on Sunday. I usually work ten-hour days, sometimes longer if we have an emergency."

He didn't like that. "You don't have any free time, do you?"

She shook her head. "I've been dedicated to the job since I got out of college."

"And no men," he murmured with a speculative glance.

She grimaced. "Well, there was one I liked very much. We went out together for four months, and I was very nearly in love with him. But he never touched me. I thought he was building up to it, or something." She sighed. "Then I saw him, with another man." She shrugged. "He thought of me as a friend. I thought of him as a boyfriend. I sort of lost confidence in myself after that."

"It happens, in the modern world," he replied quietly.

"Before that, I had crushes on boys who never noticed me, except to ask me to help them with math or chemistry." She searched his eyes. "Of course, I didn't exactly look like this until last year."

"How did you look?" he asked curiously.

She got off the bed, went to get her purse, and took out a plastic insert. She pulled a photo from behind a credit card and handed it to him.

His eyes widened. "Good heavens!"

She winced. "I was sixty pounds overweight, and I couldn't lose it at all. I guess I tried every diet known to man. Then I took nutrition classes and learned how to get it off the sensible way. That's why I know so much about low-fat cooking."

He looked from the photo to her face and smiled. "You were pretty before, too," he said slowly. "You know, Meredith, it's not the outside that attracts people. It's what you are, how you treat other people, that makes friends of them. You risked your life to save my brother, then you stayed with him until his family came. I wasn't very flattering to you when we first met, but I've had a lot of time to think about what you did. You're good people. Really good people."

She flushed and cleared her throat. "Thanks." She gave him a mischievous look. "So, would you like to get married Friday, or is Monday better for you?" she added with a grin.

He chuckled. "Sorry, I have to wash my dogs."

She sighed. "Rejected again."

He pursed his lips and let his eyes run over her slowly. "You could lie back down and we could discuss it again."

"Absolutely not. I only have so much willpower. You shouldn't throw yourself at women that way unless you're asking to be seduced. It's unfair."

"You're not bad yourself, kid," he murmured with a warm smile. He got up. "I've got to go back to work. Come here."

She went to him. "Changed your mind?" she asked. "I can get a ring today…"

He put a finger over her mouth. "How do I smell?"

"Is that all you want?" she exclaimed. "Good Lord, you got me all the way over here to *smell* you?"

He bent and kissed her hungrily, pulling her so close that she could feel him against every cell of her body. But before she could cling, he put her away. "How do I smell?" he persisted.

She sniffed him. "You smell like aftershave."

He bent and sniffed her, and frowned. "You're not wearing perfume, are you?"

She shook her head. "I'm allergic to most strong fragrances."

"You smell like flowers."

She smiled. "Herbal shampoo. Flowers don't bother me. Well, real ones do sometimes, but not flowery scent. I can use scented shampoos and wear one or two colognes, but no perfumes. They're too strong."

"At least I don't smell womanly," he said with mocking relief. "I'd never live that down."

She cocked her head and stared up at him. "There goes the shower," she sighed.

He tapped her nose. "Now, cut that out." His fingers traced the fading bruises on her cheek and jaw and his eyes narrowed. "He'll never touch you again, I swear he won't," he said in a low, dangerous tone.

Her heart lifted at the look on his face. "Oh, my, aren't we getting possessive?" she teased.

He didn't smile. "Careful," he told her quietly. "I'm not teasing."

Her eyes widened with something like wonder.

"Hasn't anyone ever stood up for you?" he asked curiously.

"Just my brother. But he never had to protect me from Daddy. I know it looks really bad, but my father was the most gentle man on earth until we lost Mama and Mike. He goes crazy when he drinks, and he never remembers what he did." Her eyes fell to his chest. She toyed with his shirt buttons, wondering absently how it would feel to smooth her fingers over his bare chest. "I miss my brother terribly," she added simply.

"I'm sure you do. And your mother."

She grimaced. "She and I weren't really very close," she confessed. She searched his eyes. "You see, what Daddy yelled about her that night you were at the house was pretty much true. She was a very attractive woman, and she had lovers." She winced. "I hated knowing that. You can't imagine what it did to Daddy. She even bragged about them."

"She doesn't sound like much of a wife," he murmured.

"She didn't act like one, either. She did love to spend money, though. That's why she picked rich lovers." Her face clouded. "I was so ashamed of her. I guess she saw herself as a modern woman. I'm not. There's a big difference between sleeping with someone you truly love, and jumping into bed with anyone who has some money."

He nodded and touched her soft, swollen mouth. “She’s soured you on men, hasn’t she?”

“Sort of. Until you came along, at least,” she admitted, without looking at him. She stared at his shirt button. “Bad temper and all, you’ve got some wonderful qualities.”

He gave her a wry look. “I’ll have to tell my brothers. They didn’t know.”

She chuckled. “Thanks for letting me come here to heal, anyway.”

He felt uneasy. “That sounds like goodbye, Meredith.”

She sighed. Her fingers stilled on his buttons. “I can’t stay much longer,” she said sadly. “Even though I’d like to. My boss is shorthanded as it is, and the woman filling in for me doesn’t like leaving her kids in day care. She retired when she had the second one.”

“Retired?”

“Yes. She said keeping two kids in day care ate up her whole paycheck.” She lifted her eyes to his. “Since her husband got a raise, it was actually cheaper for her to stay home with the kids than it was to work. She loves it.”

There was a strange look on his face. He rubbed his fingertips over her short fingernails absently. “Would you want to stay home with your kids?”

She stared up at him, transfixed. “Yes, I would. Those first few years are so important. If I could find any way to do it, I would, even if I had to sacrifice some little luxuries.”

“That would be tricky. You’re a highly trained professional.”

“One of my friends was a highly trained doctor,” she

replied. "She gave up her job and stayed home with her little boy until he was in kindergarten. Even then, she arranged her schedule so that she'd be there when he got home in the afternoons."

He was frowning, and his fingers were still smoothing over hers. He wanted to ask if she thought she could get used to ranch life and snakes. He was afraid to say it. The act of commitment was still very new to him. He couldn't rush her.

He sighed, troubled. "What does your father do, by the way?" he asked suddenly.

"Oh, he teaches in the veterinary department of his college in Houston."

His hand stilled on hers. "He's a veterinarian?"

"He has a doctorate in veterinary medicine, yes. Why?"

Wheels were turning in his head. He stared at her thoughtfully. "Will he have a job to go back to, after all the trouble he's had with the law?"

"You're very perceptive," she said after a minute. "Actually, no, he won't. The college phoned before his last bender and told him not to come back. You can't blame them, either," she added sadly. "What would it do to the college's image, to have an alcoholic on staff with a dangerous temper?"

"Not much," he had to admit. "Did he drink before the shooting?"

"Never. Not even a beer," she replied. "But he's set records in the past six months. I couldn't get him near a treatment center. At least he's in one, now."

"Not only in it, but improving by the day," Rey said unexpectedly. "He'd like you to come see him. I can run you up there Sunday, if you'd like to go."

That was surprising. "You've spoken to him?" she asked.

He nodded. "I had Leo phone Colter. He has contacts who helped arrange it." He drew in a deep breath. "Your father seems pretty rational right now. Of course, he isn't drinking, either." His eyes darkened. "I meant exactly what I said. He'll never touch you again in anger."

"When he's sober, he never would. I can't believe… he really wants to see me?" she asked haltingly.

He brushed his hand against her cheek. "He loves you. I'm sure you love him, too. You don't throw people away because they make a mistake—even a bad one. You get help for them."

"I tried."

"Sure you did. But it's better this way. When he comes home, we'll decide where to go from there. For now, I'll drive you to Houston on Sunday to see him. Want to go?"

"Oh, yes," she said. Her expression was soft, wondering. "You'd do that, for me?"

He smiled. "Anything you want, kiddo," he murmured. "It's the least I can do for the only woman who's ever proposed to me."

She pursed her lips and gave him an impish look. "We could lie down and talk about it."

"No, we couldn't," he told her firmly, and chuckled as he removed her hands from his shirt. "I have to get back to work. I was in the middle of a meeting when you did your snake charmer routine. I left twelve employees sitting in the boardroom with glasses of water and no ashtrays. At least six of them smoke, despite all the regulations. I expect they've attacked the other six with chairs by now, or vice versa. I've got to get back. Quick."

"I'd love to go Sunday," she said.

"Fine. I'll run you up there Sunday afternoon. We can go to church first."

Her eyebrows lifted. "I'm Methodist."

He grinned. "So are we. It's a date." He opened the door. Before he went out it, he glanced back over his shoulder. "And stay out of the henhouse for the rest of the day, will you?"

"Anything for my prospective fiancé," she said with a theatrical gesture of her arm.

He shook his head and walked out, still chuckling.

LATER, SHE WONDERED what he'd meant, about making decisions when her father got out of rehab. She didn't dare think too hard about it. But it sounded very much as if he wanted to go on looking out for her.

She was a modern woman. She could look out for herself. But it was kind of nice to have a man act protective and possessive, especially one like Rey, who didn't seem the sort to do it habitually. She remembered the hunger in his lean body when he held her, when he kissed her. She remembered the strange tenderness he reserved for her. It was an adventure, just being around him. They'd known each other such a short time, really, but she felt as if she'd known him all her life. The thought of going back to Houston without him was suddenly frightening.

She did the routine things until Sunday, except that when she gathered eggs, she was overly cautious about going into the henhouse. She'd learned from Rey that snakes often traveled in pairs, so she was careful to look before she stepped anywhere that the ground was covered.

She'd become something of a legend among the Hart

ranch hands already. They removed their hats when she walked by, and they spoke to her in respectful tones.

"It's really strange," she remarked at the dinner table on Saturday evening, glancing from Leo to Rey. "The men seem sort of in awe of me."

Rey chuckled and exchanged an amused look with his brother. "They are. None of them has ever picked up a copperhead on a stick."

"It let me," she reminded him.

"That's the awesome thing," Leo remarked. "You see, Meredith, copperheads have a nasty reputation for attacking without provocation. It's kind of mystic, what you did." He pursed his lips and gave her a teasing glance over his buttered biscuit. "Any snake charmers in your family?"

"No, but Mike had a pet boa for a while, until it ate one of the neighbor's rabbits," she sighed.

"Yuccch!" Rey said, and shivered.

"It was an accident," Meredith insisted. "It escaped out the window and was gone for three weeks. We figured it was starving, because it hadn't been fed in so long. Besides that," she added, "the rabbit was vicious. It attacked everybody who opened the cage."

"Why did the neighbor keep rabbits?"

"He sold them for meat to a specialty grocery store."

Rey chuckled. "Maybe the boa was a reincarnated taste-tester," he mused.

Leo made a face. "I wouldn't eat a rabbit if I was starving. On the other hand, snake's not so bad. Remember when we were in Arizona on that hunting trip, camping out, and our guide caught that big, juicy rattler?"

"Sure do," Rey agreed, nodding. "Tasted just like chicken!"

Obviously that was a private joke, because the brothers looked at each other and burst out laughing.

"What became of the boa?" Leo asked, interested.

"Mike had just sold it to a breeder," she recalled sadly. "He was engaged to the sweetest, kindest girl I ever knew. It devastated her when he was killed. They had to sedate her for two days, and she couldn't even go to the funeral." She shook her head. "I felt as sorry for her as I did for Dad and me."

"What happened to her?" Leo asked.

She finished her coffee. "She became a missionary and went to South America with a group of them." She winced. "She had the worst luck…it was that plane that was mistaken for drug smugglers and shot down. I think she was one of the survivors, but she didn't come back to America with the others."

"Poor kid," Rey said.

"Colter was upset over the shooting for a long time, too," Leo recalled. "Just between you and me, he was sweet on Mike's girl, but too much a gentleman to do anything about it. He thought the sun rose and set on Mike."

"I never knew," Meredith said softly.

"Neither did Mike. Or the girl," Leo added with a smile. "Colter's a clam. He never talks."

"Is he still with the Texas Rangers?" Meredith asked.

Leo nodded. "Got promoted to lieutenant just recently. He's good at his job."

She pushed back from the table. "If you two are through, I'll just wash up. Rey's going to drive me up to see my dad tomorrow."

"What a sweet guy!" Leo exclaimed with a wide-eyed look at his brother.

"He's being nice to me, because I'm the only woman who ever proposed to him," Meredith volunteered with a wicked grin. "He feels guilty because he turned me down."

"Good. I'll marry you, Meredith," Leo volunteered at once. "You just name the time and place, and I'll buy a new suit…!"

"Shut the hell up!" Rey said curtly, and hit his brother with his Stetson.

Leo protected his shoulder. "Meredith, he's picking on me!" he wailed.

"Do you want biscuits for breakfast?" she asked Rey.

He stopped flogging his brother. "All right. But only for biscuits," Rey said. He got up and deliberately bent and kissed Meredith, right in front of Leo. "Don't stay up too late. Leo and I have to check the livestock in the barn."

"Okay. Wear a jacket," she said, smiling up at him.

He bent and brushed his mouth against hers one more time. "It's not cold."

"It is. Wear a jacket," she insisted.

He sighed and made a face, but he picked up his lightweight denim jacket from the hat stand by the back door as he went out.

Leo followed him, but with a new expression on his face. He'd seen something he hadn't expected during that teasing exchange. He wondered if Rey realized that he was in love with that sweet little biscuit-making woman. And unless he missed his guess, it was mutual.

CHAPTER TEN

THE NEXT MORNING, Meredith sat next to Rey in church and felt his hand holding hers almost all the way through the service. She felt different with him than she'd ever felt with anyone else. Rey made her feel as if she could do anything. He made her feel strong and confident and safe.

She glanced up at him while they shared a hymnal and he forgot what he was singing. They searched each other's eyes slowly, until they realized that everybody else had stopped singing and were sitting down. Smiling sheepishly, Rey sat down and tugged her down beside him.

After the service, they got amused, affectionate looks from bystanders who knew Rey and had heard about his new cook.

But he didn't seem to be the least bit embarrassed by the attention. In fact, he made a point of introducing Meredith to several people, adding the little known information that she was a licensed nurse practitioner as well as a great biscuit chef.

Meredith flushed, because it sounded as if he were very proud of her, especially when he related how her quick thinking had probably saved Billy Joe's life at the target range. Billy Joe was well-known and liked locally, so that brought even more smiles. She clung to his hand with unashamed delight when they left.

"See, you're already a local celebrity," he teased. "And I didn't even get around to mentioning the snake."

"We should forget the snake," she said quickly.

He chuckled. "No, we shouldn't. It wins me points if I have a…cook who isn't even afraid of poisonous snakes."

She heard that hesitation before "cook," as if he wanted to say something else instead. It made her tingle all over. She couldn't stop smiling, all the way to the Jaguar convertible he drove when he wasn't working.

"This is a very flashy car," she commented as he put her in on the passenger side.

"I like sports cars," he said with a grin.

"So do I," she confessed. She didn't even put on a scarf. In fact, she pulled the pins out of her hair and let it fall around her shoulders.

"Won't it tangle in the wind?" he asked when they were seat-belted in place.

"I don't care." She looked at him and smiled warmly. "I like to feel the wind."

"Me, too."

He started the car, put it in gear, and pulled out onto the highway. When they were on the interstate, heading toward Houston, he let the powerful car do its best.

"Now this is a HORSE!" he called over the roar of the wind.

She laughed with pure delight. It was the most wonderful day of her life. She even forgot where they were going in the excitement of being with him in the elegant vehicle.

But all too soon, they were pulling up at an impressive brick building with its function discreetly labeled on a metal plate near the door. It was a substance abuse rehabilitation center, three stories tall, and staffed impressively with psychologists, psychiatrists, and health professionals, including physicians.

Rey held her hand to the information desk and then up to the second floor waiting room, where her father would be brought to visit with them.

"They don't like visitors the first week," Rey explained to her. "You probably knew that," he added, remembering her profession.

"I've never had anybody in here," she said quietly. She was nervous and she looked it.

He caught her fingers in his again and held them tight. "It's going to be all right," he said firmly.

She met his eyes and took a deep breath. "Okay," she said after a minute, and her body lost some of its rigidity.

There were footsteps and muffled voices. A minute later, her father came in the door, wearing slacks and a knit shirt, and behind him was a uniformed woman with a clipboard.

"Miss Johns? I'm Gladys Bartlett," the woman introduced herself with a firm handshake. "I'm the staff psychologist on your father's case."

"Hello, Merry," her father said hesitantly. He winced when he noticed the faded bruises on her face. "I'm sorry, my dear," he choked.

Meredith let go of Rey's hand and went forward to hug her father warmly. Mr. Johns closed his eyes and hugged her back, hard. His lips trembled as he forced them together, but tears ran down his lean, pale cheeks. "I'm so sorry," he sobbed.

She patted him on the back and tears fell hotly from her own eyes. "It's okay, Daddy," she whispered brokenly, comforting him the way he'd once comforted her and Mike when they were little, and something had hurt them. He'd been a wonderful father. "It's okay," she said again. "You're going to be fine. We both are."

"My son. My boy!" He shook all over. "I said I was too busy to take her to the bank. I asked him… I *asked* Mike…to go instead. He'd be alive, but for me!"

"Now, Mr. Johns," the counselor said gently, "we've been over this several times already. You can't assume blame for the lawless acts of other people. Ninety-nine times out of a hundred, nothing would have happened if you'd asked your son to go to the bank on your behalf."

"But this was the one out of a hundred," he husked. "And I can't live with the guilt!"

"I've had my own problems with it," Meredith confessed. "I could have refused to go in to work that day and taken her instead."

"And you'd be lying dead instead of Mike," her father replied curtly. "And I'd be just as eaten up with guilt!"

"You're both missing the point," Rey said, standing up. "You can't control life. Nobody can."

They all looked at him. He stood quietly, his hands deep in his slacks pockets, and stared back. "Einstein said that God didn't play dice with the universe, and he was right. Even in seeming chaos, there's an order to things, a chain of events that leads inevitably to conclusions. People are links in the chain, but people don't control the events. Life has a pattern, even if we don't see it."

"You've studied philosophy," Mr. Johns said quietly.

Rey nodded. "Yes, I have."

The older man, with thinning hair and glasses and a faintly stooped posture, moved away from Meredith and smiled. "I took several courses in it, myself. You have a degree, haven't you?"

"I do, in business. A master's, from Harvard," Rey volunteered, something that Meredith hadn't even known.

"Mine is in medicine. Veterinary medicine. I'm…"

"I know. You're Dr. Alan Johns," Rey said, shaking hands. "Your daughter is staying with us on the ranch in Jacobsville, baking biscuits, while she recovers."

Dr. Johns winced and flushed. "They told me what I did to you," he said, glancing shamefaced at his daughter. "I swear before God, I'll never take another drink as long as I live!"

"You won't get the chance," Rey said. "I intend to watch you like a red-tailed hawk."

"Excuse me?" Dr. Johns stammered.

Rey studied his boots. "We don't have a vet on staff. We have to call one down from Victoria, because our vets are overworked to death. It would be nice to have our own vet. We pay competitive salaries and you'd have your own house."

Dr. Johns sat down quickly. "Young man, I…!"

Rey lifted his head and stared him in the eyes. "You made a mistake. People do. That's why they put erasers on pencils. You can work for us. We'll keep you straight, and you won't have to take some sort of menial job in Houston just to make ends meet. You'll like the ranch," he added. "We have a good crew."

"Someone might know what I did," Dr. Johns stammered.

"Everybody knows already," Rey said, and shrugged.

"It's no big deal to us. We've got one man who came back from cocaine addiction—let me tell you, that was a story and a half—and another one who was a habitual DWI for six years until we hired him and helped him get straight." He smiled. "We don't hold a man's past against him, as long as he's willing to stay straight and work hard."

Dr. Johns was having a hard time keeping control of himself, and it was obvious. "Young man, I'll work without a salary, if that's what it takes. And I promise, you'll never have cause to regret giving me a job."

"Not unless you keep calling me 'young man,'" Rey said with a grin. "I'm Reynard Hart, but everybody calls me Rey."

"Glad to meet you," the older man said. "Rey."

Rey nodded. "How much longer will they keep you?" he asked, and glanced at the woman with the clipboard.

"Another week should do it," she said with a big smile. "And how nice, to see him with a settled environment to look forward to the day he leaves! I believe in minor miracles, but I don't see many. This is certainly one."

Rey gave her a complacent smile. "Miracles only happen for people who believe in them," he said, chuckling.

"Thanks, Rey," Meredith said huskily.

He only shrugged. "How could I ignore the father of the only woman who ever proposed to me?" he said, matter-of-factly, and with a smile that made her blush.

"You proposed to him?" her father asked with raised eyebrows.

"Several times," she said with mock disgust. "But he has to wash his dogs, so he can't marry me."

Dr. Johns laughed heartily.

The counselor relaxed. This was going to work out. Dr. Johns was never going to end up in rehab again, she was certain of it. She only wished she could say the same for more of her poor patients.

ON THE DRIVE back to Jacobsville, Meredith was on top of the world. "Not only does he get a new job, but one doing what he always loved best, working around large animals."

"He likes cattle, does he?" Rey asked absently, enjoying Meredith's animated company.

"He grew up on a cattle ranch in Montana," she explained. "He was even in rodeo for six or seven years before he went to college."

Rey expelled a breath. This was going to work out even better than he'd dreamed. Amazing, he thought, how a single act of kindness could expand like ripples around a rock dropped into a pond.

"He's not much good on a horse anymore," she continued chattily, "but he really knows veterinary medicine."

"He might go back to teaching one day. Not in Houston," he added gently. "But Texas is a big state, and when he's been away from alcohol a couple of years, who knows?"

"The ranch will be good for him. You did mean it, didn't you?" she added quickly. "It wasn't something you said to help him want to get better?"

"I very rarely say things I don't mean, Meredith," he replied. "Well," he added with a frown, "I wasn't exactly telling the truth about washing the dogs."

"Excuses, excuses." She toyed with her purse. "Rey, thank you for giving him a second chance."

He laughed gently. "I've got an ulterior motive," he murmured dryly. "When you come to the ranch to visit him, you can make me a pan of biscuits."

"Just you? Not one to share with Leo?"

He shifted behind the wheel. "He can go find someone to make him biscuits," he said. "Surely, somewhere in Texas, there's a woman who'd do it just for him."

"Your other brothers, do their wives bake?"

"Dorie and Tess do," he said. "But Tira hasn't got a clue how to," he added on a sigh. "Simon doesn't mind. They have a cook who can. Although he's really not much on biscuits, so it doesn't matter." He grinned. "You should see him with his sons. Two of them now. They're still toddlers, and he's a whiz at fatherhood. Dorie and Corrigan have a boy and a girl and Cag and Tess have a son. That makes me an uncle five times over! Christmas is going to be a real treat this year."

She thought about Christmas. It was going to be a lonely one for her, with her father down here on the ranch.

He saw the look on her face and reached out to catch her hand in his. "Hey," he said softly, "you're invited for Christmas, you know. We'll pack up the kids and go over to the annual Christmas party at the Doctors Coltrain. They have huge layouts of Lionel trains that they run every year, especially with a little boy of their own who'll be big enough to play with them in a couple of years. Draws a big crowd. Do you like train sets?"

She smiled. "I do." It lifted her heart to know that she was going to be included in the family get-together. She loved children. It would make the season less traumatic for her and her father, because they were missing two members of their immediate family.

"We'll make it a happy Christmas," he said softly.

She tangled her fingers into his. "I'll have that to look forward to, when I go back."

"It's premature right now, but if you decide to move down here, too, I'd bet good money that Micah Steele would offer you work."

She looked at his big, warm hand holding hers. "I like Jacobsville."

His fingers grew possessive. "I like *you.*"

"Thanks. I like you, too, and if you'll loan me your cell phone, I'll call the minister right now and we can set a date," she added with wicked haste.

He chuckled. "Hold on, tiger, I may have been lying about washing the dogs, but marriage is a big step. You have to look out for me. I know you can tame snakes and handle heart attacks, and you bake good biscuits. But how do you look in a suit, and can you dance?"

"I look great in a suit," she said firmly, "and I can do Latin dances."

He grimaced. "I can't. How about a nice, slow two-step?"

"I can do that, too!"

He glanced at her. "What do you like to read?" he asked.

The next few minutes were spent in gleeful harmony, going over things they had in common. They liked the same basic forms of relaxation, and they even thought alike on politics and child-raising. It was a very good start. Meredith had seen far too many relationships start out with nothing more than sex for a foundation, and they didn't last. It took common interests, common beliefs, friendship, to make a lasting marriage.

Marriage. That word, once so warily approached, now seemed as natural as letting Rey hold her hand all the way back to Jacobsville. She wondered where they were going together in the future, and hoped it was someplace nice.

SHE HAD TO go back to work the following week. Friday morning she had her suitcase packed. She was wearing her tailored beige suit with her blond hair in a neat ponytail when she followed Rey out the front door. He carried her suitcase to his car and put it in the trunk.

"I'll be back late this afternoon," he told Leo. "If you need me, I'll be on my cell phone." He patted the cell phone carrier on his belt.

"Oh, I think I can cope," Leo drawled with a wink at Meredith. "Don't be a stranger, Meredith," he added. "We'll miss you. But thanks for making us all those pans of frozen biscuits!"

"It's a good thing you have a walk-in freezer, is all I can say," she mused, chuckling. "But don't forget the directions on how to cook them," she added. "They're only dough until then."

"I'll have it all down pat in no time," Leo promised. "Meanwhile," he added, rubbing his big hands together with visible delight, "there are still six biscuits left over from breakfast!"

"No use asking you to save me a couple, is there?" Rey asked on a sigh.

"Blood is thicker than water, except where biscuits are involved," Leo shot back. "Sorry."

Rey got in the car and started the engine without another word.

MEREDITH WAS QUIET most of the way to Houston. She was oddly reluctant to go back to work, although she loved her job. She was going to miss Rey and Leo and Mrs. Lewis. She was even going to miss the chickens.

"You can come down anytime you want to," Rey reminded her, when he noticed that she was brooding. It had been hard, but he'd kept his hands to himself for the duration of her stay at the ranch. He was planning a frontal assault in the near future. This wasn't the time, though.

"I know." She stared out the window at the bare trees and chilly flat landscape. "Thanksgiving comes along pretty soon."

"Your father will be working for us by then. You can come and spend a few days while you're off."

"I might still be on call," she worried.

He was grim and silent himself, after she said that. The rest of the way to Houston, he had the radio on, letting it fill the cool silence.

He dropped her off at her father's house. It looked cold and unwelcoming as she unlocked the front door so that he could sit her suitcase inside.

She turned back to him, her grey eyes wide and sad as they met his dark ones. He hadn't removed his hat, and it was hard to see his face in the shadow of it.

"Well, thanks for everything," she began.

He stared down at her with a sense of loss. After their ride up to Houston to visit her father, there seemed to be a curtain between them. They'd been very close that Sunday. But he'd gotten cold feet, he admitted to himself, and he'd drawn back. He felt the threat of her in his heart and he was trying to run from it. Suddenly it was like trying to run from himself.

"You'll be here alone," he said quietly. "Make sure you keep your door locked. We haven't had any reports that they caught the guys who rolled Leo. Just in case, don't let your guard down."

"I'll be fine," she promised him.

She looked so small and vulnerable standing there. He hated leaving her.

"You wear your jacket when it's cold like this," she told him firmly, noticing that he was standing in the cold wind in just the shirtsleeves of his chambray shirt.

"And my raincoat when it's raining," he said with a mocking smile. "You wear yours, too."

She hesitated. "Well, goodbye," she said after a minute.

"You and I won't ever say goodbye, Meredith," he replied. "It's 'so long.'"

She forced a smile to her lips. "So long, then."

He was still hesitating. His face was absolutely grim.

"I know where a jeweler's is open this early," she said suddenly, with mischievous enthusiasm.

It warmed him to hear her tease, to see that wonderful smile. "Do you, really?"

She nodded. "You can even have a diamond. But it would have to be a small one."

His dark eyes twinkled. "You just hold that thought," he said gently. "One of these days we might talk about this marriage hang-up of yours. Meanwhile, I've got to…"

"If you say 'wash the dogs,'" she interrupted, "I'll slug you!"

He chuckled. "I wasn't going to say that. I've got to get back and finish my marketing strategy for the next year before we have our year-end board meeting."

"I guess that's pretty complicated."

"No more than treating diseases and plotting nutrition," he replied. He studied her quietly. "I'll miss you. Don't stay away too long."

"Why?" she prodded.

"You have to save me from attacks on my virtue from hordes of amorous, sex-crazed women," he said without cracking a smile. "Who knows when I might weaken and give in to one of them, and then where would we be?"

"I've got my heart set on a virgin," she informed him.

He laughed helplessly. "Sorry, honey, you missed the boat by a decade or so."

She snapped her fingers. "Damn!"

"On the other hand, I didn't," he said in a deep, soft voice, and moved closer. He framed her face in his lean hands and studied it hungrily for several seconds. "You make me ache every time I touch you," he whispered, bending. "I'll starve to death before you get back."

"Starve…?" She wasn't thinking. She was watching his long, hard mouth come closer. She held her breath until it settled, ever so softly, on her parted lips. And then she didn't think at all for several long, tempestuous seconds.

Too soon, he caught her by the arms and pushed her away. "You stop that," he muttered breathlessly. "I refuse to be seduced on the front lawn."

She was trying to catch her own breath. "No problem. There's a nice soft carpet just five steps this way," she indicated the hall.

"I'm not that kind of man," he said haughtily.

She made a face at him.

He chuckled and kissed her one last time, teasingly, before he pulled back and started toward his car. "I'll call you."

"That's what they all say!" she cried after him.

"Then you call me, honey," he said in that deep, sexy voice that made her melt. "You've got my number, even if you don't know it yet." He winked and went on to the car. He didn't look back, even as he drove away. Meredith's eyes followed the car until it was out of sight. She didn't cry until she was inside, behind the closed door.

SHE WAS BACK at work and going crazy in no time, overrun by people with everything from stomach viruses to the flu. She had a good immune system, and she didn't catch any of the ailments, but she missed Rey terribly.

Three days before Thanksgiving, her father telephoned her from the ranch, full of excitement about his new job. He seemed like a different person. He told her he was still going to therapy sessions, but in Jacobsville with a psychologist. He was doing much better, and he was going to make everything up to his daughter, he swore it. And wasn't she coming for Thanksgiving?

It took real nerve to tell him the truth, that she hadn't been able to get off because of the time she'd already missed. There was simply nobody available to replace her. She'd have Thanksgiving Day, but nothing more.

She'd tried to beg the time off to have a long weekend, but her boss hadn't been pleased and he refused. He wanted her on call that weekend, and she couldn't be and go to Jacobsville. The office held a huge clinic for the local immigrant population on Saturdays, as well as Sunday afternoons, and Meredith was competently bilingual in medical terms. It made her indispensable. Not that she minded. These people were desperately in need of even the most basic health care, and Meredith was a whiz at preventive medicine. She counseled them, advised them on nutrition and wellness, and tried not to let her heart break at the sight of little children with rotting teeth and poor vision and a dozen other ailments that money could have corrected easily. The disparity between the rich and the poor was never more evident than in minority communities.

But the fact was, she had one day off for Thanksgiving and no real time for herself. It was a reminder of just how pressured her job really was, and how demanding. She loved what she did, but she hated being made to feel guilty when she asked for time off—something she hadn't done since her brother's and mother's untimely deaths. Actually it had been a battle royal to get time off for bereavement leave, and the funerals, and she'd had to go right back to work the day after the burials. It had been too soon, but she'd thought work would be good medicine.

Perhaps it had been, but she was living on nerves. The weeks at the Hart ranch had given her a taste of a whole other life. It was one she recalled with joy and missed every day. Most of all, she missed Rey. Now she wouldn't even see him. Her father said that he'd ask someone to loan him a vehicle, and he'd come to have Thanksgiving with her. That cheered her up a little, but it would mean she wouldn't see Rey. It was a bad blow. She told her father that she'd make dinner, which cheered him up as well.

THANKSGIVING DAY CAME, and Meredith got up before daylight to start cooking. She was determined that she and her father were going to have the best Thanksgiving dinner she could manage. She'd bought a turkey and a small ham, and raw ingredients to make dressing and sweet-potato soufflé, green beans, ambrosia, homemade rolls and cherry and pumpkin pies.

She'd just taken the last pie out of the oven when she heard a car pull up in front of the house. She didn't stop to take off her apron or run a brush through her disheveled hair. She ran to the front door and opened it, just in time to see her father and Rey come up on the porch.

"Happy Thanksgiving, Merry," her father said, and hugged her warmly.

Rey grinned. "We thought you might like company to help you eat all that food," he told her.

"I didn't make any biscuits," she said worriedly. "Just homemade rolls."

"I love rolls." He held out his arms. "Well, come on," he chided when she hesitated. "You can't treat a red-hot matrimonial prospect like me to the cold shoulder! You'll never get me to say 'yes' from arm's length!"

Her father coughed. "I'll just, uh, check on the turkey," he said with an impish smile and went into the kitchen.

Rey nudged Meredith back inside the house, closed the door, and kissed her to within an inch of her life. He barely stopped to breathe before he was kissing her again, enfolding her in a bearish embrace while he made up for what seemed like years of abstinence.

"You'll smother me," she complained weakly.

"Stop complaining and kiss me," he murmured against her swollen lips. He kissed her ever harder.

"I'm not…complaining!" she gasped when he finally stopped.

He bit her lower lip ardently. "I am," he groaned. "Come on, woman, ravish me!"

"Here?" she exclaimed, wide-eyed.

"Well, give your father a quarter and send him to the store for cigarettes!" he asked with comical desperation between kisses.

"Nobody here smokes," she pointed out.

"Excuses, excuses," he murmured against her lips, using her own favorite complaint. His arms tightened and he only stopped when he had to breathe. "What a long, dry spell it's been, Merry," he whispered huskily. "Come back here…"

She kissed him and kissed him with no thought of the future. It was wonderful to be held and cuddled and wanted. She thought she'd never felt so much joy in her whole life as she did here, in Rey's hard arms.

"There's that carpet you mentioned when I left here last time," he said breathlessly, indicating the floor. He wiggled both eyebrows. "We can lock your father in the kitchen and you can ravish me, right here!"

"Not on your life." She linked her arms around his neck. "I won't ravish you until you agree to marry me," she managed unsteadily.

"Is that a proposal?" he murmured huskily.

"Sure. You can have a ring. I think there's a ten-year-old cigar around here somewhere with a band on it…"

He was still kissing her between words. "I'll phone the minister first thing tomorrow. You can have a blood test at work. I already had Micah Steele do one on me. He said he'd love to have a nurse practitioner of his very own, by the way, if you're interested. We can have a Christmas wedding in Jacobsville."

Her mind was spinning. She couldn't quite understand what he was saying. Of course, he was kissing her and she could hardly think at all. "Blood test…work for Micah… Christmas wedding?" she murmured.

"Mmm-hmm," he whispered, kissing her again. "You can get me a ring whenever you like, but I got you one already." He fumbled in his jacket pocket and pulled out a velvet-covered jeweler's box. He opened it and showed it to her. Inside was a glorious emerald solitaire, and a diamond and emerald wedding band. "If you don't like it, we can throw it in the fishpond and go buy you something else..."

"I love it!" she exclaimed, flustered by the sudden turn of events.

"Good. Here." He took out the engagement ring, pocketed the box and slid it gently onto her ring finger. "Now it's official. We're engaged. Remember what you just promised," he added with a wicked grin. "The minute your father leaves, I'll let you ravish me on the carpet!"

CHAPTER ELEVEN

"BUT, REY, DADDY won't leave," she whispered. "There's a turkey in the kitchen!"

"He can take it with him," he said generously.

She laughed and hugged him very hard. "I can't believe this."

"Neither can I," he said, nuzzling his cheek against hers. His arms tightened. "Even when I was suspicious of you, I couldn't bear you out of my sight. I still can't. This past week has been endless. I thought we could cool it for a few weeks, while I got things into perspective. But the only thing I got into perspective was how lonely I was without you." He lifted his head and looked down into her wide, rapt eyes. "I love my freedom. But not as much as I love you."

"And I love you, Rey," she said huskily. "I was lonely, too. I feel as if I've known you for centuries."

"Same here," he replied. "We're going to make a good marriage."

"A very good marriage," she agreed, and lifted her face so that he could kiss her again. He did, at length and very nicely, until her father came out of the kitchen with a turkey leg in one hand and asked if there were plans to take the dressing out of the oven before it got any blacker. Rey told him their news while Meredith took off at a dead run to rescue dinner.

MEREDITH WORKED OUT a two-week notice and gave up her job, to the dismay and regret of her boss, who hadn't wanted to lose her. He did see that she couldn't have a husband in Jacobsville and a job in Houston, however, and he made them a wedding present of a beautiful faceted crystal bowl.

Micah Steele offered her a job at his office, which she accepted with pleasure, on the understanding that she could work three days a week instead of six. Micah understood being a newlywed, since he and his Callie were still newlyweds as well, even with a baby on the way.

The only hitch was that all Rey's brothers got together and took over the wedding plans, to his dismay and Meredith's horror.

"It's going to be a humdinger of a wedding," Leo promised with relish, rubbing his hands together. "Cag had this great idea for entertainment."

"I don't want to hear it," Rey said firmly.

"You'll love this," Leo continued, unabashed. "He's got this great hard-rock band from Montana coming down to play their new hit record. They just had a hit single about getting married," he added with a rakish grin. "And they're having a caterer from San Antonio bring down the buffet lunch. The wedding gown is coming from one of the couture houses in Paris…"

"But you don't even know my size!" Meredith protested breathlessly.

"We looked in your dresses," he said imperturbably. "Got your shoe size, too, and we also looked in your drawers and got the, ahem, other sizes." He grinned sheepishly. "Everything is couture, and silk. Only the best for our new sister-in-law," he added sweepingly.

Meredith didn't know whether to laugh or scream.

"We booked you a room at a five-star hotel for your honeymoon," he continued, glancing at Rey. "You still speak French, don't you?"

"French?" Meredith gasped.

"Well, your rooms are in Nice," he said. "The French Riviera. You've got a suite, overlooking the beach. Monaco is just on down the beach from there."

Rey whistled. "Not bad, for a rush job."

"We try to be efficient," Leo said, and his eyes twinkled. "We even ordered her a trousseau with formal gowns and casual clothes. Lots of pinks and blues and soft beige colors. We thought pastels would suit her."

Her mouth was open. She was trying to take it all in without fainting. She was only beginning to realize that the horror stories she'd heard from Tess about weddings and the brothers were true.

"You did kidnap Dorie and tie her in a sack with ribbon and carry her home to Corrigan!" she gasped.

"He didn't have a Christmas present," Leo explained patiently. "We gave him one. Look how well it worked out!"

"You hooligans!"

"Our hearts are all in the right place," Leo protested. "Besides, Dorie could bake. Which brings us to Tess, who could also bake…"

"You blackmailed Callaghan into marrying her, I heard!" Meredith was getting her second wind now.

"He's very happy. So is Tess."

"And poor Tira," she continued, unabashed. "You arranged her wedding and she didn't even get to choose her own gown, either!"

"She was pregnant. We had to hurry, there was no time," Leo explained matter-of-factly.

"I am not pregnant!" she exclaimed, red-faced.

Leo gave Rey a quick, speculative glance. "Yet," he replied. He grinned.

"If you would just give me a little time to organize my own wedding," she began, exasperated, and thought, I'm being nibbled to death by ducks…!

Leo checked his watch. "Sorry, I'm running late. The printer is waiting for me to check the proofs."

"Of what?" she burst out.

"Oh, just the wedding invitations. We're overnighting them to the people we invited. The governor's coming, so is the lieutenant governor. The vice president wanted to come, but he has to be in Singapore…" He frowned and checked his back pocket. "There they are! I almost forgot the interview questions. Here." He handed Rey two folded sheets of paper. "You'll have time to look them over before the camera crews move in."

Meredith and Rey exchanged wide glances. "What camera crews?" she asked.

"Just a few reporters," Leo waved them away with a lean hand. "You know, CNN, Fox, the international press…got to run!"

"International press!" Meredith choked.

"We've just signed an important export deal with Japan, didn't I mention it?" Leo called back. "They love organic beef, and we've got some. I mentioned it to our public relations people and they called the news people for us. Your father's writing the statement we're giving them. He's sure got a way with words, hasn't he?"

He waved again, climbed into his truck and sped off.

"Invitations," Meredith said haltingly. "Clothes. Honeymoons. Reporters."

"Now, now," he said, pulling her into his arms. "Just

think of all the work they've saved you. You'll have nothing to do but dress and say yes, and fly off to the Riviera with your brand-new husband!"

"But, but," she blurted.

"I want to marry you right away," he added. "You're a qualified health professional, and I have a terrible pain that you can cure in only one night."

She got the idea, belatedly, and hit him.

He chuckled, bending to kiss her gently. "It's no use trying to stop them," he said. "Besides, they're very good at it. I used to be, too." He scowled. "Somehow, it's not as much fun being on the receiving end, though."

She just shook her head.

THE WEDDING WAS beautiful, despite her misgivings. Meredith wore the most gorgeous gown she'd ever seen, with yards and yards of exquisite lace over satin, with a long veil made of the same lace and a bouquet of pure white roses. Her father gave her away, and all four of Rey's brothers were best men. Tess, Cag's wife, stood with Meredith as her matron of honor. In a very short time, the two women had become close friends.

Most of Jacobsville turned out for the affair, but Meredith had eyes only for her handsome husband, who was dressed to the hilt as well. They exchanged rings and Rey lifted the veil very slowly. He'd been romantic and gentle and teasing over the days before the wedding. But when he looked at her now, his eyes were quiet and loving and very solemn. He bent and kissed her with such tenderness that she knew she'd remember the moment for the rest of her life.

They clasped hands and ran down the aisle and out of the church together, laughing gaily as they were pelted with rice and rose petals. At the waiting limousine, Meredith turned and tossed her bouquet. Surprisingly it was caught by Janie Brewster, notorious locally for her rubber chicken dinners and trying to catch Leo Hart's eye. She blushed vividly and clutched the bouquet, her eyes on it and not on anyone nearby. Which was as well, because Leo looked suddenly homicidal as the ranch foreman elbowed him and grinned.

The newlyweds waved and dived into the limousine, already packed and ready to take them to the airport. They'd already announced that the reception would have to go on without them, to the brothers' shock and dismay.

"I hated for us to miss it," Rey told her on the way to the airport, "but I know my brothers. They'd have found some way to embarrass us."

She chuckled, snuggling close to him. "Well, we're safe now."

THE FLIGHT TO France was long and boring. They held hands and couldn't sleep as the little computers above the seats marked the long trail on a map, showing the progress of the flight. When the jumbo jet finally landed, they walked like zombies into the airport to go through passport control and then on to wait for their luggage so that they could get through customs and to the waiting car that would take them to their hotel. The driver, holding a sign that read Hart Newlyweds had met them at the gate and arranged to meet them at customs. Meredith was yawning visibly when they found the driver and followed him and the wheeled luggage out the door. He and Rey exchanged comments that went right over Meredith's head.

"I don't speak French," she said worriedly when they were in the car. "I took a double minor in German and Spanish."

"No Latin?" he teased.

"There's a special course of it for nursing students," she replied with a smile. "Fortunately you don't have to learn the whole language anymore, although I wouldn't have minded. I'm so tired!"

"We'll have a nice long rest when we get to the hotel." He pulled her close. "I could use a little sleep myself!"

The car pulled up under the covered entrance and a bellboy came out to get the luggage. Rey paid the driver and made arrangements to contact him when they were ready to go sightseeing in a day or two.

Meredith followed Rey and the luggage to the desk clerk and waited while he got the key to their suite.

It didn't take long. Rey unlocked the door and opened it. And the bellhop burst into helpless laughter.

There, on the bed, very obviously courtesy of the Hart boys, were two life-size blow-up dolls, a blonde female and a dark-haired male, in the midst of a garden of thornless roses of every color known to man. They were obviously engaged in a notorious newlywed ritual.

Rey tipped the bellhop and opened the door himself, waving the man out while he tried not to bend over double laughing.

When he closed the door again, Meredith was removing the dolls and roses with tears of mirth running down her cheeks.

"Just wait until they break something, anything," she threatened. "We can have them put in body casts for a sprained ankle…!"

He came up behind her and caught her around the

waist. "And I'll help you. But, later, sweetheart," he added in a soft, hungry tone as he turned her into his arms. "Much, much…later!"

SHE WAS A professional health care worker. She knew all the mechanics of marriage. In fact, she counseled young wives in them. This was totally out of her experience.

Rey undressed her with slow precision, while he kissed every soft inch of skin as he uncovered it. He never rushed. He seemed to have committed the whole night to her arousal, and he went about it like a soldier with a battle plan.

She was teased, caressed, kissed until she felt as if there wasn't a bed under her at all. The roses were scattered over the carpet by now, along with half the bed linen. She was under him and then over him as he increased the insistence of his hands and mouth on her body. She heard high-pitched little cries of pleasure and barely realized that they were coming from her own throat.

One particularly enthusiastic embrace landed them on the carpet, cushioned by the sheet and blanket and, under them, the thick comforter.

"The bed," she whispered, trembling with unsatisfied hunger.

"It will still be there when we're finished," he replied breathlessly as his mouth bent again to her taut, arching breasts. "Yes, do that again, sweetheart!" he added when she pulled his head down to her.

He guided her hands along his lean, fit body to his hips and pressed them there as he suddenly shifted between her soft legs and his mouth ground into hers with intent.

The abrupt shift in intensity took her by surprise and lessened the sharp pain of his possession of her. His hard mouth absorbed the tiny cry that pulsed out of her tight throat, and his hands moved under her hips to caress her.

After a few seconds, she began to relax. He shifted again and found the place, and the pressure, that made her lift toward him instead of trying to escape the downward rhythm of his hips.

She clung to his damp shoulders as the little bites of pleasure became great, shivering waves. She could feel him in every cell of her body, and she wanted to look at him, to see his face, but she was intent on some distant goal of pleasure that grew by the second. Her mouth opened against the hollow of his shoulder and she moaned, her eyes closed, her body following the lead of his own as the heated minutes lengthened.

Her nails suddenly stabbed into his back and she gasped.

"Yes," he groaned at her ear. "Now, baby, now, now…!"

As if her body had given him some secret signal, his hips became insistent and the rhythm increased to madness. She reached, reached…reached…until the pleasure exploded inside her and began to spread in racking hot waves from her head to her toes. She rippled with him, sobbed against his skin, as the ecstasy she'd never known flamed through her with hurricane force.

"Rey!" She cried out pitifully as the wave peaked, and she felt her body go incandescent with joy.

His hands gripped her hips as he riveted her to his insistent hips. She heard his breathing become raspy and hoarse and then stop as he groaned endlessly against her throat and his entire body convulsed over her.

She felt him shake as the madness began to drift away.

"Are you all right?" she whispered urgently.

"I'm...dying," he choked.

"Rey!"

She held him close until the harsh contractions of his body slowed and then stopped. He collapsed on her with his whole weight, his breathing as labored as his heartbeat. His mouth burrowed into her throat hungrily.

"Never like that, Mrs. Hart," he whispered huskily. "You just made me a whole man!"

"Did I, really?" she whispered with a silly giggle.

He laughed, too. "That's what it felt like." He sighed heavily and lifted his head to look at her. His hair was as damp as hers, and he looked exhausted. He brushed loose blond strands away from her cheeks. "I'm glad we waited. I hope you are."

"Yes." Filled with wonder, she touched his hard mouth, which was swollen from its long contact with hers. "I think I swallowed the sun," she whispered. "It was...glorious!" She hid her face in his throat, still shy of him, especially now.

He laughed again, lazily brushing his mouth over her closed eyes. "Glorious," he agreed with a long sigh. He rolled away from her gently, onto his back, and pulled her against him. "We fell off the bed," he remarked after a minute.

"I thought we were thrown off it," she murmured sleepily. "You know, by the hurricane."

"Hurricane." He kissed her forehead gently. "That's what it felt like."

"I'm sleepy. Is it normal?"

"Yes, it is, and it does worlds for my masculinity," he drawled. "Feel free to tell anyone you like that you ravished me to such an extent that I fell out of bed in my excitement, and you went to sleep from the tidal wave of pleasure!"

She managed one tired little chuckle. "I'll take out an ad in a magazine," she promised. She wrapped her arms and one leg around him, completely uninhibited now. "I love you, but I have to go to sleep now."

"Suit yourself, but I hope you're not throwing in the towel. I'm a brand-new bridegroom, remember, you can't just roll over and go to sleep once you've had your way with me… Meredith? Meredith!"

It was no use. She was sound asleep, worn-out by the pace of the wedding and her first passion. He lay watching her sleep, his eyes quiet and tender and loving. It had already been, he mused, one hell of a wedding night, even if they hadn't waited for it to get dark.

WHEN SHE WOKE up, she was wearing a nightgown and lying on the bed, under the covers. Rey was sipping coffee and sniffing freshly cooked food under silver lids. He glanced up as Meredith sat up in bed and blinked her eyes sleepily.

"Supper?" she asked.

He grinned. "Supper. Come and eat something."

She pulled herself out of bed, feeling a little uncomfortable and grinning as she realized why. She sat down beside Rey, who was wearing a pair of blue silk pajama bottoms and nothing else, and looked under lids.

"Seafood," she sighed, smiling. "My favorite."

"Mine, too. Dig in, honey." He reached over and kissed her softly and gave her a wicked grin. "It's going to be a long, lovely night!"

And it was.

THEY CAME BACK to the ranch after several magical, wonderful days together to find the house deserted. There was a note propped up on the kitchen table, obviously left by Leo, because his name was signed to it.

"Goodbye, cruel world," it read. "Have run out of biscuits. No relief in sight. Can't go on. Have gone into Jacobsville to kidnap a cook or beg door-to-door for biscuits. If I fail, drag the river. P.S. Congratulations Meredith and Rey. Hope you liked the wedding present. Love, Leo."

"He wouldn't really kidnap a cook," Meredith said.

"Of course not," Rey agreed. But he had a very odd look on his face.

"Or beg door-to-door for a biscuit."

"Of course not," Rey repeated.

Meredith went to the telephone. "I'll call Dad."

He waited while she dialed the cottage her father occupied and tapped his foot while it rang and rang.

"Dad?" she asked suddenly. "Have you seen Leo?"

There was a pause, while Rey gestured with his hands for her to tell him something. She flapped a hand at him while she listened and nodded.

"Okay, Dad, thanks! Yes, we had a lovely honeymoon! We'll have you up for supper tomorrow. Love you, too!"

She hung up and sighed. "Well, Leo's gone to San Antonio."

"What the hell for?" he exclaimed.

"Apparently he walked out of Barbara's café with a cook in his arms and put him in the ranch truck…"

"Him?" Rey exclaimed.

"Him." She sighed. "The cook escaped out the other door and ran to get Chet Blake."

"The chief of police?" Rey looked horrified.

"Chet was laughing so hard that he didn't get to the café before Leo took off in a cloud of dust, barely escaping public disgrace. He tried to hire the little man to bake him some biscuits, but the cook refused, so Leo took harsh measures." She chuckled. "Dad said he phoned halfway to San Antonio and said he'd be back in a few days. He thinks he'll go to that genetics workshop until the heat dies down here."

"We'll never live that story down," Rey sighed, shaking his head.

"There is a solution," she remarked. "We can find him a nice wife."

He laughed even harder. "Leo's the one of us who'll have to be dragged to the altar behind a big horse," he told her. "For all that Janie Brewster is desperate to marry him, he's as elusive as smoke."

"Janie's pretty," she recalled, because the girl caught her bridal bouquet at the wedding.

"She's a doll, but she can't boil water," Rey told her. "He'd never get a biscuit if he married Janie. Besides, she's not mature enough for him."

"She could change."

"So could he, sweetheart," he drawled, pulling her close to kiss her. "But I wouldn't hold my breath in either case. Now here we are, at home, and all alone, and I'll give you one guess what I'd like you to do next," he whispered suggestively.

She smiled under his lips. "Would it have something to do with flour and olive oil and skim milk and a hot oven?" she whispered back.

He actually gasped. "Darling!" he exclaimed, and kissed her even harder.

She linked her arms around his neck. “So,” she whispered, moving closer, “Just how badly do you want that pan of biscuits, sweetheart?” she teased.

Chuckling, he bent and lifted her clear of the floor and turned down the hall. “Let me show you!”

Eventually he got a pan of fresh biscuits and a whole jar of fresh apple butter to go on them—along with a nice pat of low-fat margarine. And he didn’t even complain!

* * * * *

STUART

CHAPTER ONE

IT WAS LATE, and Ivy was going to miss her class. Rachel was the only person, except Ivy's best friend, who even knew the number of Ivy's frugal prepaid cell phone. The call had come just as she was going to her second college class of the day. The argument could have waited until the evening, but her older sister never thought of anyone's convenience. Well, except her own, that was.

"Rachel, I'm going to be late," Ivy pleaded into the phone. She pushed back a strand of long, pale blond hair. Her green eyes darkened with worry. "And we've got a test today!"

"I don't care what you've got," her older sister snapped. "You just listen to me. I want that check for Dad's property, as soon as you can get the insurance company to issue it! I've got overdue bills and you're whining about college classes. It's a waste of money! Aunt Hettie should never have left you that savings account," she added angrily. "It should have been mine, too. I'm the oldest."

She was, and she'd taken everything she could get her hands on, anything she could pawn for ready cash. Ivy had barely been able to keep enough to pay the funeral bills when they came due. It was a stroke of luck that Aunt Hettie had liked her and had left her a small inheritance. Perhaps she'd realized that Ivy would be lucky if she was able to keep so much as a penny of their father's few assets.

It was the same painful argument they'd had for a solid month, since their father had died of a stroke. Ivy had been left with finding a place to live while Rachel called daily to talk to the attorney who was probating the will. All she wanted was the money. She'd coaxed their father into changing his will, so that she got everything when he died.

Despite the fact that he paid her little attention, Ivy was still grieving. She'd taken care of their father while he was dying from the stroke. He'd thought that Rachel was an angel. All their lives, it had been Rachel who got all the allowances, all the inherited jewelry—which Rachel pawned immediately—all the attention. Ivy was left with housework and yardwork and cooking for the three of them. It hadn't been much of a life. Her rare dates had been immediately captivated by Rachel, who took pleasure in stealing them away from her younger, plainer sister, only to drop them days later. When Rachel had opted to go to New York and break into theater, their father had actually put a lien on his small house to pay for an apartment for her. It had meant budgeting to the bone and no new dresses for Ivy. When she tried to protest the unequal treatment the sisters received, their father said that Ivy was just jealous and that Rachel needed more because she was beautiful but emotionally challenged.

Translated, that meant Rachel had no feelings for anyone except herself. But Rachel had convinced their father that she adored him, and she'd filled his ears with lies about Ivy, right up to accusing her of sneaking out at night to meet men and stealing from the garage where she worked two evenings a week keeping books. No protest was enough to convince him that Ivy was honest, and that she didn't even attract many men. She never could keep a prospective boyfriend once they saw Rachel.

"If I can learn bookkeeping, I'll have a way to support myself, Rachel," Ivy said quietly.

"You could marry a rich man one day, I guess, if you could find a blind one," Rachel conceded, and laughed at her little joke. "Although where you expect to find one in Jacobsville, Texas, is beyond me."

"I'm not looking for a husband. I'm in school at our community vocational college," Ivy reminded her.

"So you are. What a pitiful future you're heading for." Rachel paused to take an audible sip of her drink. "I've got two auditions tomorrow. One's for the lead in a new play, right on Broadway. Jerry says I'm a shoo-in. He has influence with the director."

Ivy wasn't usually sarcastic, but Rachel was getting on her nerves. "I thought Jerry didn't want you to work."

There was a frigid pause on the other end of the line. "Jerry doesn't mind it," she said coolly. "He just likes me to stay in, so that he can take care of me."

"He feeds you uppers and downers and crystal meth and charges you for the privilege, you mean," Ivy replied quietly. She didn't add that Rachel was beautiful and that Jerry probably used her as bait to catch new clients. He took her to party after party. She talked about acting, but it was only talk. She could barely remember her own name when she was on drugs, much less remember lines for a play. She drank to excess as well, just like Jerry.

"Jerry takes care of me. He knows all the best people in theater. He's promised to introduce me to one of the angels who's producing that new comedy. I'm going to make it to Broadway or die trying," Rachel said curtly. "And if we're going to argue, we might as well not even speak!"

"I'm not arguing..."

"You're putting Jerry down, all the time!"

Ivy felt as if she were standing on a precipice, looking at the bottom of the world. "Have you really forgotten what Jerry did to me?" she asked, recalling the one visit Rachel had made home, just after their father died. It had been an overnight one, with the insufferable Jerry at her side. Rachel had signed papers to have their father cremated, placing his ashes in the grave with those of his late wife, the girls' mother. It was rushed and unpleasant, with Ivy left grieving alone for a parent who'd never loved her, who'd treated her very badly. Ivy had a big, forgiving heart. Rachel did manage a sniff into a handkerchief at the graveside service. But her eyes weren't either wet or red. It was an act, as it always was with her.

"What you said he did," came the instant, caustic reply. "Jerry said he never gave you any sort of drugs!"

"Rachel!" she exclaimed, furious now, "I wouldn't lie about something like that! I had a migraine and he switched my regular medicine with a powerful narcotic. When I saw what he was trying to give me, I threw them at him. He thought I was too sick to notice. He thought it would be funny if he could make me into an addict, just like you...!"

"Oh, grow up," Rachel shouted. "I'm no addict! Everybody uses drugs! Even people in that little hick town where you live. How do you think I used to score before I moved to New York? There was always somebody dealing, and I knew where to find what I needed. You're so naive, Ivy."

"My brain still works," she shot back.

"Watch your mouth, kid," Rachel said angrily, "or I'll see that you don't get a penny of Dad's estate."

"Don't worry, I never expected to get any of it," Ivy said quietly. "You convinced Daddy that I was no good, so that he wouldn't leave me anything."

"You've got that pittance from Aunt Hettie," Rachel repeated. "Even though I should have had it. I deserved it, having to live like white trash all those years when I was at home."

"Rachel, if you got what you really deserved," Ivy replied with a flash of bravado, "you'd be in federal prison."

There was a muffled curse. "I have to go. Jerry's back. Listen, you check with that lawyer and find out what's the holdup. I can't afford all these long-distance calls."

"You never pay for them. You usually reverse the charges when you call me," she was reminded.

"Just hurry up and get the paperwork through so you can send me my check. And don't expect me to call you back until you're ready to talk like an adult instead of a spoiled kid with a grudge!"

The receiver slammed down in her ear. She folded it back up with quiet resignation. Rachel would never believe that Jerry, her knight in shining armor, was nothing more than a sick little social climbing drug dealer with a felony record who was holding her hostage to substance abuse. Ivy had tried for the past year to make her older sibling listen, but she couldn't. The two of them had never been close, but since Rachel got mixed up with Jerry, and hooked on meth, she didn't seem capable of reason anymore. In the old days, even when Rachel was being difficult, she did seem to have some small affection for her sister. That all changed when she was a junior in high school. Something had happened, Ivy had never known what, that turned her against Ivy and made a real enemy of her. Alcohol and drug use hadn't helped Rachel's already abrasive personality. It had been an actual relief for Ivy when her sister left for New York just days after the odd blowup. But it seemed that she could cause trouble long-distance, whenever she liked.

Ivy went down the hall quickly to her next class, without any real enthusiasm. She didn't want to spend her life working for someone else, but she certainly didn't want to go to New York and end up as Rachel's maid and cook, as she had been before her sister left Jacobsville. Letting Rachel have their inheritance would be the easier solution to the problem. Anything was better than having to live with Rachel again; even having to put up with Merrie York's brother, Stuart, in order to have one true friend.

It was Friday, and when she left the campus for home, riding with her fellow boarder, Lita Dawson, who taught at the vocational college, she felt better. She'd passed her English test, she was certain of it. But typing was getting her down. She couldn't manage more than fifty words a minute to save her life. One of the male students typing with both index fingers could do it faster than Ivy could.

They pulled up in front of the boardinghouse where they both lived. Ivy felt absolutely drained. She'd had to leave her father's house because she couldn't even afford to pay the light bill. Besides, Rachel had signed papers to put the house on the market the same day she'd signed the probate papers at a local lawyer's office. Since Ivy wasn't old enough, at almost nineteen, to handle the legal affairs, Rachel had charmed the new, young attorney handling the probate and convinced him that Ivy needed looking after, preferably in a boardinghouse. Then she'd flown back to New York, leaving Ivy to dip into a great-aunt's small legacy and a part-time job as a bookkeeper at a garage on Monday and Thursday evenings to pay for her board and the small student fee that Texas residents paid at the state technical and vocational college. Rachel hadn't even asked if Ivy had enough to live on.

Merrie had tried to get Stuart to help Ivy fight Rachel's claim on the bulk of the estate, but Ivy almost had hysterics when she offered. She'd rather have lived in a cardboard box by the side of the road than have Stuart take over her life. She didn't want to tell her best friend that her brother terrified her. Merrie would have asked why. There were secrets in Ivy's past that she shared with no one.

"I'm going to see my father this weekend." Lita, dark-haired and -eyed, smiled at the younger woman. "How about you?"

Ivy smiled. "If Merrie remembers, we'll probably go window-shopping." She sighed, smiling lazily. "I might see something I can daydream about owning," she chuckled.

"One day some nice man is going to come along and treat you the way you deserve to be treated," Lita said kindly. "You wait and see."

Ivy knew better, but she only smiled. She wasn't anxious to offer any man control of her life. She was through living in fear.

She went in the side door, glancing over to see if Mrs. Brown was home. The landlady must be grocery shopping, she decided. It was a Friday ritual. Ivy got to eat with Mrs. Brown and Lita Dawson, the other tenant, on the weekends. She and Lita took turns cooking and cleaning up the kitchen, to help elderly Mrs. Brown manage the extra work. It was nice, not having to drive into town to get a sandwich. The pizza place delivered, but Ivy was sick of pizza. She liked her small boardinghouse, and Lita was nice, if a little older than Ivy. Lita was newly divorced and missing her ex-husband to a terrible degree. She fell back on her degree and taught computer technology at the vocational college, and let Ivy ride back and forth with her for help with the gas money.

She'd no sooner put down her purse than the cell phone rang.

"It's the weekend!" came a jolly, laughing voice. It was Merrie York, her best friend from high school.

"I noticed," Ivy chuckled. "How'd you do on your tests?"

"I'm sure I passed something, but I'm not sure what. My biology final is approaching and lab work is killing me. I can't make the microscope work!"

"You're training to be a nurse, not a lab assistant," Ivy pointed out.

"Come up here and tell that to my biology professor," Merrie dared her. "Never mind, I'll graduate even if I have to take every course three times."

"That's the spirit."

"Come over and spend the weekend with me," Merrie invited.

Ivy's heart flipped over. "Thanks, but I have some things to do around here..."

"He's in Oklahoma, settling a new group of cattle with a sales barn," Merrie coaxed wryly.

Ivy hesitated. "Can you put that in writing and get it notarized?"

"He really likes you, deep inside."

"He's made an art of hiding his fondness for me," Ivy shot back. "I love you, Merrie, but I don't fancy being cannon fodder. It's been a long week. Rachel and I had another argument today."

"Long distance?"

"Exactly."

"And over Sir Lancelot the drug lord."

"You know me too well."

Merrie laughed. "We've been friends since middle school," she reminded Ivy.

"Yes, the debutante and the tomboy. What a pair we made."

"You're not quite the tomboy you used to be," Merrie said.

"We conform when we have to. Why do you want me there this weekend?"

"For selfish reasons," the other woman said mischievously. "I need a study partner and everybody else in my class has a social life."

"I don't want a social life," Ivy said. "I want to make good grades and graduate and get a job that pays at least minimum wage."

"Your folks left you a savings account and some stocks," Merrie pointed out.

That was true, but Rachel had walked away with most of the money and all of the stocks.

"Your folks left you Stuart," Ivy replied dryly.

"Don't remind me!"

"Actually, I suppose it was the other way around, wasn't it?" Ivy thought aloud. "Your folks left you to Stuart."

"He's a really great brother," Merrie said gently. "And he likes most women…"

"He likes all women, except me," Ivy countered. "I really couldn't handle a weekend with Stuart right now. Not on top of being harassed by Rachel and final exams."

"You're a whiz at math," her friend countered. "You hardly ever have to study."

"Translation—I work math problems every day for four hours after class so that I can appear to be smart."

Merrie laughed. "Come on over. Mrs. Rhodes is making homemade yeast rolls for supper, and we have all the pay per view channels. We can study and then watch that new adventure movie."

Ivy was weakening. On weekends, it was mostly takeout at the boardinghouse. Ivy's stomach rebelled at the thought of pizza or more sweet and sour chicken or tacos. "I could really use an edible meal that didn't come in a box, I guess."

"If I tell Mrs. Rhodes you're coming, she'll make you a cherry pie."

"That does it. I'll pack a nightgown and see you in thirty minutes, or as soon as I can get a cab."

"I could come and get you."

"No. Cabs are cheap in town. I'm not destitute," she added proudly, although she practically was. The cab fare would have to come out of her snack money for the next week. She really did have to budget to the bone. But her pride wouldn't let her accept Merrie's offer.

"All right, Miss Independence. I'll have Jack leave the gate open."

It was a subtle and not arrogant reminder that the two women lived in different social strata. Merrie's home was a sprawling brick mansion with a wrought-iron gate running up a bricked driveway. There was an armed guard, Jack, at the front gate, miles of electrified fence and two killer Dobermans who had the run of the property at night. If that didn't deter trespassers, there were the ranch hands, half of whom were ex-military. Stuart was particular about the people who worked for him, because his home contained priceless inherited antiques. He also owned four herd sires who commanded incredible stud fees; straws of their semen sold for thousands of dollars each and were shipped all over the world.

"Should I wear body armor, or will Chayce recognize me?"

Chayce McLeod was the chief of security for York Properties, which Stuart headed. He'd worked for J.B. Hammock, but Stuart had offered him a bigger salary and fringe benefits. Chayce was worth it. He had a degree in management and he was a past master at handling men. There were plenty of them to handle on a spread this size. Most people didn't know that Chayce was also an ex-federal agent. He was dishy, too, but Ivy was immune to him.

Stuart's ranch, all twenty thousand acres of it, was only a part of an empire that spanned three states and included real estate, investments, feedlots and a ranching equipment company. Stuart and Merrie were very rich. But neither of them led a frantic social life. Stuart worked on the ranch, just as he had when he was in his teens—just as his father had until he died of a heart attack when Merrie was thirteen. Now, Stuart was thirty. Merrie, like Ivy, was only eighteen, almost nineteen. There were no other relatives. Their mother had died giving birth to Merrie.

Merrie sighed at the long pause. "Of course Chayce will recognize you. Ivy, you're not in one of your moods again, are you?"

"My dad was a mechanic, Merrie," she reminded her friend, "and my mother was a C.P.A. in a firm."

"My grandfather was a gambler who got lucky down in the Caribbean," Merrie retorted. "He was probably a closet pirate, and family legend says he was actually arrested for arms dealing when he was in his sixties. That's where our money came from. It certainly didn't come from hard work and honest living. Our parents instilled a vicious work ethic in both of us, as you may have noticed. We don't just sit around sipping mint juleps and making remarks about the working class. Now will you just shut up and start packing?"

Ivy laughed. "Okay. I'll see you shortly."

"That's my buddy."

Ivy had to admit that neither Merrie nor Stuart could ever be accused of resting on the family fortune. Stuart was always working on the ranch, when he wasn't flying to the family corporation's board meetings or meeting with legislators on agricultural bills or giving workshops on new facets of the beef industry. He had a degree from Yale in business, and he spoke Spanish fluently. He was also the most handsome, sensuous, attractive man Ivy had ever known. It took a lot of work for her to pretend that he didn't affect her. It was self-defense. Stuart preferred tall, beautiful, independent blondes, preferably rich ones. He was vocal about marriage, which he abhorred. His women came and went. Nobody lasted more than six months.

But Ivy was plain and soft-spoken, not really an executive sort of woman even if she'd been older than she was. She lived in a world far removed from Stuart's, and his friends intimidated her. She didn't know a certificate of deposit from a treasury bond, and her background didn't include yearly trips to exotic places. She didn't read literary fiction, listen to classical music, drive a luxury car or go shopping in boutiques. She lived a quiet life, working and studying hard to provide a future for herself. Merrie was in nursing school in San Antonio, where she lived in the dorm and drove a new Mercedes. The two only saw each other when Merrie came home for the occasional weekend. Ivy missed her.

That was why she took a chance and packed her bag. Merrie wouldn't lie to her about Stuart being there, she knew. But he frequently turned up unexpectedly. It wasn't surprising that he disliked Ivy. He'd known her sister, Rachel, before she went to New York. He was scathing about her lifestyle, which had been extremely modern even when she was still in high school. He thought Ivy was going to be just like her. Which proved that he didn't know his sister's best friend in the least.

Jack, the guard on the front gate at Merrie's house, recognized Ivy in the local cab, and grinned at her. He waved the cab through without even asking for any identification. One hurdle successfully passed, she told herself.

Merrie was waiting for her at the front steps of the

sprawling brick mansion. She ran down the steps and around to the back door of the cab, throwing her arms around Ivy the minute she opened the door and got out.

Ivy was medium height and slender, with long, straight, pale blond hair and green eyes. Merrie took after her brother—she was tall for a woman, and she had dark hair and light eyes. She towered over Ivy.

"I'm so glad you came," Merrie said happily. "Sometimes the walls just close in on me when I'm here alone. The house is way too big for two people and a housekeeper."

"Both of you will marry someday and fill it up with kids," Ivy teased.

"Fat chance, in Stuart's case," Merrie chuckled. "Come on in. Where's your bag?"

"In the boot…"

The Hispanic driver was already at the trunk, smiling as he lifted out Ivy's bag and carried it all the way up to the porch for her. But before Ivy could reach into her purse, Merrie pressed a big bill into the driver's hand and spoke to him in her own, elegant Spanish.

Ivy started to argue, but the cab was racing down the driveway and Merrie was halfway up the front steps.

"Don't argue," she told Ivy with a grin. "You know you can't win."

"I know," the other woman sighed. "Thanks, Merrie, but…"

"But you've got about three dollars spare a week, and you'd do without lunch one day at school to pay for the cab," came the quiet reply. "If you were in my place, you'd do it for me," she added, and Ivy couldn't argue. But it did hurt her pride.

"Listen," Merrie added, "one day when you're a fabulously rich owner of a bookkeeping firm, and driving a Rolls, you can pay me back. Okay?"

Ivy just laughed. "Listen, no C.P.A. ever got rich enough to own a Rolls," came the dry reply. "But I really will pay you back."

"Friends help friends," Merrie said simply. "Come on in."

THE HOUSE WAS huge, really huge. The one thing that set rich people apart from poor people, Ivy pondered, was space. If you were wealthy, you could afford plenty of room in your house and a bathroom the size of a garage. You could also afford enough land to give you some privacy and a place to plant flowers and trees and have a fish pond…

"What are you brooding about now?" Merrie asked on the way up the staircase.

"Space," Ivy murmured.

"Outer?"

"No. Personal space," Ivy qualified the answer. "I was thinking that how much space you have depends on how much money you have. I'd love to have just a yard. And maybe a fish pond," she added.

"You can feed our Chinese goldfish any time you want to," the other girl offered.

Ivy didn't reply. She noticed, not for the first time, how much Merrie resembled her older brother. They were both tall and slender, with jet-black hair. Merrie wore her hair long, but Stuart's was short and conventionally cut. Her eyes, pale blue like Stuart's, could take on a steely, dangerous quality when she was angry. Not that Merrie could hold a candle to Stuart in a temper. Ivy had seen grown men hide in the barn when he passed by.

Stuart's pale, deep-set eyes weren't the only indication of bad temper. His walk was just as good a measure of ill humor. He usually glided like a runner. But when he was angry, his walk slowed. The slower the walk, the worse the temper.

Ivy had learned early in her friendship with Merrie to see how fast Stuart was moving before she approached any room he was in. One memorable day when he'd lost a prize cattle dog to a coyote, she actually pleaded a migraine headache she didn't have to avoid sitting at the supper table with him.

It was a nasty habit of his to be bitingly sarcastic to anyone within range when he was mad, especially if the object of his anger was out of reach.

Merrie led Ivy into the bedroom that adjoined hers and watched as Ivy opened the small bag and brought out a clean pair of jeans and a cotton T-shirt. She frowned. "No nightgown?"

Ivy winced. "Rachel upset me. I forgot."

"No problem. You can borrow one of mine. It will drag the floor behind you like a train, of course, but it will fit most everywhere else." Her eyes narrowed. "I suppose Rachel is after the money."

Ivy nodded, looking down into her small bag. "She was good at convincing Daddy I didn't deserve anything."

"She told lies."

Ivy nodded again. "But he believed her. Rachel could be so sweet and loving when she wanted something. He drank…" She stopped at once.

Merrie sat down on the bed and folded her hands in her lap. "I know he drank, Ivy," she said gently. "Stuart had him investigated."

Her eyes widened in disbelief. "What?"

Merrie bit her lower lip. "I can't tell you why, so don't even ask. Suffice it to say that it was an eye-opening experience."

Ivy wondered how much information Stuart's private detective had ferreted out about the private lives of the Conley family.

"We just knew that he drank," Merrie said at once, when she saw her friend's tortured expression. She patted Ivy's hand. "Nobody has that perfect childhood they put in motion pictures, you know. Dad wanted Stuart to raise thoroughbreds to race in competition. It was something he'd never been able to do. He tried to force Stuart through agricultural college." She laughed hollowly. "Nobody could force my brother to do anything, not even Dad."

"Were they very much alike?" Ivy asked, because she'd only met the elder York a few times.

"No. Well, in one way they were," she corrected. "Dad in a bad temper could cost us good hired men. Stuart cost us our best, and oldest, horse wrangler last week."

"How?"

"He made a remark Stuart didn't like when Stuart ran the Jaguar through the barn and into its back wall."

CHAPTER TWO

IVY COULD HARDLY contain her amusement. Merrie's brother was one of the most self-contained people she'd ever known. He never lost control of himself. "Stuart ran the Jag through the barn? The new Jaguar, the XJ?"

Merrie grimaced. "I'm afraid so. He was talking on his cell phone at the time."

"About what, for heaven's sake?"

"One of the managers at the Jacobsville sales barn mixed up the lot numbers and sold Stuart's purebred cows, all of whom were pregnant by Big Blue, for the price of open heifers," she added, the term "open heifer" denoting a two-year-old female who wasn't pregnant. Big Blue was a champion Black Angus herd sire.

"That was an expensive mistake," Ivy commented.

"And not only for us," Merrie added, tongue-in-cheek. "Stuart took every cattle trailer we had and every one he could borrow, complete with drivers, went to the sales barn and brought back every single remaining bull or cow or calf he was offering for sale. Then he shipped them to another sales barn in Oklahoma by train. That's why he's in Oklahoma. He said this time, they're going to be certain which lots they're selling at which price, because he's having it written on their hides in magic marker."

Ivy just grinned. She knew Stuart would do no such thing, even if he felt like it.

"The local sales barn is never going to be the same," Merrie added. "Stuart told them they'd be having snowball fights in hell before he sent another lot of cattle to them for an auction."

"Your brother is not a forgiving person," Ivy said quietly.

The other girl nodded. "But there's a reason for the way he is, Ivy," she said. "Our father expected Stuart to follow in his footsteps and become a professional athlete. Dad never made it out of semipro football, but he was certain that Stuart would. He started making him play football before he was even in grammar school. Stuart hated it," she recalled sadly. "He deliberately missed practices, and when he did, Dad would go at him with a doubled-up belt. Stuart had bruises all over his back and legs, but it made him that much more determined to avoid sports. When he was thirteen, he dug his heels in and told Dad he was going into rodeo and that if the belt came out again, he was going to call Dallas Carson and have him arrested for beating him. Dallas," she reminded Ivy, "was Hayes Carson's father. He was our sheriff long before Hayes went into law enforcement. It was unusual for someone to be arrested for spanking a child twenty years ago, but Dallas would have done it. He loved Stuart like a son."

It took Ivy a minute to answer. She knew more about corporal punishment than she was ever going to admit, even to Merrie. "I always liked Dallas. Hayes is hard-going sometimes. What did your father say to that?" she asked.

"He didn't say anything. He got Stuart in the car and

drove him to football practice. Five minutes after he left, Stuart hitched a ride to the Jacobsville rodeo arena and borrowed a horse for the junior bulldogging competition. He and his best friend, Martin, came in second place. Dad was livid. When Stuart put his trophy on the mantel, Dad smashed it with a fire poker. He never took the belt to Stuart again, but he browbeat him and demeaned him every chance he got. It wasn't until Stuart went away to college that I stopped dreading the times we were home from school."

Involuntarily, Ivy's eyes went to the painting of Merrie and Stuart's father that hung over the fireplace. Stuart resembled Jake York, but the older man had a stubborn jaw and a cruel glimmer in his pale blue eyes. Like Stuart, he'd been a tall man, lean and muscular. The children had been without a mother, who died giving birth to Merrie. Their mother's sister had stayed with the family and cared for Merrie until she was in grammar school. She and the elder York had argued about his treatment of Stuart, which had ended in her departure. After that, tenderness and unconditional love were things the York kids read about. They learned nothing of them from their taciturn, demanding father. Stuart's defiance only made him more bitter and ruthless.

"But your father built this ranch," Ivy said. "Surely he had to like cattle."

"He did. It was just that football was his whole life," Merrie replied. "You might have noticed that you don't ever see football games here. Stuart cuts off the television at the first mention of it."

"I can see why."

"Dad spent the time between football games running the ranch and his real estate company. He died of a heart attack when I was thirteen, sitting at the boardroom table. He had a violent argument with one of his directors about some proposed expansions that would have placed the company dangerously close to bankruptcy. He was a gambler. Stuart isn't. He always calculates the odds before he makes any decision. He never has arguments with the board of directors." She frowned. "Well, there was one. They insisted that he hire a pilot to fly him to business meetings."

"Why?"

Merrie chuckled. "To stop him from driving himself to them. Didn't I mention that this is his second new XJ in six months?"

Ivy lifted her eyebrows. "What happened to the first one?"

"Slow traffic."

"Come again?"

"He was in a hurry to a called meeting of the board of directors," Merrie said. "There was a little old man driving a motor home about twenty miles an hour up a hill on a blind curve. Stuart tried to pass him. He almost made it, too," she added. "Except that Hayes Carson was coming down the hill on the other side of the road in his squad car."

"What happened?" Ivy prompted when Merrie sat silently.

"Stuart really is a good driver," his sister asserted, "even if he makes insane decisions about where to pass. He spun the car around and stopped it neatly on the shoulder before Hayes got anywhere near him. But Hayes said he could have killed somebody and he wasn't getting out of a ticket. The only way he got his license back was that he promised to go to traffic school and do public service."

"That doesn't sound like your brother."

Merrie shrugged. "He did go to traffic school twice, and then he went to the sheriff's department and showed Hayes Carson how to reorganize his department so that it operated more efficiently."

"Did Hayes actually ask him to do that?"

"No. But Stuart argued that reorganizing the chaos in the sheriff's department *was* a public service. Hayes didn't agree. He went and talked to Judge Meacham himself. They gave Stuart his license back."

"You said he didn't hit anything with the car."

"He didn't. But while it was sitting on the side of the road, a cattle truck—one of his own, in fact—took the curve too fast and sideswiped it off the shoulder down a ten-foot ravine."

"I don't guess the driver works for you anymore," Ivy mused.

"He does, but not as a driver," Merrie said, laughing. "Considering how things could have gone, it was a lucky escape for everyone. It was a sturdy, well-built car, but those cattle trucks are heavy. It was a total loss."

"Even if I could afford a car, I don't think I want to learn how to drive," Ivy commented. "It seems safer not to be on the highway when Stuart's driving."

"It is."

They snacked on cheese and crackers and finger sandwiches and cookies, and sipped coffee in perfect peace for several minutes.

"Ivy, are you sure you're cut out to be a public accountant?" Merrie asked after a minute.

Ivy laughed. "What brought that on?"

"I was just thinking about when we were still in high school," she replied. "You had your heart set on singing opera."

"And chance would be a fine thing, wouldn't it?" Ivy asked with a patient smile. "The thing is, even if I had the money to study in New York, I don't want to leave Jacobsville. So that sort of limits my options. Singing in the church choir does give me a chance to do what I love most."

Merrie had to agree that this was true. "What you should really do is get married and have kids, and teach them how to sing," she replied with a grin. "You'd be a natural. Little kids flock around you everywhere we go."

"What a lovely idea," she enthused. "Tell you what, you gather up about ten or twelve eligible bachelors, and I'll pick out one I like."

That set Merrie to laughing uproariously. "If we could do it that way, I might get married myself," she confessed. "But I'd have to have a man who wasn't afraid of Stuart. Talk about limited options…!"

"Hayes Carson isn't scared of him," Ivy pointed out. "You could marry him."

"Hayes doesn't want to get married. He says he likes his life uncluttered by emotional complications."

"Lily-livered coward," Ivy enunciated. "No guts."

"Oh, he's got guts. He just doesn't think marriage works. His parents fought like tigers. His younger brother, Bobby, couldn't take it, and he turned to drugs and overdosed. It had to affect Hayes, losing his only sibling like that."

"He might fall in love one day."

"So might my brother," Merrie mused, "but if I were a betting woman, I wouldn't bet on that any time soon."

"Love is the great equalizer."

"Love is a chemical reaction," Merrie, the nursing student, said dryly. "It's nothing more than a physical response to a sensory stimulus designed to encourage us to replicate our genes."

"Oh, yuuuck!" Ivy groaned. "Merrie, that's just gross!"

"It's true—ask my anatomy professor," Merrie defended.

"No, thank you. I'll take my own warped view of it as a miracle, thanks."

Merrie laughed, then she frowned. "Ivy, what are you eating?" she asked abruptly.

"This?" She held up a cookie from the huge snack platter that contained crackers, cheese, cakes, little finger sandwiches and cookies. Mrs. Rhodes loved to make hors d'oeuvres. "It's a cookie."

Merrie looked worried. "Ivy, it's a chocolate cookie," came the reply. "You know you'll get a migraine if you eat them."

"It's only one cookie," she defended herself.

"*And* there's a low pressure weather system dumping rain on us, *and* you've had the stress of Rachel worrying you to death since your father's funeral," she replied. "Not to mention that your father's only been dead for a few weeks. There's always more than one trigger that sets off a migraine, even if you don't realize what they are. Stuart gets them, too, you know, but it's red wine or aged cheese that causes his."

Ivy recalled one terrible attack that Stuart had after he'd closed a tricky big business deal. It had been the day after he'd attended a band concert at Ivy and Merrie's school soon after the girls had become friends.

They were both in band. It had been Ivy who'd suggested strong coffee and then a doctor for Stuart. He'd never realized that his terrible sick headaches were, in fact, migraines, much less that there were prescriptions for them that actually worked. Ivy had suffered from them all her life. Her mother and her mother's father had also had migraine headaches. They tended to run in families. They ran in Stuart's, too. Even though Merrie hadn't had one, her father had suffered with them. So had an uncle.

"The doctor gave Stuart the preventative, after diagnosing the headache," Merrie commented.

"I can't take the preventative," Ivy replied. "I have a heart defect, and the medication causes abnormal heart rhythms in me. I have to treat the symptoms instead of the disease."

"I hope you brought your medicine."

Ivy looked at the chocolate cookie and ruefully put the remainder down on her plate. "I forgot to get it refilled." Translated, that meant that she couldn't afford it anymore. There was one remedy that was sold over the counter. She took it in desperation, although it wasn't as effective as the prescription medicines were.

"Stuart has pain medicine as well as the preventative," Merrie said solemnly. "If you wake up in the night screaming in pain because of that cookie, we can handle it. Maybe when your father's estate is settled, Rachel will leave you alone."

Ivy shook her head. "Rachel won't rest until she gets every penny. She convinced Dad that I was wilder than a white-tailed deer. He cut me out of his will."

"He knew better," Merrie said indignantly.

She laughed. "No, he didn't." Nor had he tried to find out. He drank to excess. Rachel encouraged him to do it. When he was drunk, she fed him lies about Ivy. The lies had terrible repercussions. That amused Rachel, who hated her prim younger sister. It made Ivy afraid every day of her life.

She pulled her mind from the past and forced a smile. "If having the estate will keep Rachel in New York, and out of my life, it will be worth it. I still have Aunt Hettie's little dab of money. That, and my part-time job, will see me through school."

"It's so unfair," her friend lamented. "It's never been like that here. Stuart split everything right down the middle between us. He said we were both Dad's kids and one shouldn't be favored over the other."

Ivy frowned. "That sounds as if one was."

She nodded. "In Dad's will, Stuart got seventy-five percent. He couldn't break the will, because Dad was always in his right mind. So he did the split himself, after the will was probated." She smiled. "I know you don't like him, but he's a great brother."

It wasn't dislike. It was fear. Stuart in a temper was frightening to a woman whose whole young life had been spent trying to escape male violence. Well, it was a little more than fear, she had to admit. Stuart made her feel funny when she was around him. He made her nervous.

"He's good to you," Ivy conceded.

"He likes you," she replied. "No, really, he does. He admires the way you work for your education. He was furious when Rachel jerked the house out from under you and left you homeless. He talked to the attorney. It was no use, of course. It takes a lot to break a will."

It was surprising that Stuart would do anything for her. He always seemed to resent her presence in his house. He tolerated her because she was Merrie's best friend, but he was never friendly. In fact, he stayed away from home when he knew Ivy was visiting.

"He's probably afraid of my fatal charm," Ivy murmured absently. "You know, fearful that he might succumb to my wiles." She frowned. "What, exactly, are wiles anyway?"

"If I knew that, I'd probably have a boyfriend," Merrie chuckled. "So it's just as well I don't. I'm going to get my nursing certificate before I get involved with any one man. Meanwhile, I'm playing the field like crazy. There's a resident in our hospital that I adore. He takes me out once in a while, but it's all very low-key." She eyed Ivy curiously. "Any secret suitors in your life?"

Ivy shook her head. "I don't ever want to get married," she said quietly.

Merrie frowned. "Why not?"

"Nobody could live with me," she said. "I snore."

Merrie laughed. "You do not."

"Anyway, I'm like you. I just want to graduate and get a real job." She considered that. "I've dreamed of having my own money, of supporting myself. In a lot of ways, I led a sheltered life. Dad didn't want to lose me, so he discouraged boys from coming around. I was valuable, free hired help. After all, Rachel couldn't cook and she'd never have washed clothes or mopped floors."

Merrie didn't smile. She knew that was the truth. Ivy had been used her whole young life by the people who should have cherished her. She'd never pried, but she noticed that Ivy hardly ever talked about her father, except in a general way.

"You really do keep secrets, don't you?" Merrie asked

gently. She held up a hand when Ivy protested. “I won’t pry. But if you ever need to talk, I’m right here.”

“I know that.” She smiled back. “Thanks.”

“Now. How about a good movie on the pay channels? I was thinking about that fantasy film everyone’s raving about.” She named it.

Ivy beamed. “I really wanted to see that one, but it’s no fun going to the movies alone.”

“I’ll ask Mrs. Rhodes for some popcorn to go with it. In fact, she might like to watch it with us. She doesn’t have a social life.”

“She’s married, isn’t she?” Ivy probed gently.

“She was,” came the reply. “He was an engineer in the Army and he went overseas with his unit. He didn’t come back. They had no kids; it was just the two of them for almost twenty years.” She grimaced. “She came to us just after it happened, looking for a live-in job. She’d lost everything. He got a good salary and was career Army, so she hadn’t worked except as a temporary secretary all that time. When he was gone, she had to go through channels to apply for widow’s benefits, and the job market locally was flat. She came to work for us as a temporary thing, and just stayed. We all suited each other.”

“She’s very sweet.”

“She’s a nurturing person,” Merrie agreed. “She even gets away with nurturing Stuart. Nobody else would dare even try.”

Ivy wouldn’t have touched that line with a pole. She just nodded.

SHE WAS LOOKING through the program guide on the wide-screen television when Merrie came in with a small, plump, smiling woman with short silver hair.

"Hi, Mrs. Rhodes," Ivy said with a smile.

"Good to see you, Ivy. I'm making popcorn. What's the movie?"

"We wanted to see the fantasy one," Merrie explained.

"It's wonderful," came the surprising reply. "Yes, I went to the theater to see it, all by myself," Mrs. Rhodes chuckled. "But I'd love to see it again, if you wouldn't mind the company."

"We'd love it," Ivy said, and meant it.

"Then I'll just run and get the popcorn out of the microwave," the older woman told them.

"I'll buy the movie," Merrie replied, taking the remote from Ivy. "This is the one mechanical thing I'm really good at—pushing buttons!"

THE MOVIE WAS wonderful, but long before it was over, Ivy was seeing dancing colored lights before her eyes. Soon afterward, she lost the vision in one eye; in the center of it was only a ragged gray static like when a television channel went off the air temporarily. It was the unmistakable aura that came before the sick headaches.

She didn't say a word about it to Merrie. She'd just go to bed and tough it out. She'd done that before. If she could get to sleep before the pain got bad, she could sleep it off most of the time.

She toughed it out until the movie ended, then she yawned and stood up. "Sorry, I've got to get to bed. I'm so sleepy!"

Merrie got up, too. "I could do with an early night myself. Mrs. Rhodes, will you close up?"

"Certainly, dear. Need anything else from the kitchen?"

"Could I have a bottle of water?" Ivy asked. "I always keep one by my bed at home."

"I'll bring it up to you," Mrs. Rhodes promised. "Merrie?"

Merrie shook her head. "No, thanks, I keep diet sodas in my little fridge. I drink enough bottled water at school to float a boat!"

"You said you could lend me a nightgown?" Ivy asked when they were at the top of the staircase.

"Can and will. Come on."

Merrie pulled a beautiful nightgown and robe out of her closet and presented it to Ivy. It was sheer, lacy, palest lemon and absolutely the most beautiful thing Ivy had ever seen. Her nightgowns were cheap cotton ones in whichever colors were on sale. She caught her breath just looking at it.

"It's too expensive," she protested.

"It isn't. It was a gift and I hate it," Merrie said honestly. "You know I never wear yellow. One of my roommates drew my name at Christmas and bought it for me. I didn't have the heart to tell her it wasn't my color, I hugged her and said thank you. Then I hung it in the closet."

"I would have done the same," Ivy had to admit. "Well, it's beautiful."

"It will look beautiful on you. Go on to bed. Sleep late. We won't need to get up before noon if we don't want to."

"I never sleep past seven, even when I try," Ivy said, smiling. "I always got up to make breakfast for Dad and Rachel, and then just for Dad after she left home."

"Mrs. Rhodes will make you breakfast, whenever you want it," Merrie said. "Sleep well."

"You, too."

Ivy went into the bedroom that adjoined Merrie's. There was a bathroom between the guest room and Stuart's room, but Ivy wasn't worried about that. Stuart was out of town and she'd have the bathroom all to herself if she needed it. She probably would, if she couldn't sleep off the headache. They made her violently ill.

She put on the nightgown and looked at herself in the full-length mirror. She was surprised at how she looked in it. Her breasts were small, but high and firm, and the gown emphasized their perfection. It flowed down her narrow waist to her full hips and long, elegant legs. She'd never worn anything so flattering.

With her long blond hair and dark green eyes and silky, soft complexion, she looked like a fairy. She wasn't pretty, but she wasn't plain, either. She was slender and medium height, with a nice mouth and big eyes. Only one of the big eyes was seeing right now, though, and she needed sleep.

There was a soft knock at the door. She opened it, and there was Mrs. Rhodes with the water. "Dear, you're very pale," the older woman said, concerned. "Are you all right?"

Ivy sighed. "It was the chocolate. I've got a headache. I don't want Merrie to know. She worries. I'll just go to sleep, and I'll be fine."

Mrs. Rhodes wasn't convinced. She'd seen Ivy have these headaches, and she'd seen Stuart suffer through them. "Have you got something to take?"

"In my purse," Ivy lied. "I've got aspirin."

"Well, if you need something stronger, you come wake me up, okay?" she asked gently. "Stuart keeps medicine for them. I know where to look."

She smiled. "Thanks, Mrs. Rhodes. I really mean it."

"You just get some sleep. Call if you need me. I'm just across the hall from Merrie."

"I will. Thanks again."

SHE DROPPED DOWN on the queen-size bed and pulled the silken covers up over her. The room was a palace compared to her one-room apartment. Even the bathroom was larger than the room she lived in. Merrie took such wealth and luxury for granted, but Ivy didn't. It was fascinating to her.

The pain was vicious. The headaches always settled in one eye, and they felt as if a knife were being pushed right through the pupil. Some people called them "headbangers" because sufferers had been known to knock their heads against walls in an effort to cope with the pain. Ivy groaned quietly and pushed her fist against the eye that had gone blind. The sight had returned to it, and the pain came with it.

Volumes had been written on the vicious attacks. Comparing them to mild tension headaches was like comparing a hurricane to a spring breeze. Some people lost days of work every year to them. Others didn't realize what sort of headaches they were and never consulted a doctor about them. Still others wound up in emergency rooms pleading for something to ease the pain. Hardly anything sold over the counter would even faze them. It usually took a prescription medicine to make them bearable. Ivy had never found anything that would stop the pain, regardless of its strength. The best she could hope for was that the pain would ease enough that she could endure it until it finally stopped.

Around midnight, the pain spawned nausea and she

was violently sick. By that time, the pain was a throbbing, stabbing wave of agony.

She dabbed her mouth and eyes with a wet cloth and laid back down, trying again to sleep. But even though the nausea eased a little, the pain increased.

She would have to go and find Mrs. Rhodes. On the way, she'd stop in the bathroom long enough to wet the cloth again.

She opened the door, half out of her mind with pain, and walked right into a tall, muscular man wearing nothing except a pair of black silk pajama bottoms. Blue eyes bit into her green ones as she looked up, a long way up, into them.

"What the hell are you doing here?" Stuart York demanded with a scowl.

CHAPTER THREE

IVY HADN'T SEEN him in months. They didn't travel in the same circles, and he was never at home when she was visiting Merrie. The sight of him so unexpectedly caused an odd breathlessness, an ache in the pit of her stomach.

He was watching her intently, and there was an odd glint in his pale blue eyes, as if she'd disappointed him. He rarely smiled. He certainly wasn't doing it now. His wide, sexy mouth was thin with impatience. She couldn't take her eyes off him. His chest was broad and muscular and thick with black, curling hair that narrowed on its way down his belly. The silk pajama bottoms clung lovingly to the hard muscles of his thighs. He was as sexy as any television hero. Even with his thick, straight black hair slightly tousled and his eyes red from lack of sleep, he was every woman's dream.

"I was…looking for something," she faltered.

"Me?" he drawled sarcastically, and he reached for her. "Rachel told me all about you before she left town. I didn't believe her at first." His eyes slid down her exquisite body in the revealing gown. "But it looks as though she was right about you all along."

The feel of all that warm strength so close made her legs wobbly. There was the faint scent of soap and cologne that clung to his skin, and the way he was looking at her made it even worse. Over the years, she'd tried very hard not to notice Stuart. But close like this, her heart ran away with her. She felt sensations that made her uneasy, alien sensations that made her want things she didn't understand. She couldn't take her eyes off him, but he was misty in her vision. Her head was throbbing so madly that she couldn't think.

A split second later, she was standing with her back against the cold wall with Stuart's hard body pressing down against hers. His hands propped against the wall, pinning her, while his eyes took in the visible slope of her breasts in the wispy gown. He couldn't seem to stop looking at her.

"I need..." she began.

"...me?" he taunted. His voice was deep and velvety soft, husky with emotion as his head bent. His pale eyes went to her parted lips. "Show me, honey."

She'd never been so close, so intimately close, to a man before. His mouth was demanding, twisting on hers as though he wanted more than he was getting.

She really should protest the way he was holding her, so that she felt every inch of muscle that pressed against her. But his mouth was erotic, masterful. She'd only been kissed a few times, mostly at parties, and never by a boy who knew much about intimacy. It had been her good fortune that she'd never felt violent attraction to a man who wouldn't accept limits. But her luck had just run out, with Stuart. He knew what he was doing. His mouth eased and became coaxing, caressing. His teeth nipped tenderly at her lower lip, teasing it to move down so that he had access to the whole of her soft, warm mouth.

She shivered a little as passion grew inside her. She felt his bare chest under her hands, and she loved the warmth and strength of him so close. Her fingers burrowed through the thick hair that covered the hard muscle, making them tingle even as she felt the urgent response of his body to the soft caress. She let her lips part as he pressed harder against them and she moved, involuntarily, closer to the source of the sudden pleasure she was feeling.

It was like an invitation, and he took it. His hips ground into hers and she felt the sudden hardness of him against her with real fear. He groaned harshly. His body became even more insistent.

The throbbing delight she felt turned quickly to fear as his hands dropped to her hips and dragged them against the changing contours of his body with intent enough that even a virgin could feel his rising desire. Frightened by his headlong ardor, she pushed at his chest frantically, trying to drag her lips away from the hard, slow drugging pressure of his mouth.

He was reluctant to stop. He could feel his own body betraying his hunger for her. He couldn't help it. She was exquisite to touch, and she tasted like sweet heaven. He couldn't think past her body under him in the bed behind them. But finally the violence of her resistance got through to his foggy brain. He managed to lift his head just long enough to meet her eyes.

When he saw the fear, he began to doubt for the first time what Rachel had said about her little sister. If this was the permissive behavior that had been described to him, it was unlikely that she'd had many boyfriends. On the contrary, she looked as if she was scared to death of what came next.

"No," she choked huskily, her eyes bright with feeling, pleading with his. "Please don't."

For just an instant, his hands tightened on her waist.

But her gasp and stiffening posture told its own story. Promiscuous? This little icicle? Just on the strength of her response, he would have bet his life on her innocence.

As his head began to clear, anger began to smolder in his chest. He'd betrayed his hunger for her. He couldn't pretend that he hadn't felt desire while he was kissing her. She'd felt his momentary weakness. His own raging desire had betrayed him, with this innocent child-woman who was only eighteen years old. Eighteen!

Anger and shame and guilt overwhelmed him. He pushed her away from him roughly, his eyes blazing as he looked down at her body in the revealing nightgown. Despite everything, he still wanted her, desperately.

"What did you expect, when you go looking for a man, in the middle of the night, dressed like that!?" He emphasized her attire with one big hand.

Shivering, her arms crossed over her breasts. She swayed, putting a hand up to her eye. She'd forgotten the headache for a few seconds while he'd been kissing her, but it came back now with a fury. She leaned back against the wall for support. Stronger than shame, than anger, was pain, stabbing into her right eye like a heated poker.

Her face was white and contorted. It began to occur to him that she was unwell. "What's the matter with you?" he asked belatedly.

"Migraine," she whispered huskily. "I was looking for aspirin."

He made a rough sound in his throat. "Aspirin, for a migraine," he scoffed. He bent suddenly, swung her up into his arms and strode back into his bedroom with her. The feel of her softness in his arms was intoxicating. She was as light as a feather. He noticed that she wasn't protesting the contact. In fact, her cheek was against his bare chest and he could hear her breathing change, despite the pain he knew she was feeling. "You'll get something stronger than aspirin to stop the pain, but not before I've checked with your doctor. Sit." He put her down on the bed and went to the dresser to pick up his cell phone.

"It's Dr. Lou Coltrain," she began.

He ignored her. He knew who her doctor was. "Lou? Sorry to bother you so late. Ivy Conley's spending the weekend with Merrie, and she's got a migraine. Can she take what you give me for it?"

There was a pause, during which he stared at Ivy, trying not to look at her the way he felt like looking. She was beautifully formed. But her age tortured him. She was too young for him. He was thirty, to her eighteen. He didn't dare touch her again. In order to keep his distance, he was going to have to hurt her. He didn't want to, but she was looking at him in a different way already. The kiss had been very much a shared pleasure until he'd turned up the heat and frightened her.

A minute later he shifted, listened, nodded. "Okay. Yes, I'll send her in to the clinic tomorrow if she isn't better by morning. Thanks."

He hung up. "She said that you can have half the dose I take," he said, pulling a prescription bottle from his top drawer and shaking out one pill. He poured water from a carafe into a crystal glass and handed her the pill and the glass. "Take it. If you're not better in the morning, you'll need to go to her clinic and be seen."

"Could you stop glaring at me?" she asked through the pain.

"You aren't the only one who's got a pain," he said bluntly. "Take it!"

She flushed, but she put the pill in her mouth and swallowed it down with two big sips of water.

He took the glass from her, helped her up from the bed and marched her back through the bathroom to her own room. He guided her down onto the bed.

"I didn't know you'd be home," she defended herself. "Merrie promised you wouldn't. I didn't expect to walk into the bathroom and run into you."

"That goes double for me. I didn't know you were on the place," he added curtly. "My sister has a convenient memory."

In other words, she hadn't told him Ivy was here. Ivy wondered if her friend knew he was due back home. It would have been a dirty trick to play, and Merrie was bigger than that. So maybe she hadn't known.

"Thank you for the pill," she said tautly.

He let out a harsh breath. "You're welcome. Go to bed."

She slid the covers back and eased under them, wincing as the movement bumped the pain up another notch.

"And don't read anything romantic into what just happened," he added bluntly. His eyes narrowed. "Your sister fed me a pack of lies about you. Why?"

"Why were you even talking to her about me?" she countered. "You always said you couldn't stand her, even when you were in the same class in high school."

"She phoned me when your father died."

"Ah, yes," she said, closing her eyes. "She didn't want to take any chances that you might come down on my side of the fence during the probate of the will." She laughed coldly. "I could have told her that would never happen."

"She thought you might ask Merrie for help."

She opened her eyes. The pain was throbbing. She could see her heartbeat in her own eyes. "She would have. Not me. I can stand on my own two feet."

"Yes," he said slowly, studying her pale face. "You've done remarkably well."

That was high praise, coming from him. She looked up into his lean face and wondered how it would have felt if she hadn't pulled back. Warm color surged into her cheeks.

"Stop that," he muttered. "I won't be an object of desire to some daydreaming teenager."

His tone wasn't hostile. It was more amused than angry. Her eyebrows arched. "Are you sure?" she asked, returning the banter. "Because I have to have somebody to cut my teeth on. Just think, I could fall into bad company and become a lost sheep, and it would all be your fault, because you wouldn't let me obsess over you."

At first he thought she was being sarcastic. Then he saw the twinkle in those pretty green eyes.

"You're too young to be obsessing over a mature man. Go pick on a boy your own age."

"That's the problem," she pointed out, pushing her hand against her throbbing eye. "Boys my own age are *just* boys."

"All men started out that way."

"I guess so." She groaned. "Could you please hit me in the head with a hammer? Maybe it would take my mind off the pain."

"It takes pills a long time to work, doesn't it?" he

asked. He moved to sit beside her on the coverlet. "Want a cold wet cloth?"

"I'd die before I'd ask you to go and get one."

He laughed shortly. But he got up, went into the bathroom and was back a minute later with a damp washcloth. He pressed it over her eyes. "Does it help?"

She held it there and sighed. "Yes. Thank you."

"I have to have heat," he replied conversationally. "I can't bear cold when my head's throbbing."

"I remember."

"Where did you get the chocolate, Ivy?" he asked after a minute.

She grimaced. He really did know too much about her. "There was a cookie this afternoon. I didn't realize it was chocolate until I'd eaten half of it. Merrie warned me."

"I can eat ten chocolate bars and they don't faze me."

"That's because chocolate isn't one of your triggers. But Merrie says you won't drink red wine."

"Wine is no substitute for a good Scotch whiskey. I gave it up years ago."

"Aged cheese probably has the same effect."

He grimaced. "It does. I love Stilton and I can't eat it."

She smiled. "A weakness! I thought you were beyond them."

"You'd be surprised," he replied, and he was looking at her with an expression he was glad she couldn't see.

The door opened suddenly and Merrie stopped, frozen, in the doorway. "Are you having a pajama party?" she asked the occupants of the room.

"Yes, but you're not invited. It's exclusive to migraine sufferers, and you don't have migraines," he added with a faint smile.

She closed the door and came in, to stand by the bed. "I was afraid of this," she told Ivy. "I should have noticed there was chocolate on the tray."

"She's the one who should have noticed," Stuart said harshly.

"Well, talk about intolerance," Ivy muttered from under the washcloth. "I'll bet nobody fusses at you for what you ate when you've got one of these. I'll bet you'd throw them out the window if they did."

"You're welcome to try throwing me out the window," he offered.

"Don't be silly. I'd never be able to lift you."

"Do you need some aspirin, Ivy?" Merrie asked, sending a glare at her brother.

"I've already given her something."

Merrie was outraged. "We're taught that you never give anything to another person without consulting their physician…!"

"I'm glad you know procedure, but so do I," Stuart replied. "I phoned Lou before I gave it to her." He glanced toward the clock on the bedside table. "It should be taking effect very soon."

It was. Ivy could hardly keep her eyes open. "I'm very sleepy," she murmured, amazed at the sudden easing of the pain that had been so horrific at first.

"Good. When you wake up, your head will feel normal again," Stuart told her.

"Thanks, Stuart," she said, the words slurring as the powerful medication did its job.

"You're welcome," he replied. "I know a thing or two about migraines."

"And she taught you a thing or two about seeing the

doctor for medicine that actually helped them," Merrie couldn't resist saying.

He didn't reply. His eyes were on Ivy's face as she went to sleep. He lifted the washcloth and took it away. Her eyes were closed. Her breathing regulated. He was glad that the cover was up to her chin, so that he didn't have to see that perfect body again and lie awake all night remembering it.

He got up from the bed, gently so as not to awaken her, the washcloth still clutched in his hand.

"That was nice of you, to get her something to take," Merrie said as they left Ivy's room.

He shrugged. "I know how it feels."

"How did you come out in Oklahoma?" she asked.

"Everything's ready for the auction," he replied. "I still can't believe they let me down like that at the Jacobsville sales barn."

"They don't have a history of messing up the different lots of cattle they sell," she said in their defense.

"One mistake that big can be expensive," he reminded her. "In this economic climate, even we have to be careful. Losing the Japanese franchise hurt us."

"It hurt the Harts and the Dunns worse," she replied. "They'd invested a lot in organic beef to send over there. They were sitting in clover when the ban hit."

"But they recovered quickly, and so did we, by opening up domestic markets for our organic beef. This organic route is very profitable, and it's going to be even more profitable when people realize how much it contributes to good health."

"Our signature brand sells out quickly enough in local markets," she agreed.

"And even better in big city markets," he replied. "How's school?"

She grinned. "I'm passing everything. In two years, I'll be working in a ward."

"You could come home and go to morning coffees and do volunteer work," he reminded her with a smile.

She shook her head, returning the smile. "I'm not cut out for an easy, cushy life. Neither are you. We come from hardworking stock."

"We do." He bent and brushed his mouth over her cheek. "Sleep tight."

"Are you home for the weekend?"

He glanced at her. "Are you wearing body armor?"

"You and Ivy could get along for two days," she pointed out.

"Only if you blindfold me and gag her."

She blinked. "Excuse me?"

"It's an in-joke," he said. "I have to fly to Denver tomorrow to give a speech at the agriculture seminar on the subject of genetically engineered grain," he added.

She grimaced. "Don't come home with a bloody nose this time, will you?"

He shrugged. "I'm only playing devil's advocate," he told her. "We can't make it too easy on people who want to combine animal cells and vegetable cells and call it progress." His pale eyes began to glitter. "One day, down the road, we'll pay for this noble meddling."

She reached up and touched his face. "Okay, go slug it out with the progressives, if you must. I'll treat Ivy to the new *Imax* movie about Mars."

"Mars?"

"She loves Mars," Merrie told him.

"I'd love to send her there," he replied thoughtfully. "We could strap her to a rocket..."

"Stop that. She's my best friend."

He shook his head. "The things I do for you," he protested. "Okay, I'll settle for sending her to the moon."

"She's only just lost her father, her house and she'll soon lose her inheritance as well," she said solemnly. "I could strangle Rachel for what she's done."

He could have strangled Rachel himself, for the lies she'd fed him about Ivy. He should have known better. She'd never been forward with men, to his knowledge. He was certain now that she wasn't. But he wondered why Rachel would make a point of downgrading her to him. Perhaps it was as Ivy said—her sister wanted him to stay out of the probate of her father's will. Poor Ivy. She'd never get a penny if Rachel had her way.

"You look very somber," Merrie observed.

"Ivy should have had the house, at least," he said, betraying the line of his thoughts.

"She couldn't have lived there, even if she'd inherited it," she told him. "There's no money for utilities or upkeep. She can barely keep herself in school and pay her rent."

His eyes narrowed. "We could pay it for her."

"I tried," Merrie replied. "Ivy's proud. She won't accept what she thinks of as charity."

"So she works nights and weekends to supplement that pitiful amount of money her aunt left her," he grumbled. "At least one of those mechanics she keeps books for is married and loves to run around with young women."

"He did ask Ivy out," Merrie replied.

He looked even angrier. "And?"

"She accidentally dropped a hammer on his foot," Merrie chuckled. "He limped for a week, but he never asked Ivy out again. The other men had a lot of fun at his expense."

He felt a reluctant admiration for their houseguest. If she'd been older, his interest might have taken a different form. But he had to remember her age.

"Rachel called her today harping about the probate," she said slowly. "I expect that's why she had the migraine. Rachel worries her to death."

"She needs to learn to stand up to her sister."

"Ivy isn't like that. She loves Rachel, in spite of the way she's been treated by her. She doesn't have any other relatives left. It must be lonely for her."

"She'll toughen up. She'll have to." He stretched. "I'm going to bed. I probably won't see you before I leave. I'll be back sometime Monday. You can reach me on my cell phone if anything important comes up."

"Chayce handles the ranch very well. I expect we'll cope," she said, smiling. "Have fun."

"In between fistfights, I might," he teased. "See you."

"See you."

He went back to his room and closed the door. He had to put Ivy out of his mind and never let history repeat itself. Maybe it wouldn't hurt to have himself photographed with some pretty socialite. He didn't like publicity, but he couldn't take the chance that Ivy might warm up to him.

He recalled reluctantly the dossier a private detective had assembled on Ivy's father. The man had been a closet alcoholic and abusive to his late wife as well as Ivy, although he'd never touched Rachel. He'd wanted to know why Ivy had backed away from him once when he'd been yelling at one of the cowboys. He was never going to tell her what he'd learned. But he was careful not to yell when she was nearby. Still, he told himself, he had to discourage her from seeing him as her future. It would be a kindness to kill this attraction before it had a chance to bloom. She was years too young for him.

The rest of the weekend passed without incident. The two women worked on Merrie's anatomy exam. They watched movies and shared their dreams of the future. On Monday morning, Merrie dropped Ivy off at the local college on her way to San Antonio.

"I'll phone you the next time I have a free weekend," Merrie promised as they parted. "Don't let Rachel make you crazy, okay?"

"I'll try," Ivy said, smiling. "It was a lovely weekend. Thanks."

"I had fun, too. We'll do it again. See you!"

"See you!"

IVY SPENT THE week daydreaming about what had happened in the guest room at Merrie's house. The more she relived the torrid interlude with Stuart, the more she realized how big a part of her life he was. Over the years she'd been friends with Merrie, Stuart had always been close, but in the background. Because of the age difference, he didn't really hang out in the places that Merrie and Ivy frequented. He was already a mature man while they were getting through high school.

But now, with those hard, insistent kisses, everything between them had changed. Ivy had dreams about him now; embarrassing, feverishly hot dreams of a future that refused to go away. Surely he had to feel something for her, even if it was only desire. He'd wanted her. And she'd wanted him just as much. It was a milestone in her young life.

But toward the end of the week, as she waited in line at the grocery store to pay for her meager purchases, she happened to look at one of the more lurid tabloids. And there was Stuart, with a beautiful, poised young woman plastered against his side, looking up at him adoringly. The caption read, Millionaire Texas Cattleman Donates Land to Historical Trust. Apparently the woman in the photo was the daughter of a prominent businessman who was head of the trust in question. She was a graduate of an equally prominent college back east. The article went on to say that there was talk of a merger between the millionaire and the socialite, but both said the rumors were premature.

Ivy's heart shattered like ice. Apparently Stuart hadn't been as overwhelmed by her as she had been by him, and he was making it known publicly. She had no illusions that the story was an accident. Stuart knew people in every walk of life, and he numbered publishers among his circle of friends. He wanted Ivy to know that he hadn't taken her seriously. He'd chosen a public and humiliating way to do it, to make sure she got the point. And she did.

Merrie called her to ask if she'd seen the story.

"Oh, yes," Ivy replied, her tone subdued.

"I don't understand why he'd let himself be used like that," Merrie muttered irritably. It was obvious that she knew nothing of what had happened between her brother and her best friend, or she'd have said so. She never pulled her punches.

"Even the most reclusive person can fall victim to a

determined reporter," Ivy said in his defense. "Maybe the photographer caught him at a weak moment."

"Maybe he's giving a public cold shoulder to some woman who's pursuing him, too," Merrie said innocently. "It would be like him. But there hasn't been anybody in his life lately. Nobody regular, I mean. I'm sure he takes women out. He just doesn't get serious about any of them."

"How did you do on your exam?" Ivy asked, deliberately changing the subject.

"Actually, I passed with flying colors, thanks to you."

"You're welcome," came the pert reply. "You can do the same for me when I have my finals."

"That won't be for a while yet. Coming over next weekend?"

Ivy thought quickly. "Merrie, I promised my roommate that I'd drive up to Dallas with her to see her mother. She doesn't like to make that drive alone." It wasn't the whole truth. Lita had asked her to go, and Ivy had promised to think about it. Now, she was sure that she'd agree.

"Well, it's nice of you to do it." There was a pause. "I'm not going to be able to come home much, once I take the job I've been offered at the hospital here. I'll be working twelve-hour shifts four days a week, and a lot of them will be on weekends."

"I understand," Ivy said quickly, thankful that she wouldn't have to come up with so many excuses to escape seeing Stuart again. "When I graduate, I'll be doing some weekend work myself, I'm sure. But when I can afford a car, I can drive up to see you and we can go to a movie or out to eat or something."

"Of course we can." There was a pause. "Ivy, is anything wrong?"

"No," she said at once. "The lawyer is ready to hand over Dad's estate to Rachel. I'm to get a small lump sum. Maybe Rachel will leave me alone now."

"I hope so. Please keep in touch," Merrie added.

"I will," Ivy agreed. But she crossed her fingers. It was suddenly imperative that she find a way to avoid Stuart from now on. She couldn't afford to let her heart settle on him again, especially now that he'd made his own feelings brutally clear. She'd miss Merrie, but the risk was too great. Broken hearts, she assured herself, were best avoided.

CHAPTER FOUR

Two years later...

"IVY, WOULD YOU like a cup of coffee while you work?" her latest client asked from the doorway of the office where she was writing checks and balancing bank statements.

She looked up from her work, smiling, her long blond hair neatly pinned on top of her head. Her green eyes twinkled. "I'd love one, if it isn't too much trouble," she said.

Marcella smiled back. "I just made a pot. I'll bring it in."

"Thanks."

"It's no trouble at all, really. You've saved me from bankruptcy!"

"Not really. I just discovered that you had more money than you thought you did," she replied.

The older woman chuckled. "You say it your way, I'll say it mine. I'll bring the coffee."

Ivy contemplated the nice office she was using and the amazing progress she'd made in the past two years since her disastrous weekend at Merrie's house. She'd been able to give up the part-time job at the garage when Dorie Hart offered her a bookkeeping service, complete with clients. Dorie had enjoyed the work very much, and she'd kept handling the books for her clients long after her marriage to Corrigan Hart. But her growing family kept her too busy to continue with it. Ivy had been a gift from heaven, Dorie told her laughingly. Now she could leave her clients in good hands and retire with a clear conscience.

Dorie had some wonderful accounts. There was a boutique owner, a budding architect, the owner of a custom beef retail shop, an exercise gym and about a dozen other small businesses in Jacobsville. Ivy had met the businesspeople while she was in her last semester of college, when Dorie had approached her with the proposal. Dorie and Lita, who carpooled with Ivy, were friends. Lita had mentioned Ivy's goals and Dorie had gone to see her at the boardinghouse. It had been an incredible stroke of good luck. Ivy had resigned herself to working in a C.P.A. firm. Now she was a businesswoman in her own right.

And as if her blessings hadn't multiplied enough, she'd also volunteered to do the occasional article for the Jacobs County Cattlemen's Association in what little free time she had. She would have done it as a favor to the Harts, since Corrigan was this year's president, but they wouldn't hear of it. She got a check for anything she produced. Like her math skills, her English skills were very good.

Merrie was nursing at a big hospital in San Antonio. The two spoke on the phone at least twice a month, but they stayed too busy for socializing. Ivy had never told her friend what had happened that last night she spent under Stuart's roof. She never asked about Stuart, either. Merrie seemed to sense that something had gone wrong, but she didn't pry. She didn't talk about her brother, either.

Autumn turned the leaves on the poplars and maples beautiful shades of gold and scarlet. Ivy felt restless, as if something was about to change in her life. She did her job and tried not to think about Stuart York, but always in the back of her mind was the fear of something unseen and unheard. A premonition.

There was a party to benefit a local animal shelter, which Shelby Jacobs had organized. Ivy wouldn't have gone, but Sheriff Hayes Carson was on the committee that had planned the party, and he was showing an increasing interest in Ivy.

She didn't know if she liked it or not. She was fond of Hayes, but her heart didn't do cartwheels when he was around. Maybe that was a good thing.

When he showed up at her boardinghouse late one Friday afternoon, she sat on the porch swing with him. Her room contained little more than a bed and a vanity, and she was uncomfortable taking a man there. Hayes seemed to know that, because he sat down in the swing with no hesitation at all.

"We're having the benefit dance next Friday night," he told her. "Go with me."

She laughed nervously. "Hayes, I haven't danced in years. I'm not sure I even remember how."

His dark eyes twinkled. "I'll teach you."

She studied him with pursed lips. He really was a dish. He had thick blond hair that the sun had streaked, and a lean, serious face. His dark eyes were deep-set, heavy browed. His uniform emphasized his muscular physique. He was built like a rodeo rider, tall, with wide shoulders, narrow hips and long, powerful legs. Plenty of single women around Jacobsville had tried to land him. None had succeeded. He was the consummate bachelor. He seemed immune to women. Most of the time, he looked as if he had no sense of humor at all. He rarely smiled. But he could be charming when he wanted to, and he was turning on the charm now.

Ivy hadn't been asked out in months, and the man who'd asked had a reputation that even Merrie knew about, and Merrie didn't live at home anymore.

Having turned down the potential risk, Ivy kept to herself. Now Hayes was asking her to a dance. She walked around in jeans. She looked and acted like a tomboy. She frowned.

"Come on," he coaxed. "All work and no play will run you crazy."

"You ought to know," she tossed back. "Didn't you take your last vacation day four years ago?"

He chuckled deeply. "I guess so. I love my job."

"We all noticed," she said. "Between you and Cash Grier, drug dealers have left trails of fire behind them running for the border."

"We've got a good conviction rate," he had to admit. "What's holding you back? Nursing a secret passion for someone hereabouts?"

She laughed. It was half true, but she wasn't admitting it. "Not really," she said. "But I'm not used to socializing. I didn't even do it in college."

He frowned. "I know why you don't date, Ivy," he said unexpectedly. "You can't live in the past. And not every man is like your father."

Her face closed up. Her hands clenched in her lap. She stared out at the horizon, trying not to let the memories eat at her consciousness. "My mother used to say that she thought he was a perfect gentleman before they married. They went together for a year before she married him. And then she discovered how brutal a man he really was. She was pregnant, and she had no place to go."

He caught one of her small hands in his big one. "He was an outsider," he reminded her. "He moved here from Nevada. Nobody knew much about him. But you know people in Jacobsville." He pursed his lips. "I daresay you know all about me."

That droll tone surprised her into laughing. "Well, yes, I do. Everybody does. The only brutal thing about you is your temper, and you don't hit people unless they hit you first."

"That's right. So you'd be perfectly safe with me for one evening."

She sighed. "You're hard to refuse."

"You'll have fun. So will I. Come on," he coaxed. "We'll help add some kennel space to the animal shelter and give people something to gossip about."

"It would be fun," she came back. "You don't date anybody locally."

He shrugged. "I like my own company too much. Besides," he said ruefully, "there's Andy. He stunts my social life."

She shivered. "I'm not going home with you," she pointed out.

"I know. I haven't found a single woman who will." He sighed resignedly. "He's really very tame. He's a vegetarian. He won't even eat a mouse."

"It won't work. Your scaly roommate is going to keep you single, just like Cag Hart's did."

"I've had him for six years," he said. "He's my only pet."

"Good thing. He'd eat any other pet you brought home."

He scowled. "He's a vegetarian."

"Are you sure? Have any dogs or cats disappeared on your place since you got him?" she teased.

He made a face at her. "It's silly to be afraid of a vegetarian. It's like being afraid of a cow!"

Her eyebrows arched. "Andy doesn't look like any cow I ever saw," she retorted. "His picture was on the front page of the paper when you took him to that third grade class to teach them about herpetology. I believe there was some talk about barring you from classrooms…?"

He glowered. "He wasn't trying to attack that girl. She was the tallest kid in the room, and he tried to climb her, that's all."

She had to fight laughter. "I'll bet you won't take him out of the cage at a grammar school ever again," she said.

"You can bet on that," he agreed. He frowned thoughtfully. "I expect he'll have a terror of little girls for the rest of his life, poor old thing."

She shook her head. "Well, I'm not going into the room with him unless he's confined."

"He hates cages. He's too big for most of them, anyway. Besides, he sits on top of the fridge and eats bugs."

"You need to get out more," she pointed out.

"I'm trying to, if you'll just agree," he shot back.

She sighed. "All right, I'll go. But people will gossip about us for weeks."

"I don't care. I'm immune to gossip. So are you," he added when she started to protest.

"I guess I am. Okay. I'll go. Is it jeans and boots?"

"No," he replied. "It's nice dresses and high heels."

"I hate dressing up," she muttered.

"So do I. But I can stand it if you can. And it's for a good cause," he added.

"Yes, it is."

"So, I'll pick you up here at six next Friday night."

She smiled. "I'll buy a dress."

"That's the spirit!"

WORD GOT AROUND town that she was going to the dance with Hayes. Nobody ever knew exactly how gossip traveled so fast, but it was as predictable as traffic flow in rush hour.

Even Merrie heard about it, although Ivy had no idea how. She phoned her best friend two days before the dance.

"Hayes actually asked you out?" Merrie exclaimed. "But he doesn't date anybody! At least, he hasn't dated anybody since that Jones girl who dumped him for the visiting Aussie millionaire."

"That was two years ago," Ivy agreed, "and I still don't think he's really over her. We're only going to a dance, Merrie. He hasn't asked me to marry him."

"You never know, though, do you?" the other girl wondered aloud. "He might be feeling lonely. He loves kids."

"Slow down!" Ivy exclaimed. "I don't want to get married any more than Hayes does!"

"Why not?"

"I like living by myself," she said evasively. "Anyway, I expect Hayes doesn't know that many single women."

"There are plenty of divorced ones around," came the droll reply.

"The dance will benefit our animal shelter," Ivy told her. "It will add new kennels. We've got so many strays. It's just pitiful."

"I like animals, too, but Hayes isn't asking you to any dance because of stray dogs, you mark my word. Maybe he's going to flash you to deter some woman who's chasing him. That's the sort of thing my brother does."

"Your brother is better at it than Hayes is," Ivy said, not wanting to think of Stuart. She hadn't seen him in a long time.

"Well, of course he is. He gets plenty of practice." There was a sigh. "Except he doesn't seem to be dating anybody lately. I asked him why and he said it wasn't fun anymore. If I didn't know him better, I'd think he'd found someone he wanted to get serious about."

"That's unlikely," Ivy said, but she wondered if Merrie was right. It made her sad.

"Unlikely, but not impossible. I think I might come to the dance, too," she said out of the blue. "I can get someone to work my shift. Everybody owes me favors."

"Who will you come with?"

"I'll come by myself," Merrie returned. "I don't need a date. Tell Hayes to save me a dance, though."

Ivy laughed. "He can take both of us. That will really shake people up locally. They'll think he's putting around a new sort of double-dating."

Merrie laughed, too. "I had a flaming crush on Hayes when we were in high school, but he couldn't see me for dust. That was about the time he fell in with the she-tiger who ditched him for the Aussie. Served him right. Anybody could see that she was only a gold digger."

"Hayes owns his own ranch," she began.

"And he inherited a trust from his grandfather," Merrie agreed. "But Hayes isn't the sort to live on an income he didn't earn. He's like Stuart. They're both independent."

"Same as you," Ivy accused.

She laughed. "I guess so."

"How do you like being a nurse?"

"I love it," Merrie said honestly. "I've never enjoyed anything so much. I love knowing that I helped keep someone alive. It's the best job in the whole world."

"Merrie, you work all day with sick people," Ivy pointed out.

"Sick people? Me? Are you sure?"

"You work in a hospital," Ivy returned.

"No kidding? No wonder there are sick people everywhere!"

Ivy laughed. "Okay, you made your point. You're in the right place. I'm glad you like your job. You might not believe it, but I like mine just as much. I'm working with some really interesting people."

"So I've heard," Merrie replied. "I'm glad you're happy. But speaking of pleasant things, have you heard from Rachel?"

Ivy's happy face fell. She drew in a long breath. "As a matter of fact, I haven't. Not in over two months. The last I heard, she was trying to get away from Jerry the drug dealer so that she could shack up with a richer man. She wouldn't tell me his name. She did mention that he was married."

"Married. Why doesn't that surprise me?"

"I could barely make sense of what she said," Ivy replied. "She slurred her words so badly that she was incoherent. I can't imagine what a rich man would see in a woman who stays stoned all the time. How she can still act in that condition is beyond me."

"As long as she's leaving you alone, that has to be a bonus."

"I suppose. I just worry about her. She's the only living relative I have," she added. "Maybe the rich guy will wean her off drugs and get her away from Jerry for good. Unless his wife finds out." She groaned. "That's just what it would take to send Rachel over the edge. I'm sure she's convinced herself that he'll divorce his wife to stay with her. I don't think he will."

"Most of them don't," Merrie agreed. "Did she argue with the drug dealer?"

"I have no idea. But from what I understood, she thinks she's landed in a field of clover. The rich guy buys her diamonds."

"I won't ask what he gets in return."

Ivy grimaced. "Neither would I."

"Well, I'll see you at the dance. Where is it, and when?"

Ivy gave her the particulars, but she was morose when she hung up. What if Rachel was involved with someone well-known and the wife found out and went after her in the press? Rachel was brassy and demanding and totally lacking in compassion. But she was weak in every other way. A scandal would drive her over the edge. There was no telling what she might do.

There had been something unusual in their last conversation as well. Rachel had asked her to pass a message along to the owner of the only bakery in town, the Bun Shop. It hadn't made sense to Ivy; something about a shipment of flour that hadn't arrived on schedule. She wanted to know why Rachel was concerned with a bake shop. Rachel said it was a friend who needed the message passed along.

That conversation had been more volatile than she felt comfortable divulging to Merrie. Rachel had mentioned the ultimatum she'd given her rich lover, that either he divorce his wife or she'd go public with the truth of their relationship. Ivy had pleaded with her to do no such thing, that if the man was that rich, his wife could hire someone to hurt her. Rachel had only laughed, saying that the wife was a cold fish who was half out of her mind, and that she posed no threat at all. But in case that fell through, she said, she'd discovered another good way to get a lot of money. She taunted Ivy with her newfound sources of wealth, intimating that Ivy couldn't get a man even if she had millions. Ivy didn't care. She was tired of Rachel's sarcasm.

They'd parted on not good terms. Rachel had accused her of being jealous. She'd never gotten the attention Rachel had, not even from their father. Ivy was just a loser, Rachel said, and she'd never be more than a clerk. Ivy had agreed that Rachel had gotten more attention at home, by lying about Ivy to their father and letting her take the punishment their father had deemed appropriate for her supposed sins.

Rachel had sounded shocked at the description of their father's idea of punishment. Ivy was lying, she'd accused. The old man hadn't had a violent bone in his body. He loved Rachel, Ivy reminded her sister bitterly. Ivy was just the servant, and the more Rachel denounced her, the more critical and angry he became.

For a few seconds, Rachel actually sounded regretful. But it passed, as those rare bouts of sympathy always did. Rachel hung up abruptly, mumbling that her lover was at the door.

Ivy put down the phone and realized that she was shaking. Reliving those last days Rachel was at home made her miserable. Her memories were terrible.

SHE DID GO shopping for a dress, but the boutique owner she kept books for insisted on letting her borrow one of her own designs for the affair.

"It's my display model," Marcella Black insisted, "and just your size. Besides, it's the exact shade of green that your eyes are. You come by here at five, and I'll help you into it and I'll do your hair and makeup as well. No arguments. You're going to be a fairy princess Friday night."

"I'll turn into the frog at midnight," Ivy teased.

"Fat chance."

"All right. I'll come by at five on Friday. And thanks, Marcella. Really."

The older woman wrinkled her nose affectionately. "You just tell everybody who made that dress for you, and we're even."

"You bet I will!"

HAYES WASN'T WEARING his uniform. He had on a dark suit with a white cotton shirt and a blue patterned tie. His shoes were so shiny that they reflected the porch light at Mrs. Brown's rooming house.

Ivy had just returned in the little used VW she'd bought and learned to drive two years earlier from Marcella's boutique, where she'd been dressed and her long blond hair had been put up in a curly coiffure. She had on just enough makeup to make her look sensational.

She was shocked at the results. She'd never really tried to look good. Her mirror told her that she did.

Hayes gave her a long, appreciative stare. "You look lovely," he said quietly. He produced a plastic container with a cymbidium orchid inside. He offered it with a little shrug. "She said that women wear them on their wrists these days."

"Yes," she said, "so they don't get crushed when we dance. You didn't have to do this, Hayes," she said, taking the orchid out of the box. "But thank you. It's just beautiful."

"I thought you might like it. Ready to go?"

She nodded, pulling the door closed behind her. She had a small evening bag that Marcella had loaned her to go with the dress. She really did feel like Cinderella.

THE COMMUNITY CENTER was full to the brim with local citizens supporting the animal shelter. Two of the veterinarians who volunteered at the animal clinic were there with their spouses, and most of the leading lights of Jacobsville turned up as well. Justin and Shelby Ballenger came with their three sons. The eldest was working at the feedlot with Justin during the summer and working on his graduate degree in animal husbandry the rest of the year. The other two boys were still in high school, but ready to graduate. The three of them looked like their father, although the youngest had Shelby's blue-gray eyes. The Tremayne brothers and the Hart boys came with their wives. Micah Steele and his Callie came, and so did the Doctors Coltrain, Lou and her husband "Copper." J. D. Langley and Fay, and Matt Caldwell and his wife Leslie, and Cash Grier with his Tippy were also milling around in the crowd. Ivy spotted Judd Dunn and his wife, Christabel, in a corner, looking as much in love as when they'd first married.

"Amazing, isn't it, that the hall could hold all these people?" Hayes remarked as he led Ivy up the steps into the huge log structure.

"It really is. I'll bet they'll be able to add a whole new kennel with what they make tonight."

He smiled down at her. "I wouldn't doubt it."

They bumped into another couple, one of whom was Willie Carr, who owned the bakery. Then she remembered Rachel's odd message that she was supposed to give him.

"Willie, Rachel asked me to tell you something," she said, frowning as she struggled to remember exactly what it was.

Willie, tall and dark, looked uncomfortable. He laughed. "Now why would Rachel be sending me messages?" he asked, glancing at his wife. "I'm not cheating on you, baby, honest!"

"Oh, no, it wasn't that sort of message," Ivy said quickly. "It was something about a shipment of flour you were expecting that didn't arrive."

Willie cleared his throat. "I don't know anything about any shipment of flour that would go to New York City, Ivy," he assured her. "Rachel must have been talking about somebody else."

"Yes, I guess she must have. Sorry," she said with a sheepish smile. "She's incoherent most of the time lately."

"I'd say she is, if she's sending me messages about flour!" Willie agreed. He nodded at her and then at Hayes, and drew his wife back out onto the dance floor.

Hayes caught her hand and pulled her aside. "What

shipment of flour was Rachel talking about?" he asked suddenly, and he wasn't smiling.

"I really don't know. She just said to tell Willie one was missing. She doesn't even eat sweets..."

"How long ago did she tell you to give Willie that message?" he persisted.

"About two days ago," she said. She frowned. "Why?"

Hayes took her by the hand and drew her along the dance floor to where Cash Grier was standing at the punch bowl with his gorgeous redheaded wife, Tippy.

"How's it going?" Cash greeted them, shaking hands with Hayes.

Hayes stepped closer. "Rachel sent Willie over there—" he jerked his head toward Willie, who was oblivious to the attention he was getting "—a message."

Cash was all business at once. "What message?"

Hayes prompted Ivy to repeat it.

"Code?" Cash asked Hayes.

The other man nodded. "It was two days ago that Ivy got the message."

Cash's dark eyes twinkled. "What a coincidence."

"Yes."

"Which proves that connection we were discussing earlier." He turned to Ivy. "If your sister sends any more messages to Willie, or anyone else, by you, tell Hayes, would you?"

She was all at sea. "Rachel's mixed up in something, isn't she?"

"Not necessarily," Hayes said at once. "But she knows someone who is, we think. Don't advertise this, either."

Ivy shook her head. "I'm no gossip." She grimaced. "Rachel's getting mixed up with some rich man, and she's trying to get away from her boyfriend, who deals drugs. The rich man is married. I'm afraid it's all going to end badly."

"People who get involved with drugs usually do end badly," Hayes said somberly.

"Yes, they do," Ivy had to agree. She smiled at Tippy, who was wearing a green and white dress made of silk and chiffon. "You look lovely."

"Thanks," Tippy replied, smiling. "So do you, Ivy. Marcella made my dress, you know. She made yours, too, didn't she?"

Ivy nodded, grinning. "She's amazing."

"I think so, too," Tippy agreed. "I've sent photos of her work to some friends of mine in New York. Don't tell her. It's a surprise."

"If anything comes of it, she'll be so thrilled. That was sweet of you."

Tippy waved away the compliment. "She's so talented, she deserves a break."

"Well, I came here to dance," Hayes informed them, taking Ivy's hand.

Cash pursed his lips. "Really?"

"I know I'm not in your league, Grier," Hayes said dourly, "but I can do the Macarena, if we can get somebody to play it."

"You can?" Cash chuckled. "By a strange coincidence, so can I. And I taught her." He indicated Tippy.

"In that case," Hayes replied, grinning, "may the best sheriff win."

And he went off to talk to the bandleader.

The band stopped suddenly, talked among the members and they all started grinning when Hayes came back to wrap his arm around Ivy.

"One, two, three, *four,*" the bandleader counted off, and the band broke into the Macarena.

Ivy knew the steps, having watched a number of important people dance it on television some years before. She wasn't the only one who remembered. The dance floor filled up with laughing people.

Hayes performed the quick hand motions with expertise, laughing as hard as Ivy was. They got through the second chorus and Ivy almost collapsed into Hayes's strong arms, resting her cheek against his chest.

"I'm out of shape!" she exclaimed breathlessly. "I need to get out more!"

"Just what I was thinking," he replied, smiling down at her.

Ivy happened to glance toward the doorway at that moment. Her gaze met a pair of pale blue eyes that were glittering like a diamondback rattlesnake coiling. Ivy's heart ran away as Stuart York gave her a look that could have fried bread.

CHAPTER FIVE

IVY HAD NEVER seen that particular expression in Stuart's pale eyes, and she was amazed that he seemed so furious. Beside him, Merrie was also watching her with Hayes, and even though she smiled, she seemed a little shocked.

The two Yorks moved through the crowd, pausing now and again to exchange greetings as they came to stand beside Ivy and Hayes, who had broken apart by then. Ivy stared helplessly at Stuart. It had been a long time since she'd seen him. She knew that he'd been avoiding her ever since the unexpected and explosive interlude that last night she'd spent at Merrie's house, over two years ago.

If she was self-conscious, he wasn't. His pale eyes were narrow, glittering, dangerous as they met hers.

"I thought you didn't dance, Hayes," Merrie said. She was smiling, but she seemed ill at ease.

"I don't, as a rule," he agreed, smiling back. "But I can manage it once in a while."

"We're all here to support the local animal shelter," Ivy told Merrie. "From the looks of this crowd, they're going to end up with plenty of donations."

"I send them a check every year," Stuart said curtly.

"Did you two come together?" Hayes asked curiously.

"We were both at a loose end tonight," Merrie replied.

"I got someone to cover for me at the hospital. I really came because I knew Ivy would be here. I haven't seen her in so long!"

Ivy was bemused. She wondered why Merrie seemed so unlike herself.

"I never believed you'd make a nurse," Hayes told Merrie with a grin. "I still remember you fainting when we had to sew up a wound on that old horse you used to trot around on."

"I wish I could forget." Merrie groaned. "It wouldn't have been so bad, except for where I landed."

"It was the only fresh manure on the place," Stuart inserted with a chuckle. "I swear she took three baths that day before she got rid of the smell."

The band started up again, this time playing a dreamy slow tune. Hayes looked down at Merrie. "Want to dance?"

She hesitated.

"Go on," Ivy coaxed, smiling.

Merrie relaxed a little and let Hayes take her hand. He led her onto the dance floor and into a lazy box step. Was it Ivy's imagination, or did Merrie look as if she'd landed in paradise, wrapped up in Hayes Carson's strong arms?

"Do you dance, Mr. York?" Tippy asked.

He shook his head, sliding his big hands into his pockets. "Afraid not."

She smiled. "Neither do I. At least, not very well. I'm learning, though."

Cash drew her to his side. "Yes, you are, baby," he said affectionately. "Come on. We can always do with a little practice. See you both later," he added.

Which left Ivy alone with Stuart for the first time in over two years. She was ill at ease and it showed.

He turned and looked down at her deliberately, his pale eyes narrow and searching. "I like the dress," he said, his voice deep and slow.

"Thanks," she said, a little self-conscious because of the way he was looking at her. "I keep books for a boutique owner. It's a model she's hoping to sell."

"So what are you, walking advertising?" he asked.

She smiled. "I suppose so."

He glanced at his sister dancing with Hayes. "She used to have a horrific crush on him," he said out of the blue. "I was glad when she outgrew it. Hayes takes chances. He's been in two serious gun battles since he became sheriff. He barely walked away from the last one. She'd never make a lawman's wife."

"She made a nurse," she pointed out.

"Yes, well, patients go home when they've healed. But a lawman's wife waits up all hours, hoping he'll come home at all." He looked down at her. "There's a difference."

She felt guilty when she remembered the way Merrie had looked when Hayes asked her to dance, as if she'd trespassed on someone else's property. Considering Stuart's attitude, it wasn't out of the realm of possibility that Merrie might be hiding her interest in Hayes. Stuart liked him, but he'd always said that Hayes was too old for his sister, not to mention being in one of the more dangerous professions. Merrie idolized her brother. She wouldn't deliberately cross him.

"Why are you here with Hayes?" he asked abruptly.

She blinked at the boldness of the question. She should have told him it was none of his business. But she couldn't. He had that air of authority that had always opened doors for him.

"He didn't want to come alone and neither did I," she said.

"He's well off, and he's a bachelor," he replied.

"Are you making a point?" she asked.

His eyes narrowed on her face. "You'll be twenty-one soon."

She was surprised that he kept up with her age. "Yes, I suppose so."

He didn't blink. "Merrie said you wanted to study opera."

"Then she must have also said that I don't want to leave Jacobsville," she replied. "It would be a waste of time to train for a career I don't want."

"Do you want to keep books for other people for the rest of your life?"

"I like keeping books. You might remember that I also do the occasional article for the local cattlemen's association."

He didn't reply to that. His eyes went back to his sister, moving lazily around the dance floor with Hayes. After a minute, his big hand reached down and caught Ivy's. He tugged her gently onto the dance floor and slid his hand around her waist.

"You said you didn't dance," she murmured breathlessly.

He shrugged. "I lied." He curled her into his body and moved gracefully to the music, coaxing her cheek onto his chest. His arm tightened around her, bringing her even closer.

She could barely breathe. The proximity was intoxicating. It brought back that one sweet interlude between them, so long ago. It was probably a dream and she'd wake up clutching a pillow in her own bed. So why not enjoy it, she thought? She closed her eyes, gave him her weight, and sighed. For an instant, she could almost have sworn that a shudder passed through his tall body.

She felt his lips against her forehead. It was the closest to heaven she'd ever come.

But all too soon it was over. The music ended and Stuart stepped away from her.

She felt cold and empty. She wrapped her arms around herself and forced a smile that she didn't really feel.

Stuart was watching her intently. "That shade of green suits you," he said quietly. "It matches your eyes."

She didn't know how to handle a compliment like that from him. She laughed nervously. "Does it?"

He smiled slowly. It wasn't like any smile she'd ever had from him. It made his pale eyes glitter like sun-touched diamonds, made him look younger and less careworn. She smiled back.

Merrie joined them, an odd little smile touching her lips. "Having fun?" she asked Ivy.

"It's a very nice dance," Ivy replied, dragging her eyes away from Stuart.

"It is," Merrie agreed.

Hayes had been stopped on the way off the dance floor by a somber Harley Fowler, who motioned Cash Grier to join them. Hayes made a face before he rejoined them, disappointment in his whole look.

"We've had word of a drug shipment coming through," he said under his breath. "Harley was watching for it. He says they've got a semi full to the brim with cocaine. I have to go. We've been setting this sting up for months, and this is the first real break we've had." He stared at Ivy. "I can get one of my deputies to swing by and take you home," he began.

"She can ride with us," Stuart said easily. "No problem."

"Thanks," Hayes said. He grinned at Ivy. "Our first date and I blew it. I'll make it up to you. I promise."

"I'm not upset, Hayes," she replied. "You go do your job. There will be other dances."

"You're a good sport. Thanks. See you, Merrie," he added with a wink, nodding to Stuart as he headed for the front door.

Merrie was biting her lower lip, her eyes on Hayes's back as he left. Ivy noticed and didn't say a word.

"How about some of this punch?" Ivy asked her best friend. "It looks very good."

Merrie was diverted. "Yes. I'll bet it tastes good, too. But I want a word with Shelby Ballenger before I indulge. I'll be right back." She went toward Shelby. Ivy filled two glass cups with punch and handed one to Stuart.

He made a face. "It's tropical punch, isn't it? I hate tropical punch."

"They have coffee, too, if you'd rather," Ivy told him, putting the punch down on the table.

He met her searching eyes. "I would. Cream. No sugar."

She poured coffee into a cup, adding just a touch of cream. She handed it to him, but her hands shook. He had to put his around them, to steady them.

"It's all right," he said softly. "There's nothing to be afraid of."

She didn't understand what was happening to her.

The feel of his big, warm hands around hers made her heart race. The look in his pale eyes delighted, thrilled, terrified. She'd never had such a headlong physical reaction to any other man, and especially not since that incredible night when he'd held her and kissed her as if he couldn't bear to let her go. It had haunted her dreams for more than two years, and ruined her for a relationship with any other man.

She let go of the cup with a nervous little laugh. "Is that enough cream?" she asked.

He nodded. He sipped it in silence while she sipped at her punch. The music was playing again, this time a slow, bluesy two-step.

Merrie came back to them, grinning. "I asked Shelby if she'd save me one of those border collies she and Justin are breeding. They're great cattle dogs."

Stuart scowled at her. "What the hell do you need with a cattle dog?"

"It's not for me," she replied. "There's a sweet little girl on my ward who has to have a tumor removed from her brain. She's scared to death. I asked her parents what might help her attitude, and they said she'd always wanted a border collie. It might be just what she needs to come through the surgery. You see," she added sadly, "they don't know if it's malignant yet."

"How old is she?" Ivy asked.

"Ten."

Ivy winced. "What a terrible age to have something so deadly."

"At least she'll have something to look forward to," Stuart added. "You really are a jewel, Merrie."

She made an affectionate face at him. "So are you.

Now let's dance or eat or something so we don't burst into tears and embarrass Ivy."

He cocked an eyebrow and gave Ivy a mischievous look. "God forbid that we should embarrass her." He put down his coffee cup. "Dancing seems more sensible."

He took Ivy's glass of punch and put it down, only to draw her back onto the dance floor.

IT WAS THE sweetest evening of Ivy's life. She danced almost exclusively with Stuart, and he didn't seem to mind that people were watching them with fond amusement. It was well-known that Stuart played the field, and that Ivy didn't date anyone. The attention Stuart was showing her raised eyebrows.

Merrie didn't lack for partners, either, but she seemed subdued since Hayes had left. Ivy wondered if there wasn't something smoldering under Merrie's passive expression that led back to that old crush she'd had on Hayes.

When it came time to leave, Merrie informed Stuart that she was going to ride home with one of the Bates twins, who passed right by their house. She didn't give a reason, but Stuart didn't ask for one, either. He linked his fingers into Ivy's and drew her outside to his big, sleek Jaguar.

"I can't remember when I've enjoyed a party more," he remarked.

"It was fun," she agreed, smiling. "I don't get out much at night. Usually I'm trying to keep up with the accounts, including doing estimated taxes for all my clients four times a year. It keeps me close to home."

"You and Merrie have lost touch since she went to work in San Antonio."

"A little, maybe," she replied. "But Merrie is still the best friend I have. That doesn't go away, even when we don't see each other for months at a time."

He was quiet for a minute. "Have you heard from Rachel?" he asked.

She drew in a painful breath. "Yes. Last week."

"How was she?"

She wondered why he was asking her questions about her sister, whom he hated. "Pretty much the same, I guess." Except that she was steadily higher than a kite when she called Ivy, and she was running around with someone else's rich husband, she added silently.

He shot a glance at her. "That isn't what I hear."

Her heart welled up in her throat. She'd forgotten that he moved in the same circles as other rich, successful men. Rachel's garden slug of a boyfriend knew such people in New York. Stuart might even know Rachel's latest lover. "What do you hear?" she asked.

"That she's about to create a media sensation," he said flatly. "Which is why I brought Merrie to the dance. Hayes mentioned that he was bringing you, and I wanted to talk to you without the whole town knowing. Your boardinghouse isn't private enough, and my Mrs. Rhodes is a terrible gossip. That left me looking for a neutral spot. Here it is."

Her heart was hammering. Rachel again. It was always something, her whole life. Would she ever be free of her sister's messy problems?

"Don't look like that," he said curtly. "I know you don't have any influence on her. I just don't want you to be surprised by some enthusiastic journalist out of the blue, asking you personal questions about your sister for print. Scandals pay well, especially if the victim's relatives can be shocked into a printable reaction."

She put her face in her hands. "How bad is it?" she asked.

"Bad enough." He pulled the car off the main road onto a dirt road and cut off the engine. When she looked around, disturbed, he added, "This is on my land. I don't want to sit in front of Mrs. Brown's boardinghouse and have curtains fluttering the whole time we're talking." He freed his seat belt and turned to her, one arm curved around the back of her bucket seat. "You need to know what you're up against before the story hits the tabloids."

She grimaced. Tippy Moore had gone through the tabloid mills before her marriage to Cash Grier. So had Leslie, Matt Caldwell's wife. She knew the devastating effect they could have on people's lives. But she never dreamed that she could become a victim of them. Surely Rachel's sister wouldn't be interesting news to anyone? On the other hand, Rachel had actually landed a few roles on Broadway, despite her drug habit, and one review had called her talent "promising." After years of auditions, it seemed that Rachel might actually make it as an actress. But Stuart looked uncomfortable.

"Tell me," she prodded gently.

"She's been supplying drugs to an elderly recluse who fancies himself in love with her," he replied curtly. "The problem is that he's recently married to a former beauty queen who doesn't want to share him and his fortune with anyone, least of all a minor actress with a drug dealer for a boyfriend. A mutual friend says she's about to go public with the story. If she does, it will ruin Rachel's chances of any more roles on Broadway, and it may put her drug-dealing boyfriend in prison. It might even put her there, if the wife decides to go public with what her very expensive private detective dug up on Rachel. She found a connection to some very big drug lords across the border; some of the same ones Hayes and Cash and Cobb of the DEA are trying to catch."

By now, Ivy was noticeably pale despite the semi-darkness of the front seats. That message Rachel had given her for the baker had been code, after all. Her sister was a drug dealer. Her heart ran away with fear. She pulled at a curl beside her ear. "I wonder if I could get lost in the Amazon jungle before Rachel gets it in the neck?"

"You'd have to come home one day. Running away never solved a problem."

She leaned back against the seat, sick to her soul. In a small town like Jacobsville, a tabloid story would be a gossip fest. There wouldn't be a place she could go where people wouldn't be talking about her.

She wrapped her arms around herself, feeling a sudden chill.

"Rachel told a lot of lies about you around town, when you were in high school," he said after a minute, his eyes narrow and thoughtful. "She fed me a dose of them, too. I actually believed her, until two years ago. But just the same, I made sure that she left town."

She felt her cheeks go hot, and she hoped he couldn't see. So that was why Rachel had gone away so suddenly, why her attitude toward Ivy had changed. She thought Stuart was protecting her little sister, and she was jealous!

"Copper Coltrain says that you were in his office frequently with injuries from 'falls' when you were in school," he persisted.

Her heart jumped. “I was clumsy,” she said quickly.

“Bull! Your father drank to excess and Rachel fed him the same lies she fed other people about you,” he countered. “She bragged about getting you in trouble with your father. It suited her to have you constantly out of favor, so that she’d inherit everything. Which she did.”

The news that he knew all her problems, although she’d secretly suspected as much, made her sick. “Dad thought she was wonderful.”

“Yes, and he was fairly certain that you weren’t his child.”

She gasped aloud, her eyes as wide as saucers. “What?!”

“I didn’t think you knew that,” he murmured, watching her. “Rachel said that your mother told her, before she died, that she’d had an affair and you were the result.”

Of all the things Rachel had done to her, that was the absolute worst. She couldn’t even find words to express how horrified she was. “Is it…is it true?” she asked unsteadily.

He was hesitant. “I don’t know. There’s an easy way to find out, if you want to know for sure. If you can get a hair from your father’s brush, or if Coltrain has a blood sample from him on file, we can have a DNA profile done. If there isn’t a sample, but if Coltrain has his blood type on file, we can have your blood typed. Paternity can be determined by blood groups. It won’t prove anything for sure, unless we could get a DNA sample from your father, but it would at least show if you could have been your father’s child.”

"You'd do that, for me?" she asked, surprised at his indulgence.

"Of course," he said matter-of-factly.

It was a lot to swallow at once. No wonder her father had been so brutal to her! He thought she wasn't his child. And Rachel had used that knowledge—if it wasn't a lie—to cheat Ivy out of anything that belonged to her family. Rachel had inherited it all, and sold it all.

"She must hate me," Ivy said aloud.

"She was jealous of you," he corrected flatly.

"Oh, sure, I'm such a peach of a beauty, why wouldn't she be?" she asked sarcastically.

He reached out and tugged a lock of her hair. "Stop that. You're no ugly duckling, except in your own mind. But I wasn't talking about looks. Rachel was jealous because of the way you are with people. You're always looking for the best in people, making them feel good about themselves, making them feel important. You never gossip or tell lies, and you're always around if anyone's in trouble or grieving. Rachel has never given a damn for anyone except herself. You made her feel inferior, and she hated you for it."

"She was beautiful," she said. "All the boys loved her."

"Even boys you tried to date," he added, as if he knew. He nodded. "Yes, I heard about that, too. Rachel delighted in stealing away any boy you brought home. She turned your girlfriends against you, everyone except Merrie. She told Merrie some whoppers about your social life." He looked away, his body stiffening. It didn't take a mind reader to know that Merrie had repeated the lies to him.

"I'm amazed you didn't forbid Merrie to have anything to do with me."

"I did," he said surprisingly, glancing at her. "She wouldn't listen, of course. And I stopped pressuring her about it when I realized how badly Rachel had lied about your character."

She knew what he was talking about, and it made her uneasy. He was remembering what a novice she was in a man's arms.

"Copper doesn't usually talk about patients," he continued. "But we're second cousins as well as good friends, and I've felt responsible for you since your father's death. He thought I should know about your home life. Just in case Rachel ever came down here and tried to start trouble. He didn't know I'd already gotten the news from a private detective I hired."

She couldn't look at him. It felt as if all the bruises and lacerations were plainly visible to anyone looking.

"You've never talked about it, have you?"

She shook her head. "Not even to Merrie."

"Merrie is more perceptive than you realize. She knew why you covered your legs when you went to school. You didn't want anyone to see the bruises he left on you with that doubled-up belt."

She bit her lower lip and looked up at him. She was remembering what Merrie had said about his own childhood, and how his father had punished him for refusing to give his life to football.

"You got your share, too, didn't you?" she asked quietly.

He hesitated for a moment. His dark brows drew together. "Yes," he replied finally. "I've never talked about it to anyone outside my family. The memories sting, even now."

"They would have locked my father up and thrown away the key if he'd done it today."

"Mine, too," he agreed. He smiled faintly. "Our fathers would probably be occupying adjoining jail cells." He sighed and traced a pattern at her throat, making her heartbeat throb. "Nobody's using a belt on my kids."

"Mine, either," she replied at once.

He smiled down at her. "We're all products of our upbringing. Pity we don't get to choose our relatives."

"You can say that again." She searched his eyes. "Rachel isn't afraid of anything except losing her chance to act in a starring role on Broadway. But if she gets caught up in a public scandal, it will kill her career stone dead. And she might go to prison for drug dealing. I don't know what she'd do if she had all that to contend with. She's not very strong emotionally."

"Only when she's on the receiving end," he agreed. "But she chose her own path, Ivy. We all do. Then we take the consequences of those choices."

She cocked her head. "What path did you choose that had consequences?"

"It was one I didn't choose," he said enigmatically. His hand slid under the silken fist of hair at her nape, warm and strong. "But we've done enough talking for one night."

As he spoke, he tugged her face gently under his. "Don't panic," he whispered against her mouth as his lips teased at it. "There are some things you just can't do in bucket seats…"

She went under in a daze of throbbing pleasure. It was like the first time he'd held her and kissed her, but much more explosive. The long years between kisses made her bold, made her hungry. She slid her arms around his neck and opened her mouth under his. He groaned. A shudder went through him. He hesitated, but only for a split second. Then he gathered her up whole and dragged her over the console and into his lap, and the kisses grew harder and more insistent.

She felt his big hand under the neckline of her gown, gently tracing patterns down into the soft flesh under her bra. She gasped.

He lifted his head and looked into her wide, shocked eyes, with affectionate amusement. "Think of it as exploration into new territory," he teased gently. "You've got a lot of catching up to do."

"And you're offering to guide me through the undergrowth?" she gasped.

"Frilly undergrowth," he murmured, looking down at the quick beat of her heart that was echoed in the trembling of her bodice as her pulse increased madly.

"I'm not sure," she began breathlessly.

"Neither am I," he agreed as he bent again to her mouth. "But it's been a long, dry spell and I've waited as long as I can and stay sane."

While she was trying to figure that out, his mouth opened on her parted lips and his hand trespassed right under her bra onto her soft flesh with a sureness and mastery that chased any thought of protest right out of her head. She clung to him and gave in to the sweetness of the moment.

CHAPTER SIX

Just as Ivy was seeing stars, there was the purr of a big cat somewhere in the jungle of pleasure she was exploring.

Stuart must have heard it, too, because he raised his head and frowned as he looked into the rearview mirror. "I don't believe it!" he burst out.

She followed his gaze and saw flashing blue lights coming at breakneck speed right down the dirt road behind them.

"Hayes!" he muttered, and let out a word that made her blush.

The all-white Jacobs County Sheriff's car pulled up past them, whipped around, and came back again, so that Hayes and Stuart were facing each other through open drivers' windows. In the time it had taken Hayes to turn around, Ivy had slid discreetly back into her own seat, straightened her clothing and smoothed her hair. She was grateful that it was dark, so that Hayes wouldn't be able to see the lingering traces of Stuart's demanding passion on her lips and hair.

"Aren't you a little far out of your territory?" Stuart drawled. "This is my land."

Hayes just stared at him. "We flushed a drug transport with three armed men inside," he said at once. "We got two of them, but one escaped not far from here. He's carrying an automatic weapon."

"Good God," Stuart exclaimed.

"I didn't think he'd be driving a Jag," he continued dryly, "but you can't rule out a carjacking. And this car was all alone in a field." He scowled. "What the hell are the two of you doing out here?"

"Talking about DNA profiles," Stuart shot back.

Hayes pursed his lips. "Oooookay," he said, but clearly not believing it. "Just the same, I'd take her home, if I were you. These guys don't play nice. One of my deputies is in the emergency room with a bullet in his hip."

"I hope you get them," Stuart said.

"Me, too. See you."

He roared away, sirens still going.

Stuart glanced wryly at Ivy. "I suppose we've talked enough for one night. I don't fancy fighting off drug dealers at this hour."

"Neither do I," she agreed, but there was disappointment about having to come down from the clouds. It had been a sweet few minutes.

"I'm not anxious to leave, either, Ivy," he said as he started the car. "But there's a time and place, and this isn't it."

With that enigmatic statement, he pulled the car back into the highway, and sped toward her boardinghouse. They arrived there too soon.

He got out of the car, opened her door and walked her to her front door. He noted the quick flutter of a curtain with an amused smile, and then positioned them where no windows intruded. He took her by the waist and looked down into her sad eyes in the porch light. "I shouldn't have told you about your father like that," he said apologetically. "I'm sorry."

"The tabloids wouldn't have been very kind about it, if I'd had to hear it from them," she said philosophically. "Thanks for the heads-up."

His big hands tightened on her small waist. "Go see Copper," he coaxed. "He'll do what he can to help you find out, one way or another. I'll take care of the bill. I'll tell him that, too," he added.

"All right."

"And don't worry yourself to death about your sister," he said firmly. "If the situation was reversed, I promise she wouldn't waste a night's sleep about you."

"I know that. But she's still the only family I have left in the world."

He drew in an audible breath. "That doesn't help, I'm sure." He bent and brushed his mouth gently over her soft, sensitized lips. She stood on her tiptoes to increase the pressure, shivering a little when he accepted the silent invitation and gathered her in close, so that they were riveted together, hip to hip.

She'd never known such pleasure. It felt as sweet as it had in his car, but much more intense. Her nails dug into the hard muscles of his shoulders as she gave in to the sheer delight of being close to him.

When she moaned, he drew back. His hands were briefly cruel as he fought the need to back her into the wall and devour her. He had to force himself to let her go.

She saw that, and was fascinated by the sudden change in him. It was so sweet to kiss him, beyond her wildest dreams of delight.

"We can't do much more of that," he whispered. "Not in public."

"Are we in public?" she whispered back, dazed.

He drew in a long breath. "If I don't stop kissing you, we're going to be. It's sweet, Ivy. Sweeter than my dreams."

"Sweeter than mine, too," she confessed, aching to have his mouth on hers again.

He knew that, but he had to be strong for both of them. It wasn't the place. He held her gently by the waist. "I have to fly to Denver for a conservation workshop. I'll call you when I get there."

She stared up at him with her heart flipping around. Her surprise was noticeable.

He searched her wide eyes. "Times change. So do people. You're twenty-one next month, aren't you?"

She nodded, spellbound.

He looked very somber for a minute. "Still years too young," he murmured as he bent his head. "But what the hell..."

He lifted her up against him and kissed her until her mouth felt bruised. She didn't complain. She held on for dear life, her arms tight around his neck, her feet just barely touching the floor at all. If this was a dream, she never wanted to wake up.

When she moaned softly, he put her back on her feet and let her go abruptly. His breathing was noticeably faster. "Stay out of trouble," he told her.

"I don't ever get into trouble," she replied dimly, her eyes on his hard mouth.

He smiled slowly. "Yes, but that was before."

"Before what?" she asked.

He bent and kissed her quickly. "Before me. Lock the door behind you."

He was walking away before she realized what he'd said. He was hinting at a new relationship between them. It made her breath catch in her throat. Her eyes followed him hungrily all the way to his car. He started it and turned on the lights, but he didn't budge. Finally she realized that he wasn't going until she was inside. She smiled at that protectiveness, which was so alien to their relationship. She waved, went inside and closed the door. Only when she turned off the porch light did she hear the car driving away.

NEXT MORNING AT breakfast, Mrs. Brown and Lita were beaming at her, both affectionately amused.

"Have fun last night, dear?" Mrs. Brown asked. "I noticed that Sheriff Hayes didn't bring you home. Wasn't that Stuart York's car?"

"Yes, it was," Ivy confessed, and hated the warm color that blushed her cheeks. "Hayes had a call and had to leave."

"We heard on the radio that there was a shootout," Lita said. "Deputy Clark was admitted to the hospital with a gunshot wound."

"So was one of the suspects," Mrs. Brown said shortly. "They said Hayes got him."

"We saw him on the way home," Ivy confessed, but not how they'd seen him, or where. "He said the deputy was shot in the hip. He didn't mention the drug dealers getting shot, too."

"It was the one who went missing when they stopped the truck," Mrs. Brown said. "My daughter works as a dispatcher," she reminded the other women. "She said he was hiding in a chicken coop just off the highway. Hayes saw chickens flying out of the coop and went to investigate." She chuckled. "People shut their chickens up at sunset to keep them from getting eaten by foxes or raccoons. Nobody turns them out at night. Sure enough, there was this miserable little drug dealer, hiding there. He shot at Hayes and missed. Hayes didn't."

Ivy shook her head. "He takes so many chances," she said. "It will take a brave woman to marry him."

"Probably why no woman ever has," Lita remarked. "He was always a hothead, even when he was in high school. Always taking risks. He joined the police force when he was just seventeen. I guess his father influenced him."

"His father was a lovely man," Ivy remarked with a smile. "He loved flowers, did you know? He always had the most beautiful garden of them, and everybody thought it was his wife who did all the planting. But it wasn't."

"I'll bet Hayes doesn't raise flowers," Mrs. Brown remarked.

"He had a younger brother," Lita continued, frowning, "who died of a drug overdose. You know, they never found the person who bought him that bad batch of cocaine that did him in. They say that Hayes is out to get his brother's killer, that he'll never quit until the drug dealer goes to prison." She sighed. "He still thinks that Minette Raynor gave that drug to Bobby Carson, but I don't. Minette isn't the sort."

Ivy nodded. "I know, but he won't see it that way. He never stops once he's got a suspect in view. That's sort of scary, in a way."

"Makes me feel safe," Mrs. Brown chuckled. "I like knowing he doesn't let criminals get away."

"Me, too," Ivy had to admit. But she was thinking about Stuart and their changed relationship, going through the motions of eating and behaving normally. Inside, she was blazing with new hungers, new hope.

SHE WENT OUT to see her clients that day, but she was missing Stuart and waiting, hoping, for a phone call. She knew that he could have been joking. Maybe he'd just said it to tease. But the look in his eyes on the porch had been possessive, acquisitive. Her heart jumped every time she remembered how that last, desperate kiss had felt. Surely something so powerful had to be shared. After all, she hadn't been the only one breathing hard after the hungry kisses they'd shared. It was just that Stuart was older and more experienced. Maybe to him it was just a pleasant few minutes. To her, it was a taste of heaven.

Merrie called her at lunchtime, just to talk. Ivy was having a sandwich at Barbara's Café, but she didn't taste it. When the phone rang, she jumped to pull it out of her purse and answer it. It had to be Stuart. It had to be!

"Hi," Merrie said cheerfully.

"Oh. Hi," Ivy replied, trying to compose herself and not let her disappointment show. "How are you?"

"Lonely. You need to come spend a weekend with me," Merrie said. "I'm coming home next weekend. How about it?"

Once, Ivy would have jumped at the chance. Now, she was keeping secrets from her best friend. She didn't know whether she should agree. What she felt for Stuart might show, if she was under his roof. She didn't want

Merrie to see it. Not yet. It was too new, too private, too precious to share. And what if he didn't want her around there at all? What if he'd just been playing some sophisticated game to which she didn't know the rules? Her insecurities floated to the top like cream in a churn.

"Ivy, you don't have to worry about me," Merrie said before Ivy could speak. Her tone was subdued, quiet. "I won't interfere."

"Excuse me?"

Merrie drew in a breath. "Hayes is a great catch."

Ivy was speechless. "Hayes?"

"He seems to like you a lot. He was really happy last night."

Now here was a problem she didn't know how to resolve. She couldn't admit that she was crazy about Merrie's brother, for fear that her friend might tease Stuart or do something to make him draw back from Ivy. On the other hand, she wasn't involved with Hayes and wasn't ever likely to be.

"Hayes is very nice," she compromised. "But he doesn't want to get serious about anyone, and neither do I. I don't want to get married for years yet. I want to enjoy being out on my own, and being single."

There was another sigh, but this one sounded strange. "Then, you're not involved with Hayes?"

"We're friends, Merrie. That's all."

"I'm glad," she said. "By the way, have you heard anything, about how he is?" Merrie added after a minute. "I heard that there was a shootout and someone got shot apprehending a drug dealer. Was it Hayes?"

"No!" Ivy said. "It was one of his deputies. One of the suspects got shot, too. Hayes is fine."

"Thank God."

“You’ve known Hayes a long time,” Ivy recalled.

“Yes, since he used to stay with us when his father and mother had to go out of town to see about her parents in Georgia. Even though he was Stuart’s friend, I always felt as if he were part of my family. He’s a lot older than me, of course. Like someone I know in San Antonio,” she added enigmatically.

The age difference between Merrie and Hayes was about the same as that between Stuart and Ivy. Stuart didn’t seem to have a problem with it anymore, if his new attitude toward Ivy was any indication. So maybe there was hope for Merrie.

“He’s not that much older, Merrie,” Ivy said gently.

“Stuart thinks he is.”

There was an edge in that usually calm tone. “He’s your brother. He loves you. He just thinks…” She stopped at once.

“He thinks what?” Merrie prompted.

“He thinks that Hayes’s profession puts him out of the running for you,” she said reluctantly. “Hayes does take chances, Merrie. He can be a lot of fun, but under it all is a man who takes risks, who walks right into gun battles. Stuart’s just thinking about what’s best for you.”

“So that’s what’s been eating him lately,” Merrie said dryly. “Old worrywart. But no relative, no matter how caring, can decide your life for you, you know.”

“I know that. Merrie, Stuart loves you. He’d want you to marry someone you love.”

There was a husky laugh. “Think so?”

“Yes.”

“Well. That’s something.”

“You’re very depressed. Why don’t you come to the

boardinghouse and have supper with us tonight? You know Mrs. Brown wouldn't mind. I could phone her."

"No. Thanks, anyway, but we've got a flu epidemic. I can't be spared, with so many health care workers out sick."

"Maybe when it's all over..." She let her voice trail off.

"Yes. I'd love it."

"Take care of yourself," Ivy said. "And stop worrying about everything. Life evens out. Wishes come true."

"Sure they do," Merrie said cynically.

"I mean it. They do!"

Merrie sighed. "You always did believe in fairies."

"Angels, too, don't forget."

"If I have a guardian angel, he's asleep at the wheel."

"Stop that. Come and see me when you can."

"How about that invitation to spend the weekend?" Merrie persisted. "You and Stuart weren't fighting, for a change, at the dance. You might enjoy it."

"I'll let you know," Ivy said, stalling. "I've got a new client."

"You and your blessed clients. Okay, then. Call me?"

"I'll call you. Take care, Merrie."

"You, too."

Ivy hung up. Poor Merrie.

SHE WAITED AND WAITED, but there was no other phone call. She even checked to make sure the phone was working. By late evening, she was certain she'd misunderstood what Stuart had said. He was probably just joking. But he wasn't a man who usually cracked jokes.

She got ready for bed, climbed under the covers and

was just about to turn out the light when the phone began to ring noisily.

Heart pounding, she leaped out of bed and upended her purse to find the small flip phone. She opened it with trembling hands and put it to her ear. "Hello?"

There was a deep, soft chuckle. "Dived for the phone, did you?"

She laughed breathlessly. "Yes," she confessed.

"I would have waited. I told you I'd call."

"Yes, but I thought maybe you got busy," she began.

"So you gave up on me."

She fidgeted on the bed. "Not really. Well, maybe. I wasn't sure that you weren't teasing."

There was a brief pause. "It's early days, isn't it, Ivy?" he asked quietly. "We're only beginning to learn each other."

She wasn't sure what he meant. Her hand tightened on the phone. "Merrie invited me to spend the weekend."

"What did you tell her?"

"I said I'd let her know," she hesitated.

There was a short pause.

She felt insecure. "I didn't know if you'd approve."

The pause grew.

She felt her spirits hit the floor. She drew in a slow, shivery breath. "Stuart?"

There was a clink, like that of ice in a glass. "You don't know me at all."

"Of course I don't," she replied. "You've avoided me for two whole years."

"I had to," he said harshly.

She didn't understand what he meant. She was shy with him. It wasn't helping things.

He drew in another harsh breath. "Oh, hell." Ice sloshed in liquid again.

"I should go," she said sadly.

"Is it Hayes?" he asked harshly.

"What?"

"Are you in love with Hayes Carson?"

"I most certainly am not!" she exclaimed before she stopped to think.

There was a sigh. "Well, that's something, I guess." Another pause. "When I come back, we'll go for a drive and talk."

"That would be…nice."

"Nice."

She was lost for words. She loved the sound of his deep, slow voice. She didn't want him to hang up. But she didn't know what to say, to keep him talking.

"What are you doing?"

"Sitting on the bed in my nightgown, talking to a madman."

He burst out laughing. "Is that how I sound?"

"I feel like apologizing, but I don't know what for."

"I've had a long day," he told her. "We always get at least one tree hugger who comes to these conferences and demands that we set up special homes for our cattle where they can be properly housed and clothed and educated. This guy thinks we should learn to communicate with them."

She burst out laughing. "If you could, they'd say, 'don't eat me.'"

"You stop that," he muttered. "You know I don't raise beef cattle."

That was true. He had purebred Black Angus cattle. He knew the names and pedigrees of all his bulls, and they were as tame as dogs. The pedigree cows were treated almost as gently as the bulls. He was dangerous to cowboys who thought they could mistreat his livestock.

"I know that," she said gently. "What did you say to the tree hugger?"

"Oh, I didn't say anything to him."

There was an odd inflection in his voice. "But somebody else did?"

"One of the delegates from the national association invited him outside. The guy thought they were going to share a nice discussion. The delegate picked him up and put him down in the ornamental fountain."

She gasped. "But it's freezing in Colorado! There's snow!"

He chuckled. "I know."

"The poor man!"

"They gave him a blanket and a bus ticket," he said. "Last I saw of him, he was shivering his way back west into the sunset."

"That wasn't kind."

"Last year, it was a global warming advocate who said that we needed to find ways to stop cattle from belching and destroying the ozone layer. But I won't mention what happened to him."

"Why not?"

He only laughed. "You'll read all about it in the book he's writing. Last I heard, he was still looking for a publisher."

"Poor man."

"Poor man, hell. Humans belch as much as cattle do."

"I have never belched."

"Baloney," he shot back.

She sighed. "Well, I've burped quietly. But I never considered that it was doing damage to the planet."

He laughed. "I'm kidding. They actually let him present his program. One cattleman even bought him a drink."

"That was nice."

"It wasn't. The drink he bought him was a 'Wallbanger.'"

"What's that?"

"You wake up eventually with a hell of a hangover."

"You guys are terrible."

"I don't buy drinks for advocacy groups."

"You might influence them if you did."

"Not a chance." There was another pause. "I've got to go. There's someone at the door."

"An advocacy group?" she teased.

He laughed again. "No. A buddy of mine from Alaska."

"Does he raise cattle up there?"

"He's stationed at a military base there. Active military."

"Oh."

"I'll talk to you when I get back. Take care."

"You, too," she said, her voice softening.

"Good night, sugar."

He hung up before she was sure she'd really heard that. He'd never called her a pet name in all the time they'd known each other. It sounded as if they were actually going to be friends. Maybe even more. She slept finally in a welter of delightful, impossible dreams.

THE NEXT MORNING, her whole world fell apart. She answered her phone, thinking drowsily that it might be Stuart again, when a stranger addressed her.

"Miss Conley?" the voice inquired. And when she said yes, he continued, "I had this number from your police chief. I'm Sergeant Ed Ames, of the New York Police Department, Brooklyn Precinct. It's about your sister."

Her heart fell. "Is she all right?" she asked at once. "Has she been arrested?"

There was a loaded pause. "I'm sorry to tell you that she was found dead in her apartment this morning… Miss Conley? Miss Conley!"

She could barely breathe. She'd known this was coming, deep in her heart. But she wasn't ready to face it.

"Yes," she said heavily. "I'm still here. Sorry. It's… it's a shock…"

"I can imagine," he replied.

"You said she was found dead. Did she commit suicide?" she asked. "Or did someone else…"

"We don't know. There's going to have to be an autopsy, I'm afraid, to decide that. We'll need you to identify the body, to make sure it is your sister. Then someone has to arrange for disposition of her personal effects and her burial, or cremation."

"Yes. Of course. I'll have to come up there and deal with it." She hesitated, her mind spinning. "I'll come today. As soon as I can get a flight."

He gave her his telephone number and contact information. She wrote it all down and said goodbye.

She sat back down on her bed, rocking quietly with her arms wrapped around herself. Rachel was dead. Rachel was dead. She hadn't even gotten to say goodbye. And now she had to go and deal with the funeral arrangements. Worse, she didn't even know if her sister had killed herself, or if someone had murdered her.

She thought of Jerry, her sister's drug-dealing boyfriend. Had he tired of her habit and killed her with an overdose? Had the millionaire's wife sent someone to kill her? Her head buzzed with all sorts of horrible images.

Then came the thought that she was all alone. Rachel had been the last living member of her family. The anguish of her sister's machinations and lies was over, but so was the last bond of kinship she had.

She thought of their father and wondered if he'd been there to meet Rachel when she crossed over. He'd loved the other sister so much. He hadn't loved Ivy. He didn't think Ivy was his. Was she? Had Rachel lied about that, too, as she'd lied about so many other things?

Maybe Rachel had left a note, a letter, something, to explain her hatred of Ivy. If she went to New York, maybe she could find it. Maybe she could understand the other woman, at long last.

She started packing.

CHAPTER SEVEN

LUCKILY, IVY HAD enough in her savings account to cover a reduced fare round-trip airline ticket to New York. But once there, she would have expenses. She'd have to find somewhere to stay—she couldn't bear to stay at Rachel's apartment with the drug-dealing boyfriend lurking nearby—and there would be cab fare and then the cost of bringing Rachel home. It was a nightmare. If Stuart had been at home, she might have been bold enough to call him and ask for help. But it was too soon in their changing relationship for that.

On the other hand, she could call Merrie. But Ivy was too proud. It would sound as if she needed charity. No, she had to stand on her own two feet and do what was necessary. She was a grown woman, not a child. She could do this.

She'd never been on an airplane in her life. It was an adventure, from going through security to takeoff, which she compared in her mind to blasting off in a spaceship. She was sitting next to a nice elderly couple in tourist class. They were friendly, and seemed amused at her fascination with air travel.

Once at La Guardia, she took a cab to a modestly priced hotel that Lita had told her about, which was in Brooklyn, not too far from Rachel's apartment. She also had the number of the police sergeant who'd told her about her sister's death.

She checked in at the hotel and took time to go upstairs with her single suitcase. The room was small, but neat and clean, and there was a lovely view of the city skyline. She wondered how she was going to bear the loneliness of it, though, after she went to the morgue to identify her sister's body. The ordeal was one she dreaded.

Sergeant Ames wasn't in his office when she got there, so she took a seat in the waiting room. The police precinct seemed in a constant case of chaos. People came and went. Lawyers came to see clients. Reporters came to talk to detectives. Uniformed officers came and went. It was a colorful mix of people, especially to Ivy, who was used to living in a town of only two thousand people. A few minutes later, a tall, dark-haired, good-looking man in a suit approached her.

"Miss Conley?" he asked, smiling.

She stood up. "Yes. Are you Sergeant Ames?"

"I am." They shook hands. "Sorry I was late," he added, leading her to his cubicle and offering her a seat. "I had to testify in a murder trial. Court just let out."

"Have you learned anything else about my sister's death?" she asked.

"Just that her boyfriend has a record as long as my desk," he replied curtly. "He has clients in high places around town. Apparently your sister was involved with one of them, a married man, and the client's wife was none too happy about the affair. She made threats against your sister's life. Then there's the boyfriend. A neighbor of theirs told one of our investigators that your sister and her boyfriend had frequent violent arguments.

During their latest one, he told her to leave his client alone and she threatened to go to the police with information she said could convict him of drug smuggling." He folded his hands on the cluttered desk. "As you can tell, there's no shortage of suspects if it does turn out to be a case of murder." He frowned. "Is someone with you? Family? A boyfriend, perhaps?"

She shook her head. "I don't have any relatives, except Rachel," she replied. She thought about Stuart, but kisses didn't make relationships. "And no boyfriend," she added reluctantly. "There was no one I could ask to come with me."

He grimaced. "You're not going to try to stay in your sister's apartment?" he asked quickly.

"No," she told him. "I couldn't bear to stay there. I have a room in a small hotel for the night."

"Have you ever had to deal with a death in your family before?"

"My father died two years ago," she said. "But Rachel made all the arrangements. I just paid the bills. I don't know exactly what to do," she confessed.

"I'll walk you through the procedure," he said in a gentler tone. "What can you tell me about your sister's private life?"

"Probably no more than you know already," she said apologetically. "Rachel was older than me, and she didn't like me. She only got in touch with me when I could do something for her."

He studied her quietly. "You weren't close?"

She shook her head. "Rachel didn't want to live in a small town. She wanted to be an actress on Broadway." She felt a terrible emptiness in the pit of her stomach. "I knew that she used drugs. She's done that for a long time, ever since high school. But I never thought she'd die so young." Tears ran down her cheeks. "It's just been so sudden."

"May I make a suggestion?"

She wiped her eyes. "Of course."

"You said that you have a hotel room?"

"Yes," she replied.

"Go to it and rest for a couple of hours. Call me when you're ready and I'll take you to the morgue to identify her. How about that?"

She almost argued. But he was a kind man, she could see it in his dark eyes. She smiled. "I would like to do that. Thank you."

He stood up. "I'll have one of the guys drop you off at your hotel," he added, as if he knew how limited her funds were.

"Thank you," she said gently.

He smiled. "No problem. I'll see you later."

IT WASN'T EVEN lunchtime yet. She wasn't hungry. The flight had taken away her appetite. She lay down on the bed covers and closed her eyes. The ordeal was still in front of her. But the sergeant had been right, a few minutes' rest might help her face the morgue.

She must have drifted off, because a persistent knocking sound brought her back to the present. She climbed off the bed, wiping at her sleepy eyes, and went to the door. She looked through the peephole and couldn't believe her eyes.

She threw open the door and ran into Stuart's warm, strong arms. She held on for dear life, sobbing, so happy to see him that she couldn't even pretend.

"It's all right, honey," he said softly, drawing her into

the room. He closed and locked the door and then lifted her, carrying her to the bed. He sat down on it and cradled her across his knees. "I know it's hard. Whatever else she was, she was still your sister."

"How did you know?" she sobbed into his shoulder.

"The cabdriver who took you to the airport is Mrs. Rhodes's second cousin. He phoned her and she phoned me." His arms tightened. "Why didn't you call me?" he asked. "I would have been there like a shot."

She didn't have that much self-confidence, especially where he was concerned. But miraculously, here he was. She'd never needed someone this much in her life. She wasn't alone anymore.

She cuddled up against him, shivering a little with relief. "I have to call Sergeant Ames and he'll take me to identify…identify the body."

"I'll do that for you," he said softly.

She looked up into his pale blue eyes. "I can do it," she said. "If you'll go with me."

He smiled. "Of course I will." The smile faded. "How did she die?"

"I don't know. The police aren't sure, either. He said they'll have to do an autopsy to find the cause of death." She laid her cheek against his broad chest. "Her apartment will have to be gone through and her things removed. Then I have to decide whether to have her cremated or bring her home to Jacobsville and bury her there, near our parents."

"Rachel wouldn't have cared what you did with her," he said coldly.

"I'd really rather have her cremated," she told him sadly. She didn't want to mention that the expense of transporting a coffin to Jacobsville was too overwhelming for her. She was sure that Rachel had no health insurance, or life insurance. And even if she had, there was no doubt that Jerry would have had himself put on the policy as beneficiary. But that still left Ivy with the funeral expense.

"Then, we'll see about doing that," Stuart said after a minute. "But first things first. We'll go to the morgue, then we'll find a funeral home. After we've made the arrangements, we'll go back to her apartment and see what needs doing there."

"You make everything sound so simple," she remarked.

"Most things are. It's just a matter of organization."

She sat up on his lap, dabbing at her eyes. "Sorry. I just lost it when I saw you. I thought I'd have to do all this alone."

He pulled out a white handkerchief and put it in her hands. "Dry your eyes. Then we'll call your sergeant and get the process started. Okay?"

She smiled. "Okay."

STUART TRIED TO keep her from looking at Rachel, but she insisted. She wanted to see how her sister looked.

It was bad. Rachel was gray. There was no expression on her face, although it was pockmarked and very thin. She looked gruesome, but it was definitely Rachel.

Stuart and Sergeant Ames escorted her back to Ames's office, where they sat around his desk drinking cups of black coffee until Ivy was fortified enough to talk.

"We're going to have an autopsy done," Ames told them, "but the medical examiner says it's pretty conclusive that she died of a massive overdose of cocaine."

"Is that why she looks the way she does?" Ivy asked, dabbing at her eyes with Stuart's handkerchief. "I mean, her face looks pockmarked."

"That's the crystal meth she'd been using," he replied. "It's the most deadly drug we deal with these days. It ravages the user. A few months on it and they look like zombies."

"Why?" she asked suddenly. "Why would anyone use something like that in the first place?"

"People have been asking that question for years, and we still don't have an answer. It's one of the most addictive drugs," the detective told her gently. "Once it gets into their systems, people will literally kill to get it."

"How horrible," she said, and meant it.

"How long had she been using?" he asked Ivy.

"Since she was in high school," she told him dully. "I told my father, but he didn't believe me. He said Rachel would never do drugs." She laughed hollowly. "She'd come to see us when she was high as a kite, and my father never even noticed."

"Her father drank," Stuart interrupted solemnly. "I don't think he noticed much."

Ivy grimaced. "I never imagined she'd end up like this."

"What about her boyfriend?" Stuart wanted to know.

Ames shrugged. "We've managed to get a couple of convictions against him, but even so, he gets out of jail in no time, and goes right back to his old tricks. A couple of his clients are powerful figures in the city."

"On all the best television shows, the drug dealers go away for life," Ivy pointed out.

Ames chuckled. "I wish it was that way. It's not. For

hundreds of reasons, drug dealers never get the sentences they deserve."

"When will they do the autopsy?" Ivy asked.

"Probably tonight," Ames said. "They don't have a backlog, for the first time in months. Once we have a cause of death, we can decide where to go from there."

"What about her apartment?" Ivy asked. "Is it all right for us to go there?"

"Yes," he replied and, reaching into his middle desk drawer, produced a key. "This is a copy of the key to her apartment, which we have in the property room. I thought you'd need access, so I had this one made. We've already processed her apartment."

"I'll need to clean it out and pack up whatever little family memorabilia she kept, so I can take it home with me," Ivy said dully.

"How well do you know Jerry Smith?" the detective asked her.

"I've seen him a few times," she replied. "I never liked him. I have migraine headaches," she added. "He came home with Rachel when our father died. I had the headache and he switched my medicine for some powerful narcotics. I realized he'd substituted something for my prescription pills, and I refused to take what he gave me. He thought it was funny."

Stuart looked murderous. "You never told me that," he accused.

"I knew what you'd do if you found out," she replied. "That man looks to me like he has some really dangerous connections."

"I have a few of my own," Stuart replied curtly. "Including two Texas Rangers, an FBI agent and our local sheriff. You should have told me."

She grimaced. “I was glad when Rachel and Jerry went back to New York.”

“I’m not surprised,” the sergeant said. “I have your sister’s effects in the property room. If you’ll come with me, I’ll get them for you. You’ll have to sign them out.”

“All right.” She stood up, feeling numb. “Thank you for being so kind.”

“It goes with the job description,” he assured her.

STUART HAD HIRED a limousine. Ivy found it fascinating. She wished she wasn’t so transparent to him. He seemed amused that she wanted to know everything about the expensive transportation.

He had the driver wait for them at Rachel’s apartment building. He escorted Ivy up the stairs to the second floor apartment and opened the door. It was just the way Rachel had left it, except for the white outline that showed where her body had been.

Ivy was taken aback at the graphic evidence of her sister’s death. She stood there for a moment until she could get her emotions under control. “I don’t know where to begin,” she said.

“Try the bedroom,” Stuart suggested. “I’ll go through the drawers in the living room.”

“Okay.”

She wandered into Rachel’s bedroom, her eyes on the ratty pink coverlet, the scattered old shoes, the faded curtains. Rachel had always told everybody back home that she was getting good parts in Broadway plays and making gobs of money. Ivy had even believed it.

But she should have realized that Rachel wouldn’t have been so persistent about their father’s money unless she was hurting for it. A rich woman would have less need for a parent's savings.

Ivy opened the bedside table, feeling like a thief as she looked inside. There was a small book with an embroidered cover. A diary. Absently, Ivy stuck it in the pocket of her jacket and moved to the dresser.

There was hardly anything in the dresser except for some faded silk lingerie and underwear. The closet, however, was a surprise. Inside were ten exquisite and expensive evening gowns and two coats. Ivy touched them. Fur. Real fur. There were expensive high heeled shoes in every color of the rainbow on the floor of the closet.

She opened the jewelry box on the dresser and gasped. It could be costume jewelry, of course, but it didn't look cheap. There were emeralds and diamonds and rubies in rings and necklaces and earrings. It looked like a king's ransom of jewelry. What in the world had Rachel done to get all this, she wondered?

Stuart came in, his hands deep in his pockets, frowning. "She's got a big plasma television, a top-of-the-line DVD player and some furniture that came from exclusive antique shops. How did she manage all that without visible means of support?"

"That's a good question," Ivy replied. "Look at this."

Stuart looked over her shoulder at the jewels. He picked up a ring and looked at the inscription inside the band. "Eighteen karat gold," he murmured. "The stones are real, too."

"Do you think she stole them?" Ivy asked worriedly.

"I don't think it's likely that she owned them," he replied. "There's about a hundred thousand dollars worth, right here in this tray."

Her gasp was audible. "I thought it might be costume jewelry."

He tilted her chin up to his eyes. "You don't know a lot about luxury, do you, honey?" he asked softly. He bent and touched his mouth gently to hers. "I like you that way."

The touch of his mouth was almost her undoing, but she couldn't forget the task at hand. "Where do you think she got all this?" she persisted.

"If she was hanging out with a millionaire, I imagine he gave it to her."

"His wife will want it all back."

He nodded. "If she knows it's here." He frowned. "I'm surprised that Ames didn't take it and put it in the property room."

"Maybe he thought it was fake, too."

He chuckled. "No. That guy knows his business. He may have some sort of surveillance camera in here, waiting to see if anyone carries off the jewels."

"That's not a bad idea," she mused.

He closed the lid of the jewelry box. "No, it isn't." He checked his watch. "It's going on lunchtime. We can go back to my hotel and have room service send something up to us."

"I have my own room," she reminded him.

"We'll cancel it and pick up your suitcase," he replied. "I'm not letting you out of my sight," he added somberly. "Especially while we don't know exactly why your sister died."

She started to argue. He held up a hand. "I won't give up or give in. Just come along and don't fight it."

"You're very domineering," she accused.

"Years of working cattle has ruined me for polite society," he said with a twinkle in his pale eyes.

She laughed, as she was meant to. "All right," she said after a minute. She didn't mind being guided at the moment. She was worn. He picked up the jewelry box and put it in her hands.

"Her boyfriend will say these belong to him," he said. "But he's not getting them without a fight. We'll put them in a safe-deposit box for the time being."

"That's a good idea," she agreed. "He may not have killed her, but he helped her get where she is now. He shouldn't profit from her death."

"I agree."

ON THE WAY to the hotel, he stopped at a bank where he obviously had an account and asked for access to his own safe-deposit box. They deposited the jewelry box in it. He asked to speak to one of the vice presidents of the bank, who came out of his office, smiling, to motion Stuart and Ivy into it. Stuart asked him about funeral parlors in the city and was referred to a reputable one. The bank officer gave Stuart the number.

When they were back in the limousine, Stuart dialed the number and spoke to one of the funeral directors. He made an appointment for them later that afternoon to speak about the arrangements. The funeral home would arrange for transport of Rachel's body when the medical examiner released it. Then they went by Ivy's hotel and picked up her suitcase. Stuart, despite her protests, paid for the room.

"We can argue about it when we're back home," he told her.

His hotel room made hers look like a closet. It was a

penthouse suite, one of those that figured in presidential visits, she guessed. Stuart took it for granted. He phoned room service and ordered food.

"You should have asked for more than that," he said when she was through a bowl of freshly made potato soup.

"It was all I thought I could eat," she said simply. "It hasn't been the best day of my life." She put down the spoon. "I don't think it's hit me yet," she added solemnly. "I feel numb."

"So did I, when my father died," he said, putting down his fork. He poured second cups of coffee for them both before he spoke again. "I was sure that I hated him. He'd spent his life trying to force me to become what he couldn't. But when it happened, I was devastated. You never realize how important a parent, any parent, is in your life until they're not there anymore."

"Yes," she agreed. "Nobody else shares your memories like a parent. My father was bad to me. He always preferred Rachel, and he never tried to hide it." She sighed. "Maybe it's a good thing that I know he didn't believe I was his child. It makes the past a little easier to bear. I wish I knew for sure, though."

"We'll find out. I promise you we will."

She stared at him across the table. "You must be letting deals get by while you're up here with me," she said.

He shrugged. "There's nothing any of my managers can't handle. That's why I hire qualified people, so that I can delegate authority when I need to."

She smiled. "I'm very glad. I could have done this by myself. But I'm glad that I didn't have to."

He finished his coffee and put his napkin on the table. His pale eyes caught hers from the other side of the table. "I'd never have let you go through this alone," he said quietly.

The words were mundane, but his eyes were saying things that made her heart jump up into her throat. A faint wave of color stained her cheeks.

He smiled slowly, wickedly. "Not now," he said in a deep, slow drawl. "We've got too much to do. Business now. Diversions later."

The blush went nuclear. She got up from the table, fumbling a little with her coffee cup in the process.

He laughed. She was as transparent as glass to a man with his experience. It made him feel taller to see that helpless delight in her face. He was glad he'd come to New York. And not just because Ivy needed help.

THEY SAT IN the funeral director's office, going over final arrangements for Rachel. Ivy decided on cremation. It was inexpensive, and Stuart had already mentioned that he was flying his own twin-engine plane home. There wouldn't be any problem with getting the urn containing Rachel's ashes through security.

She picked out an ornate black and gold brass urn. "I can have our local funeral director bury it in the space next to Daddy," she told Stuart.

"Some people keep the ashes at home," the director remarked.

"No, I don't think I could live in the house if Rachel was sitting on the mantel," Ivy said quietly. "My sister and I didn't get along, you see."

The director smiled. "I have a brother I couldn't get along with. I know how you feel."

They went back into his office and Ivy signed the

necessary papers and wrote a check for the cost of the expenses, despite Stuart's protests.

Later, in the limousine, he voiced his disapproval. "You've got enough to do supporting yourself," he said curtly. "Rachel's funeral cost is pocket change to me."

"I know that," she replied. "But you have to understand how I feel, Stuart. It's my sister and my responsibility."

He caught her hand in his and held it tight. "You always were an independent little cuss," he mused, smiling at her.

She smiled back. "I like the feeling that I can stand on my own two feet and support myself," she replied. "I never had a life of my own as long as Rachel was alive. She was even worse than Dad about trying to manage me."

He pursed his lip. "Do I detect a double meaning?"

She laughed. "No. Well, yes. You do try to manage me." She stared at him curiously. "And I don't know why. You were just going around with some beautiful debutante. There was a photograph of you in a tabloid two weeks ago," she added and then flushed because that sounded like jealousy.

But he only smiled. "That photo was taken four years ago. God knows where they dug it up."

She blinked. "Excuse me?"

"The photograph was taken years ago. See this?" He indicated a tie tack that she'd given him for his birthday three years ago. "I always wear it with my suits. Look in the photo and see if you see it."

In fact, she hadn't seen it in that photo. It amazed her that he prized such an inexpensive present. And that he wore it constantly. "You like it that much?" she asked, diverted.

Instead of a direct answer, his hand slipped to her collar and dipped under it to produce a filigree gold cross that he'd given her for Christmas three years past. "You never take it off," he said, his voice deep and slow. "It's in every photo of you that my sister takes."

"I…it's very pretty," she stammered. The feel of his knuckles against her soft skin was delightful.

"Yes, it is. But that isn't why you wear it, any more than I wear the tie tack because it's trendy."

He was insinuating something very intimate. She stared into his pale eyes as they narrowed, and darkened, and her breath began to catch in her throat.

"We're both keeping secrets, Ivy," he said in a deep, soft tone. "But not for much longer."

She searched his pale eyes, looking for a depth of feeling that matched her own. He was familiar, dear. When she and Merrie were in high school, she'd felt breathless when he walked into a room. She hadn't realized, then, that the feelings she got when he was around were the beginnings of aching desire.

He traced the outline of her soft lips with his forefinger, making her tingle all over. He smiled, so tenderly that she felt she could fly. Any idea she'd had that he was playing a game with her was gone now. No man looked at a woman like this unless he cared, even if only a little.

CHAPTER EIGHT

Ivy felt as if the ground had been pulled out from under her as she stared into Stuart's pale eyes. His gaze dropped to her soft, full mouth and lingered there until she thought her heart would burst out of her chest. She stared at his hard mouth and remembered, oh, so well, the feel of it against her own. The need was like a desperate thirst that nothing could quench. She started to lean toward him. His hand contracted. His face hardened. She could see the intent in his eyes even before he reached for her.

And just then, the car lurched forward as the traffic light changed, separating them before they'd managed to get close.

Ivy laughed breathlessly, nervous and shy and on fire with kindling desire.

He cocked an eyebrow. "You're safe," he murmured, although he still had her hand tight in his. "But don't get too comfortable."

She only smiled. His eyes were promising heaven. It seemed impossible that they'd been enemies for so long. This familiar, handsome, compelling, sexy man beside her had become someone she didn't know at all. The prospect of the future became exciting. But even as she felt the impact of her own feelings for him, she remembered why she was in New York City. Dreams would have to wait for a while.

They went back to Rachel's apartment to arrange things. Stuart went down to talk to the apartment manager. Ivy stayed in the apartment and began going through drawers again.

She found a photo album. She sat down with it on the couch and opened it. As she expected, the photos were all of Rachel. There was one of their father, sitting on the porch swing at his house. There were a few of their mother. There wasn't one single picture of Ivy anywhere in the album. It stung. But it wasn't unexpected.

She put the album aside and picked up a letter, addressed to Rachel and marked Private. It was trespassing. She felt guilty. But she had to know what was in the letter, especially when she read the return address. It was an expensive stationery, and the return address was that of a law firm in Texas.

Just as she started to open it, she heard footsteps. They weren't Stuart's. She stood up and slipped the letter into her slacks' pocket just as the door flew open.

Jerry Smith walked into the apartment as if he owned it. He was somber and angry. His narrow eyes focused on Ivy with something like hatred.

"What are you doing here?" Ivy asked coldly.

He shut the door behind him and smiled. The smile was sleazy, demeaning. He looked at Ivy as if she were a streetwalker awaiting his pleasure.

"So, it's the little sister, come looking for buried treasure, is it? Don't get too comfortable here, sweetheart. Everything in this apartment is mine. I paid for all this." He swept his arm around the room. "Mustn't steal things that don't belong to you," he added in a sarcastic undertone.

She would have backed down even a year ago. But she'd spent too much time around Stuart to cave in, especially when she knew he was nearby and likely to return any minute. This sleazy drug dealer didn't know that, and it was her ace in the hole.

"Any photographs and quilts and paintings in here are mine," she returned icily. "You don't get to keep my family heirlooms."

"Quilts." He made the word sound disgusting. "Rachel thought they were worth a fortune, because they were handmade. She took them to an antique dealer. He said they were junk. She tried to give them away, but nobody wanted them. She used them to pack her crystal in, for when she planned to move next month." He shrugged. "I guess she won't be moving anywhere."

Her relief at knowing the quilts weren't trashed disappeared when he made that odd statement. "Rachel never said anything about moving. Where was she moving to?"

"Back to your little hick town, apparently," he said. "She owned a house there."

"She didn't," Ivy returned, and felt guilty as relief flooded her. Rachel had planned to come home and let Ivy be her personal slave. "She sold the house two years ago."

"Whatever. She didn't remember much. I warned her about that damned meth. I don't even sell it, because it's so dangerous, but she got hooked on it and wouldn't quit."

"Did you kill her?" Ivy asked curtly.

"I didn't have to," he muttered. "She stayed comatose half the time, ever since she lost that big part she'd just landed in a play that's starting on Broadway in a couple of months. Her lover's wife knew the producer. She had him drop Rachel, then she called and told her all about it. She promised Rachel that she'd never get a starring role ever again. That was when she hit bottom."

"They're doing an autopsy."

He shrugged. "They usually do, when people die suddenly. I didn't kill her," he repeated. "She killed herself." He looked around, his eyes narrowing. "Don't take anything out of here until I have time to go through her things."

"I've already taken her jewelry to a bank for safekeeping," Ivy returned.

"You've what?" He moved toward her, his hands clenched at his sides. "That jewelry is worth a king's ransom! She wheedled it out of that old man she was sucking up to!"

"Which means it belongs to him," Ivy replied.

"You'd really give it back to him, wouldn't you?" he taunted. "God, what an idiot you are! Tell you what, you give me half of it and I'll forget where it went."

"You can only bribe dishonest people," she said quietly. "I don't care that much about money. I only want to make a living."

"Rachel would have kept the lot!"

"Yes, she would have. She took and took and took, all her life. The only human being she ever cared about was herself."

"Well, you're not blind, are you?" He moved into the bedroom and opened drawers while Ivy hoped that Stuart would come back soon. Seconds later, Jerry barreled out of the bedroom. "Where is it?"

She blinked. "Where is what?"

"The account book!"

She frowned. "What account book? There wasn't any account book here!"

He went white in the face. "It's got to be here," he muttered to himself. He started going through drawers in the spacious living room, taking things out, scattering them. "It's got to be here!"

She couldn't understand what he was so upset about. Obviously there would be some sort of record of rent and other expenditures, but who kept a journal in this day and time?

"Wouldn't it be on the computer?" she asked, indicating the laptop on the dining room table.

"What? The computer?" He turned on the computer and pulled up the files, one by one, cursing harshly as he went along. "No, it's not here!" He stared at her over the computer. "You took it, when you took the jewelry, didn't you?" he demanded. "Did you get my stash, too?"

He strode into the bathroom. Loud noises came from the room. He appeared again with some small bags of white powder. "At least only one is missing," he said, almost to himself. He stuffed the bags into his pants pockets. He glared at Ivy. "I don't know what your game is, but you'd better find that journal, and quick, if you know what's good for you."

"What journal?" she demanded. "For heaven's sake, my sister just died! I'm not interested in your household accounts!"

He glared back.

"Did she have any life insurance?" she asked, forcing herself to calm down. "A burial policy?"

"She didn't expect to die this young," he returned. "No, there's no life insurance." He smiled coolly. "You can leave the apartment and its contents to me. Now take whatever you want of her 'heirlooms,' and then get the hell out of this apartment."

She wanted to argue, but Stuart would be here soon, and after Jerry got his comeuppance, he wasn't likely to let her back in again. She retrieved the quilts out of the closet, leaving the crystal stacked neatly on the floor. She took the photo album, although the photos were mostly of Rachel. She took none of the dresses or gowns or shoes or furs. Rachel's whole life boiled down to frivolous things. There wasn't a single book in the entire apartment.

Clutching the quilts and the photo albums, she moved back into the living room, where Jerry was still pulling open drawers, looking for the mysterious journal.

He seemed surprised when he saw what she had. "There were evening gowns in the closet. Weren't you interested in them? You and Rachel were almost the same size."

"I can buy my own clothes," she replied. It was a sore spot. Just once, when she was sixteen, she'd asked to borrow one of Rachel's gowns to wear to the prom. Rachel had asked why, and Ivy had confessed that a nice boy from the grocery store had invited her to the prom. So when he came to the house, Rachel had flirted with him and before he left, Rachel had teased him into driving her to Houston to see some friends on the same night as the prom. Then Rachel had mocked Ivy about borrowing the gown, adding that she hardly needed one since she no longer had a date.

"Did Rachel send you anything to keep for her?" Jerry persisted.

"Rachel only phoned me when she wanted me to send

her something," she replied. "She wouldn't have trusted me with anything. She never did."

"Yeah, she said you stole her stuff when she was living at home."

Ivy's face went red with bad temper. "I never took anything of hers. It was the other way around. She could tell a lie to anyone and be believed. It was her greatest talent."

"I guess you were jealous of her, because she was so beautiful," he replied.

"I'm not jealous of people who don't have hearts."

He laughed coldly. "Beauty makes up for character."

"Not in my book."

He moved toward her, noting her quick backward movement. He smiled tauntingly. "Maybe you and me could get together some time. You're not pretty, but you've got spirit."

"I'd rather get together with a snake."

He lifted an eyebrow. "Suit yourself. I guess you'll grow old and die all alone in that hick town you come from." He touched her long, blond hair. "You could have some sweet times if you stayed here with me."

The door flew open and Jerry's face went rigid as the tall, dangerous man saw what Jerry was doing, stalked right up to him, took his hand from Ivy's hair and literally pushed him away.

"Touch her again and I'll break your neck," Stuart said, his whole demeanor threatening.

"Hey, man, I'm cool!" he said, backing even further away with both hands raised, palms out.

The flippant, cocksure young man of seconds before was flushed with nerves. Ivy didn't blame him. Stuart in a temper was formidable. He never lost control of himself, but he never flinched when confronted. The meanest of his cowboys walked wide around him on the ranch.

Ivy felt relief surge up inside her. Instinctively she moved closer to Stuart—so close that she could feel his strength and the warmth of his body. His arm slid around her shoulders, holding her near. She felt safe.

"I was just telling Ivy that this stuff is mine," Jerry said, but not in a forceful tone. "My money paid for it."

"And I told him," Ivy replied, "that all I wanted was whatever heirlooms from my family that Rachel kept here. I've got them…three quilts and a photo album." She was holding them.

"Ready to go?" Stuart asked her calmly, but his cold eyes were pinning Jerry to the wall.

"Yes," she said.

"All right, then."

She grabbed her purse from the table and went through the doorway. Stuart gave Jerry one last, contemptuous look before he closed the door behind them.

"The drug dealer, I take it?" he asked, relieving Ivy of the quilts.

"Yes. He was being very nasty until you showed up. Thanks for saving me."

He chuckled. "You were doing pretty well on your own, from what I saw." He led the way into the elevator and pressed the button for the lobby. "At least you won't have to dispose of the apartment and its contents."

"Yes, that's one worry gone." She looked up at him. "He was desperate to find some sort of account book he said Rachel had. He was frantic when he couldn't locate it."

"Did you find it?" he asked.

She shook her head. "There weren't any account books that I could see. He was furious about the jewelry, too," she added.

"He can try to get them back, if he likes. I have some great attorneys."

"I told him they were going back to the millionaire who gave them to her," she replied.

He laughed. "That must have given him hives."

"He was upset. I meant it, though." She grimaced. "But how am I going to find out who he is?"

"I'll take care of that," he said, so easily that Ivy relaxed. "All you have to worry about is the funeral. And I'll help with that."

"You've been so kind," she began.

He held up a hand. "Don't start."

She smiled. "Okay. But thanks, anyway."

"I couldn't leave you to do it alone." He led her out of the elevator when it stopped and out to the limousine, which was waiting for them just beyond the entrance. Stuart motioned to the driver and he pulled out of his parking space and around to the front of the apartment building.

The quilts were placed in the trunk and Stuart helped Ivy into the limousine.

They went back to the hotel. Ivy felt drained. She hadn't done much at all, but the stress of the situation was wearing on her nerves.

"You can have the master bedroom," he offered. "I'll have the one across the living room…"

"But I don't need all that room," she protested. "Please. I'd really rather have the smaller of the two."

He shrugged. "Suit yourself." He put her suitcase onto the bed in the smaller room and left her to unpack.

"Why don't you lie down and rest for a while? I've got some phone calls to make. Then we'll see about supper."

"I haven't got anything fancy with me," she said as she opened the suitcase. "Oh, no," she muttered, grimacing as she realized that she'd only packed another pair of slacks and two blouses and an extra pair of shoes. She'd forgotten that she was going to spend the night.

"What's wrong?" he asked.

"I didn't pack a nightgown…"

"Is that all?" He pursed his lips, letting his eyes slide down her body. "I can take care of that. You get some rest. I'll be back in a little while. Don't answer the door," he added firmly. He didn't add why. He was sure the tabloids would pick up the story, and some enterprising reporter could easily find out that Ivy was in town to see to her sister's burial arrangements. He didn't want Ivy bothered.

"I won't answer the door." She wanted to offer to give him some money to get her a nightgown, but she didn't have it. The airfare and taxis had almost bankrupted her.

He was gone before she could even make the offer. She kicked off her shoes and put the open suitcase on the folding rack. Then she sank down onto the comfortable bed, in her clothes. She didn't mean to doze off, but she did. The long day had finally caught up with her.

SHE WOKE TO the smell of freshly brewed coffee. She started sitting up even before she opened her eyes, and a deep, masculine chuckle broke the silence.

"That's exactly how I react to fresh coffee when I've been asleep," he murmured, standing over her with a cup and saucer. The cup was steaming. He handed it to her. "Careful, it's hot."

She smiled drowsily as she took it. The color told her that he'd poured cream in it. He'd remembered that she only liked cream in her coffee. It was flattering. It was exciting. So was the way he was looking at her.

"Hungry?"

"I could eat," she replied.

"I had room service send up a platter of cold cuts," he told her. "Come on in when you're ready."

She took a minute to bathe her face and put her hair back up neatly before she joined him in the suite's living room. The table held a platter of raw vegetables with several dips, as well as cold meats, breads and condiments.

"Have a plate." He offered her one. "I like a steak and salad, but it's too late in the day for a heavy meal. Especially for you," he added, studying her. "You need sleep."

She grimaced. "I haven't really slept since this happened," she confessed. "I always knew Rachel could overdose. But she'd been using drugs for years without any drastic consequences."

"Anyone can take too many pills," he said, "and die without meaning to."

"Yes, like Hayes Carson's brother did," she remarked. "Hayes still isn't over that, and it's been years since his brother died."

He didn't like the reference to Hayes, and it showed. He didn't answer her. He loaded a plate and sat down with his own cup of coffee.

She sat at the table alone, nibbling on food she didn't taste. He was more taciturn than usual. She wondered why the mention of Hayes set him off like that. Perhaps they'd been rivals for a woman's affection. Or maybe it was just because he didn't want to see his sister get serious about Hayes.

"He's not a bad person," she ventured.

He glowered at her. "Did I say that he was?"

"You can't tell Merrie who to date," she pointed out.

He looked totally surprised. "Merrie?"

"She and Carson are friends," she persisted. "That doesn't mean that she wants to marry him."

He didn't answer. He frowned thoughtfully and sipped coffee.

She didn't understand his odd behavior. She finished her food and her coffee. She was worn-out, and the ordeal wasn't over. She still had the cremation ahead of her. There was something else, too. She would be truly alone in the world now. The thought depressed her.

"Are you going to call that man about the jewelry Rachel had?" she asked.

He nodded. "Tomorrow. We'll get everything else arranged then as well." His eyes narrowed. "I'm curious about that ledger Rachel's boyfriend mentioned."

"Me, too," she said wearily. "If he wants it that bad, it must have something to do with his clients."

He didn't say anything immediately. He looked thoughtful, and concerned. "I've heard it mentioned that Rachel knew where to buy drugs in Jacobsville. We both know that it's been a hub for illicit drug trafficking in the past. It still is." He frowned. "That ledger might have some incriminating evidence in it, and not just about Rachel's boyfriend." He stared at her. "You don't have any idea what it looks like?"

She shook her head. "I didn't ask. He was being obnoxious." She smoothed back her hair. "I wish I could feel something," she said dully. "I'm sorry she died that way, but we were never close. She did everything she could to ruin my reputation. I used to think we might grow closer as we aged, but she only got more insulting."

"Rachel liked living high," he said. "She didn't care how she achieved status."

There was something in his tone that made her curious. "She was in your class in high school, wasn't she?"

"Yes." His dark eyes narrowed. "She made a play for me. I put her down. She was vengeful, and you and Merrie were best friends."

That explained why Rachel had suddenly turned against Ivy; she thought Ivy's friendship with Merrie gave her access to Stuart. If Rachel had wanted Stuart, it must have galled her that Ivy was welcome in his house. Rachel might even have guessed how Ivy felt about him, which would have given her a motive to try to convince Stuart that Ivy was promiscuous.

"So she set out to make you think I was running wild," she guessed.

He grimaced. "Yes, she did. I'm sorry to say she might have succeeded, except that Merrie knew you and defended you."

She smiled. "Merrie was always more like a sister to me than Rachel ever was."

"She likes you, too." He got up. "Bed. You need rest."

She hesitated.

He guessed why and chuckled. "I didn't forget." He produced a bag from Macy's and handed it to her. "Sleep well."

"I'll pay you back," she said with determination.

He shrugged. "Suit yourself. Good night."

"Good night." She hesitated at the door to her room. "Stuart…thanks. For everything."

"You'd do the same for anyone who needed help," he replied easily.

She smiled. "I guess so."

She went into her room and closed the door. When she opened the bag, she caught her breath. He'd purchased a gown and peignoir set for her. The gown was pale lemon silk with white lace trim, ankle-length, with a dipping bodice and spaghetti straps. The peignoir had long sleeves and repeated the pattern of the gown. She'd sighed over similar styles in Macy's herself and dreamed of owning something so beautiful. It was even prettier than the set Merrie had loaned her that long-ago night. She'd never have been able to afford something like this on her budget. She didn't know how she was going to repay Stuart for it, but she had to. She couldn't let him buy something so intimate for her.

She put on the ensemble and brushed out her blond hair so that it haloed around her shoulders and down her back. When she looked in the mirror, she was surprised at how sensual she looked. That was a laugh. What she knew about men would fit on the back of an envelope.

She climbed into bed and turned out the light. She wished she had something to read. She wasn't even sleepy. Her mind went back to the sight of Rachel in the morgue. She forced the memory out and replaced it with lines from a book she'd read about meteorites. That amused her and she laughed to herself. Stuart probably didn't know how fascinated she was about the space rocks, or that she was constantly borrowing books from the library about their structure. She loved rocks. She had boxes of them at her apartment. Everyone teased her about their number and variety. She was forever looking for anything unusual. Once she walked right out into a plowed field to search for meteorites and came away with projectile points instead. Merrie said she should be studying archaeology, and Ivy had replied that chance would be a fine thing.

Even if she didn't study it formally, she knew quite a lot about the subject. Everyone should have a hobby, after all.

She closed her eyes and thought about the projectile points. She'd taken them to a professor of anthropology at the community college, who'd surprised her by dating them at somewhere around six thousand years old. It had never occurred to her that they were more than a hundred years old. That prompted her to get more books from the library about projectile points. She was surprised to learn that you could date them by their shape and the material from which they were made.

She thought back to the summer she was eighteen. Stuart had been out on the ranch with his cowboys rounding up the bulls, to move them to greener pastures. She'd watched him stand up in the saddle and ride like the wind. The picture had stayed with her when he'd come in for lunch. He had seen her rapt attention as he'd swung down out of the saddle with lazy grace.

He'd looked at her in a curious way, his pale eyes glittering. "Staring at me like that will get you in trouble," he'd said in a deep, slow tone.

She'd laughed nervously. "Sorry. I love to watch you ride," she'd added. "I've never seen anybody look so much at home in the saddle."

He'd given her a strange look. "I did rodeo for several years when I was in my teens," he'd said.

"No wonder you make it look so easy."

He'd reached out and touched her soft hair. His eyes

had been intent on her face, and he hadn't smiled. Some odd magnetism had linked them at that moment, so that she could hardly breathe. Even now, almost three years later, she could still feel the pure intensity of that look he gave her. It was when she'd realized how she was starting to feel about him.

For just a few seconds, his pale eyes had dropped to her soft mouth and lingered until she flushed. She waited, breathless, for his head to bend. And it had started to. Then one of the cowboys had called to him. He'd walked away as if nothing at all had happened. After that, he'd avoided Ivy. Right up until that fateful night she'd spent with Merrie in a borrowed lemon-colored gown…

Somewhere music was playing softly. Perhaps Stuart had the radio on in the adjoining part of the suite. It was sweet music, sultry and slow. As she listened to it, she began to drift away.

She was a little girl again, running out through the fields around the house where she'd grown up. She was wearing jeans and an old white shirt and, as usual, she searched for unusual rocks.

Behind her, Rachel was dancing around in a full white gown and high heeled shoes, singing off-key and stumbling around.

Ivy turned and called to her, cautioning her about the sudden deep crevasses in the field. Rachel made a face and replied that she knew what she was doing. Just then, she tripped and fell into one of the deep trenches.

Ivy ran toward her. Rachel was hanging on to a small bush at the edge of the crevasse, screaming at the top of her lungs.

"If I fall, I'll tell everyone that you pushed me!" she threatened.

"I'll save you, Rachel!" Ivy shouted. "Here. Grab my hand!"

"Your hands are dirty," Rachel shouted back. "Dirty, dirty, dirty! You're dirty. You aren't my sister! I hate you! Go away! Go away!"

"Rachel, please…" she pleaded.

But Rachel jerked her hand back. She made a rude gesture with her hand and leaned back, falling deliberately into the darkness below.

"You killed me, Ivy. You killed me!" she yelled as she fell faster. Then there was a scream, piercing and terrifying. It went on and on and on…

CHAPTER NINE

"IVY. IVY! WAKE UP!"

Strong hands held her by the wrists. She was being lifted, higher and higher. Rachel had fallen to her death, but this determined voice wouldn't let Ivy follow her. She took a deep breath and slowly opened her eyes.

Stuart's eyes were there, filling the world. She blinked sleepily.

"Wake up, sweetheart," he said gently. "You were having a nightmare."

She searched his face. "Rachel wouldn't let me help her. She fell into a crevasse. I couldn't save her."

His hands became caressing on her wrists. "It was only a dream. You're safe."

"Safe."

His gaze dropped to her bodice and his face seemed to clench. "You're sort of safe," he amended.

She was awake now, and she realized suddenly why Stuart was staring at her like that. Her bodice had dropped so that one of her pretty, firm breasts was on open display. Stuart had a ruddy color across his high cheekbones and his teeth were clenched, as if he were exerting maximum self-control.

"You...you shouldn't look at me, like that," she stammered as color shot into her own cheeks.

"I can't help it," he said huskily. "You have the most beautiful breasts I've ever seen, Ivy."

She couldn't have uttered a word to save her life. He knew it, too. His big hands let go of her wrists and took her by the shoulders instead. His thumbs eased the tiny straps over her shoulders and down her arms. The bodice fell to her waist.

He was only wearing silk pajama bottoms. His broad, hair-covered chest was almost touching her bare breasts.

"As I recall," he whispered, "this is about where we left off, two years ago. I even got the color of the gown right."

He had, but she couldn't answer him. She couldn't breathe. The clean, sexy scent of his body wafted up into her nostrils. She felt his breath against her lips as his hands became lightly caressing on her upper arms. The tension between them twisted like a cord. Ivy trembled all over as the slow, exquisite pleasure began to grow.

"What the hell," he whispered at her mouth. "It's this or go crazy..."

His mouth opened on her soft lips in a hard, insistent pressure that held traces of desperation. His arms swallowed her, grinding her bare breasts against the warm muscles of his chest.

She moaned jerkily at the rush of sensation.

He hesitated. "Did I hurt you?" he whispered.

"Oh, no," she whispered back, shyly lifting her arms around his neck. "I didn't know...it would feel like this."

He smiled slowly. "Didn't you?" He bent again, but this time his mouth was less desperate. It was tender, teasing. He nibbled her lower lip and smiled again as she parted her lips to lure him closer. His thumb probed gently, coaxing her mouth to open. When it did, his tongue slowly trespassed inside. “No, don’t fight it,” he whispered against her lips. “It’s as natural as breathing...”

She felt him lift and turn her, so that she was lying on her back. His powerful body eased down over hers, one long leg insinuating itself between both of hers over the gown.

She stiffened, wanting more and afraid of it, all at once.

He lifted his head and searched her wide, apprehensive eyes. He brushed the hair back from her temples. His body was half over her and half beside her on the wide bed. But he didn’t seem to be in a hurry. He bent and brushed his mouth over her eyelids, closing them. She felt her breasts go tight, pressed so hard up against him. She was aching for something she didn’t understand.

He seemed to know it. “Ivy?”

“What?” she managed shakily.

“Lie back and think of England,” he murmured wickedly.

A laugh jerked out of her tight throat.

He lifted his head, grinning down at her. He propped on an elbow while his other hand began to trace lightly, boldly, around a distended nipple. “Or, in our case, lie back and think of Texas.” He bent again, brushing his open mouth along her collarbone. He felt her body shudder. He smiled against her soft skin as his mouth slowly trespassed down, close to but never touching the nipple. She began to twist helplessly as the sensations overwhelmed her. She was new to this kind of physical pleasure. Her reactions were unexpected, even to herself.

Her short nails bit into his shoulders as his mouth teased at her breast.

"You haven't done this before," he murmured, savoring her response.

"No," she agreed. She shivered as his mouth grew slowly insistent. "Stuart…!" she ground out as his lips traced very lightly closer and closer to the nipple.

"What do you want?" he whispered against her breast. "Tell me."

"I…can't," she moaned.

His hand slid under her, lifting her hips up against the slowly changing contour of his powerful body. "Tell me," he coaxed. "You can have anything you want."

She moaned aloud. "You…know!"

"Stubborn," he pronounced. He lifted his head to look down into her misty, fascinated eyes staring blindly up at him. Her whole body was trembling with passion. "You can't imagine how badly I've wanted your breasts under my mouth, Ivy," he told her as his gaze fell to her bodice. "But even in dreams, it was never this good." He moved closer. "I like feeling you tremble when I do this," he whispered as his mouth began to open on the soft flesh. "But it's going to be like a jolt of lightning when I do what you really want me to do…"

As he spoke, his warm mouth moved right onto the nipple and pressed down, hard.

She arched off the bed, crying out. Her whole body shuddered as the pleasure bit into her. She clutched him helplessly, whimpering as his mouth became demanding.

He rolled onto her, nudging her long legs out of the way so that she could feel him from hip to breast in an intimacy that burst like sensual fireworks in her body.

"Yes," she groaned. "Please, Stuart, please…!" Her

voice rose as he pressed her down into the mattress. "Oh, please, don't stop!"

His mouth slid up to cover hers, devouring it, possessing it, as his body moved sensuously over hers. She hung on for dear life. She was losing it. She wanted him. She wanted him so badly that it was almost painful when he suddenly rolled away from her and got to his feet.

She lay there, bare to the waist, shivering in the aftermath, too weakened by her own surrender to even manage to cover herself. She stared at his long back, watching him fight to regain control.

After a minute, he took a long, shuddering breath, and then another, before he turned. He stared at her hungrily, his eyes making a meal of her as she lay there, bare-breasted, her hands by her head on the pillow. He stood over her with eyes that burned like dark fires.

She moved helplessly on the bed.

"No," he said quietly. "There's a time and place. This isn't it."

"You want to," she said with new knowledge of him.

"Good God, of course I do!" he ground out. "I hurt like a teenager after his first petting session. Just for the record, I don't seduce virgins. Ever."

She drew in a short, jerky breath. "How do you know…?"

"Don't be absurd," he interrupted.

Which meant that she was as transparent as glass to him, with his greater experience. Oddly she didn't feel embarrassed or self-conscious. He was looking at her boldly, and she loved his eyes on her body.

"I ache all over," she whispered.

"So do I." He sat down beside her and blatantly traced her breasts with the tips of his fingers. "I could do anything I wanted to you. But in the morning, you'd hate both of us."

It was the truth. She wished it wasn't. "Everybody else does it. They had a poll…"

"Polls can be manipulated." He bent and put his mouth tenderly against her breasts. "Virginity is sexy," he whispered. "I lie awake nights thinking about how I'd take yours."

She flushed.

He laughed. "Tell me you've never thought about doing it with me," he dared.

The flush got worse.

He drew in a long breath. "One of us has to be sensible, and I'm giving up on you," he mused, watching her body move on the sheets. "Come here."

He slid under the covers and tucked her close against his side. He turned out the light and cuddled her closer. "You can take my word for the fact that I'm violently aroused and desperate for relief. So just lie still, recite multiplication tables and try to sleep."

"You're staying?" she whispered, fascinated.

"Yes. And you won't have any more nightmares. Now go to sleep."

She closed her eyes. She was sure that she couldn't sleep with his warm, powerful body so close to her. But she drifted off almost at once and slept until morning.

WHEN SHE WOKE, it was to a throbbing pain in her right eye and nausea that made her lie very still. The headache wasn't unexpected. Stress often combined with other factors to cause them.

Stuart came in with a cup of coffee, but he stopped

smiling when he saw Ivy holding her head and pushing against her right eye. "Migraine," he murmured.

She nodded, swallowing hard to keep the nausea down. "I'm so sorry."

"Don't be ridiculous, you don't plan to have headaches. Lie back down."

When he came back, scant minutes later, he had a doctor with him. The doctor smiled pleasantly, asked her a few questions, listened to her heart and lungs and popped a shot into her arm. She closed her eyes, unable even to thank him, the pain was so severe. She eventually dozed off.

The second time she awoke, the pain had reduced itself to a dull echo of its former self. She sat up, drowsy, and smiled at Stuart.

"Thanks," she said huskily.

"I know how those headaches feel," he reminded her. "Can you eat some scrambled eggs and drink some coffee?"

"I think so." She got out of bed and staggered a little from the drugs. "It was just all the pressure," she added. "I always get headaches when I'm under stress."

"I know. Come on." Instead of letting her walk to the table, he swung her up in his arms, in the pale gown, and carried her there. He sat down with Ivy in his lap, within reach of the late breakfast he'd ordered, and began to spoon-feed her eggs and bacon.

She was amazed at the transformation of their relationship, as well as his sudden tenderness. She reacted to it hungrily, never having had anyone treat her so gently in all her life.

He smiled down at her, his dark eyes soft and full of strange lights. When he finished, he cuddled her close and shared a cup of coffee with her. Neither of them spoke. Words weren't even necessary. She felt safe. She felt…loved.

Later, the limousine took them to the funeral home where Rachel's cremated remains were already interred in an ornate bronze urn. The limousine took them from there to the airport, where Stuart's pilot was waiting to fly them home in the Learjet.

It was like a beginning. He held hands with her on the jet. When they loaded her few possessions into his car, which had been left parked at the airport, he held her hand as he drove toward her boardinghouse.

She didn't question it. The feeling was too new, too precious. She was afraid that words might shatter it.

He pulled up in front of Mrs. Brown's house and cut the engine. He helped her out first, then he carried her suitcase and her bags of quilts and photo albums up onto the porch for her. He sat Rachel's urn carefully beside the suitcase.

It was dark. Mrs. Brown hadn't left on the porch light.

"Are you going to be all right?" he asked gently, holding her by the shoulders.

"Yes. My head's fine, now. Stuart," she added slowly, "thank you, for all you've done."

"It was nothing," he replied. "If you hear from that drug-dealing boyfriend of Rachel's, you call me. Okay?"

She nodded. "I will."

"And if you remember anything about where that journal might be, call me."

"I'll do that."

He lifted his hand to her face and traced her soft cheek. "We didn't get to do anything about those jewels, but I promise you I'll get in touch with the man in a day or so and arrange to get them back to him. If you're sure that's what you want."

"It's what's right," she countered quietly. "Rachel had no scruples. I do."

He smiled. "Yes, I know."

She didn't want him to leave. She'd gotten used to being with him, almost intimately, in the past couple of days. Tonight she'd sleep alone. If her headache came back, she'd have to take aspirin and pray for sleep, because he wouldn't be there.

"Don't look like that, or I won't be able to leave you," he said suddenly, his jaw tautening. "I don't want to go home alone, either."

Her soft expulsion of breath was audible.

"Blind little woman," he whispered tenderly, and bent his head. He lifted her completely against his hard body while he kissed her. It took a long time, and when he finally let her down, she shivered with the overwhelming desire he'd kindled in her.

A sudden flash of lightning lit up the sky, followed by a crash of thunder. She jumped. "You be careful going home," she said firmly.

He smiled. "Wear a raincoat if it's still raining in the morning when you go to work," he countered.

She smiled back. Rain was blowing onto the porch, getting them both wet. Neither was wearing a raincoat.

"Go inside," he said, giving her a gentle push toward the door. "I'll phone you tomorrow."

"Okay. Good night."

"Sleep tight," he replied, and winked at her.

She watched him from the open door, after she'd put all her things inside, including the urn with Rachel's ashes. It was as if her life was just now beginning.

MRS. BROWN HAD gone to bed. Apparently, so had Lita. Ivy moved all her things into her room and placed Rachel's ashes on the mantel. The next day, she was going to see about having them interred in the cemetery next to their father.

She lay awake for a long time, thinking about her new relationship with Stuart. She hoped his attitude meant that they had a shared future ahead. She wished for it with all her heart.

THE NEXT DAY, she remembered that she'd put Rachel's diary in her purse. So before she started her rounds of clients, she took it out and read it. What she'd thought was an ordinary recitation of events turned out to be something quite different. There were names, phone numbers and other numbers that seemed more like map coordinates than anything else.

She read them over and over, and grew even more puzzled. Then she pulled out the letter Rachel had received from a San Antonio law firm. It was dynamite. The letter referenced certain materials she'd put in a safe-deposit box in Jacobsville, to be opened if anything unexpected happened to her. The attorneys wrote to remind her that she hadn't forwarded them the key.

She sat back with a harsh sigh. Rachel was involved in something illegal, she just knew it. And she was clearly blackmailing someone else. Was it the millionaire whose jewels she'd kept? Or was it her boyfriend? Or one of his clients?

She knew immediately that this was too big for her to handle. She phoned Sheriff Hayes Carson and had him come to the boardinghouse. She met him on the porch, smiling as she invited him into the house and into the kitchen, where she had coffee brewing.

"Thanks for coming so quickly," she said, sitting down after she'd poured coffee for them both. "I'm in over my head on this stuff. Here. See what you make of it."

She handed him the journal and the letter from the attorneys in San Antonio that she'd found in Rachel's apartment. He read them, frowning. "These are GPS coordinates," he remarked, running his finger along the columns in the diary. "I recognize two of the names, too," he added. His dark eyes met hers. "They're deep in the Mexican drug cartel that Cara Dominguez was running until her arrest. One of the Culebra drug cartel named here," he added, "is Julie Merrill. The other is Willie Carr, the baker you gave the message about flour to."

She grimaced. "Oh, boy."

"This information is worth its weight in gold, all by itself. But the key she mentioned is missing," he continued. "That key is dynamite. Your life could be in danger if any of her associates even think you might have it. We're talking multimillion dollar drug shipments here."

"But I don't know where the key is," she said miserably. "I looked through all the stuff I got from her apartment. I even checked the quilts to make sure she hadn't slipped it into the backing." She shook her head. "I can't imagine where she might have left it."

"Was there anything else that you took from the apartment?" he asked.

"Just the jewelry she was hoarding," she said miserably. "From that elderly millionaire she was involved with. Stuart and I put them in a safe-deposit box in New

York City, under his name. He's arranging to get them back to the man."

He frowned. "Was there a locket, or any sort of thing a key could be hidden in?"

"No," she assured him.

He sipped coffee, frowning. "I don't want to spook you, but isn't there someone you could move in with until we find that key?"

She would have said Stuart and Merrie only a day before. But Stuart hadn't called her, as he'd promised he would. She hadn't heard from Merrie, either. She couldn't just invite herself to be a houseguest under the circumstances.

"No," she said sadly.

"Okay," he said with resolution. "I want to know where you are day and night for the next few days. I'm going to get in touch with Alexander Cobb at DEA and talk to our police chief, Cash Grier, as well. We'll arrange to keep you under surveillance." He picked up the padded diary. "Will you trust me with this?" he asked.

"Of course."

His thumb smoothed over the back of it. Suddenly he went still. His eyes went to the diary. He put it on the table and pulled out his pocketknife. Before she could ask what he was doing, he opened the diary with the pages down on the table and slit the fabric of the back. Seconds later, he pulled out a safe-deposit box key.

"Good heavens!" she exclaimed. "How did you…?"

"Sheer luck," he said. "I felt it under my thumb. I'll have to contact those attorneys in San Antonio and see what the key fits. I may need you, as next of kin, to authorize me to access it."

"Before I can do that, I'll need to meet with Blake

Kemp," she replied, "and see about the paperwork to get Rachel's estate—such as it is—into probate."

"If you're not busy right now, I'll drive you over there," he said. "I'd like to talk to him as well."

She grinned. "That would be terrific. Thanks."

Hayes went out onto the porch while she phoned Blake Kemp's office and found him free if they could make it there within the half hour. She assured his new secretary—he'd only recently married his old secretary Violet and they were expecting a child—that she and Hayes would be right over.

SHE CLIMBED INTO the unmarked sheriff's car with Hayes, cradling the diary and the attorney's letter with her purse on her lap.

As they pulled out of the driveway, a car that had been sitting parked by the side of the road was quickly started. It pulled onto the road, following slowly behind Hayes Carson's car.

Hayes sat in the waiting room while Ivy spoke to Blake Kemp about Rachel's estate. She didn't have bank statements or any documentation about her possessions, but the attorney's letter intimated that they did. He read the letter, frowning.

Blake shook his head. "She was nothing like you," he said quietly.

"She told Dad that I wasn't his," she replied. "Is there a way to find out…?"

"Not his?" he exclaimed. His blue eyes darkened. "For God's sake, your mother would never have cheated on your father! She worshipped him, despite his bad temper and the way he knocked her around. Besides all that, he'd have killed any man who touched her!"

"Are you sure?" she asked, relieved.

"Yes, I am," he said flatly. "Rachel got exactly what she deserved, Ivy. She was a horror of a human being. Why in God's name would she tell a lie like that?"

"Can't you guess? I can. She wanted everything Dad had when he died. If he thought I wasn't his blood daughter, why would he want to leave me anything?" she asked sadly.

"How many lives did that woman shatter?" he wondered aloud.

"Quite a few, I expect. Her boyfriend was trying to find the journal she kept. He was frantic about it," she recalled, "but it turned out to be her diary. I gave it to Hayes," she added. "He says it has some vital information about drug smuggling, of all things."

"There's one more thing about Rachel I don't imagine you know," he began, his face solemn. "She didn't just use drugs, Ivy. She sold them, beginning when she was a senior in high school. She always had a direct pipeline to the local drug trade. If she has the documentation mentioned in this letter, it probably names names. That would give Cash Grier a heads-up while he's trying to shut down the newest drug cartel members locally."

"That's what Hayes said," she replied with a smile. "He thinks it may show the position of some drug caches."

"I hope it does," he said. "This little community has gone through some hard times because of drug smuggling. I'd love to see the suppliers shut down."

"So would I."

"Don't worry about the rest of this," he told her. "I'll handle it. But I should talk to Stuart York about that jewelry."

"Yes," she said, concerned that he hadn't phoned her yet. She had her cell phone turned on and she'd been checking it all morning to make sure it was working. It was.

"Let's call Hayes in." He touched the intercom button and had the receptionist send Hayes down the hall to his office.

Hayes showed him the journal. It really was dynamite. It would be wonderful, Ivy thought, if they could really use it to shut down the drug dealers.

"Rachel's boyfriend knows this journal exists," Hayes said somberly. "I wouldn't put it past him to come down here if he thinks Ivy might have it. If Rachel gave her attorneys something damaging about him, and he knows it, he won't have a lot to lose. No evidence, no case."

Both men looked at Ivy.

"I can buy a gun," she began.

"No, you can't," Hayes said firmly. "I have an idea, about where you could stay."

"I can get a motel room…"

"You aren't thinking of Minette and her brood?" Blake asked hesitantly.

Hayes's face went taut. "She lives out of town, where anybody coming to the house would be immediately visible, and her ranch manager was a Secret Service agent some years ago."

"But Merrie York is your best friend," Blake interrupted, eyeing Ivy. "Surely you could stay with her. Stuart has an ex-fed working for him, too."

Her face colored. "Merrie lives in San Antonio," she said. "And I don't think Stuart's home…"

"Sure he's home," Hayes returned. "I saw him driving by this morning with that debutante from Houston he's been seeing."

Ivy felt the life drain out of her. The words kept repeating in her head. Stuart had held her and kissed her and treated her with such tenderness that she thought they were going to be together for life. Instead, the minute they got home from New York, he made a beeline for his latest conquest. He probably hadn't given Ivy a second thought. Maybe he even thought of the way he'd taken care of her as an act of mercy.

She closed her eyes. Pain echoed through her nerves.

"ARE YOU ALL right?" Hayes asked, concerned. They had left the office and were now in the car.

She forced a smile. "I'm fine. Tell me about this Minette."

He seemed reluctant. "She owns the Jacobsville newspaper. You know that."

"But I've never met her," she pointed out.

He shrugged. "She lives with her aunt and two siblings, a half brother and a half sister. She's off today because there was a fire in the office and they had to call in a cleaning crew to pick up the mess and deal with the fire damage."

"Was it an accidental fire?" she asked.

"I don't know. She's been running some articles about the drug trade. I warned her that her new ace reporter was going to bring down some heat on the paper, but she wouldn't listen. The eager-beaver reporter is fresh out of journalism school looking for his first shrunken head to flaunt."

"If he points a finger at the wrong people, he'll get her sued."

"Been there, done that," he murmured. "She got Kemp to represent her and won the suit. But she's letting the kid push the wrong people. Sooner or later, there's going to be a tragedy. I tell her so, but she won't listen."

"She's a crusader," she mused.

He gave her a tight glare. "She's showing me that she doesn't take advice if it comes from my general direction. It may get her killed, in the end."

"You should find her some protection," she pointed out. "If she's trying to shut down the drug lords, you and Cash Grier might thank her for the help."

"You don't understand," he growled. "She isn't doing any of us any good. She's pointing out possible hiding places for the influx of illegal drugs and hammering home that foreign nationals are financing the traffic."

"They are."

"Ivy," he said heavily, "at the same time she's hammering the drug trade, she's holding out olive branches to illegal immigrants. She's making enemies on both sides of the drug issue."

Ivy's face softened. "You know Mario Xicara, don't you?"

He slowed for a turn. His lips thinned. "Yes."

"And his wife, Dolores, and their four little kids?"

"I know the family."

"In the village they came from in Guatemala, one man turned in a drug dealer and his whole family was gunned down. To punctuate the threat, they killed six other families as well. Mario escaped with his wife and children, but his parents and grandparents were among the dead, along with their new baby who was in the house when the drug dealer's minions came in firing."

"I know that, but..."

"They're applying for citizenship," she continued. "But now they have to be sent back to Guatemala until they can get temporary papers. The drug dealers are still around their village."

He grimaced. "There are always two sides to every issue," he reminded her.

"I know." She smiled. "But people are more than statistics."

He gave a turn signal. "I'll talk to Homeland Security. I know a man who works in ICE," he said with resignation, naming the enforcement arm of the immigration service.

"Thanks, Hayes."

"Any other small favors I can do you?" he teased.

"I'll make a list. Hayes, this isn't the way to my boardinghouse," she announced suddenly, as she realized they were heading out of town in the wrong direction.

"I know. I've got an idea."

CHAPTER TEN

MINETTE RAYNOR WAS twenty-four. She was managing editor of the weekly *Jacobsville Times,* the newspaper of Jacobs County. Her mother had inherited the paper from Minette's grandfather, and she ran it until her death. After that, her father and stepmother ran it. He'd died three years previously. Minette had grown up knowing how to sell ads, write copy, set type and paste up copy in the composing room. It was easy for her to step into her parents' shoes and run the paper. She was tall, slender, dark-eyed and blond, with a scattering of freckles over her nose. Her hair was her most incredible asset. It looked like a thick flow of pale gold that inched down her back almost to her waist. It was much longer than Ivy's.

From a deceased uncle, she'd inherited a ranch that raised steers for beef, and it was ramrodded by her late father's wrangler and two part-time cowboys who were students at the local community college. Her great-aunt Sarah lived with her and helped take care of Minette's half brother, Shane, who was eleven, and her half sister Julie, who was five. Minette's mother had died when she was ten, and her father had married Dawn Jenkies, a quiet librarian who adored him and Minette. Over their years together, she presented Dane with a son and a daughter, upon whom Minette doted. When Dawn died, and her father soon after of a heart attack, Minette was left to raise the children. It seemed to be a labor of love.

Hayes pulled up at her front steps, where she and the children were wielding paintbrushes, touching up the fading white of the door facing and wood trim. Minette, in jeans and a sweatshirt, got up, glaring at Hayes.

He glared back. “I need to ask a favor.”

She looked furious. “I don’t owe you any favors, Sheriff Carson,” she said icily.

“I know that. But I have to put Ivy someplace where she’ll be safe. Drug dealers may be after her.”

Minette’s eyes narrowed. She seemed to be biting her tongue.

Carson just looked uncomfortable. “The county will pay for her upkeep,” he said curtly. “It’s only for a few days.”

Minette looked worriedly at her siblings.

“I’m going to have one of my deputies stay here, too,” he added. “If you don’t mind.”

“I always wanted to open a hotel,” Minette told him irritably. But when she saw Ivy’s consternation, she went to her and smiled. “I’m sorry. You may have noticed that the sheriff and I don’t get along. But you’re welcome to stay. Aunt Sarah would love the company. I’m at work most days until late.” She looked at Hayes viciously. “When I’m not overdosing men, that is.”

“Cut it out,” he bit off, avoiding her eyes.

Ivy knew at once that Merrie York was out of luck where Hayes was concerned. Something powerful was at work between these two. And it wasn’t business.

The little girl, Julie, walked over to Hayes and looked up at him. “Do you got any little kids?” she asked softly.

"Careful, baby," Minette said softly, eyeing Hayes. "Rattlesnakes bite."

He glared at her. She glared back.

He looked down at Julie, who was blond like her half sister. "No, I don't have any kids," he said a little stiffly.

The child cocked her head at him. "That's very sad," she replied, sounding very grown up. "My sister says little kids are sweet." She frowned. "You don't look like a rattlesnake."

"Julie, would you get me a rag from the kitchen, please?" Minette asked her.

"Okay, Minette!" She ran up the steps and into the house.

"You're very welcome to stay with us," Minette told Ivy, her smile welcoming.

"I'll run you back to the boardinghouse to pack a bag," Hayes said.

Ivy hesitated. "Listen, are you sure this is necessary?"

"Mrs. Brown isn't going to be much protection if Rachel's boyfriend comes looking for you," he said.

She grimaced. "All right, then." She smiled at Minette. "I can cook," she said. "If you need help in the kitchen."

The other woman laughed. "Always. Aunt Sarah and I share kitchen duty, but neither of us is overly skilled. Still, we haven't poisoned anyone."

"Yet," Hayes enunciated coldly.

She stood up, eyes blazing. "Someday," she said slowly, "the truth is going to bite you in the neck! I didn't kill your brother. He killed himself. That's what you can't accept, isn't it, Hayes? You want a scapegoat…!"

"You bought the drug for him that he overdosed on!" Hayes shot back.

Minette stood erect, her face pale. "For the twentieth time, I never used drugs, or got drunk, or put a foot out of line in my life," she said proudly. "So how exactly do you think I'd know where to find illegal drugs in this town?"

He looked odd.

"Never mind," she continued. "I'm tired of beating a dead horse. Ivy, we'll get a room ready for you. The one thing we do have plenty of in this white elephant," she indicated the two-story Victorian house, "is room."

"Thanks," Ivy replied. "Hayes?"

He was staring at Minette, frowning. "What? Yes. We'll go now. Minette, I'd like to speak with Marsh."

"He's out in the barn, fixing a saddle."

Hayes took Ivy to the car, and he went to the barn. He was back in a couple of minutes. He got in the car and drove away.

Ivy didn't ask about his feud with the other woman, but she gathered that it had something to do with his brother's death. Everyone knew that Bobby Carson had died of a drug overdose three years earlier, just before Rachel went to New York. Why he thought Minette was responsible was curious. She was known locally for her hard stand on drug use and her support of antidrug programs in the schools.

"She's very nice," Ivy began.

Hayes didn't answer. "You'll be safe. Marsh will keep you safe. Nobody would think of looking for you out there, but even if they did, you'd see them coming a mile away. Not that I think the boyfriend will come all the way down here, since he isn't sure you've got that journal. But it's best to be cautious." He glanced at her. "I still think Merrie and Stuart would have let you stay with them."

She didn't answer him, either.

THE NEXT DAY, she authorized Hayes to open the safe-deposit box in the Jacobsville bank, with Police Chief Cash Grier and DEA Agent Alexander Cobb as witnesses. He picked her up and brought her to the bank.

It was a haul. Rachel had names, locations, dates, quantities of drugs shipped and the point of origin for a huge cocaine shipment. Implicated in the drug trafficking were her boyfriend, a local Jacobsville resident and two men who sat on Jacobsville's city council two years earlier.

"This is great." Cash Grier spoke for the other men as he read through the documentation. "This is enough evidence to shut down one of the biggest pipelines of illicit drugs in south Texas."

"We can certainly use it," Cobb agreed.

"Amen." Hayes smiled at Ivy. "Rachel made up for a lot with this," he said. "Regardless of her motive."

Ivy wondered about that motive. She didn't say it aloud, but she had a feeling that Rachel had been blackmailing somebody. She probably never expected to die, or to have played a big part in shutting down the drug trade in Jacobs County. It was the one noble act of Rachel's life.

It was decided that Ivy would stay at Minette's house. When she packed up her few things and told Mrs. Brown and Lita what was going on, they both tried to get her to stay.

"I have my father's old shotgun," Mrs. Brown said.

"I'm not afraid of drug dealers," Lita added.

"I know that, but it's going to take professionals to keep this from escalating," Ivy told them. "I don't want either of you in danger. Okay?"

They agreed, reluctantly.

Ivy left Rachel's ashes in her room for the time being. Once the fear of retribution from Rachel's boyfriend was past, she could take care of the funeral.

She was given a room next to Minette's, and she became part of the family overnight. Aunt Sarah, a tiny little woman with white hair, was a live wire. The children had sweet, loving natures. Minette had a wicked sense of humor.

"I'm surprised that Hayes would bring you here," she commented over steak and biscuits. "He really hates me."

"Maybe that's why," Ivy chuckled. "He seems to think I might be a target." She shook her head. "If anything happened to the kids," she added worriedly.

"Don't you worry," Minette assured her. "We have Marsh Bailey out in the bunkhouse. He was an IPSIC shooter. That's pistol competition," she clarified. "He worked for the U.S. Marshals Service, and he never misses. God help the outlaw who shows up here uninvited."

"I hope he won't," Ivy said. "But Rachel's boyfriend has more to lose than most people. He might figure out that I have the journal she left, and come after me."

"I don't think he's that stupid," Minette ventured, sipping coffee. Her soft eyes pinned Ivy's across the supper table. "Think about it. There's a journal floating around that has names and addresses and the potential to explode the local drug trade. You don't know who's got it or where it is, but you know you'll get blamed if the authorities find it. Would you walk into the arena, or would you run for your life?"

Ivy felt better. "You know," she said, "I think I'd run."

Minette smiled. "I think I would, too."

FOR THE NEXT two days, Ivy stayed with the Raynors. She got her ledgers from the boardinghouse and drove her little VW back to Minette's house. Hayes came by to check on her and mentioned that they'd heard nothing from their informants about the New York connection to the drug trade. However, he did say that the baker had been arrested and charged with drug trafficking. Julie Merrill was still on the loose, however, and nobody, including her father, had any idea where she'd gone.

"We did phone the Brooklyn precinct that worked your sister's death," he added. "It seems that her boyfriend was involved in an accident yesterday. He's in the hospital and not expected to live."

"What happened to him?" she exclaimed.

"It seems he walked into an elevator shaft in his own apartment building," Hayes told her. "There were two eyewitnesses. They have mob ties, of course. The word on the street is that Smith was trying to trespass on another drug dealer's territory."

"Tough," Ivy said, without any real regret. The man who'd helped Rachel feed her habit had gone the same way she had. It was a fitting sort of end. She said so.

"I have to agree."

"Then, do you think I could go home?" she ventured.

He hesitated. "I can't stop you. Smith won't be a problem, but there are some shadowy members of the drug cartel still on the loose. You won't know who they are."

"I have an answer to that," she replied.

"What?"

"Let Minette do a story about the Jacobsville drug link and say that all Rachel's records are now in the hands of law enforcement," she suggested. "That should put a kink in their operation—and keep them out of Jacobsville."

He began to smile. "I like the way you think. Okay. I'll talk to her about it."

"And I can go home? I still have Rachel's funeral to arrange."

He nodded. "Go ahead. If you need me, you know where I am."

"Yes, I do. Thanks, Hayes."

"No problem."

She did go back to the boardinghouse, but she was nervous, even under the circumstances. She didn't want to endanger Mrs. Brown and Lita. On the other hand, she hadn't felt right about endangering Minette's young siblings. If only Stuart was still speaking to her. She agonized over his defection to the pretty debutante. He'd just dropped Ivy like a rock, and when she needed him most. If she only knew why!

THE NEXT DAY, she drove out to the cemetery, where the funeral home director and his assistant were waiting. The trees were all bare. It was a gray day. It was misting rain as well. It looked such a forlorn place with the cold wind whipping Ivy's hair around.

A small grave had been dug next to her father's, to receive Rachel's urn. There wasn't anyone there except herself. She had thought of putting the obituary notice in the paper, but Rachel had left plenty of enemies in Jacobsville, and few friends.

She was wearing a long gray dress with an equally long tweed coat. The wind was crisp and cruel. She'd been awake half the night thinking about Stuart and wondering what she'd done to make him stay away. They'd been so close in New York. Now, he didn't seem to remember her at all. At least when he'd disliked her, she'd seen him from time to time. She ached to be with him. Even just the sight of him at a distance would feed her hungry heart. But apparently that wasn't going to happen.

The wind blew coldly around her as she stared at the bronze urn that contained the only human remains of her sister. She'd never felt so alone.

The funeral director's assistant, who was also a lay minister, said the words over Rachel's ashes. As Ivy listened, she was sorry that her sister's life had been so wasted, so full of selfish greed. If only Rachel had been different. If only she'd cared about Ivy. She closed her eyes as the prayer ended, hoping that it had helped the older woman in her path to the other side of life.

When she looked up, she was astonished, delighted, shocked to see Stuart York striding toward her. He wasn't smiling. His wide-brimmed dress hat was pulled down low over his eyes. He was dressed in city clothes, a gray suit that made him look distinguished. He paused at the graveside and looked down at Ivy, who couldn't hide her delight, or her wounds.

"I'm sorry I'm late," he said curtly. "I couldn't find out what time you were having the service. If I'd known, Merrie would have come down, too."

"I didn't think anyone would come," she said simply.

His eyes narrowed. "You didn't think, period," he said shortly. His big hand caught her small one and held it tight. She looked up at him, feeling suddenly safe and confident, and tears misted her eyes.

The funeral home director gave Ivy his condolences, along with the lay minister, and then beckoned to the workman to put the urn in its resting place.

"Do you want to stay for this?" Stuart asked.

She nodded. "It's such a sad way to die," she said.

His hand tightened. He didn't say anything.

He walked with her to her vehicle, and his eyes said what he thought of it. "You'd be safer riding a one-wheeled bicycle," he said flatly.

"It doesn't look like much," she agreed, "but it does run. Mostly."

He turned her to him, taking her gently by the shoulders. "I saw you ride off with Hayes Carson the morning after we got in," he said coldly. "You were with him again the next day."

"Yes," she said, surprised, "because he and Chief Grier…"

"…had to oversee the opening of the safe-deposit box," he finished for her, dark eyes flickering. "You could have called and told me that, Ivy."

"Yes?" Her own eyes began to glitter. "And you could have called me, instead of riding around town with your pretty debutante visitor!"

The hard look on his face melted. He began to smile. "Were you jealous?" he taunted softly.

"Were you?" she shot right back.

He laughed. It was a wicked sort of laugh.

It made her cheeks color. She lowered her eyes to

his chest. "I thought you'd had second… I mean, I thought…"

He put his forefinger gently across her lips. "So did I," he whispered.

She met his eyes and couldn't look away. He bent and drew his lips tenderly across her soft mouth. She started to reach up, but he caught her arms and held them down.

"No," he whispered. "Not in a cemetery."

She cleared her throat. "You started it."

"And you have no willpower," he teased. "I love it."

She laughed shyly.

"Why did you go out to Minette Raynor's house with Hayes?"

"How did you…?"

"Two thousand pairs of curious eyes live in this town," he said with affection. "The druggist and the clerk at the bank mentioned it, even before Cash Grier told me the whole story. Which you could have done," he added shortly.

She started to argue, but she realized that he was right. She moved restlessly and didn't look at him. "My pride was hurt, when I heard about you riding around with that woman."

"She was visiting her uncle. I'm doing a business deal with him. She needed a ride to town, and I obliged." He tilted her chin up. "Which I could have let Chayce do. But I'd seen you with Hayes and I figured somebody would see me with her. In fact," he added wickedly, "I drove right by Hayes Carson's office with her. He saw us."

"Rachel gave us enough information to hang the local drug lords out to dry," she said. "Maybe, in one way, she redeemed herself. How about the jewelry?" she added.

"I flew up there yesterday and had the millionaire's attorney meet me at the bank," he told her. "He was astonished that you'd want to give him back what amounted to a king's ransom. He wants to give you a reward."

"I wouldn't take one," she said.

He smiled. "I told him that. Know what he said?"

"What?"

"That you were one in a million, and I was a very lucky man."

"You weren't thinking that, I bet."

"Not at the time, no." He frowned. "You haven't said why you went to Minette's with Hayes. He hates her. Everybody knows he thinks she gave his brother the drugs that killed him."

"He said that Marsh would watch out for me, and that the place was situated so that you could see someone coming two miles away. There's no way to sneak up on it."

"He's right, there—Marsh was a federal agent. But so was Chayce, who works for me. You'll be safer at my house."

"Are you sure about that?"

He grimaced and took a long breath. "I asked Merrie if she could take a few days off and come home to chaperone me with a woman. She laughed her head off when I had to admit that it was you."

"She would."

He brought her hand to his mouth and kissed the palm. "I'll follow you to your boardinghouse. You can leave your car there and come with me in mine."

She hesitated. "I've only just come home from Minette's place, and I've been worried about my boardinghouse friends. Rachel's boyfriend is on his way out of the world," she added, pausing to explain what had happened. "But it's still possible that one of the cartel people could come looking for me. If they see my car there, it might put Mrs. Brown and Lita in danger," she cautioned.

"Suppose we leave it at Hayes's office?"

"Would he mind?"

"Hell, no. Hayes only lives for the adrenaline rushes his job gives him. That's why he's never married. No woman in her right mind would marry him."

"He and Minette are like flint and steel together," she commented.

"Yes, I know," he replied. "One day, there's going to be a fearful explosion between them, and anything could happen. That's why I've discouraged Merrie."

"Merrie isn't stupid, you know," she said gently.

"Well, not in most ways. Come on. Let's go."

LIFE WAS SWEET AGAIN. Ivy forgot the cartel, Rachel's burial, everything as she and Stuart dropped her car off at the sheriff's office.

"I wondered why she wasn't staying with you," Hayes commented to Stuart. "She and Merrie have been friends forever."

"We had a misunderstanding," Stuart replied. He caught Ivy's hand in his, to make the point, just in case Hayes had missed it. "But we've cleared things up. Merrie's coming home for a few days, too. Chayce and I, and the boys, will make sure Ivy's safe."

Hayes grinned wickedly. "What about the pretty debutante?"

Stuart raised an eyebrow. "Her fiancé is waiting for her back in Houston."

"Oh," Hayes remarked, with a speculative look at Ivy, who flushed.

"Thanks for letting me keep my car here," Ivy said. "I was worried about leaving it at my boardinghouse."

"No problem," Hayes said. "It might work to our advantage if they think you're staying here in my office." He grinned. "In fact, I hope they do think it. I'll call Cash and tell him, too."

"Let me know if you catch anyone," Ivy asked.

"Of course."

"WILL HE REALLY call me, do you think, if he catches somebody?" Ivy asked as they drove to Stuart's house.

"I imagine so. You're involved, whether you want to be or not." He took her hand in his and held it tightly. "I found out something else in New York that I didn't share with Hayes."

"What?" she asked, certain that it was something unpleasant.

"The millionaire was concerned enough to hire a private detective. He shadowed Rachel before she took the overdose. She led him to one of the bigger names in drug distribution in the country. The detective said that she was blackmailing the man with information she'd gleaned from her boyfriend. She'd hidden the evidence, and nobody could find out where."

"Did they kill her?" she asked worriedly.

"It wouldn't have been wise to do that, considering that they didn't know exactly what she had on them, or where it was kept."

"She'd used drugs for years," she argued. "She wouldn't have taken an overdose deliberately."

"There were no signs of force on her body," he replied. "I checked with the medical examiner."

"Then, how…?"

"They did a toxicology screen, though," he added. "The stuff she injected was a hundred percent pure. She used too much."

"Did she have help using too much?" she asked warily.

"Her boyfriend was right in the middle of her schemes," he said. "It's possible that he deliberately gave her the pure drug, instead of the drug that had been cut, to save himself. He might not have known about the evidence she had. He might have thought she was bluffing. She would have used her regular dose, which was fatal because of the substitution. It would still look like suicide."

"Tough luck for him, if it's true," she said curtly. "Because when the drug pipeline gets shut down by the DEA, they're going to want to punish someone, and he's the only one left alive that they can get to. If he lives, he may wish he'd died."

"Yes." He glanced at her. "Poetic justice, you might say."

She had to agree that it was. "Poor Rachel," she said, shaking her head. "She was always greedy."

"Always." He squeezed her hand. "She was at that party with Hayes's brother Bobby, you know," he added. "She knew the dealers and where to get the drugs, and she had a case on Bobby at the time because he was rich. She might have thought she was doing him a favor, so when it went bad, she put it around that Minette did the dirty work."

"That would be like her," she agreed. "But Hayes still thinks Minette did it."

"God knows why," he said. "Minette sings in the choir at church, teaches a Sunday school class and she's never had so much as a speeding ticket. She never even knew any kids who were on the wrong side of the law."

"Hayes is blind when it comes to her," she said.

He smiled. "Men tend to be that way when they're afraid of being caught," he told her. "Freedom becomes a religion when you're over thirty."

"I guess most men don't want to settle down."

"Oh, we do, eventually. Especially when we realize that some other man might be poaching on our territory." He glanced at her. "I was ready to punch Hayes."

She felt her cheeks go hot. She smiled. "Were you?"

"Are you sure there's nothing between you?" he persisted.

"I'm very sure," she replied, linking her fingers closer into his.

He smiled.

MERRIE WAS ALREADY at the house when they got there, to Ivy's faint disappointment. She'd hoped to have some time alone with Stuart.

He got out and opened her door, helping her out. He led her up the steps, leaving the car in the driveway.

"I didn't believe him when he told me," Merrie teased, hugging her friend.

"I still can't," Ivy confessed, with a shy glance at Stuart.

"Come on in," Merrie said. "Mrs. Rhodes has already made some tea cakes and coffee for us."

"I'd love something hot to drink," Ivy replied. "It was cold at the cemetery."

"I would have been there, too, if I'd known," Merrie said gently. "I just got here about twenty minutes ago. I'm sorry about Rachel."

"Me, too," Ivy replied. "I wish she'd made better choices in her life."

"I hope that information she furnished helps close doors around here for the drug trade," Stuart said as he sat beside Ivy on the sofa. "It's more dangerous than ever when you have two factions fighting for supremacy."

"Rachel actually turned informant?" Merrie exclaimed.

"She did," Ivy replied, and told her the whole story, interrupted briefly by Mrs. Rhodes bearing a silver tray with coffee and tea cakes, milk and sugar and china.

"But why did Hayes take you to Minette's house?" Merrie asked curiously. "He hates her."

"I wouldn't take any bets on that," Stuart replied, munching on a tea cake.

"They're very explosive together," Ivy said warily.

Merrie sighed. "I had a feeling about that," she confessed. She grinned. "I had a real crush on Hayes when I was about sixteen, but I'm not stupid enough to think we'd do well as a couple. We're too different. Besides," she confessed with a shy smile, "there's a very handsome divorced doctor I work with at the hospital."

"Tell me all about him," Ivy coaxed.

Stuart finished his coffee and stood up. "I'll pass," he said with a grin. "I have things to do. Don't go away," he told Ivy.

"I won't," she promised.

He winked at her, leaving her flushed and delighted.

"I still can't believe it!" Merrie exclaimed when he'd gone out of earshot. "You and my brother! I thought you hated each other!"

"So did I," Ivy confessed. "I've loved him since I was eighteen."

"I think he feels something similar. He was livid about seeing you around town with Hayes. No man gets that mad about a woman he hates." She laughed. "You can't imagine how relieved I was! I was sure you were falling for Hayes, and I knew that he and Minette were passionate about hating each other. One day, mark my words, there's going to be an explosion between the two of them. I didn't want you to be hurt," she added gently.

Ivy felt the relief all the way to her toes. She just smiled. "Thanks. But I wasn't kidding when I said Hayes was a friend. I've loved Stuart forever, it seems. I can't believe he feels the same."

Merrie chuckled. "I can."

Ivy leaned forward. "Well, now that we've got Hayes out of the way, tell me about this sexy doctor you work with!"

AFTER SUPPER, MERRIE discreetly went upstairs to watch a movie on pay-per-view with Mrs. Rhodes while Stuart went into his study with Ivy and closed the door. As an afterthought, he locked it behind him.

Ivy was nervous and delighted, all at once, as he drew her into his arms.

"I'm starving," he whispered as his mouth covered hers.

She realized quickly that he wasn't talking about

food. She held on for dear life and kissed him back with her whole heart. She felt him lift her, carry her, to the long leather sofa. He put her down on it and joined her, drawing her completely against his powerful body.

She shivered at the sensations that rose like a flood, almost searing her as passion consumed them both.

He ground her hips into his, groaning when she jerked and gasped into his demanding mouth. She made no protest at all when she felt his lean hands go under her blouse, against her bare skin.

"Your body is softer than silk," he breathed into her mouth. "Warm and sweet to touch. I want you, Ivy."

She wanted him, too, but they were getting in over their heads and she was an old-fashioned woman. She grew more nervous as his ardor increased. Helpless, she stiffened.

He hesitated, lifting his head to look down into her wide, apprehensive eyes. His own narrowed. "Yes," he whispered. "You want me. You'd give in, if I asked you to. But you don't want it to happen like this, do you?"

She swallowed, knowing she might lose him forever if she told the truth. "I… I was raised to believe that some things are still wrong even if the whole world says they're right."

She looked up at him nervously, waiting for him to get up and walk out, or just to make some sarcastic comment. He was a worldly man in his thirties. He'd said he wasn't a marrying man, and she wasn't capable of sleeping with him out of wedlock. Her heart fell to her knees. She couldn't go on living if she lost him, now. What would she do? Her eyes pleaded with his as the silence grew around them. It was, truly, the moment of truth.

CHAPTER ELEVEN

AND THEN, WHEN Ivy was certain she'd lost, Stuart began to smile. It wasn't a sarcastic smile, either. He rolled over onto his side and traced patterns on her soft, swollen mouth. His shirt was open and her fingers were tangled in the thick hair that covered his chest. She didn't remember unfastening buttons, but she must have. Her own blouse and bra were down around her waist.

"I told you, I don't seduce virgins," he whispered deeply.

"I remember," she whispered back.

"I do, however, marry them," he murmured against her lips.

Her eyes widened. "You want to…to marry me?"

He kissed her eyelids closed. "Of course I do," he replied huskily. "I wanted you when you were just eighteen. I've gone almost out of my mind wanting you since then, and hating myself for it. You're so young, Ivy," he told her, hugging her close. "But I can't live without you."

She clung to him, burying her face in his warm throat. "I can't live without you, either, Stuart," she confessed on a broken sob. "I love you…!"

His mouth stopped the words. He kissed her until her mouth was sore and they were both on the verge of surrender.

Whether it was by accident or by design, a loud knock at the door announced Merrie.

"Who wants cake and ice cream?" she called.

Stuart laughed. "Both of us!" he called back, winking at Ivy, who was delightfully flushed.

"Coming right up. You two coming out to get it?"

Stuart made a face. "Sure," he replied.

"Okay! Five minutes!"

Her footsteps died away.

Stuart's eyes began to glitter wickedly as he eased Ivy onto her back and slid over her. "Five whole minutes," he murmured against her soft mouth. "Let's make the best of them, sweetheart."

They did, too.

AMID PLANS FOR a big, society wedding that Ivy really didn't want, Chief Cash Grier and Sheriff Hayes Carson came to talk to Ivy. Stuart had gone out onto the ranch because there was a problem with some equipment, and Merrie was in town ordering invitations and a wedding cake.

Mrs. Rhodes led them into the living room, where Ivy was making a list of people she wanted to invite to the wedding.

"What can I do for you?" she asked them, smiling as she offered them chairs around the big, open fireplace that was blazing, cozy and warm in the large room.

"We thought you might like to know how things are going since we got Rachel's packet of information," Hayes told her.

"Would I ever!" she replied.

"It turns out that her boyfriend's main supplier was from Jacobsville," Cash Grier said. "Do you remember back last year when two of my patrol officers arrested a drunk politician and his daughter slandered me in the press?"

"Everybody remembers that," she said.

"Well, his daughter, Julie Merrill, was up to her neck in drug trafficking, along with the two commissioners who resigned from the city council and vanished."

"Julie was arrested and accused of arson for trying to burn down Libby Collins's house, wasn't she?" she replied. "And then she skipped bond and vanished, about the same time that Dominguez woman took over Manuel Lopez's old drug territory."

"Good memory, Ivy," Hayes chuckled.

"Better than mine," Cash agreed, grinning. "Anyway, we couldn't find her anyplace and, believe me, we looked. So this information Rachel left pointed to a hotel in downtown San Antonio where one of her drug-dealing boyfriend's contacts lived. Guess who the contact turned out to be?"

"Julie Merrill?!"

"The very same," Cash told her. "We've got her in custody. She's lodged in the county jail awaiting arraignment."

"Will that shut down the drug trade locally?" Ivy asked. "And what about those two councilmen?"

"They're still hiding out somewhere," Hayes drawled. "But we'll turn them up sooner or later. Meanwhile, Dominguez has a successor."

"Do you know who it is?" she asked.

Cash and Hayes glanced at each other and some silent message passed between them. "We have an idea," Cash said. "We're working on proof. One of Cy Parks's old friends is going to help us out. He's a Mexican national with some long-held grudges."

"Rodrigo Ramirez," Ivy murmured thoughtfully.

"How do you know about him?" Cash asked suspiciously.

"I know Colby Lane's new wife, Sarina," she said. "She mentioned that Colby and Rodrigo had some, shall we say, problems during the time they were working on breaking the Dominguez case."

"Translated," Hayes said with a droll smile at Cash, "that means that Colby and Rodrigo could hardly stay in the same room together without exchanging threats of violence."

"Well, Rodrigo and Sarina had been partners for three years, after all," Cash pointed out.

"Yes, well, Colby and Sarina had been married and had a child together. Anyway," Hayes continued, "we have a lead on where Dominguez's lieutenant, who's taking over the Culebra cartel, is hiding out. Rodrigo's going to infiltrate it."

"What's Sarina going to say to that?" Ivy asked. "She and Rodrigo worked together busting up Dominguez's operation. Sarina's DEA, too, you know."

Cash chuckled. "Cobb doesn't want to let her resign. He says she can go undercover as Rodrigo's contact. Colby wants her to work for me. So do I," he added. "I only have one investigator, and it's a big county. I was hoping that she'd start right away. But Cobb offered her this peach of a case and she walked right over Colby and took it."

"Colby's really crazy about her," Ivy mentioned.

"Yes, and vice versa," Cash said. He sighed. "Well, maybe one day Colby will find a way to convince her to resign. Meanwhile, he and Bernadette hold down the fort on their ranch in Jacobsville while Sarina works nights."

"Is he still teaching tactics for Eb Scott?" she asked.

They nodded. "There was one other confession in Rachel's papers," Cash added slowly. "We thought you ought to know. She admitted that she gave Bobby Carson the drug that killed him."

Ivy's gasp was audible. She glanced at Hayes, whose face was as closed as a clam shell. "She confessed? But why?"

"Who knows?" Cash replied. "Maybe she had a premonition. Whatever her reason, she made amends for a lot of bad things she'd done in her life."

"Was there anything about me?" Ivy wanted to know. She hadn't even asked to read the papers, certain that they were all about drug trafficking and not about personal matters.

Cash hesitated.

"No," Hayes replied quietly. "She just noted that she guessed all her things would go to her sister at her death. It wasn't a will. She wasn't planning to die. But she knew that blackmailing drug lords is an iffy business. I guess she wanted to make the point."

Ivy felt her heart sink. She'd hoped for more than that.

"Don't lie to her," Cash said coldly. "Telling the truth is always the best way, even if it seems brutal." He looked at Ivy. "She said she'd told her boyfriend that you'd have all the blackmail information in case something happened to her."

"Dear God!" Ivy exclaimed, feeling sick.

"That wasn't necessary," Hayes said curtly.

"It was," Cash disagreed. "Mean people don't usually change, Ivy," he added. "If anything, they get meaner.

She put you in the line of fire deliberately by telling Jerry Smith she'd given you the evidence."

"I'm not surprised," she said sadly. "She always hated me, from the time I was old enough to know who she was. My life was hell when I was a child."

Hayes pursed his lips. "Not anymore," he mused. "I noticed that Merrie York was at the engravers ordering wedding invitations this morning for you and Stuart."

She burst out laughing. "There's no such thing as a secret in Jacobsville."

"Damned straight," Cash agreed. "Are we getting invited?"

"Everybody's getting invited," Ivy replied with a smile. "I would have liked to elope, but Stuart says we're going to have all the trimmings."

"I love weddings," Hayes said. "It's the only time I get decent cake."

"No fair," Ivy protested. "Barbara makes wonderful cakes at her café."

"I eat on the run, mostly," Hayes said.

"Are Jerry's friends going to come after me, when they know about Rachel's confession?" she worried.

"Not likely," Cash said with a grin. "Jerry survived his fall, against all the odds, and he's turning state's evidence. He pointed out his management-level supplier, who was picked up in New York City this morning and charged with drug trafficking. It seems this supplier had enough methamphetamine and crack cocaine in a rented, vacant apartment to qualify him for superdealer status. Federal charges," he continued, "and they carry long prison sentences. Cobb and the DEA had already picked up the ex-state senator's daughter in San Antonio, and we hear that the two ex-councilmen implicated in the scheme are trying to make it to Mexico."

"If they do, Rodrigo will push them back across the border and yell for the police," Hayes chuckled.

"I'm just glad it's over," Ivy said quietly. "It's been a long week."

"It certainly has," Hayes agreed.

Ivy wondered how he'd taken the news that Minette had never given his little brother the drugs that cost him his life. He might not believe it just yet. His vendetta against the woman had gone on for some time. Maybe he liked hating her.

They left a few minutes later, and she went back to her list.

THE WEDDING, PREDICTABLY, was the social event of the season. The church was decorated in white and red poinsettias, because it was only a few weeks before Christmas. Ivy wore a white gown with a train and a trailing veil that Stuart had bought for her at Neiman Marcus. She looked in the mirror and couldn't believe that this was her. She'd never dreamed that Stuart would want to marry her one day, when she was cocooned in her daydreams. She smiled at her reflection, flushing a little with happiness.

She walked down the aisle alone. She'd had offers from townspeople to give her away, but it seemed right to make the walk all by herself. You couldn't really give people away in these enlightened times, she'd told Stuart. If anything, she was giving herself.

Stuart stood at the beautiful arbor of poinsettias where the minister was waiting. He looked down the aisle as Ivy walked toward him and the look on his face was fascinating to her. This worldly, experienced man looked very much like a young boy on his first date. His eyes were eloquent.

She stopped beside him with her bouquet of white roses and lily of the valley and faced him shyly, with her veil draped delicately over her face, while the minister read the vows.

Finally the ring was on her finger, and on his. He lifted the beautiful lacy veil to look upon her for the first time as a bride.

"Beautiful," he whispered, as he bent to kiss her with exquisite tenderness. "Mrs. York," he added, smiling.

She beamed. She could have walked on air. She was the happiest woman in Texas, and she looked it.

EVERYONE IN TOWN was there. The big families, the little families, friends and acquaintances filled the church and flowed out into the yard.

"At least," she whispered to him at the reception, "nobody started a mixer, like they did at Blake Kemp's wedding to his Violet."

"It's early, yet," he cautioned, nodding toward a fuming Minette Raynor glaring up at a taciturn Hayes Carson.

"He doesn't believe she wasn't responsible, does he?" she mused.

"He doesn't want to believe it," he corrected. "Here, precious, take a bite of the cake so the photographer can make us immortal."

She flushed at the endearment and nibbled the white cake as the flash enveloped them. The camera captured similar exquisite moments until the happy couple finally climbed into a waiting white limousine and sped away toward the airport.

JAMAICA, IVY THOUGHT as she lay exhausted in Stuart's strong arms, was a dreamy place for a honeymoon. Not that they'd seen much of it yet. The minute the bellboy had deposited their luggage, received his tip and left the room, they'd ended up in the bed.

Ivy knew the mechanics of it, from her romantic novels and blunt articles in women's magazines. But reading about it and doing it were two very different things.

The sensations Stuart drew from her untried body were so powerful that they frightened her. She lost control of herself almost at once. His mouth and his hands coaxed a response out of her that would make her blush afterward. He teased her, encouraged her, praised her as he drew her with him from one peak to an even higher one.

There was one tiny flash of pain, and then nothing except sheer heat and passion that built on itself until she was shivering, exploding with pleasure, begging for relief from the tension that pulled her poor body so taut that it felt likely to explode.

And it did, in a maelstrom of excited delight that was beyond rational description. She cried out endlessly as her body arched up to receive his in helpless trembling thrusts.

He found his own relief just as she did, and then collapsed over her. She cradled him in her arms, drunk on ecstasy, blind with satiation.

After a few breathless minutes, he managed to lift his head and look down into her misty, happy eyes.

"Now I know you're disappointed," he said dryly, "that we rushed it like this. But later, I promise, I'll torture you with passion and make you scream like a wildcat when I satisfy you."

"Dis…appointed?" she asked, blank-eyed.

He pursed his lips. "You're not disappointed?"

"Good Lord, Stuart!" she exclaimed, barely able to breathe even now. "I thought I was going to die!"

He chuckled. "I must be better than I thought I was," he told her. He bent and kissed her eyelids. "I wanted to go slow, but I just lost it. I've waited so long for you, little one. Years and years. For the past year or so," he added huskily, "I've been as celibate as a man stranded on a desert island. I wasn't able to want anyone but you. So I couldn't draw it out the way I meant to, tonight."

She was delighted with the confession. Her long legs curled around his and her eyes half-closed in satisfaction. If she were a cat, she mused, she'd be purring. "I don't have a single complaint."

"It didn't hurt?" he persisted.

"Only a little. Mostly, I was too busy to notice."

He nibbled her lower lip. "I'm good," he drawled.

She grinned and punched him in the ribs. "Very good. I think. My memory seems to be slipping." She glanced up at him, drawing her fingers through the thick hair on his chest. "Could you do all that again, do you think, so I can make up my mind?"

"Darlin'," he whispered into her parting lips, "I would be delighted…!"

THE NEXT DAY, holding hands and walking along the beach while the waves crashed on the sand beside them, she wondered if anyone had ever been as happy as she was right now.

She leaned her head against his bare shoulder and kissed it. "Did I mention that I loved you?" she asked softly.

"I believe you did," he replied, and pulled her close.

He looked down into her wide, radiant eyes. "But I didn't." He traced a path down her soft cheek, and his eyes were solemn. "I could have told you anytime in the past two years that I loved you. I still do. I always will."

It was powerful, hearing the words. She could hardly breathe. "Really?"

"Really." He bent and kissed her eyelids closed. "We've had a nice breakfast and some comfortable exercise. What would you like to do next, Mrs. York?"

She grinned wickedly, tugged his head down and whispered in his ear.

His eyebrows arched. "Do you know, that's exactly what I'd like to do next, too!"

She pulled away, laughed and went running back down the beach. Stuart gave a shout of laughter and ran after her.

Years later, she could still draw a smile from him when she reminded him of that bright, sweet morning on a Jamaican beach, when their lives together were just beginning. It was, she thought, the best morning of her life.

* * * * *

In the small Texas burg of Rambling Rose, real estate investor Callum Fortune is making a big splash. The last thing he needs is any personal complications slowing his pace—least of all nurse Becky Averill, a beautiful widow with twin baby girls!

Read on for a sneak preview of
Fortune's Fresh Start
by Michelle Major, the first book in
The Fortunes of Texas: Rambling Rose continuity.

"I didn't mean to rush off the other day after the ribbon cutting," he told her as they approached the door that led to the childcare center. "I think I interrupted a potential invitation for dinner, and I've been regretting it ever since."

Becky blinked. In truth, she would have never had the guts to invite Callum for dinner. She'd been planning to offer to cook or bake for him and drop it off at his office as a thank-you. The idea of having him over to her small house did funny things to her insides.

"Oh," she said again.

"Maybe I misinterpreted," Callum said quickly, looking as flummoxed as she felt. "Or imagined the whole thing. You meant to thank me with a bottle of wine or some cookies or—"

"Dinner." She grinned at him. Somehow his discomposure gave her the confidence to say the word.

He appeared so perfect and out of her league, but at the moment he simply seemed like a normal, nervous guy not sure what to say next.

She decided to make it easy for him. For both of them. “Would you come for dinner tomorrow night? The girls go to bed early, so if you could be there around seven, we could have a more leisurely meal and a chance to talk.”

His shoulders visibly relaxed. “I’d like that. Dinner with a friend. Can I bring anything?”

“Just yourself,” she told him.

He pulled his cell phone from his pocket and handed it to her so she could enter her contact information. It took a few tries to get it right because her fingers trembled slightly.

He grinned at her as he took the phone again. “I’m looking forward to tomorrow, Becky.”

“Me, too,” she breathed, then gave a little wave as he said goodbye. She took a few steadying breaths before heading in to pick up the twins. *Don’t turn it into something more than it is*, she cautioned herself.

It was a thank-you, not a date. Her babies would be asleep in the next room. Definitely not a date.

But her stammering heart didn’t seem to get the message.